C

The trees were torn aside behind him, as Steven felt the air displaced by something there, something huge, monstrous . . .

He was almost to the top—the lip of the valley was just within his reach—when the inhuman howl came again and giant fingers of ice closed around his leg, almost jerking him from the slope. He fought in blind panic then, clawing at the dirt and weeds and trying to drag himself to the top, even as the howl grew louder and changed and became his name, his NAME for god's sake. He tried to scream, but little more than a strangled sound reached his lips . . . a single word . . .

"Windigo . . . !"

"A winner . . . the influence of Stephen King and David Morrell shows through . . . neatly mixes new elements of horror."

—J. N. Williamson
Author of *Noonspell* and *The Black School* on *Nightblood*

★

WHERE THE CHILL WAITS

ALSO BY T. CHRIS MARTINDALE

NIGHTBLOOD

Published by
WARNER BOOKS

WHERE THE CHILL WAITS

T. Chris Martindale

WARNER BOOKS

A Time Warner Company

WARNER BOOKS EDITION

Cover design by Richard Milano
Cover illustration by Bob Hickson

Warner Books, Inc.
666 Fifth Avenue
New York, N.Y. 10103

 A Time Warner Company

Printed in the United States of America

First Printing: January, 1991

10 9 8 7 6 5 4 3 2 1

DEDICATION

To Sharon Lou Martindale
For encouraging a strange imagination.
Thanks, Mom.

ACKNOWLEDGEMENT

To Kevin for a great scene ending;
and to Paula Sanders of the
Atikokan Chamber of Commerce, for
letting me borrow her town.

WHERE THE
CHILL WAITS

THERE WERE DARK PLACES IN THE FOREST.

Some were pockets of natural shadow, where the trees grew tall and close and cheated the ground of sunlight. But the other places . . . Their darkness had little to do with simple degrees of light and shade.

It was that way in the deep woods beyond the Chalako Lakes, along the tributaries and backwaters that snaked lazily through the mostly uncharted wilds. There were nooks and crannies in the Precambrian Shield that seemed somehow older than the surrounding lands, where even the animals would not go. And despite the long presence of mankind throughout the region, such places had seldom felt the tread of human feet. From the native Cree and Ojibwa to the coming of the French trappers and voyageurs, they all avoided the dead spots where the chill hung year round and the silence called their names . . .

But the forest was eternal. The forest could wait.

ONE

STEVEN WILHOIT SCRUNCHED DOWN BEHIND THE WHEEL and grumbled to himself as he drove. He had only been up for an hour or so—it was barely after six in the morning and not even light out yet—but the day was already turning to shit. And who do we have to thank for that, he thought, glancing over at his wife. She sat thin-lipped and brooding in the passenger seat, staring out the window at scenery too dark to see. The tension was still there, just as thick between them as when they'd argued the night before. A few hours' sleep had done little to relieve it. But he'd never really expected it would. One thing he'd learned after ten years of marriage, it was that Janet could nurse a good grudge for days at a time.

He peered over the edge of his glasses for a longer look this time, studying her profile in the dim glow of the dash lights. And despite the early hour and his less-than-sterling mood, he couldn't help but appreciate just how natural her beauty was. She had pulled her nape-length blond hair into an abbreviated ponytail, and that accentuated her flashing green eyes and firm-set jaw. She would have looked more herself with a smile on her lips rather than a frown. But even anger was becoming on her. In fact, she was more fetching now than when they first met . . .

His mind drifted back there for a moment, to their college days, and a bit of nostalgia seemed to temper his exasperation. *Isn't there something else I could say?* he wondered. *Something that might soothe her feelings or at least make her understand my side of the story?* But he knew better than to try. He'd said everything there was to say, argued his logic time and again for the past week and a half, ever since he'd accepted the old man's invitation for this fishing trip. *What's the big deal,* he'd thought at the time. *It's just a fishing trip, one lousy week. Surely Jan will understand.*

Oh, surely . . . Jeez, Steven. After ten years you'd think you would know better.

His foul mood reasserted itself. *Well, I can be stubborn too,* he thought. So he said nothing and they drove on in silence, and the test of wills continued.

The sun was just peeking over the Hoosier hills when he turned their Dodge Caravan onto the main drive of the Monroe County airport. It was a relatively small facility as airports go, certainly not in the same league as Indianapolis International some fifty miles to the north. But it was getting there. There were new runways going in and more small jets were making use of the facilities, including a regular shuttle that carried passengers to Indianapolis and Chicago. A few of the local Bloomington businesses had even established their own aviation wings on the airport grounds to handle shipping and company flights. And that was where Steven headed— past the small terminal building, nearly empty this early in the morning, and all the way to the end of the drive where the TUCKER AERO hangar was located. The flight office took up only one small corner of the large structure; the rest housed the two Lear jets belonging to the parent company, Tucker Pharmaceutical. Which happened to be Steven's employer as well.

He pulled through the open gate and parked in the private

lot to the side of the office. The bay doors of the hangar were standing open and one of the Lears was already outside, fueled and checked, ready to pull onto the tarmac.

Steven looked the jet over and felt a familiar queasiness in the pit of his stomach. Janet must have sensed his unease because she picked that time to say, without turning to look at him, "Did you remember your Dramamine?"

"I've got one of these instead," he answered, reaching up behind his ear to make sure the medicinal patch was still in place and hidden by his hair. "The guy at the drugstore said they really work. I sure hope so. It wouldn't do to blow my oatmeal all over the old man's plush interiors, right?" But Janet did not chuckle as she normally would have. She did not bother to respond at all. The warming spell was apparently over, and the cold front had slid back into place.

Steven fumed. "For Christ sake, Janet, it's just a fishing trip. I'll just be gone a week, one lousy week. I mean, what's the big deal? I've had business trips that lasted longer than that and you didn't pitch a fit like this." He stopped, waited for her defense. But there was only more of the tense, irritating silence. "Dammit, it's not as if I have a choice in the matter."

"You don't, huh?" Janet finally replied, still without looking in his direction. "C'mon, Steven. You're a grown man. You don't have to do anything you don't want."

"It's not that simple, Jan," he sighed. "You don't know how things work around here."

"I know enough. I know that you work as hard as anyone else in this company, probably harder, and you're damn good at what you do. You shouldn't have to brown-nose the boss like this to get along."

"I'm not brown-nosing!"

"Then what do you call it?"

Steven just looked at her and simmered a minute or two, unable to mount a defense or at least vocalize one. Janet often had that effect on him, for her arguments invariably had an edge of truth to them. Just enough to slip past all his own logic and excuses and hit home. "Look," he said, measuring his words to make the reasons sound more justifiable, even to himself. "Your freelance work is finally starting to pay off. You're building a solid career. I'm glad, I'm tickled shitless. But don't deny me the same thing, okay? This is *my* career, Janet. It's what I do. I've got five years invested in a company that's on its way up. I mean, we're moving, hon, we're nipping at the heels of the big boys—Eli Lilly, Letterle, Upjohns. This is my chance, maybe my only one. I'm not getting any younger, you know. I've got to keep climbing or I'll slide. And if that means camping with the boss and playing his little games, so be it. It's a small price to pay."

"Except for your self-respect, you mean."

Steven flinched at that. "Cold, Janet," he whispered. "Very cold."

She turned to look at him for the first time. Her head was bowed slightly and her gaze had softened since he'd last felt it. She knew she'd counterpunched a bit too effectively, struck a little too deep. "Steven," she said, this time without venom, "why don't you stand up to him for once? You don't belong on this trip. Let's face it, you're no Daniel Boone."

"What, you don't think I can cut it down in the Smokies?"

"On a weekend with some friends, sure. But this isn't a vacation, remember? You told me yourself, Elton Tucker's a competition freak. You'll be hustling the entire time—who can catch the most fish, who can make the best fire, who can pitch the best tent. Give it two days out there and you'll be taking bets on whose dong's the longest. Is that what you really want to get in to?"

He shook his head silently.

"Then just say no. Tell him you're sick or take some vacation time. We'll go out of town. Christ, he won't fire you for spending time with your wife."

"Tell that to Art Griffin," he finally replied. "You remember Art, don't you, from the office parties? Fortyish, balding? Looked like he starched his underwear? He was the golden boy when I hired on. Everyone thought the sun rose and set in his ass. But then Tucker invited him to go on some rock-climbing trip and Art turned him down—he had a softball tourney that weekend or something like that. Within six months he was buried under the shittiest accounts they could dig up, and when he couldn't keep up with the workload, they busted him back to the mailroom. I mean, Jesus, the mailroom? Is that where you want me to end up?''

Janet still held his gaze even though her reply did not come immediately, and for an instant Steven thought he'd finally gotten through to her. But then her lips pursed, thinned to a hard line, and she returned to staring out the window. ''Do what you want,'' she told him in a dull sigh that signaled the end to another round. No winner. Only casualties.

Steven frowned with frustration. ''Okay, have it your way,'' he snapped impatiently. ''The others should be here pretty soon. I'd better get my gear out.'' He left the keys in the ignition and got out, stretched his legs, reveled in the clean morning air and even more so the lack of tension in it. It was good just to distance himself, escape all the bickering they'd done of late. Who knows, he thought. After the last week, maybe this trip won't be so bad after all.

With Elton Tucker? Please!

He went around to the back of the van and opened the door to the storage area behind the rear seat, then started to stack his gear on the pavement. First the Northface backpack with internal frame (easier on your back that way, the salesman at J. L. Waters had said), then the Kelty Nimbus sleeping bag (good to ten degrees, the salesman had said), and the Daiwa fishing kit and expanding tackle box (from K-Mart, where there were no salesmen and the cashier just snapped her gum). He had all the popular lures from the TV fishing shows, the spoons and jigs and spray-on fish scent and every rubber insect known to man. He'd even bought a copy of the *Pocket Encyclopedia of Fishing*, which he now carried in his back pocket and quizzed himself on religiously. All told, the whole outfit, including the new clothes in the pack's main compartment and the overpriced hiking boots on his feet, had set him back more than he cared to admit or even think about for very long. But it was a necessary evil, he figured. After all, he had no comparable gear to take along—he'd never been camping in his life, and the old bamboo pole he'd fished with once or twice with his dad and grandpa had been discarded long ago with the rest of the souvenirs of adolescence. And besides that, this wasn't just any camping trip, was it? It was as much a beauty contest as anything else. Whoever makes the best impression, right? A picture popped into his head, a skewed vision of himself in his spanking new outdoor clothes, wearing a tiara and a big ribbon across his chest that read Mr. Pharmaceutical as he paraded down a runway . . . Steven grimaced at the thought. It would have been funny had it not been so close to the truth.

"Can I help you with that stuff?" said an older man who came out of the open hangar bay, wiping his hands on a rag. He was an unkempt sort, at least for a Tucker employee, dressed in stained coveralls with the name JERRY stitched in gold above the TUCKER AERO logo. He approached with a lanky, long-legged gait and a friendly grin, picked up Steven's gear, and slung them over a shoulder. For a moment he stood there, looking the young executive over a time or two and none to subtly at that. "So you're going fishing with Mr. Tucker, huh?" he asked, his grin looking more and more like a smirk.

Steven looked down self-consciously. Maybe I should have worn some of the new stuff, he thought, conceding that his faded jeans and torn IU sweatshirt were more suited for a pickup game of sandlot ball than a trip to the wilds. But it shouldn't have marked him as that conspicuous an amateur. For that matter, neither should his physical condition. Steven Wilhoit was not a complete desk jockey, or at least he didn't look it. He kept trim and fit, still had his college waist size and a chest that he wasn't exactly ashamed of. So what's the guy getting at, he wondered, suddenly a little irritated. He glared back at Jerry, trying to match his contemptuous expression. But now it was not there, if it had truly ever been. Too defensive, Steven told himself. Get a grip, man. "So," he muttered, shifting the conversation, "when are the others coming?"

Jerry shrugged, checked his watch. "Shouldn't be long. Mr. Tucker said to be on the runway by six-thirty sharp, and he's never late. Never." He grinned again, touched his forehead as if doffing a hat, then carried the gear toward the waiting jet.

Steven turned to close the van doors and noticed that Janet had already moved over into the driver's seat, preparing to leave. He walked toward the front of the vehicle, trying to think of something witty or calming to say, anything to let them part on a decent note. Then he saw the lit cigarette dangling from her lips. "I thought you were going to give those up."

"I said I'd try," she snapped back at him. "So sue me, okay?"

"Okay, okay, excuse the hell out of me."

She took a long silent drag in defiance, then stubbed it out on the ashtray. "So . . . I'll pick you up a week from Sunday." It was as close to a question as she was liable to get.

He nodded. "I'm not sure what time. I'll just have to call you when I get in." He leaned on the windowsill a moment, reached in and traced his fingers across the back of her hand on the steering wheel. "Look, Jan," he whispered, "I don't want to leave it like this, you know? I'll tell you what. When I get back we'll take a long weekend, just you and me. Maybe we could even go up to Wisconsin to see your folks. Would you like that?"

Janet turned and looked at him, straight in the eye. But her manner remained cool. "We'll see," she replied with a complete lack of enthusiasm as she turned the key and slipped the van into gear. Steven had to do a quick two-step to save his toes as she backed out of the parking space and left the Tucker Aero compound.

Steven stood and watched her leave the airport until the

Caravan's taillights disappeared down Kirby Road into the morning gloom. She never failed to surprise him—he knew she was mad at him, but not *that* mad. Well, it was plainly obvious to him now, for she had committed the cardinal sin: she had forgotten, or refused, to kiss him good-bye. A trifling thing, perhaps, a mere detail to most. But not to him. He knew his wife well enough to be bothered by it, for it was one of her little rituals. No matter where he was going, across town or across the country, she always kissed him good-bye—sometimes a peck on the cheek, often deeper and more soulful than that, but always a kiss, without fail. "Just in case," she would say, meaning that if his plane went down or an eighteen-wheeler went out of control on the bypass and mashed him to a fine paste, at least he'd go knowing she loved him. He'd always thought it a bit silly and old-fashioned and played along just to keep her happy. But now he began to realize how much he'd come to count on it.

She'll get over it, he thought. Besides, what's she got to be so mad about, anyway? After all, she's not the one being forced into this fool's errand of a trip. She's not the one having to . . .

Go on, say it. Brown-nose.

He could at least admit it to himself, and he didn't like it one bit. But it wasn't like he had a choice in the matter. He liked his job, despite that hairy asshole of a boss, and he intended to keep it, fight for it if need be. Or fish for it, to be more precise. Because the alternative—pounding the pavement with résumé in hand—was just unacceptable. He was thirty-five now, too damn old to cut loose and drift with the flotsam and jetsam of the business world. There was just too much competition these days, too many feral MBAs on the prowl. They came into the complex all the time, new graduates from the business school at Indiana University and other nearby colleges, sniffing around for internships or entry-level positions, any little flap of skin they could get a tooth into and hang on for dear life. Steven knew them well; he saw that steel glint, that hunger in their eyes, and he knew it was something he no longer possessed. Not to that keen degree. And experience? That wouldn't help him much either. Because his résumé would be just a scrap of paper without a good reference from Elton Tucker to cover the last five years. And if the old man suspected he was leaving just to avoid one of these trips . . .

Bye-bye, executive level, hello, McDonald's. And would you like some fries with that?

Buck up, an inner voice tried to cheer him. Look on the bright side—at least it isn't rock climbing this time. Just a little camping and a little fishing in the Smokies of Tennessee. Hell, the Cub Scouts do it all the time. You can take that, can't you? Who knows, maybe it won't be so bad. Maybe you'll have a good time, come out of this smelling like a rose.

Or like a mailroom attendant, he thought ruefully.

The roar of an engine brought him out of his reverie. He turned, half expecting the mini-van and Janet returning for that forgotten kiss. But it was a black Trans-Am this time, a car he didn't recognize from the executive lot. If this is one of my new fishing buddies, he thought sarcastically, the old man must be culling his prospects from completely different sections of the company. He watched the sleek sporter wheel through the gate as if expecting a checkered flag, then whipped into a parking space and stopped with a screech just shy of the chain-link fence. The driver's door swung open and the young man behind the tilt wheel unwedged himself, sort of rolled out onto the ground and barely got a leg under him to catch his weight. Steven didn't recognize him any more than his car. But he sighed with relief nonetheless. For one reason he'd been dreading this trip was his fear of embarrassment—what if the others are more experienced, what if I look stupid trying to keep up? But he didn't feel quite so bad anymore.

The stranger looked over at Wilhoit and smiled, came toward him. Steven could see now that the young man wasn't quite as large as he'd first thought; two hundred forty pounds maybe, no more than that. He just looked larger, because of his shorter stature and an ample gut that preceded him everywhere. It was invariably the focus of initial impression. But overall he was not that large or obese; he did not have flabby arms or wide hips or an undulating succession of chins. Just the distended abdomen, and a penchant for wheezing if he moved a bit too quickly. Steven patted his own firm, flat stomach, silently thanking Janet for the raquetball club membership on his last birthday. *I might not be Daniel Boone*, he thought, *but at least I'm in decent shape. If there are any forced marches in our immediate future, I doubt I'll be the one bringing up the rear.*

"Hiya, Steve." The man smiled and came forward with a meaty hand outstretched. Despite the morning chill in the air, he had already worked up a thin sheen of sweat just getting out of the car. "I didn't know you were in on this thing."

"Well, I wasn't expecting to see you here either," Steven replied. And he wasn't lying; he simply had no idea who the younger man was. He kept hoping a name would pop up in the back of his mind to match the face. But so far it was a total blank. So he tried to keep the conversation as general as possible. "So . . . how have you been doing?"

"Oh, fair to middlin'," the other said. "How about you?"

"Okay, I guess." And that's where the conversation died. Steven scrambled for something to fill the uncomfortable void, until he saw the man smile knowingly.

"You don't remember me, do you?" He held out his hand. "Andy Church. I'm a plant foreman at the Pharm. We met at the office party last year. Remember?"

"Oh, yeah," Steven said, lying. It still wouldn't come. Office party . . . he'd gotten a little looped that night, so the whole thing was still a bit fuzzy. Janet would have known; she had a much better memory for names and faces, and she could hold her liquor better too. *A plant foreman, huh? What would he have been doing at an office party? It just didn't jibe.* But Steven was the picture of diplomacy, so he never let his confusion show through. "Yeah, that was a wild night, wasn't it?"

"Boy, you're telling me." Church smiled. But it didn't quite match the sad look in his eyes. He glanced back toward the road. "Wasn't that your wife I passed on the way in? I waved, but I doubt she'd remember me." He leaned closer. "I could be mistaken, but she didn't look particularly happy."

Steven shrugged. "She's not real hot on this fishing trip idea."

"I can believe it. That's what wives are for, right? To piss and moan about every little thing?"

"I suppose. You're married, I take it?"

"Was. Been divorced about six months now. You probably remember Connie from the party." He didn't catch the blank look on Steven's face. "Yeah, I'm a free man these days. I can stay out late every night, I can drink all the beer my poor bladder can hold. I can piss off the back porch if I want to. And best of all, I can go fishing with the boys. What more can a man want, right?" There was a hint of sarcasm in his voice, a lack of conviction. Even he must have detected it, for he turned away, moved back toward the Trans-Am. "Better get my gear unloaded," he said over his shoulder. "You do much fishing, Steven?"

"Are you kidding? I don't even like fish. I guess I'm more of a Chicken McNugget man, you know?"

Andy laughed as he turned the key in the lock and popped the trunk lid. "Oh, I like the taste, all right. But it's a lot easier to do your trolling along the frozen food aisle than to fly off to some godforsaken lake in the boonies and do it the hard way. On the other hand, this trip has very little to do with fishing, right? More like a stroke party for the old man's ego."

"You don't like him, do you?"

Church grinned. "Who does?" He dumped an old duffle bag onto the pavement next to his backpack and a small Igloo cooler. Jerry came back about then to pick up the gear and transport it to the plane while Andy went for his spincasting rod between the bucket seats up front. "Who else is coming on this little shindig, do you know?"

Steven was about to profess ignorance when he spotted another vehicle turning on the airport's main drive. "I think we're about to find out."

An older Chrysler LeBaron came toward them through the gate. The man behind the wheel had a lean face, older than Steven, and wore reflective sunglasses and a golf hat tilted to one side like Frank Sinatra. Again, Wilhoit was at a loss. After five years he thought he knew the people at Tucker Pharms. But he was quickly realizing just how big a company it was.

Andy, on the other hand, had a different reaction. "Oh, no," he groaned, then made a gagging sound. "Not Paul Covey."

"You know him?"

"I know of him. He's a drug rep—takes the samples around to doctors' offices, brings in orders, stuff like that."

"What's wrong with that?"

"Nothing, with the job. Same as there's nothing wrong with insurance salesmen and used-car dealerships and Amway distributors. But there's always that one loudmouth that makes the rest of 'em look bad. You know, a reptile, a real . . . salesman. Cloying, obnoxious, bad jokes, the whole shebang."

"In other words, if he asks you to pull his finger, don't do it."

"Right."

The new man was just getting out of his car. His sweater and dungarees seemed baggy hanging on that tall, lanky frame. He had bushy eyebrows and a long face, would probably develop jowls later in life. And when he doffed the golf cap to run a hand through his hair, they saw that not much of it remained. Still, he did not look particularly unctuous. Contrary to Church's description, this guy looked more like a high-school math teacher than anything else.

But just then the man looked over at them and smiled. And that one expression proved Steven a poor judge of character. For it seemed well oiled and insincere, a big horse grin that was a little too wide and a little too forced.

"Well, lookee here," called the newcomer in a distinctive Hoosier drawl. "If it ain't Lewis and Clark, heading out for Louisianie. Don't you'uns tame too much of that wilderness now. Leave something for the rest of us pilgrims, okay?" He burst out laughing then, and despite a maturity that eclipsed them both, it still came out high-pitched and grating, a perfect Eddie Haskell imitation. He came over, holding out a hand. "Looks like we're in this together, huh? I don't think we've been introduced." The three exchanged names, but mostly there was a lot of hand shaking. Real shaking, so that the whole arm got a workout. Steven could tell Covey did that for a living, and the overly aggressive pumping was probably his way of getting attention or marking a territory.

"This oughta be real interesting," Covey was saying as he went back to the car to roll up the windows and lock the doors. "Nothing like taking a couple of greenhorns out into the woods. I won't have to bait you boys' hooks, now will I?" He cackled again, and the other two exchanged glances, each knowing intuitively what the other was thinking. *After a week of this, which one of us will throttle him first?*

Covey turned to get his fishing rod and tackle box from the trunk but his attention was drawn away toward the road. He shaded his eyes against the glare of the by-now rising sun. "Look alive, boys," he called to Church and Wilhoit. "The scoutmaster's coming."

It was one of the old man's new Chevy Blazers that cruised onto the company grounds, the red one he drove on Tuesdays. It stopped a few yards away and the driver stepped out, all but silhouetted against the orange horizon. He was a big man, not as tall as Covey but wider, as powerfully built now as in his prime some forty years before, and he carried himself with a youthful swagger that most considered an act but few questioned. He stood there and looked them over silently,

his squared jaw set, his eyes hidden beneath bushy grey brows
as they moved from one man to the other like a commander
inspecting his troops. The three were not surprised by this;
they were used to Elton Tucker's all-business demeanor, an
analytical, almost-aloof manner that had made him very rich
and successful and very few friends among his own work
force. They had resigned themselves to these silent, scowling
examinations sometime back. But they certainly were not
expecting the smile that suddenly greeted them. "Ahh,"
Tucker sighed. "Great day for a trip, huh?" He stretched
like a cat, breathed in the crisp morning air, then clapped his
hands with enthusiastic approval. "Well, what are we waiting
for? Let's get this show on the road. Jerry! Come here, get
this gear loaded."

The three employees exchanged bewildered looks as the
workman appeared yet again and hurried to do the boss's
bidding. Covey turned on a heel and went to gather his things
from the LeBaron, while Church and Wilhoit followed Tucker
toward the flight office. Steven leaned over to the younger
man, whispered, "Have you ever seen him grin this much?"

Church shook his head. "Gives you the creeps, doesn't
it?"

Tucker glanced back over his shoulder, grinned as if he'd
overheard their comments or at least inferred their meaning.
"We're gonna have fun, boys," he told them with a laugh.
"Don't you agree?"

Together, "Yessir."

"Please," he said, mock-flinching a little. "This isn't the
office. Call me Elton, okay?"

"Okay. Elton."

"That's better. Now you three go ahead and get on board.
I'll get the pilot and then we'll be going places."

"How long will it take us to get to Tennessee?" Andy
asked.

The old man stopped and slowly turned to look at Church,
which made Andy retreat a step or two just from inference

alone. But Tucker's smile had not disappeared. In fact, it was wider than ever. "You let me worry about our destination, Andrew," he said, even reaching out to pat the young man's shoulder reassuringly. He glanced over at Steven, said "Nice boots, Wilhoit" in passing, and headed for the hangar office.

Steven looked to Church for an explanation, but Andy just shrugged. "Too weird" was all he would venture.

Paul Covey had just finished turning his gear over to Jerry and now stood at the small steps of the jet, waiting for the others to join him. "He's pretty chipper this morning, huh?" he said, nodding to their now-absent employer. "He stays that way, and this trip might be fun after all. Hey, I'll bet the bar's well stocked. Anybody for a little nip?"

They gaped at him. "This early?"

Covey frowned at the lack of enthusiasm. "Pussies," he muttered and went on into the cabin.

"This might be fun after all," Steven said, repeating Covey's words. He looked at Church. "You think there's a chance of that?"

They both thought about it a moment, then answered in unison. "Nah!"

Andy went through the hatch while Steven hesitated on the steps, watching the roadway in the distance, hoping to see the Caravan there and Janet returning for a proper farewell. And he began to wonder if the good-bye kiss was just her ritual after all. Because right now he was the one with the real hinky feeling.

Just in case, she would have said. Just in case of what?

He reached up out of habit to check the airsickness patch again, but this time his fingertips found only a sticky spot of bare skin. The damned thing had fallen off! He immediately started scouring the ground to no avail, then remembered the spares he'd stuck in a pocket on his backpack . . . but that was already locked away with the other cargo. Damn! He started down the steps, determined to find Jerry and have him open the storage compartment. But before he could reach the bottom Elton Tucker came out of the office door with the pilot in tow.

Time to leave.

With a sinking feeling he climbed into the belly of the Lear, found a seat and strapped himself into it, and got a death grip on the armrests. Take a deep breath, he told himself, in and out, in and out, nice and steady. You're not going to be sick, you're not going to be sick . . .

A bubble of queasiness broke loose and rose into his throat. He winced. The bitter acidic taste told him his stomach was already out of sorts, and the plane hadn't even left the ground yet.

You're going to be sick, he assured himself. Get used to it.

TWO

JANET SAT AT THE DRAWING TABLE IN THE STUDY SUR-rounded by the tools of her trade; the Berol pencils and the fine camel-hair brushes, the markers and T-squares and kneaded erasers. And she did nothing. She just sat, and the large pad of newsprint before her that she used for preliminary sketches was as blank as it had been two hours before. Her pencil hovered there unmoving, had yet to touch the page completely. Instead she swiveled gently back and forth on her stool and stared vacantly out the window above the table. Her gaze was fixed on the persimmon tree in the side yard, still clinging to its fruit in anticipation of a coming chill that, being September and being Indiana, might still be months away. She looked at the tree steadily, unwavering, but she did not really see it. Instead her eyes were focused well beyond that, past the boundaries of yard and city and county, till she seemed to traverse the wilds of the Smoky Mountains two states away, searching for pieces of downed aircraft . . .

Stop it, she mentally snapped at herself, breaking that stolid trance for the first time in hours. So he hasn't called yet. Big deal. It doesn't mean there's trouble. Quit jumping to conclusions. It's only been—she checked her watch—four and a half hours since he took off . . .

Four and a half? That long?

She shook herself as if to toss off the cold hands of worry or at least lessen their grip. You've got other things to think about. You're under deadline for this book, remember? If you don't get some painting done soon . . .

Okay, okay.

She ran her pencil into the electric sharpener again, even though it didn't really need it, and then did the same for the three backup pencils lying within easy reach. She rearranged her erasers and the markers she used for color embellishing, and she swept any dust and eraser rubbings from the sketch pad. Then she took a deep breath and picked up her pencil.

And just sat there.

The blank grey newsprint glared at her knowingly, taunting her with the knowledge that her muse had departed, at least for the meantime. She tried priming her mental pump over and over in hopes that a spark of inspiration might spring full-blown from her mind and splash onto the page before her. But nothing would come. In desperation she looked to the samples of her previous work, hanging all around the room in carved wooden frames that Steven had specially ordered in nearby Nashville in Brown County. They were all scenes of her bread-and-butter characters, Chucklehead the stuffed moose and his heroic young owner, Teddy, from the three books in the series that she had already illustrated. She looked them over with a hypercritical eye and frowned;

though they were in essence the genesis of her fledgling but so-far lucrative career, they were also sources of continued consternation. Janet had always considered herself a writer as well as an artist, and she had many ideas of her own in mind, children's projects she was proud of and eager to get started on. But unfortunately her first assignment was Chucklehead, a completely derivative cross between Winnie the Pooh and the Wizard of Oz, and she did her job a little too well. The resulting success of the first book had spawned three sequels, including the one she was presently contracted for, and, to Janet's chagrin, had irrevocably identified her with a character she hated. Working with such second-rate material had stunted her creativity; it was becoming increasingly hard to squeeze any variation at all out of these stories. Each book was little more than a retread of the previous one, and she was always in danger of repeating herself. Let's face it, she sighed. You're bored with this. It's time to move on.

But she'd said that before, right after the first book. And again after the second. And the third. And now this one. And if they waved a bigger check in front of her eyes for the next Chucklehead opus, the chances were good she'd be saying it again.

She leaned down and plucked several discarded drawings from the trash basket beside the desk, unwadded them and smoothed the wrinkles with both hands. The first two were just wishful doodles—one had Chucklehead dressed as a hooker, complete with fishnet stockings, and another had the living moose-doll being strangled and de-stuffed by his beloved master Teddy. She discarded those for a second time and concentrated instead on the other she had retrieved. It was an actual scene from her latest assignment and the only honest attempt at illustration she'd made all morning, even if it was halfhearted at that. It was to have been the proverbial happy-ending scene, after Chucklehead and Teddy had rescued the princess from the Nogre King and returned her to the wondrous forest kingdom of Glitterwood. It was supposed to be a jubilant scene, festive, joyous. But what she had intended and what her pencil had eventually wrought were two entirely different things. The wrinkled scene was dark and foreboding, a sinister forest of shadow within shadow, and for a rough sketch it had a depth and mystery that almost brought a chill to her skin. The heroic moose and master looked all right in the center of the page—she could draw those two in her sleep by now—but the forest creatures gathered to greet them were very much out of character. Pixies and elves and fairies gathered there, all crouched and dark as if the very shadows were taking physical form and closing in around the intruders. And their furtive, grinning expressions, meant to be grateful at the princess's return, could just as easily have passed for wicked, malevolent . . .

"Good, Janet," she sighed. "Real good. That oughta scare the shit out of the little tykes." She started to discard it, then took one last look at the puzzling drawing. It was so different from what she'd intended . . . Where the hell did it come from, anyway?

Her eyes slid slowly across the page and centered on Chucklehead, of all things. Something about him didn't look right, stranded there in the middle of that haunted wood. It was a moose's head and antlers, all right, but the face, the eyes . . .

Janet abruptly crumpled the paper again, harder and angrier this time than when she last saw Steven's face there. She threw it all the way into the hall, where she wouldn't be tempted to look at it again. Give it up, she thought, dropping her pencil in despair. You won't get any work done today, not with this shitty mood you're in. For no matter how hard you fight it, it'll find a way of insinuating itself into every drawing and foul them up. Turn them against you.

She immediately reached for a cigarette again, the fourth in the last hour. But this time she did more than just stop herself with a mental reprimand. She grabbed up the whole pack and crushed it in her fist. "I promised Steven I'd quit,

dammit,'' she said. ''And I'm not going to disappoint him.''
No, she'd just have to find some other way of settling her
jangled nerves.

A bike ride? Janet almost smiled; that would surely do the
trick. To be on her ten-speed out on some deserted country
road, legs pumping, torso bent close to the frame to cut the
wind. That would be great. But she just couldn't leave, not
yet anyway. Not until the phone rang.

Dammit, Steven, why don't you call?!

He's still angry, she tried to rationalize. You pushed too
hard on this one, especially after he'd already made up his
mind. Now this could be his way of getting back at you.
After all, he knows how you always worry . . . But then she
frowned. For it was that very reason that convinced her he
would call. He would never put her through that on purpose.
He was just too considerate for that. Way too considerate.
This was the same guy who still held doors for ladies and
shoveled his neighbors' walks in the winter without being
asked and thanked cashiers for thanking him in the first place.
Sometimes it bordered on the compulsive, but it was always
sweet and sincere and one of the main reasons she loved him
so much.

But if he wasn't doing this on purpose . . .

. . . Plane debris littering the wilderness . . .

She forced such macabre thoughts from her mind, refusing
them weight and substance. But that was becoming increasingly difficult as the minutes ticked by. How much longer—

The phone *rang*.

Janet jolted as if shot; even though she'd been expecting
it for hours and praying for it, the sound was still remarkably
loud in the silence of her studio. She almost fell off the stool
but regained enough of her balance to land on her feet and
lunge for the handset. She wanted to yell his name into the
mouthpiece but caught herself; now that the call was here
and the urgency eased somewhat, a spark of unflagging pride
said play it cool, be nonchalant or he'll know you were

worried. So she took a deep breath and her "Hello?" came out measured and unperturbed.

"Hi, honey," came the voice from the other end of the line, but it was different from what she'd been expecting. Female. Throaty. Achingly slow.

Janet sighed wearily and sagged into the nearest lounge chair. "Hello, Mom. How are you today?"

"Oh, I'm all right," her mother's voice replied slowly, painfully. Dramatically so. "Except for my back, you know. Gave me fits all night. But I'll be okay." Her voice trailed off there for effect, which was as good a place as any since her arsenal of small talk was depleted. From there she cut right to the chase. "So," she wondered nonchalantly, "did you let him go or not?"

"I didn't *let* him do anything. He just went."

"That's what I figured," her mother said knowingly. "He's that much like your father, you know. Harry just lived for work. Never had any time for his wife or children. And Steven's his spitting image. Your father up one side and down the other."

"I don't know if I'd go that far, Mom."

"You should've stopped him, Jan."

Janet almost laughed. "He's a grown man, Mother. Just how was I supposed to do that?"

"Just put your foot down for once. Tell him where you stand."

"You mean give him an ultimatum? Over a fishing trip? Get real, Mom. This was just an argument. It's not worth putting my marriage on the line. Besides, I don't remember you ever telling Daddy anything like that."

There was a pause at the other end of the line, and Janet could almost hear her mother pursing her lips in consternation. "Look, Mom," she continued, "I'm just not so sure it's worth making threats over. Now I'll admit, I was mad that he decided to go. For two years he hasn't taken any time off with me at all, no vacation, not even a weekend trip, just the two of us. But when Elton Tucker snaps his finger, boy . . . It made me furious, okay? But now . . . I don't know, maybe I was being selfish. I mean, it is business. Sorta. And from what Steven's told me, and some of the other wives as well, it could have an impact on his future with the company. And his career *is* his identity these days, especially since my illustrating has started to pay off. I think his male pride's taken a few lumps, though he'd never admit it. He wants a promotion badly. I should've realized that from how stubborn he acted. Maybe I should've just accepted it.''

"But you're his wife. He should have considered your feelings.''

"I didn't say I agreed with him, Mother. I just have to respect his judgment, you know? He *is* my husband.''

"I suppose,'' her mother sighed skeptically. The woman's understanding did not stretch quite as far as her daughter's.

"Look, Mom, I'm kinda expecting him to call anytime, so I'm going to let you go, okay?''

"Oh. Well . . .''

"I'll talk to you later, okay? Bye-bye.'' She hung up quickly, before her mother could rekindle the conversation and stretch it out any longer. In another few minutes it would have shifted from her insensitive husband back to her insensitive father, and Janet didn't need another rehash of her parents' marital woes, especially since the poor guy had been dead for six years now. Besides, she had her own troubles.

She pulled her feet up under her and set the phone in her lap, cradled it there like a bewildered child. "C'mon, Steven,'' she whispered to it. "Call me. Now.'' But no ring.

She hadn't been completely honest with her mother. Yes, she was irritated with the way Steven followed after Tucker like a puppy. But in truth she was more worried than angry. Afraid that this trip was a sign of estrangement. Unlike other couples, she and Steven had never been just husband and wife. They were best friends. They spent almost all of their free time together. And she wasn't tired of it, not after ten years. She missed every minute they weren't together. But what about Steven? Did he still feel the same?

Quit being so insecure, she cursed herself. Steven loves you. Have a little faith.

She sat there, patting the phone on her lap. She was still angry, but now mostly at herself. She knew he'd been trying to clear the air before he left, to kiss and make up. But she had to be stubborn and make an ass of herself. And now she regretted it more than anything.

Kiss and make up . . . That may have been what bothered her the most. I didn't kiss him, she thought, over and over. And now something bad's happened, I know it . . .

The phone seemed to vibrate under her palm. And a split second later the ringing started.

She just sat there, shocked. Afraid to pick it up, afraid it might be Mom again or the publisher wondering about her paintings or . . . It rang three more times before she finally plucked the handset from its perch.

The operator's voice was distant and impersonal. "I have a collect call from a Steven Wilhoit. Will you accept the charges?"

Janet immediately yelled "Yes" into the mouthpiece, all but deafening the poor girl at the other end. "Steven? Are you there?"

The line crackled with long-distance static. Then came the voice . . . "Hi, Pud," Steven said.

Janet sank deep into the chair cushions as if her muscles had all turned to liquid. Her relief was that pronounced, and for an instant she was so incredibly giddy that she almost laughed out loud. For she knew in that instant that he was not only alive and well but no longer angry with her. When he was upset, he always used her given name. But Pud—that was his affectionate nickname for her, short for Puddin'. She swallowed and took a deep breath, steadied her voice. "I was beginning to worry."

"I'm sorry about that," he sounded sincere. "But this is the first chance I've had to use a phone."

"Is everything all right?"

There was a hesitation at the other end of the line, and that caused Janet's previous unease to sprout all over again. "Well," Steven stammered, "yes and no. We're okay. The flight was okay."

"But?"

"Well . . . there was sort of a last-minute change in plans. We didn't go to the Smokies after all."

Didn't what? "What do you mean? You're not in Tennessee?"

"Nope."

"Then where are you?"

Steven chuckled, less from humor than his own disbelief. "Would you believe . . . Canada?"

THREE

"Pud? You still there?" Steven shook the receiver, rapped it against the wall of the phone booth as if to jar it back into working order. "Janet? Did you hear me?"

A bare whisper finally sounded at the other end of the line. "Canada . . ." his wife muttered, as if saying it aloud might make it more comprehensible.

"It's crazy, isn't it?" he commiserated. "One minute we're supposed to be headed for Tennessee, and next thing I know we're pointed north and crossing into Ontario."

"But . . . Canada?"

Steven smiled to himself and gave her a moment to let things sink in. It was a little hard to swallow, he'd admit.

It had taken him a while to adjust to the idea himself. He leaned back in the corner of the booth and dug into his shirt pocket for the pack of Rolaids he'd bought from a vending machine at the small country airport where they'd landed. He was already halfway through the roll and still his guts wouldn't stop churning. But it was better now than it had been. It wasn't until he'd emptied his stomach in the men's room at the airport's little terminal building that it showed any sign of subsiding at all. One thing's for sure, he decided. When a Wilhoit gets airsick, he pulls out all the stops. He popped the antacid into his mouth and sagged against the pay phone, waited for the booth to quit spinning.

"Did you actually say Ontario?" Janet wanted to know.

"As far as I know, hon. It's hard to tell just by looking. You know me and little towns. They all look alike." He slowly turned all the way around in the booth and scanned his surroundings as if Janet might somehow witness the scene through his eyes. The town certainly qualified as small. He was standing on the main street, so named, and the buildings within his immediate view never reached beyond two stories. There were mostly shops lining the street, like Cherie's Cafe and Sunset Country Sports Ltd. and Marsha's Office Supplies, or the bar immediately behind him that everyone called Lannie's but whose sign read simply TAVERN. Steven wondered how much more town there was beyond this; he'd seen very little on the cab ride from the airport, or maybe he just hadn't bothered to look. But that reminded him . . . He began to pat down his pockets, searching for the tourist brochures he'd picked up in passing through the little terminal building. They were in the cargo pocket on his left thigh, a folded two-color sheet and a larger, glossy brochure with color pictures. "I think this place has an Indian name . . ." he told his wife as he opened the booklets, and the word he was searching for jumped immediately to his attention. "Atikokan. It means Caribou Bones. See there, Pud, you learn something every day."

Janet sounded impatient. "But where is Atikokan?" she kept after him.

"Well, gimme a minute," he said, leafing through the literature faster and reading it aloud as he went. He picked out a detail here, a tidbit there, fitted them jigsawlike and fashioned at least a passing familiarity with the town he had been thrust into. Atikokan had been an iron mining town from the mid-forties to about a decade before, when the mines closed and a big chunk of the population moved away. But the rest of the town refused to roll over and die. It hung in there thanks to the tourism of "nearby Quetico" and nowadays encouraged a growing industrial base . . .

"What's a Quetico?" Janet asked, showing that she was indeed listening.

"I don't know yet," he said, going to the more colorful brochure. Flipping through the ads for canoeing outfitters and hunting camps, even coupons for local businesses (free soft drink offer at Cherie's Cafe, ten percent discount on all meals at TJ's . . .), he finally located a full-page map of the region. And there, outlined in red, was a massive tract of real estate labeled Quetico Provincial Park, the "canoeing capital of Canada." "Hell, hon," he said into the phone, "I'm right on top of the Canadian version of Yellowstone. This place is huge." He traced a finger across the wilds of the park until he reached the southern border and realized it was the real border, where Ontario ended and the United States began. "Hey," he said, "I'm not as far away as I thought. We're just a stone's throw from Minnesota. Well, it'd be a helluva throw, but we're still fairly close."

"Steven," Janet said firmly to interrupt his little travelogue, "I still don't get it. What are you doing there in the first place?"

"Tucker," he sighed, "who else? I don't know all the details—so far he's been playing the whole thing close to the vest. But on the plane he mentioned that he'd bought some land up here. Chicano Lake, something like that. The fishing's supposed to be great. And what the hell, it was probably just pocket change to him anyway.''

"He had this planned all along?''

"You know the old man,'' Steven said with a shrug. "He gets a kick out of stringing people along. And right now he's having a real hi-ho time.''

Janet was silent for a moment. "So,'' she asked, a bit sheepishly, "what are you going to do now?''

You mean am I going to bail out and come home, he started to snap. But he knew it sounded defensive and stopped himself. She wasn't baiting him this time. It was just a simple question, one she had every right to ask. So he softened his tone. "To tell you the truth, Pud, when I first realized we were changing plans I was apprehensive. I don't like surprises like that. But now that I'm up here it is kind of exciting. I mean, fishing's fishing to me, no matter where you go. And I've never been to Canada, and it is beautiful, at least what I've seen so far, mostly from the air. Maybe after I get back we'll come back up here on vacation.''

"Not likely, buckaroo,'' Janet said. "I don't like cold weather, remember?''

"But it's not cold up here, Jan. It's just mid-September —it's not much cooler than it is down home. It's actually pretty nice. I think you'd like it. Look, I'd better be getting back before they start thinking something's happened to me . . .''

"Wait a minute. Where can I get hold of you? Is there a number or something?''

Steven had been waiting for this part and dreading it. The shit was sure to hit the fan when he told her. "I don't know yet. Right now we're waiting for somebody to pick us up and then I guess we'll be heading for the old man's little slice of heaven, wherever that is. But I kinda doubt there'll be a phone there. I might not be able to call again for a few days.'' He gave her a moment, waited for the explosion. What if there's an emergency, what if one of the kids gets sick, if we had kids, that is, or what if I can't find where you put the checkbook . . . But to his amazement she didn't say a word. "Pud," he asked, "did you hear me?"

"I heard you," she finally said, her voice surprisingly calm, "and I'm not real happy about it. But there's nothing I can do, so that's that."

Steven was shocked. "But you're not mad at me anymore?"

"Mad? Well . . . Maybe a little. But do me one favor, okay? If you can get to a phone, please call me. 'Cause I'm going to worry, whether you like it or not."

He smiled. "You're crazy about me, aren't you?"

"I just miss having you under foot is all."

"Honey, I've only been gone a few hours."

"It seems like longer than that," Janet confessed. "And I've been thinking . . . I forgot to kiss you this morning. So consider yourself kissed, okay? Just in case."

Steven's face flushed, and he felt stupid for having argued with her in the first place. Hell, he felt stupid for even being there. What sane man goes off tramping around in the woods with three bozos he barely knows when he has someone like that at home? "I love you too," he whispered into the phone. "And I'll tell you what. Maybe it's a good thing to get away once in a while. Because it sure reminds you of what you've got at home, you know? Gotta go, Pud. See you a week from Sunday." He hung up quickly, before she could say another word. It was bad enough when she was being adversarial, but now . . . Now he felt like more of a heel than ever.

From the corner of his eye he saw the door of Lannie's open and a stomach come out, followed closely by its owner. Andy Church paused there to empty a small bag of Dorito crumbs into his mouth, then crumpled the package and threw it into a trash can beside the door. He glanced around the small, mostly empty parking lot as if looking for someone . . . Steven quickly stepped out of the phone booth and was halfway across the front of the building before Andy saw him coming. "Well," he said, "we were starting to wonder about you, Steve. Where'd you disappear to?"

"Just out here, getting a breath of fresh air."

Andy nodded. "Still sick, huh?"

Wilhoit was surprised. He was so positive he'd kept it to himself. He'd even tried muffling his heaves in the airport bathroom, flushing the toilet as cover. "How did you know?"

"On the plane," the heavier man told him. "You turned a bright shade of green right after we took off. You know, my little brother used to look just like that when he got carsick on vacation."

Steven groaned. "I was hoping no one would see. I'll bet everyone had a good laugh over it."

"Not really. I think I'm the only one who noticed. Covey was too busy raiding the liquor cabinet and Tucker spent most of his time in the cockpit, probably so we wouldn't ask too many questions too early and ruin his little surprise." Andy glanced over at the phone booth, jerked a thumb in its direction. "Calling the little woman with the good news?"

Steven cursed himself. So far he was batting a thousand; everything he'd tried to conceal seemed common knowledge. He looked at the other man defensively and felt as if he'd been caught with his hand in the cookie jar. That's exactly why he hadn't called as soon as they reached Atikokan Municipal Airport. He wanted to wait and slip away, to phone in private so they couldn't accuse him of being henpecked or pussy-whipped. But now he'd blown it. Church had made a logical assumption, and any excuses he gave would only make him look worse. "Yeah, I called my wife," he admitted. "Big fucking deal."

Andy shrugged off his belligerent tone. "No deal at all, man. If I were still with Connie, I'd've called her too. There ain't much sense in letting them worry. Now, your wife is Jane, isn't it?"

"Janet."

"That's right. She seems real nice. And it doesn't hurt that she's one sharp lady, right?"

Steven smiled. "Then you do know my wife."

"Are you kidding, friend? You two are legends around the company. One of the only happily married couples left. I'm jealous, I'll admit. You know, me and Connie, we had some good times in our two years. But in the end, the bad just outweighed 'em. Like that party, right?"

Steven decided to admit that he didn't know, that he didn't remember Connie at the party or Andy for that matter, and that he'd just been placating him all day long. But then a memory came bubbling out of his subconscious. The sounds of an argument . . . There had been a squabble that night, between Jerry Burleigh's secretary and her husband. It was volatile but short, over before Mr. Tucker ever got wind of it. But it was still embarrassing. And now that he thought about it, her husband had been from out in the plant . . .

"So . . . how did she take it?"

Steven snapped out of it. "I'm sorry?"

"Your wife," Andy said. "How did she take the news of our unexpected little excursion?"

"Pretty well, actually," Steven admitted. "I was really expecting some fireworks, especially after the donnybrook we had this morning. But she was pretty calm and collected, and I just don't get it. You know, every time I think I've got her figured out, bang, she takes me completely off-guard."

Andy gave a chortle, and his stomach jostled like an amateur Santa. "Get with the game, Wilhoit. You're not supposed to understand them. That's most of the fun, so enjoy it and hope it lasts. Because when you do have her figured out, that's when the party'll be over. Take my word for it." He leaned back against the frame of the tavern door and stuck his thumbs in his belt loops, resting his gut on his forearms. It was either a philosophical pose or an attempt to keep his ill-fitting jeans from sagging down his hips any farther. "You know, if I were you, I'd be back in Bloomington right now instead of following a nut like Elton Tucker around." He glanced cautiously through the window in the tavern door, suddenly worried that his voice might have carried inside.

"It ain't worth it, man. Not screwing with your marriage. No, sir."

Steven was beginning to feel even worse—between Janet and Andy and his own conscience, he was being triple-teamed. But then, like a bolt of instant enlightenment, he realized what was happening. "Oh, boy"—he laughed wryly—"you're slick, buddy. Really slick. You had me going for a minute there."

Church looked puzzled. "What are you talking about?"

"This commiseration, that's what. The sympathy, the you've-got-a-helluva wife, you-oughta-be-home bullshit. Trying to make me homesick, guilt me into turning back. You'd like that, wouldn't you? Thinning down the competition?"

The fat man laughed. "That's hogshit, man."

"Is it? Come on, Andy. We can drop the act. This trip doesn't have anything to do with fishing. It's business, pure and simple. Tucker has power and he likes to use it. He brings us up here to test us, to make us jump through hoops, and we're all prepared to do it if he dangles the right job in front of our noses. Like the regional manager position for the new southwest branch? Yeah, it'd be real convenient if I'd pull out right now. That'd leave just you and Willie Loman in there."

Church rubbed his face with exasperation. "Man, you yuppie types are pretty fucking paranoid, aren't you? You looking at me, a plant foreman, as competition for an upper office position? It doesn't usually work that way, chum."

"Not usually, no. Unless you made points with the big guy himself. Then anything's possible. I've heard of some pretty wild promotions in this company, a lot of them centered around these little scout trips of his. So I look at everyone as competition."

"Well"—Andy shrugged— "that may be your ticket, Steve, but not me. You know why? Because I don't want to move up. I don't want your southwest position. I could do the job, mind you—I can pilot a desk just as good as the next guy. But who needs the hassle? I'm happy right where I'm at. The money's good. I like the people I work with and they like me. And we're not trying to stab each other in the back all the time like you well-dressed piranha upstairs.''

Steven looked at him skeptically. "Then why are you here?''

"Survival," Andy said simply. "I want to keep what I've got right now. And if I'd turned him down . . . Well, you knew Art Griffin, right?''

"Yeah, I knew him.''

Church nodded. "Enough said then. But I've got a feeling you still don't believe me.''

Steven just smiled. He could be cagey too—especially when he wasn't sure what to believe. The man sounded sincere, but . . . "Let's just say I'm wary," he finally allowed.

Andy threw up his arms and laughed. "Oh, boy," he exclaimed sarcastically, "is this gonna be a fun trip!''

A few cars had passed along Main Street during their conversation, which seemed relatively busy for such a small town. But none of the vehicles had pulled into the tavern. At least until now. A beat-up old Land Rover clattered noisily into Lannie's parking lot, stopping just a few feet from where the two men stood. It was impossible to tell what model year the Rover was, only that it was old and rusting out along the fender wells and was covered in a thick coating of road dust, till even the original color of the paint was in question. Even the windows were stained brown and opaque except for the semicircles on the windshield that the wipers had been able to clear away. Steven couldn't quite make out the man's face behind the wheel, but had no trouble with the passenger in the backseat.

The rear window on the driver's side was down about halfway, just enough for the dog riding back there to stick its broad, bearlike head outside where the breeze could ruffle its thick grey coat. It was not an overly large dog like a German shepherd but it was powerfully built and rugged-looking, well suited to the Canadian backwoods, at least in appearance.

"What kind of dog is that?" Andy muttered aloud, and his voice attracted the dog's attention. Its ears swiveled in his direction, tall and alert, and then the dark soulful eyes fell on his and the stout animal began to wiggle in anticipation of being petted. Church stepped forward for a closer look. "I'm not sure, but I think it's a malamute . . ."

The driver's door opened just then with a loud creak, startling Andy, who took a quick step backward to rejoin his coworker. A thin, long-limbed figure climbed out of the Rover with a grunt of exertion, then turned to the Americans there and looked them over. The man was old, at least in his late-seventies, with pinched features shadowed beneath a bushy browline and thick-rimmed glasses. His hair was iron grey and cropped short, but some patches that stuck out from beneath his ball cap grew a little long and suggested either an inept barber or that he cut it himself. He was dressed in a Toronto Bluejays jacket and baggy jeans, hoisted halfway to his chin and belted there so that he looked like anyone's grandfather. Except this man was an Indian. That was what intrigued Steven the most; he had never seen a Native American (or Native Canadian) face-to-face. There was certainly no mistaking this old man's ethnic background. The dark ruddy cast of his skin, the broad nose and accentuated cheekbones, the eyes . . . Especially the eyes. There was something old about them, older than even his many years suggested.

The three of them just stood there, looking at one another, and Steven began to feel uncomfortable beneath the old Indian's blank stare. But then the man's stern features cracked into a nicotine-stained smile. He turned sideways, motioned to the still-wriggling dog in the window. "Elkhound," he told them. Then with a nod he stepped past them, hobbling a bit and favoring an arthritic hip, and disappeared into the tavern.

"That was weird, wasn't it?" Andy said, still looking after

the enigmatic senior even after he was gone. Then he turned back to the Land Rover and its captive canine. "So that's what a Norwegian elkhound looks like? I'd heard of 'em but I've never seen one. Till now, that is." He took a step nearer to the truck, and the dog's wriggling multiplied in direct proportion to his nearness. "That's one neat-looking dog."

"I don't know, Andy," Wilhoit warned him. "I don't think I'd touch it. You're not supposed to pet other people's dogs. No telling how they'll react."

"Are you kidding?" Church laughed. He pointed at the dog, who was now looking at them quizzically with ears alert and head cocked to one side. "Look at that face. Does that look like a killer to you? Jeez, Steve, you don't know much about dogs, do you?" He approached the elkhound slowly, reaching out his hand, palm down. "Hiya, pooch," he addressed it in a soft, friendly voice. "You're a nice dog, ain't ya?" The canine craned its thick neck and sniffed at his fingers, gave them a friendly lick. Church smiled with satisfaction and scratched behind its ears. "Yeah, you're a real sweetheart . . ."

The fat man tensed all of a sudden as if startled, his hand freezing on the dog's neck. Steven wasn't sure just why at first, but a moment later the growling had traveled the few feet between them and reached his ears as well. It was low and throaty, little more than a harsh exhalation, but it triggered a wariness in the two men that a louder warning would not have engendered. Steven stared at the dog, shocked that its demeanor could change so abruptly, but he found it still wriggling with delight, its tongue lolling from its mouth and happily licking at Church's arm. So where was the growl . . . Then his eyes shifted just slightly, off the dog itself and through the window into the truck's interior. Just past the elkhound's sturdy shoulder he caught the glare of two more eyes; just as dark and expressive as the first dog, but conveying a completely different emotion . . .

He took a quick step forward and grabbed the confused Church by the belt, jerked him back a step just as the other dog's head poked through beside the first like an enraged jack-in-the-box, jaws open, black lips pulled back from its teeth. It was an elkhound like the other, only larger, a male this time, and its personality was a polar extreme. It growled another warning and eyed the strangers heatedly even as the first dog mewled for Andy to come closer and play some more.

"Fucking mongrel," Church muttered under his breath as he counted his fingers to make sure they were all there.

"I tried to tell you," Steven said, unable to resist rubbing it in. "Jeez, Andy, you don't know much about dogs, do you?"

"Very funny," the fat man grumbled, mostly to himself. He made a mock punch at the two dogs, which delighted the first one even more and drew an angrier warning from the second. But as he started to turn back toward the tavern his eyes slid down the side of the truck and something there grabbed his attention. He stepped forward, mindful of the one mad dog still straining against the glass, and kneeled down for a better look. Steven, standing behind him, couldn't see the source of his fascination.

"What are you up to, Church?"

"There's a sign here, under the dirt," he said, moving aside so Wilhoit could look as well. Indeed, on the main panel of the driver's door there was lettering present, all but obscured beneath the layers of road dust and grime. A few letters were discernible—a "CH," an "L," a "KE"—and somehow even those few clues struck the same chord of familiarity that it obviously had in his coworker. Andy moved in on the door panel, rubbed at the dirt and even spat into his palm a time or two to cut the buildup. And slowly the words there began to take form.

Andy stepped back so they could both survey the find. It was a hand painting of a country lake and forest, and surrounding it were block letters reading CHALAKO LAKES WILDERNESS RANCH.

The two looked at each other and nodded. It was the name

they had expected, one totally foreign to them until only a few hours before.

FOUR

ONCE CHURCH HAD GONE OUTSIDE TO LOOK FOR THEIR ER-
rant companion, Paul Covey moved over into the chair next
to the big boss himself. "Can I get you another beer, Mr.
. . . Elton?"

Tucker's head was bowed, studying a piece of paper he'd
laid on the table before him. "No thank you, Paul," he said
without looking up. He tapped the half-full bottle next to his
hand. "I still have this one."

Covey nodded, cursing himself silently. *Of course he
doesn't need another beer, nitwit. If he did he'd buy it himself, and the waitress would bring it over. What would he
need you for, to unscrew the cap for him? Don't be so stupid.
You're gonna have to be more subtle than that.*

Unfortunately, subtlety wasn't Paul Covey's forte. And he
knew it.

But you'll just have to work at it, he thought. *Because this
is too important. It's your best chance for something better,
maybe your only chance. So don't fuck it up.*

Covey was tired. Not from the plane trip, but fifteen years
with the same job. Different companies during that time, but
the same positions with each: field representative, glorified
salesman. And he'd grown to hate it. Always moving about,
always hawking his line to people who were never really
interested in the newest products or just too busy to give him

much time. He had spent his whole adult life waiting: waiting to talk to pharmacists, waiting to talk to doctors, waiting for a better job to come along. And there were other drawbacks. Doctors' offices were always crammed with children, sniffling little larvae who'd never learned the courtesy of covering their mouths before coughing, who gave their germs away so selflessly. In the last few years he'd had the flu too many times to count, till it seemed nausea and sinus drainage was his normal condition, suffering a bout of good health only now and again.

But most of all, he wanted an office.

Wouldn't it be great, he daydreamed, to sit down in a chair at nine A.M. and still be there at five P.M.? To see the same people every day, to not shake every hand that comes your way? I'm forty-one, dammit. I don't want to be on the road anymore. I just want to sit down. I want some rest.

Unfortunately, he wasn't in the proper queue for that to happen. Management and executive positions were going to the business school wonders, like Wilhoit, with their sheepskins and heads full of theoretical notions but not an ounce of work experience. And all of a sudden they're moving up the corporate ladder while working stiffs like Paul couldn't even locate the first rung. No, there was only one way to circumvent that inbred process.

And Paul was sitting beside it.

If I can just make a good impression, he thought. It wasn't unheard of; people on these trips were often jumped far ahead, just on the basis of the old man's personal opinion. He'd heard all the stories. And now it was his turn.

Now . . . how to do it . . .

He might come out ahead once they got into the woods. After all, those other two were city boys, rank amateurs, while he grew up in the country, on a farm near Oolitic. He was sure to look better there. But until then, he could kinda prime the pump a bit. Drop a hint here and there, make himself look better by making them look worse. It was a little underhanded, even by his estimation. And he didn't especially like doing something like that to Andy Church; he seemed like a nice enough kid. But that's just what he was, a kid. He had his whole life to search for the fabled ladder. As for Wilhoit, he was a college boy know-it-all, and Paul had no stomach for such upstarts. So screw him, he decided. It's dog-eat-dog out there. If they didn't teach him that in school, he ought to pack it in right now.

He sat back and put a boot on the table edge, sipped his beer with an exaggerated "Ahh" to show what a self-satisfied man he was. "This is really nice," he said aloud, supposedly to himself. "Yessir, I've been looking forward to this trip. I've always thought it'd be good to get to know the people I work with." He looked toward the door after the departed Church. "Take Andy there for instance. Helluva guy. Everybody loves him. And I trust him completely, I really do. I think he's responsible enough, no matter what people say. I mean, who puts stock in rumors these days, right?" He snuck a sly glance at Tucker for the first time to gauge his reaction.

To his chagrin, the old man wasn't even paying attention.

He just sat there in his chair, and did not acknowledge Covey's presence at all. His eyes were still glued to the tabletop. Paul leaned closer. The piece of paper there was a page torn from a hunting magazine; the folds and wrinkles it had incurred in the old man's pocket had been smoothed out nice and neat to show the conclusion of an article on the venerable .30-30 for taking whitetail buck. But surely an incomplete story wouldn't have held his attention this long . . . Paul edged closer still, till he could make out the various advertisements for wilderness outfitters and hunting expeditions into Montana and Wisconsin and even farther north. And in the middle of the left column, circled in blue ink, he glimpsed the words CHALAKO LAKES. And he realized that this was the ad the boss had read to them over the cockpit's PA system.

Tucker finally looked up from the corner of his eye. His gaze met Covey's and the latter immediately paled; he suddenly realized he was all but perched on the old man's shoulder and quickly backed into his chair. The boss continued to watch him, pressing his point. "You were saying something, Paul?"

Covey flinched. He still couldn't get used to the company president calling him by his first name—it was usually Mr. this or Mr. that—and there was always that tinge of condescension in everything the old man said. Paul coughed and tried to repeat his little monologue on Andy Church, but he was self-conscious now and the seemingly off-the-cuff remarks refused to gel correctly in his brain. "Uh, I was just talking about how I really like him, don't get me wrong, but . . ."

Tucker gave a slight smirk of understanding and cut him off with a shake of his head. "Paul, please. I thought we left that back in Indiana. Just relax, okay? This isn't a business trip."

"It isn't?"

Tucker gave him a wry smile. "What made you think it was?"

Covey sat back in his chair, trying to decide whether Tucker was being sincere or jerking him around again, and finally decided on the latter. Not a business trip my ass, he thought, disgusted. He had no patience for baiting and word games, not when the tables were turned and it was directed at him for a change. He looked away, irritated, shrugged, and downed the rest of his beer, then motioned for the waitress to bring another round. "How long do we have to wait on this guy, anyway?" he muttered under his breath. "It's been two hours already."

"Patience," Elton said evenly, returning to his magazine page. "Mr. Davejac will be here."

"Maybe he's still looking for us back at the airport."

"I told the pilot to give him our gear and send him in this direction. He'll find us, don't worry." Then he added, under his breath, "If he wants to keep his job, that is."

Paul's brow knitted at that last comment. He thought about it a moment, wondering if the old man had added that for his benefit, another veiled reinforcement of whose trip this really was. And it irked him. He grumbled and sank back in his chair, didn't say another word.

Tucker could barely conceal his amusement. There was always at least one on every trip; someone more than willing to undercut his coworkers, hoping to shine brighter by comparison. Paul Covey was more ambitious than most, though; he was starting his campaign before they'd even reached their destination.

Not that Tucker was put off by such an approach. Guile and deceit certainly had its place in business and could even be a good character trait, at least in the old man's perception. But he preferred to judge his employees on each man's natural advantages and deficiencies, rather than speculation and character assassination. After all, that was the key to his, and his father's, philosophy. Talk was infinitely cheap and credentials easy to manipulate. But on these trips, where a man depended only on himself, it was easier to gauge his true makeup. It had been Virgil Tucker's central viewpoint, and his son Elton had parlayed that very mind-set into a quarter-billion-dollar corporation.

And now he had the perfect testing ground to hone those theories completely . . .

His eyes returned to the page before him, wrinkled and much carried, the ink of the text now blurred from the natural oil of his fingertips, left with prints covering prints. Except over the single advertisement circled in blue, the focus of his attention. His eyes had pored over the words countless times, till he all but knew them by heart. In fact, when he quoted the ad to his young companions over the jet's PA, he did not even have to take the folded page from his shirt pocket.

FOR SALE: ADVENTURE!

Chalako Lakes, 2000 +/− acres located less than two hours from Thunder Bay. Bear, deer, grouse, speckles, rainbows. Ponds and lakes, waterfalls. Licensed guide on property. Hunter's paradise. Inquiries invited. Delacroix Management Ltd., P.O. Box 4540, Thunder Bay, Ontario P7C 4V8.

Something had clicked in Tucker's mind from the moment he first glimpsed the ad. In just so many words it had evoked memories in him, crystal-clear images of those days he'd spent in the woods with his father, the shaper of his world, where he'd first learned to camp and hunt and stand on his own two feet. They'd owned a hundred and fifty-five acres in Greene County, Indiana, not far from where his company now flourished in Bloomington. And there he'd spent many a weekend, out in the woods. He remembered those days often, recalled them in terms of lessons learned and values strengthened, the same way he often replayed his father's sensible tenets for inspiration. But seldom did the scenes jump full-blown into his mind like pictures from a scrapbook. Until now.

All because of the advertisement.

But Elton Tucker was fiercely practical, not one to squander a million dollars—or more—on a nostalgic whim. So he made inquiries, as the text suggested. He soon discovered that Chalako Lakes was far from a money-making venture. As a hunting outfitter, it had not shown a profit in ten years, and in that time had been owned by seven different organizations and individuals. Tucker was not impressed. He turned his attention to other more pressing matters and all but let the subject slip from his mind.

But then the photos arrived . . .

The thought made him reach into the cordura briefcase he'd left leaning against the leg of his chair and take out the manila folder from Delacroix Management. He had received it barely a week before, with a notice that the company would consider lowering the purchase price still further. But the price wasn't what caught his attention. The company had included photos of the tract in question, and a more conclusive argument could not have been made. He slid the eight-by-

tens from the folder now and laid them before him, then
marveled for the hundredth time at the idyllic settings captured there. Pristine forests, unscarred by the presence of
man. Babbling brooks, crystalline lakes, tributaries that cut
through the deep woods like veins of blue, ripe for canoeing.
Forest floors carpeted in pine needles and laced with fingers
of shadow as sunlight struggled through the lattice overhead.
And finally, the clincher. It was a view of the main lake,
with the base camp's rustic cabin just edging the photo, barely
suggesting the presence of humanity at all. And in the background, across the lake and barely visible until he looked
closer, stood a magnificent buck just peeking through the tree
line, its great antlers raised majestically.

That was all it had taken. Tucker did not hesitate or ponder
his justification any further. He simply wired them a bank
note and purchased Chalako Lakes sight unseen. What the
hell, he told himself. Why be rich if you can't be irrational?
Besides, he had all the normal toys—cars, boats, houses—
that he could stomach. And land was always a good invest-
ment. Even if it was another country.

The whole deal had transpired only a week ago and still
his enthusiasm had yet to wane. For Elton Tucker, a man
notorious for his short interest span, it must have been some
sort of record. He would sit for long hours staring at the
photos, thinking of how his father would view that same land,
what Dad would say to him now. And as he thought of his
father and the woods, the true role of Chalako Lakes took
form in his mind . . .

A proving ground, per se. Which can turn out the better
executive, he wondered, Chalako Lakes or the IU School of
Business? There was only one way to find out.

Tucker's little "survival of the fittest" trips had been in
place for seven years already, nearly the life of the company.
They had started innocently enough, as simple getaways, a
chance for a rich man to put himself to the test as his normal
profession seldom did. Scuba diving, rock climbing, wilderness hikes—anything to get the ol' hammer to pounding

again, to give him that adrenaline fix he so craved. As for companions, there was never a shortage of eager young men in his own employ, more than willing to suffer the indignities of mosquitoes and sunburn if it meant a chance to suck up. It was during the very first trip, though, that he began to watch the men with him, to observe them and note their strengths and weaknesses, their character and performance outside the office and how it had a direct correlation to their business manner as well. He learned many things that way. To Elton Tucker it became an unwritten law: a survivor translates from environ to environ, whether by wits or intellect or physical ability. If a man can take command of his situation, whether diving the Barrier Reef or dangling from the sheer face of El Capitan, then he would take equal charge in the boardroom.

In retrospect Tucker was quite pleased with his record; in seven years he had not been wrong about his charges yet. His first impressions were usually dead-on. Which brings us to our current guests, he told himself silently as he glanced over at Paul, starting to give each of the men a predictive analysis. Let's see which of them is really Tucker material . . .

The front door of Lannie's swung open just then, throwing a bar of bright sunlight across the room and demanding the attention of the few patrons within. Tucker glanced up from his photos, half expecting it to be Wilhoit back from sneaking away to call his wife, or maybe Church returning with a bagful of sandwiches from the cafe across the street. But neither of them was in sight. Instead the doorway framed a Bluejays jacket and cap, both hung on a painfully lean frame. Though Tucker was an old man according to his employees and even himself on occasion—the term equated a certain reverence he enjoyed—the man who stood there now was far older than he, enough so to easily qualify as his father. The Indian stepped just inside the door and waited for it to close so his eyes could adjust to the relative gloom of the tavern's interior. Then he craned his wizened old neck and peered through thick prescription lenses at the room around him.

Tucker had a weary feeling about who the man was and who he was looking for. And, sure enough, as soon as those weak eyes fell on the corporate president's table, the ancient face cracked into a grin of satisfaction and the Indian shuffled toward them, one hand resting on a bad hip as if to coax just a bit more performance from it.

This is what you get, Tucker sighed, chastising himself silently as he waited for the ponderous stranger's approach and did a slow burn in the meantime. This is what happens when you jump in on something without all the details. Well, the old guy's history, no two ways about it. How can you expect to hunt with a guide who can barely navigate a barroom . . .

"Tucker's people, right?" the old Indian asked upon finally drawing near. "I thought I'd find you here."

"Oh, yeah?" Covey smirked. "Did you track us?"

"No tracking to it," he said as he lowered his brittle frame into a chair, slowly, as if those bones would never stand the trauma of a sudden movement. Once he was down he sighed from the exertion and completed his thought. "At the airport they said you wanted a drink. The cabbie that picked you up was Joe Aleski, and Joe is Lannie's brother-in-law. You want a beer, Joe brings you here. Never fails." He sat back in his chair, chuckling to himself.

Tucker wasted no time. "Look, Mr. Davejac, I think there's been a mistake made . . ."

The old man suddenly snorted a laugh and slapped the table. "You thought I was Barton? You must be blinder than me, eh? Do I look spry enough to dog you kids through them woods day and night? Hell no. My name's George Wilson. Barton's my grandson. He just asked me to do him this favor today and that's why I'm here, you know? But I wouldn't a done it for nobody but the boy. My kidneys are akilling me." The old man must have realized Tucker wasn't following him completely, because he just grinned and shrugged. "I'm here—that's the important thing. The boy says I should find you and wait." He leaned closer. "He also says you should buy me a beer." He winked and gave a bigger grin, then motioned for the waitress.

Wilhoit and Church came in then, and they didn't seem too surprised to find the old man sitting at their table. "Hey, gramps," Andy said as they approached, "those dogs of yours are crazier than shit. One almost took my hand clean off."

Wilson nodded in total agreement. "Boo-Boo's a mean bastard, there's no doubt. You can pet the bitch—Yogi's a sweet pup —but Boo-Boo'll take you down. Don't trust him much myself."

"Then why do you keep him?" Steven asked.

"I don't. Them's Barton's dogs."

"Who's Barton?"

"His grandson," Covey said. "Our guide."

"And we're not talking about lap animals here either," Wilson continued. "Not your cockapoodles and schnitzers or schnauzers or whatever. These here's work dogs. Hunters. The boy uses 'em in the field. Elkhounds are good trackers and they bay the game, keep it busy for you. Last year those two dogs helped bring in two bears. Big ones too."

"Where?" Tucker wanted to know. "At Chalako Lakes?"

Wilson looked at him and nodded. "Is that what you're after, Mr. Tucker?" he asked. "Bear? Or just a whitetail or two?"

"We're not hunters," Church answered for him. "We're just here to fish. There are fish up here, right?"

"Plenty of 'em," the old Indian answered. "But I coulda sworn you were supposed to be hunting . . ." He perked up a moment, craned his head to the side, and listened intently. It wasn't long before the others heard it too, the clattering of an engine outside. "There he is now," Wilson said and turned to the door a moment before it opened. "There's your guide."

The figure who came through the door then looked like an outdoorsman, fit every expectation, every cliché. He was big, not so much in height as sheer size, and the rolled-up sleeves of his flannel shirt showed forearms that were thick and knotted with muscle. His heritage, like George Wilson's, was clearly evident, if not more so: shocks of coal-black hair fringed his own Bluejays cap, and his squared jawline and broad cheekbones and equally broad nose left little doubt. The man certainly looked Indian. But most of all he just looked rugged. Especially when he fixed the Americans with his dark unsettling gaze and strode across the tavern in their direction.

He looked to Wilhoit first. Then Church and Covey and Tucker in turn, all without a word. Finally he turned to George Wilson. "Any problems, old man?" he asked in a surprisingly soft, almost-whispery voice, one that sounded like he'd had laryngitis or been punched in the throat too many times. It was his natural tone.

"Needs a new transmission," the elderly Indian replied. "Helluva racket. And new shocks too. Them bumpy roads about shook me to death."

The young man nodded, then looked to the others. "Which one of you's the boss?" Tucker raised his hand. "Well, you heard then. One of your trucks needs work."

Tucker glared back at him, looking none too pleased with the man nor his unapologetic attitude. "You're late, Mr. Davejac," he said in a clipped, no-nonsense manner, "if that's who you are. Two hours late. I don't tolerate that."

Davejac's expression remained impassive, nonplussed. "Yeah, well," he shrugged. "Shit happens." His lack of reverence toward Tucker was not lost on Steven and Andy. "That brings us to your other truck," he continued. "It broke down on me earlier this morning. I barely got it into town. It's been over at Mel's Husky all morning being fixed, till about an hour ago. That's what kept me." He took a folded piece of yellow paper from his shirt pocket and dropped it on the table. "There's the bill. I'll let you take care of it."

Tucker just glowered while Wilhoit and Church tried to hide their snickering.

"So," the Indian guide asked, "are you ready to get some hunting done or what?"

"I was just going to tell you, boy," Wilson informed his grandson. "They're only here to fish after all. No hunting."

The guide looked puzzled. That is to say, his steely eyes unsquinted for just a moment. They had to guess the rest. "Makes no difference to me," he said, shrugging. "But why were there four rifle cases on the plane? I unloaded them myself—they're in my truck."

"Surprise, surprise," Andy muttered, but somehow he wasn't.

Steven looked at Tucker. "Rifles? I thought we were fishing."

Tucker grinned mischievously. "Don't worry, my boy. We'll do that too." Then, before they could question further, he slipped his photo packet back into his bag and shouldered it, stood as if ready to go. "How far is it to the ranch?"

Davejac estimated silently a moment. "About an hour, hour and a half as the crow flies. But the roads are pretty bad out that way, mostly old lumber trails. Could take anywhere from two to three hours, depending on whether that other truck gives us problems. Now, I'll take the dogs and the old man with me—I have to drop him off at home first —and then I'll come back after you. One of you will have to drive the other truck and—"

"Wait a minute," Tucker interrupted. "Three hours? I don't want to ride in some bumpy-assed wreck for three hours. Aren't there any bush planes around here I could charter?"

"Well, yeah," Davejac replied. "The seaplane base is out past the airport on Steep Rock Lake."

"Then why don't we just fly in?"

"First," the Indian told them, "I went to the trouble of bringing both of these damn trucks in here to pick you up. I even got my aged grandfather there to help me."

"He's right." Wilson nodded. "I am aged."

Tucker was unimpressed. "And the second thing?"

Barton looked him square in the eye. "I don't fly," he said. "Period."

The boss stared right back. "Fine with me," he said. "You

and Grandpa can just drive our gear back out there while we take a plane. How about it, old man? Up to another drive?'' He reached for his wallet. "I can make it worth your while.''

"Nope,'' Wilson was adamant. "I brought the damn truck in but I ain't about to suffer the trip back again. You just drop me off at my place and I'll bid you good day, thank you.''

Steven Wilhoit was already feeling queasy again, squeezing the arms of his chair for support. Just the thought of another airplane ride . . . "I'll drive one of the trucks,'' he blurted when it became too much to consider. They all looked at him. He just shrugged. "I don't mind. Really.''

"Going by truck's fine with me too,'' Andy Church pitched in his support. "Besides, that last flight left me a little sick to my stomach.'' He looked at Wilhoit and grinned.

"All right, all right,'' Tucker said, his surrender taking the employees by surprise. "I came up here to rough it. Might as well start now.'' He headed toward the door, still scowling because he didn't get his way.

FIVE

BARTON DAVEJAC HAD GONE TO TAKE HIS GRANDFATHER home. He said it was just out toward the airport a ways, and he'd be back in about fifteen minutes. That gave whoever was interested a chance to look around.

Steven came out of the Sunset Country Sports Ltd. store and paused by a trash basket on the street. He took the fishing encyclopedia from his pocket and tossed it in. No need for that anymore, he'd decided, not with Tucker shifting gears again. Time for a new bible. He discarded the bag from his sporting goods purchase and held up the new paperback. *The Complete Survivor: A Guide to Staying Alive in the Woods,* by Jeffrey P. Hinman. That ought to cover every contingency, he figured. It had sections on fishing, hunting, emergency aid, celestial navigation, how to recognize poison plant life, and so on. Maybe he'd finally learn what poison oak looked like, something most children back home were taught at an early age. The name Hinman didn't ring any bells, but then, this wasn't exactly his field of endeavor. Besides, the guy wrote a book on the subject. He must know what he's talking about.

Steven pocketed the book as he walked back up Main Street toward the tavern, taking in the sights as he went. It was a quaint, very homey setting, and on a lark he wondered what it would be like to live in such a small town. Would he know all the storekeepers by name? Would people call to him and wave warm greetings as he walked down the street on any given day? How would it feel to really belong there?

He came into the parking lot at Lannie's and found Covey and Tucker waiting beside a Land Rover the Indian had left behind. The old man was likewise surveying the town. But his thought processes traveled a different path altogether. "Isn't much of a town, is it?" He chuckled as Steven approached.

"Oh, I don't know—"

"It's a shithole," Covey blurted from behind them.

"Now, Paul, I wouldn't go that far," the boss said, considering. "Let's not be too critical. It does show promise, if you look hard enough. You know, if I decide to spend more time at Chalako I may want to move some of our manufacturing facilities up here as well. That should inject some real life into the local economy. In turn, it would bring in related businesses and fill out the work force, then stimulate the retail and service industries . . ." He smiled, caught up in his momentary reverie.

Tucker as savior, Steven grimaced. Not to help the community, but to bolster his own swelled ego. The man's arrogance was beginning to grate on him. He was just like Mr. Potter, the evil banker in *It's a Wonderful Life*. And Atikokan could be his Bedford Falls. Strip it of all integrity and charm, turn it into a well-oiled industrial park without a hint of soul. He could just visualize the courthouse of this newly dubbed Tuckerville, its walls bearing Leninesque murals of its founder and patron . . .

Sometimes Wilhoit felt guilty just by association.

It was another five minutes or so before Davejac's Land Rover reappeared 'round the corner of O'Brien and onto Main Street, then into the parking lot of Lannie's. The dogs were still with him but the passenger seat was empty. "The old man says it was nice meeting you," he said as he swung out of the truck. He looked at the three standing there. "Aren't we missing one?"

"Hey, that's right," Wilhoit said, looking around. "Where did Church go?"

"I saw him head that way." Tucker pointed down the street. It was about then that Andy reappeared, rounding the corner and coming down the block toward them. He was carrying a grocery bag from Tom Boy Foodland under one arm like a hard-fought trophy.

"Got a little hungry, did we?" Covey smirked.

Andy glared at him defensively, then turned to Davejac. "Are we ready to go?"

"Guess so." The Indian motioned to Wilhoit. "You said you'd drive the other truck, right? Here you go." He tossed the keys in Steven's direction.

Tucker's hand snaked out and intercepted them in midair. "I'd better do the driving," he said with just enough parental condescension to make Wilhoit grit his teeth. "Come on, boys," he barked, "get aboard. You're wasting my time."

The other men headed for the second truck, but Steven moved closer to Barton Davejac. "Uh," he stammered in a half whisper, "do you think I could ride along with you?"

The Indian fixed him with that unrelenting gaze, then shifted it just enough to look past him to the others. "Which one's getting on your nerves?"

"Which one do you think?"

Davejac almost grinned. Almost. "If you can stand the dogs, it's fine with me."

Steven peered into the backseat of the Rover. Both elkhounds regarded him quizzically, watching for his next move. He remembered Boo-Boo's response from earlier, but surely the man wouldn't let his dog do too much damage. Not too much. He swallowed his apprehensions and said, "I'll take my chances." He waited for Davejac to get in, then went 'round the other side and hesitantly climbed aboard himself.

Immediately forty pounds of muscle and fur hurtled over his shoulder and landed in the middle of his lap, pinning him to the seat back. He cringed and tried to cover up but the dog was too quick for him. Her muzzle darted past his defenses and painted his entire face with a raspy tongue. That's when he realized it was Yogi on top of him. The other elkhound was still in the backseat, growling deep under his breath. "Hey," the Indian snapped over his shoulder, "cut that shit right now." Boo-Boo immediately ceased growling. "And, Yogi, that's enough. Leave him alone."

"It's okay." Steven chuckled once he had the wriggling dog's licking under control. "She's not bothering me." He scratched the stiff fur along her back and neck, and the dog quickly settled down, content to be petted and to stare out the passenger window.

"Looks like you've got a new friend," Davejac said. "One down." Then he jerked a thumb toward the backseat. "And one to go." Boo-Boo gave a disgruntled whoof in reply, and this time the guide actually smiled.

They led the way in the two-car convoy, first from Main Street to McKenzie Avenue and then out of Atikokan to Highway 11, the southern route of the Trans-Canada Highway. They headed east and drove steady for the next half hour or so, the monotony punctuated only by the wheeze of the Land Rover's engine and the whine of rubber on pavement. Twenty-six miles from town they passed the entrance to Dawson Trail Campground, the opening to Quetico Provincial Park. At least that's what Steven gleaned from the smattering of signs he saw along the roadway. He pointed them out, genuinely interested, but Davejac seemed to shrug off his questions, a clear indication he wasn't interested in adding tours to his guiding duties. Steven gave up and stayed silent awhile longer, but he couldn't help himself; his natural need for conversation sent him fishing again.

"Beautiful country up here," he observed out loud as mile after mile of scenic forest sped past his window. "Reminds me a lot of home."

"Where's that?" the Indian asked, surprising him.

"Indiana. We've got some areas that look like this, down in the southern part of the state. But there's something different about this place. I don't know, it just looks . . . cold?"

Davejac laughed. "That's Canada. When it's ninety degrees in the shade, people say it still looks cold. That's what they expect, I guess. So, you Hoosiers get out in the woods much?"

"Some of us," Wilhoit admitted, then added sheepishly, "but I'm not one of them."

"You don't hunt?"

"Never have. This isn't my little shindig, you know. Tucker's the mastermind there. You see, he gets a kick out of taking some rank amateurs out in the woods and making asses out of them, to show how good he is in comparison. Big ego trip."

The guide nodded knowingly. "The three previous owners of Chalako were like that. You know, there's some damn good outfitters in this neck of the woods—Barry Brown's, Powell Lake, Indiaonta Resort—but people like your Mr. Tucker won't call them. They'd rather buy a half-assed ranch like Chalako Lakes, and you know why? Because a good outfitter won't take no shit. They're the boss—they're responsible for you so they watch over you like a hawk. They'll bait your hooks when you fish, they'll load your gun when you hunt, they'll take you to the animal and tell you when to shoot and pat your head when you do things right.''

Steven nodded in understanding. ''People like Tucker don't want that.''

''Hell no, they don't. Because they want control. They need it. So they buy their very own sandbox and they make up their own rules. Believe me, I know this from experience. Working at Chalako, I learned it the hard way. Nowadays I acquiesce with the best of them. Davejac's credo is simple: let 'em have their way and try to keep 'em from shooting themselves.''

''Well, good luck,'' Wilhoit sighed. ''Elton Tucker certainly is used to having things his way. I'm just surprised he relented on chartering a bush plane like he wanted.'' He returned to watching the passing countryside, but something Davejac had said about the previous owners stuck in his mind. ''I'm curious,'' he mentioned casually. ''Why has Chalako Lakes gone through so many owners?'' He grinned mischievously at the notion that the old man might have been taken. ''Is it real run-down?'' he asked hopefully. ''A swamp maybe?''

''Sorry. It's beautiful, take my word for it.''

''Then why the turnover?''

''Lots of reasons. Too big a headache, too much money for upkeep, for my salary, for provisions and advertising. Lots of advertising. And too little profit in the long run. Let's face it, you don't get into this business to get rich. You've gotta love it, really live for it. To these rich people, it's just a new toy—sounds good at first, but after a trip or two that new wears off and they sell. And then, you've got to remember that these are mostly city boys. A few of them came out here and were just spooked off.''

''Spooked?'' Steven asked. ''Now wait a minute. I *am* a city boy, so you'd better explain that. What do you mean spooked?''

Davejac just looked at him, and a faint grin crossed his

features. "Fact of life, Mr. Wilhoit. Some people just aren't meant for the woods."

It was twenty more minutes before they reached the turnoff from Highway 11, so Steven had plenty of time to think about what the Indian had said. Some people aren't meant for the woods. Did he mean me? Was he warning me or something? A chill ran along Steven's spine, an omen that maybe he should have stayed home after all. Because city boys are spooked up here, and Steven Wilhoit was about the city-est boy Chalako Lakes would ever see. It seemed ridiculous, considering he was Hoosier born and that his native state offered enough backwoods and open country for even the most ardent outdoorsman. But his childhood had been spent within the confines of a lower middle-class suburb of Indianapolis, where his idea of an adventure was to hike down to the circle and climb to the top of the Soldiers and Sailors Monument. He had missed out on the Cub Scouts, the Boy Scouts, and any other scouts there might have been; in fact, the closest he came to nature were infrequent visits to the Indianapolis Zoo or the Children's Museum. Hell, he thought, he was roughing it when he went to business school at IU fifty miles to the south. After all, Bloomington's population was only 50,000 or so, and not a high-rise to be found. A veritable berg, right?

But he'd never been to the woods. Never.

Some people aren't meant for 'em.

"Here we go," Davejac announced, but his words failed to pierce the membrane of apprehension Steven had wrapped himself in. It wasn't until the Rover turned off the highway and onto a bare, unnamed side road—not until they hit that first big chuckhole in the middle of the dry dirt lane—that he was physically bounced from his trance.

"What the hell . . ."

"Relax. We just turned off to the lakes."

Steven tried to steady himself, peered through the windshield. It was a startling transition, to have stared at well-paved highway for so long and suddenly find it replaced by packed dirt and rock, a bare swath through the forest whose deep ruts were formed by tires much larger than Davejac's Rover. "Loggers' roads," Barton answered before he could even form the question. "They've been working this area for years—you can do that if you're selective and respect the trees, take only the necessaries instead of clear-cutting. These roads here are in relatively good shape, since there's still some bush camps out this way. There's even some along the border of Chalako Lakes; on a good day and depending where you are in the woods, you can hear the saws cutting. But farther along, the roads will get worse."

Another rut, another rattling impact. The frame creaked and so did Steven's spine. "Worse?" he asked, incredulous.

"Oh, yeah. The lakes themselves haven't seen any tree-cutters for a long time, so the road's pretty grown over in places. That could change though. I imagine your boss'll try selling off the timber rights pretty soon. If he can find someone to cut for him, that is."

Steven had obvious questions based on what Davejac said— like why hadn't there been any recent cutting, and why wouldn't he find someone to do it?—but he didn't pursue it. First of all, it did not seem any of his concern. And second, he had a deep-seated suspicion that Davejac would only tell him something more unsettling (. . . they got spooked off . . .) and right now he didn't need that. Not at all.

A whooping sound caught his ear, barely discernible over the wheezing engine and the squeak of the Rover's antiquated shocks. Maybe the buzz saws Barton had mentioned, he thought. Maybe we're coming up on one of those bush camps full of loggers and flatbed transport trucks. But the sound got louder, steadily, until it all but drowned out everything. A Bell Ranger helicopter with *Fannie Mae* emblazoned on its side buzzed right over the top of the trees above them. It even dipped down into the forest itself when there was an opening so it could shake a runner at the truck below. A loudspeaker blared in a gruff female voice: *"Get off the road, you stupid Injun! 'Fore you kill somebody!"* Then a loopy laugh followed as the craft spun crazily into the sky.

Davejac leaned forward and shook a fist through the windshield good-naturedly. "That's Bailey," he explained. "She's a nutty old broad, but you can't help liking her. She works for Ati-Kut Timber Products, the company whose cutters are working out this direction. Gotta have the chopper to get into those camps. You can't land a bush plane in the woods, you know."

The whooping sound came again and strafed the trees once more, taunting them. "She must not have the boss with her this time," he surmised, "or she'd never be dicking around like that. Bosses tend to frown on having a good time."

"Tell me about it," Wilhoit mused. It was a rule that held little promise for the week to come.

The driving continued, as did the shaking and jarring. It was fifteen miles of bad road, no two ways about it. And at the end of that stretch, the going got no better. In fact, just as Barton had warned him, it actually got worse. The more frequently traveled lane they'd followed thus far had intermittently branched off to past and present log camps along the way, but now it veered for the last time. And Davejac did not follow it. He kept the Rover pointed due south and steered onto a path that had seen considerably less traffic aside from the two trucks traveling it now. It was not only rutted but badly overgrown; tree limbs groped into their path every few feet, like sentries holding out their hands in warning. Don't come this way, Steven could almost hear them, don't . . .

Keep it up, Wilhoit. You'll have yourself spooked long before you even get there.

Their speed dropped from a steady thirty-five to twenty now and even slower at times as they pushed through the overgrowth and around fallen tree limbs. They even left the road entirely at one point to circle a fallen tree that was too large for the Rovers to winch aside. Steven's legs ached from being relentlessly braced against the floorboard and his fingertips had all but buried themselves in the dash. But aside from the physical pounding, he was far more unsettled by the feeling of isolation that was building in his gut. The trees were closer here, limiting the sunlight as they hadn't before, and he caught himself shrinking into his seat, breathing heavier. Just the old claustrophobia kicking in, he assured himself. But that wasn't all that bothered him. How far out were they? How far from a hospital or help or, even worse, from home? Because even in Atikokan, home had been just a plane ride away. But here . . . He felt like a child going to camp for the first time, missing Mommy and Daddy. Welcome to the Cub Scouts, Wilhoit. About twenty-five years late.

"See that tree?" Davejac said as they passed an old spruce flanking the road on the left. It was a big tree, older than Steven could even guess. It had been struck by lightning high up on the blackened bough and split halfway down.

"Yeah, it's a tree. So?"

"That's the visual marker. Welcome to Chalako Lakes."

He looked around, searching for some change in the surroundings. There was none. "This is it?"

"Part of the property, at least. The base camp is just ahead. We'll be there 'fore long. If you look close, you might be able to make out Beaver Lake already."

Steven strained to see through the dense patchwork of trees along the road, but he couldn't make out anything. Not until they came into the clearing, and then it took his breath away.

Beaver, the biggest of the Chalako Lakes, was a ragged slash in the fabric of the forest, and it revealed a crystal blue backing to that field of green. The far shore was a gentle incline where jack pine and balsam fir grew right down to the water's edge, their branches still fully needled in the face of autumn. The near bank, however, had been cleared away within a hundred yards of the waterline, and that's where the cabin sat with five canoes stacked upside down against the near wall. Taken as a whole, the scene was visually striking.

It reminded Steven of one of those Wilderness Family movies he'd seen on the Superstation. His tenseness and anxiety of the last half hour seemed foolish now; the claustrophobic feeling was gone and his spirits were considerably lighter, almost buoyant.

"What did I tell you?" Davejac said. "It's the only thing that makes that drive tolerable. Every time I pull in here . . ." He trailed off, unable to put the feeling into words. But Steven knew what he meant.

The guide steered in close so they wouldn't have to carry their gear too far, and Wilhoit got his first look at the cabin. A real good look. And it tempered his elation. It was not some cozy cottage for weekend hunters. Even Daniel Boone would have balked at such an austere dwelling. It was little more than a one-room shack with just two windows that he could see, and small ones at that. The rest was native wood, probably the very trees cleared from the shore, and quite old from its appearance. The logs were bleached by the sun and harsher elements and splintering badly in places. From that distance Steven would have sworn the place was growing patches of stiff grey hair. "The Hilton it ain't," he sighed in resignation. "I suppose a microwave's out of the question."

"And electricity"—Barton nodded— "and a stove and an indoor toilet. That's out back. The only thing you'll find in there is a fireplace and six cots, though a couple of those are broken."

"Sounds thrilling."

The Indian grinned. "Welcome to the woods, great white hunter."

Steven opened the door and let Yogi jump off his lap just as the second truck pulled in behind them and the occupants began to disembark. Andy Church climbed out with the look of a shell-shocked veteran, his face a mask of discomfort as he massaged his butt and lower back. Paul Covey crawled from the backseat all bleary-eyed and sluggish, like he'd slept through the whole punishing trip. And then there was Elton

Tucker. He came around the driver's side all thin-lipped and
squint-eyed, wearing his patented I'm-not-amused-and-balls-
are-gonna-role expression, the one that had struck fear into
the hearts of so many salaried sheep around Tucker Pharms.
At least the Drive From Hell had taken care of that phony
enthusiasm and let's-be-buddies act, Steven noted. This is
the Elton Tucker we all know and loathe. Wait till he sees
the accommodations here, the lack of creature comforts . . .
The shit'll hit the fan then, you watch.

The boss walked silently past them and appraised the cabin,
looked it all over as he circled it on foot. Then he turned to
Beaver Lake and walked toward it, stared out across the
tranquil face of the water. "This," he said slowly, "this is
perfect. Perfect!"

Andy stretched, then moaned and grabbed his back. "I'm
glad he's happy," he grimaced. "Now if I could just lay
down somewhere around here and die . . ."

"Aw, this ain't so bad," Covey said, looking out at the
lake. "Let's get the poles out and hit the water. The fish may
be biting."

"You'd best take care of business first," Davejac called
to all of them. He was standing there with Yogi and Boo-
Boo at his side, having taken a box of his own groceries and
supplies from the truck. "First unload your gear and then
gather some firewood. It gets cold up here after dark. I'll be
back in the morning." He muttered something under his
breath and the elkhounds perked up, followed him toward
the corner of the cabin.

"Where are you going?"

Barton used the box in his arms to motion toward the woods
beyond the shack. "I've got my own place back that way.
If you need anything, just yell." He saw the surprise in the
Americans' eyes and he laughed. "Hey, I'm a guide, not a
baby-sitter. Besides, you've got the boss over there." Still
chuckling, he turned and headed into the woods, the dogs
right at his heel.

Down by the water, Elton Tucker was caught up in the

beauty of Chalako, more so than even Steven had been. Because it meant so much more to him. It was all so perfect . . . It was everything his father had ever wanted, everything Greene County had never been.

"What do you think, Dad?" he whispered softly, oblivious to the others. To everything. For in his mind's eye Virgil Tucker now stood beside him, beaming, his chest out and a smirking grin on his face. He approved.

Elton smiled as well. For nothing could have made him happier.

SIX

STEVEN WAS DOG-TIRED. HE'D TRAVELED ALL DAY IT SEEMED, and even after reaching Chalako he'd unpacked gear and gathered wood for the fireplace and helped fix supper from the groceries Davejac had provided. His eyelids had started to droop halfway through the meal, and they all turned in not long after that.

So why wasn't he asleep yet?

He lay there wide awake as the midnight hour approached, staring into the darkness that gathered in the cabin rafters. Maybe it was the rigid cot beneath him, like trying to sleep on a park bench. Or maybe the sleeping bag. It was everything the salesgirl had said it would be, soft and warm and cozy. But he hadn't taken his claustrophobia into consideration. He wasn't used to sleeping with his arms at his sides and his legs together—there just wasn't room to move, and that meant no room to breathe. He fidgeted and twisted and turned, and that only wrapped the damn thing around him like a tourniquet. He'd untangled himself twice already and the night was still young.

But it wasn't just discomfort that kept him awake and he knew it. He'd dealt with this kind of insomnia before, like his last business trip to Chicago. For the truth of the matter was, such trips were the few times he and his wife had ever really been apart. They had a certain way of sleeping—he on his side with Janet right up against him, fitted together like spoons in a row—and after ten years it was hard just being alone. He'd taken it for granted until now, and he promised himself he wouldn't do it again.

So, what should I do? he wondered. Just lie here all night? No, that wasn't getting him anywhere. Read a book by the light of the fireplace? The only one he had was Hinman's outdoor guide that he'd bought back in Atikokan, and he'd already tried a few chapters before supper. Unlike a good Mike Resnick science fiction novel, it was not the kind of book to be consumed in just a few sittings. And he'd had enough for now. Besides, firelight might have been bright enough for Abe Lincoln, but he evidently hadn't suffered from nearsightedness. Steven knew from experience that the eye strain would give him a migraine.

Maybe if I get up and move around, take a walk or something . . .

What, he thought, caught off-guard by his own suggestion. Take a walk? At night? In the dark? Are you nuts?

No. Just an adult.

Oh, yeah. I forgot.

He unzipped the bag and climbed out, sat on the edge of the cot. And even with the fire still burning, he shivered. Davejac had been right; it did get cold of a night. He was still clad in his pants and sweatshirt, but it was not enough. He had to reach for his thick down jacket. He slipped into his boots and crept across the creaky cabin floor, careful not to wake the others. He added a few more sticks to the fire and warmed himself there a moment. Then he went to the door and eased the latch open and stepped outside.

"Good Lord," he actually gasped as he took in the scene spread out there before him.

He had never witnessed such . . . vastness. It was a cloudless night, a near-full moon, and the stars were out. *Really* out. They stretched from one tree-ragged horizon to the other, and without the lights of the city to distract the eye, they burned at least three times as bright. The moon and starlight cast the landscape below in a pale glow that reminded him of those sky flares they used in the war movies on the late show. Except this didn't extinguish after a ten-minute burn. This just kept on shining . . .

Steven was awestruck. So this is how a Cub Scout feels on his first camp-out, he laughed inwardly, and he was glad he'd finally made it. To stand there in the great expanse of wilderness and look upon something infinitely greater . . . It made him feel smaller than small, a grain of salt, a follicle on a gnat's back. There was so much to see, to comprehend, certainly more than a rational, by-the-rules mind such as his could fathom. If I could miss this for thirty-odd years, he thought, what else might have escaped my notice? How many other things have I taken for granted? How many mysteries are out there just waiting for me?

The world was no longer so cut and dried, and he smiled for that. The possibilities left him a little giddy.

He walked down to the edge of the lake. It was completely still tonight, the surface an unblemished pane of glass that looked less like water than a second expanse of starry space, this one seen through a jagged rip in the earth. The illusion played with his mind, asked him what he was truly seeing and whether it was real or not, till he stooped down for a rock and tossed it out into the lake as far as he could. It struck about twenty yards out with a soft sploosh and sent ripples undulating through the reflected heavens, disrupting them, proving it water after all. Steven smiled. Reality had returned. He knew where he stood again, while the sense of wonderment had not departed with his momentary confusion. He also realized that he liked the sound of a stone hitting water, and he knelt down to find a few more. A good flat one this time, one that will skip a good ways . . .

A branch cracked.

It was not nearby; the sound was muffled to begin with, and by the time it reached his ears it had lost most of its clarity. He couldn't even tell which direction it had come from. But he looked around anyway. No one outside the cabin. Nothing between him and the trees. Nothing on the water.

Had there been a sound at all?

Snap. Crack. The whisper of tree limbs brushing together . . .

Steven stood up in silent alarm. He had heard it this time, no doubt about it. And he knew where it had come from. Across the lake. He scoured the far bank then for some sign of motion. But there was only the trees there, and the wall of shadow beyond them.

Crack. Shhh. The swirling of leaves.

Coming closer.

Big deal, he assured himself. There's a good quarter mile of water between you and it (whatever "it" is). Nothing to worry about. But despite such logic, he was already backing away from the water. Especially when the sounds grew in number and volume and the tree limbs over there seemed to shake in expectation. An icy dread clambered up his spine. That's no deer or bear, he knew. It's too big for that.

He wanted to run for the cabin. In fact, he tried to turn and look that way or at least call out to someone. But he couldn't move. Part of it was blind fear, despite the distance and the lake that shielded him. But the rest was some previously unknown curiosity (how many other mysteries are out there waiting for me . . .) that would not let him go. Not until he saw. So when the forest sounds reached their peak and the swaying limbs of the tree line suddenly jerked aside to permit passage, Steven Wilhoit steeled himself and looked right at them and held his breath . . .

A gust of wind whipped out of the forest like an arctic locomotive, just a single gust, but Steven would have sworn it was more than that. At first it seemed to have form and substance as it emerged into the moonlight, a huge amorphous shadow that loomed out over the water in a spray of leaves and dirt. But then the swirling pine needles and twigs began to settle onto the placid surface of the lake and the shadow lost its integrity, bit by bit, until there was nothing left at all. Nothing but the dusting of debris on the water and the still-swaying limbs to mark its passage.

The silence returned.

Steven finally exhaled.

Just the wind, he told himself. A sudden gust, like the dust devils you've seen down home, whipping across open fields or the expansive parking lots at K-Mart. Just the wind. Nothing to be scared of.

Then why do my goose bumps have goose bumps? Why is my scrotum suddenly hanging parallel with my navel?

"Spooky, huh?" said a voice. And it wasn't Steven's.

He jumped a step forward and cried out—not a real scream or even a yell, but more a very loud "ugh!" Then a warm flush of embarrassment tingled through him as he turned to find Barton Davejac standing there in a fat bomber jacket and ski cap, sans dogs.

"You okay, Mr. Wilhoit?" he said, stepping closer and touching Steven on the shoulder. "I didn't mean to startle you. I just came out for some air and saw someone down here."

"You didn't scare me," Steven said defensively, then qualified it with "Not much. It was that wind that just came through here . . . Did you see it?"

The guide looked across the lake where there was now no sign of the gust, and Steven had a sinking feeling he would say no, that he must have imagined it. But Davejac just nodded. "Yeah, I saw it. Not the first time, either. But I can't explain it. It's one of those freaks of nature, like wind shear or microbursts. Maybe the geography around here lends itself to stuff like that, you know, creates a natural wind tunnel or something. Who can say? But it still happens, and you never know when it's coming, either, or from what direction. At one time or another I've seen it blow from all points on the compass. But never for very long. Just a short harsh gust and then it's gone. That's why I wasn't too thrilled when your boss—our boss, I should say—wanted to charter a plane. He'd have found out right quick that the locals won't fly into Chalako Lakes. Hell, Bailey won't even touch down here, and she's crazy. It's those damn winds. They're the reason.''

He pointed down the shoreline about two hundred yards to a narrow peninsula that reached out into the water like a rocky finger. "About fifteen years ago a boatplane tried to sit down just off that point. But right as they came in low, one of those winds caught it, flipped it right over. The pilot was the only one to survive the crash. You can still see the plane about twenty feet down out there. The water's clear enough." He looked back at Wilhoit. "Now you know why I don't fly. It's not that safe to begin with. But when the cold wind blows . . ."

"I don't blame you." Steven nodded, glancing back across the lake to where the gust had appeared. The tree limbs there were no longer swaying; in fact, the whole area was completely still, and he would have been hard-pressed to tell exactly where the gust had broken through. It was as if the forest had covered itself, healed its own wound. "It still gives me the creeps," he said, rubbing his arms. "I just wish Tucker had been here. I would have liked to have seen his reaction."

"You still might," the guide said. "It isn't too common, but it could come again before your week's out."

Steven stepped back and looked around them, another sweeping survey of the whole setting. Now that the wind had come and gone, the silvered beauty of the night he'd admired before was reinstated. Nothing ominous here. "It's hard to believe this place has any kind of bad reputation."

Davejac nodded in agreement. "It's even harder to believe it's haunted."

"Excuse me?"

"Chalako Lakes is haunted. At least it's supposed to be."

Steven laughed, and the Indian did too. But the latter's was more a compliant expression. And it brought the American up short. "You're serious, aren't you?"

"Afraid so. Native legend says that this is a bad place, tainted by the spirits. A place to be avoided."

"And you believe that?"

Davejac shrugged as if to brush it off, to say, Are you kidding, of course not, don't be ridiculous. But his momentary pause was proof that it wasn't so cut-and-dried. "I'm Ojibwa, Steven, what you'd probably call Chippewa, along with a little Cree on my father's side. That's my heritage, so I try to respect its tenets and beliefs, not to scoff at them or ridicule them. On the other hand, times have changed. We're more rational now, more willing to look at things from all angles. Take these woods, for instance. My ancestors were uneducated and superstitious, and they blamed the spirits for anything they couldn't explain. So if some natural phenomena like your sudden wind were to blow up and startle a few of them while out hunting . . . well, hell, it has to be an evil spirit come to ruin the hunt. All of a sudden it's 'Help, help, the windigo's after me!' "

"Windigo?"

"One of their demons. Sorta the bogeyman of the forest."

"Have you ever seen it?"

Davejac laughed. "Are you kidding? The truth is, I've been out here for four years—five come spring. I've guided my share of trips through these woods when the owners wanted to go, and sometimes I've hunted them on my own. And nothing's ever bothered me."

"So much for being haunted . . ."

"On the other hand," Barton continued, "that doesn't automatically discount any legends. After all, I haven't seen every inch of this property—probably eighty to ninety percent, but not all of it. And besides that, I'm probably protected. My great-great-grandfather was a powerful medicine man among the Ojibwa, so his magic flows through my veins. Maybe that keeps the spirits away."

"Sounds like bullshit to me," Steven scoffed. "Superstitious hokum."

"You're entitled," the guide agreed. "But just wait a few days, Steven, till we're way out there someplace, away from everything, even the questionable comforts of your sad-assed cabin over there. When you hear the forest speaking around you but you can't understand its words, when you hear something in the night that you think is an owl but you're just not sure . . . Then you can put yourself in my ancestors' moccasins. Then the legends might not sound so farfetched after all. You know?" He smiled then, knowing and devilish in the moonlight, and Steven recognized his intent. He knew then and there that once in the woods the Indian would make sure there were plenty of unsettling sounds to be heard. Even if he had to make them himself.

Go ahead, Wilhoit thought with a smile as he took up the gauntlet. Try to scare me, mister. If I can take Tucker's shit, I can take yours too.

Davejac looked at the dial of his watch, which glowed luminescent in the nonlight. "Getting late," he reported. "Morning's not too far away, and the boss'll want to get started at first light. So I think I'll turn in. G'night." He strode silently across the well-lit ground, past the cabin and into the darkened woods.

Steven stood there awhile longer, thinking about the Indian's stories. Haunted . . . how ridiculous. At least it would have been if he were back home in Bloomington, in the safe confines of his own home, his own world when the rules were neat and set and nothing surprised him. But here . . .

Hell, he thought, here even the stars take you off-guard. If you can stand and stare skyward with your jaw hung in wonder, how can you dismiss anything?

Just wait a few days, Steven, till we're out there someplace . . .

Boy, that's something to look forward to, he fretted as he walked back to the cabin, zipping his jacket up 'round his neck.

SEVEN

BEEP BEEP BEEP

It was a slight electronic sound, barely noticeable even in the amplifying silence of the cabin. But it was enough to rouse Elton Tucker from his slumber. His hand wrested itself from the confines of the bedroll and grabbed for the digital watch on the crate beside his cot, pressed the button to silence the pestering alarm. He didn't bother looking at the face with its flashing LED numbers. He already knew it was five-thirty A.M. Rise and shine.

He didn't hesitate at getting up, didn't linger there in his quilted warmth or make excuses. He got out of bed immediately, because he'd made up his mind to do so last night. And to go back on his word, even to himself, was unthinkable.

The cabin was still murky with shadow, especially since the fire had ebbed to nothingness sometime in the last few hours. But the windows did show that dawn was coming, albeit slowly. There was still no hint of morning redness, but at least the night had lessened by several degrees of shade.

Tucker perched on the edge of the cot, clad only in his long thermal underwear, and he quickly learned it was not enough for the chill in the air. He reached for the clothing he'd laid out the night before, slipped into a heavy pair of jeans and a thick denim shirt, then stalked to the big stone fireplace that dominated one wall of the cabin. There were embers still glowing there amid the fine grey ashes. He stirred them with a stick, then added it as fodder, along with a handful of twigs from the hearth pile. The sparks burned brighter, caught here and there and finally birthed new flames. Before long the fire was crackling loud and strong and returning a modicum of heat to the bone-aching morning.

A cup of coffee would go down good right now, he thought as he warmed his hands before the hearth. A good hot cup . . .

Get the pot, boy.

The memory was so clear, so vivid, he almost swore for an instant that his father's voice had actually echoed through the cabin. A grin of familiarity crossed his features. It had been some time since he'd heard that. Since he'd made coffee last. The brewing machine at the office with the crinkly paper filters was a piss-poor substitute; it was weak and, worst of all, automatic. Convenient. There was no ritual involved.

He sorted through the many bags and duffels and packs they had stowed around the empty shack until he located the mess kit where the coffeepot and the Folgers had been stowed. It was a new pot, the blue-flecked enamel so far unscathed by flame, and for an instant he felt remorse. Too bad he didn't still have the old one, the pot he'd used to fix coffee for his father. That one was special . . . Oh, well. The preparation was still the same. He scooped in the coffee and added water from the hand pump in the corner, the only true amenity in the cabin, then hung the pot in the fireplace just over the flames. The aroma wasn't long in coming; it filled the air around him, almost thick enough to chew, and he couldn't wait to pour himself a cup of bubbling coal blackness. No sugar for him, no sir. No cream either. Drink it black. The

blacker the better. He cradled the steaming cup, using his
sleeve cuffs to protect his hands, and blew into it several
times before taking a sip.

He winced . . .

Drink it down, boy. That'll put hair on your balls.

. . . just as he had at the ripe old age of ten when he first
went hunting with his father. Dad only made it that once.
The rest of the time the responsibility fell to young Elton,
and he bore the ritual with childish enthusiasm. The same
taste, the same way every time. Just the way Dad liked it.
Strong enough to walk on its own. And he had the hair on
his balls to prove it.

He grinned at that. Another Virgil Tuckerism proven fact.
Chalk it up again.

He'd been lucky to have such a mentor in his youth, someone to show him what was important in the world and in a
man, really important, and what was not. How to depend on
only one person—himself—and how to see his own worth,
his own potential, even where he thought there was none
before. The sorry truth was that people these days didn't have
access to that wisdom early on, were not given the leadership
and that gentle nudge in the right direction that had made
him what he was today. He looked at the men sleeping fitfully
across the room from him. Take them for instance, he
thought. How would they have turned out differently if the
proper guidance had been available, if they'd been disciplined
when necessary, kept in line . . . In that regard he almost
felt a tinge of sympathy for them.

But at least they have this opportunity, he thought. At least
they have you to help them. And if they're willing to work
hard and to listen, you won't let them down.

No, I won't.

He concentrated his gaze on each of the men in turn, and
in his mind he finished the preliminary analysis he had started
to gather back at a bar table in Atikokan. Which of them
would measure up, he asked himself. Which of the three had
true executive potential, even more than that? Though he had

yet to see them in the true testing environment of the Chalako woods, he felt he knew enough to make some predictions.

Paul Covey was the best bet, he estimated. Though the man was a bit of a loudmouth and a know-it-all and could be genuinely grating at times, those were behavioral bugs that could be ironed out with subsequent training. What was important was the basic material, the makeup of the man, and there Covey excelled. Because he had drive. He'd never had to rely on a college education; just hard and steady work over a long period of time. Tucker had a feeling that Mr. Covey would acquit himself well on this little venture.

The rotund Mr. Church was the most obviously out of shape, he thought, and thereby the least likely to succeed in any matter remotely physical in nature. Like a hunting trip. But Tucker knew better than to dismiss such a person. In his opinion, Church had imprisoned himself in a shell of bad habits and attitudes, and that was what limited his potential, tainted his self-image. But Tucker was sure he could remedy that if he kept after the boy, if he pushed and probed and needled him until the shell was broken and Church fought back. And the old man was confident. From his experience he knew just what buttons to push.

Then he looked at Steven Wilhoit. This man was the flip side of Andrew Church—on the surface a very appealing candidate, with his MBA from Indiana University and his immaculate attendance record with the company. A good worker. So far. But Tucker was skeptical. Scratch the well-groomed surface, he estimated, and you would find an alarming lack of substance beneath. First of all, he wore glasses. Not a damning testimony in and of itself, but to the old man's mind it had always denoted a certain weakness of character. That was further evidenced by his henpecked behavior, like sneaking away from Lannie's to call the little woman. He'd tried to hide it but Tucker knew exactly what he was up to. Pussy-whipped, that was the term. Can't get his legs untangled from the old apron strings, even in another country. And strings that long always trip a man up, sooner or later. Finally, he doubted Wilhoit's ability to stand alone in a changing environment. After all, the ability to adapt was the real test in life. And while IU may have trained him well for the boardroom, Chalako would be a different matter altogether. The signs were already in place, like the constant complaining ("oh, man, it's cold; my cot's too hard; there's no heat in the outhouse . . ."), and all before the hunt had even started. Two more days, Tucker estimated. *Once we get into the woods he'll balk. Davejac will end up driving him back to town before it's all over.*

Of course, he'd known all of this back in Bloomington, long before they boarded the plane. But he invited Wilhoit just the same. Why? He told himself it was to give the boy a chance, that he could always be wrong about him and should let him prove himself. But that wasn't really it. Because as much as he liked helping a qualified disciple to realize his true potential as he himself had under his father's tutelage, he also took a perverse pleasure in watching others fail. He couldn't explain it and never really tried. He just liked it. And for that, Wilhoit, with his educated smugness and his storybook marriage, was the most qualified candidate.

Tucker finished his second cup of coffee and waited for the men to wake up. But they were still sleeping too deep to come around anytime soon. Church's snoring attested to that. A mischievous grin spread across the old man's lips. *This ain't a vacation,* he thought. *These boys have to learn there won't be any sleeping in on this trip.* And he knew just the way to teach them.

He kneeled beside his cot and reached beneath it, took out the hardshell gun case that held his prized Weatherby Euromark. He took out the custom rifle with its hand-rubbed stock and high-power scope, then opened the carrying case's ammo compartment and withdrew a single .340 WM cartridge. *That ought to do the trick,* he nodded with satisfaction as he walked over to the cabin window and pushed open the shutters.

He saw that the darkness outside was giving way to morning faster than he'd realized upon first rising. It was already a muted grey out, that transitional phase between night and day when everything appears strangely intangible and the world itself peopled only by ghosts and shades. The impression was reinforced by the appearance of Beaver Lake. Tendrils of steam danced on the glassy surface like a waving garden of white seaweed. It was the cold ethereal quality of the landscape that caught Tucker's attention, made him pause in the middle of his mischief. The early morning tableau was so completely different from the hard green and blue majesty he had witnessed upon arriving the previous day. Just another of Chalako's many faces, he supposed. You got more than your money's worth here, my friend.

He worked the Weatherby's bolt open, slowly so as not to make too much noise. Then he slipped the single cartridge into the action and chambered it. "Rise and shine, boys." He chuckled as he pointed the rifle out the window and across the lake.

And that's when he caught sight of something through the lake mist. An indistinct shape from the corner of his eye. The flicker of movement. He fixed his vision on the spot over there, not completely convinced that he'd witnessed anything at all. Perhaps the unfurling grey had tricked his eye . . .

No, there it was again. A spot of brown through the mist, a subtle shifting of position and weight. "What the hell is that?" Tucker whispered. He moved toward the door and went outside, headed for the waterline at a half run. The lake mist seemed to have dispersed a bit by then, especially along his line of sight. That left him with a clear view of the far shore where the trees stood right at the lake's edge and dabbled their roots in the water. The movement came again, and this time he had no trouble making out its source. Standing amid the boughs of the jack pine and spruce was a whitetail buck, the largest he'd ever seen. It was at least sixteen points, maybe more. It held that tremendous rack of antlers proudly as it stood and looked at him, straight at him. There was no doubting that. He could even see its breath, short puffs of white vapor that hung from its muzzle like fine old whiskers. It just stood there, unalarmed by his presence.

Tucker was full of excitement, suddenly giddy as a schoolboy, and he wasn't exactly sure why. It did prove that he'd made a good deal after all, that Chalako did have above-average game. But this was more than that. A tingling impression of déjà vu . . .

The photo, he suddenly realized. It's exactly the same. The position in the trees, the stance. The very same buck. He was sure of it. There were no characteristic marks to identify it, but he still had no doubt. The same buck. And it was waiting for him.

Tucker was not a devotee of predestiny. But he knew that this great animal had been meant for him. He would take it, the first day, before the hunt had even begun. That would show those three amateurs inside. That would make his father proud.

Don't just stand there, boy. Raise your gun.

He looked down at the Weatherby, as if he'd forgotten he still had it. He put it to his shoulder, feeling a flush of nostalgic joy. Okay, Dad. I've got my gun.

Don't get anxious. Just sight it out, nice and easy.

He peered through the scope. It brought the massive animal up close enough to touch. The cross hairs were right on target, flush over the heart-lung kill zone.

Don't jerk the trigger, boy. Squeeze it.

Elton Tucker smiled in remembrance as his finger tightened on the trigger. I'll get it, Dad. I'll get it for you.

You'd better, boy. 'Cause if you screw up, you know what'll happen . . .

The threat was implicit, and it cut through Elton Tucker like a scalpel. His heart nearly skipped a beat; his hands were shaking, making the cross hairs jump erratically. His finger jerked on the trigger, and the shot went wild.

The whitetail stiffened at the sound. Tucker could only watch as it bolted into the trees and disappeared.

. . . you know what'll happen . . .

"I'm sorry, I'm sorry," he whined, throwing his arms over his head defensively. But when he finally turned and looked up from the corner of his eye, he found no one standing behind him. There never had been. The other men were just coming out of the cabin, alarmed by the gunshot.

"What is it?" Wilhoit called. "Is something wrong?"

Tucker couldn't tell them about the buck. Then they'd know he'd missed his shot, and they'd laugh. They'd never let him live it down. The bastards . . . "Just some target practice," he lied. "I needed something to do while you people lolled around in bed. This is a hunting trip, remember? Not a fucking slumber party. Go on, get your shit together. We've got a busy day ahead."

The three exchanged irritated glances, then sighed and went back into the cabin.

Elton Tucker looked across the lake once more, through the ever-lightening veil of morning mist, and he searched for a sign of his quarry. But it was gone, and likewise the threatening voice in his head. One had melted back into the forest. The other into the shadowy corners of his memory.

Breakfast was like supper the night before—precooked and in a plastic bag. Space food, Davejac had called it. All they had to do was heat the pouches in boiling water and, voilà, a four-serving meal. Except that the hash browns tasted like cardboard and the western omelettes were identical to the hash browns. They picked at their food with finicky distaste until the guide finally showed up. "Better get used to it," he told them. "When we're out on the trail, we eat fish if we catch it and meat if we shoot it. But if not, this is all you get."

But they couldn't be threatened. Only Church cleaned his plate.

With breakfast finished, Elton Tucker decided it was time to introduce the men to "their new friends." He presented each of them with a hard plastic rifle case, then led them outside to the clearing along the lake. He instructed two of them to drag a wooden bench along, one they could use as a shooting rest, while Davejac walked off a hundred yards down the shoreline and pinned several targets to a rotten stump at the water's edge.

But Steven couldn't wait for all of this preparation. The urge to peek into the case he carried was too strong.

He'd always wanted a gun. Especially when he was a youngster. But his parents had never been too keen on the subject, whether it was .22, pellet, or even the BB variety. So the curiosity carried on into adulthood, where it still went unfulfilled. He never seemed able to justify owning one; after all, he didn't hunt or plink at cans, and had no land to shoot on even if he wanted to. Besides, Janet was vocally antigun (what if a burglar comes in and takes it away from you—an argument whose logic he could never quite grasp) and he felt little need to antagonize her further. But the interest continued nonetheless. Often in the local K-Mart store he would purposely lose Janet in the maze of aisles, just long enough for him to slip into the sporting goods section and ask to hold one of the rifles he'd so often dreamed of.

And now, here, far from Janet's disapproving glare, he was finally going to shoot one!

While Tucker and Davejac discussed the organization of their impromptu shooting course, Steven kneeled down on the grass, laid the case on his lap, and loosened the clasps. Inside were two liners of egg-carton foam for shock protection, with the rifle sandwiched between them. He lifted it out carefully, conscious to keep his fingers well away from the trigger guard, just in case. It was a bolt action, much heavier than the .22s he'd hefted at K-Mart. It had a shoulder strap and the buttstock was a polished hardwood, checkered around the grip and the fore end for a good purchase when firing. A scope was already mounted on top of the receiver, on big see-through rings that gave him the option of forgoing the fancy optics in favor of the factory's simple iron sights. A most impressive model indeed, especially to one as uninitiated as Steven. He lifted it to his shoulder and pretended to sight through the scope (the lens caps were still in place), and a tingle of anticipation raced through him.

"A beauty, isn't it?" said Elton Tucker. He had approached unnoticed and now stood at Steven's shoulder. His expression was one of surprise. He had never expected Wilhoit to be even tolerant of these test-shots, let alone eager. Could he have misjudged? He reached over and took the rifle from Steven's hands, retracted the heavy bolt, and showed it to all three of them. "Go ahead," he told the other two, "get yours out as well. They're all the same model. A Remington 700, chambered for the 30.06 cartridge. One of the best all-around hunting arms in the world."

"Thirty-aught-six," Steven mulled it over, trying to remember the smattering of gun talk he'd heard on TV. "That's bigger than a forty-four Magnum, right?"

The others smirked and snickered under their breath, even Davejac, making him feel suddenly stupid and very small. To his credit, Elton Tucker didn't join in the chiding. But when he answered Steven's question, he spoke in a slow and measured tone as if instructing a child. "A forty-four is primarily a pistol caliber." He reached into his jacket pocket, laid a metallic cartridge in Steven's hand. "This is a 30.06."

Steven examined it. The shell was long and thin, a bit shorter than his index finger. Way too big for a pistol, Steven could see. This would make a rather nasty hole indeed.

"You sure that'll bring down something big?" Church asked, unashamed to show his own ballistic naivete. "Like a bear maybe?"

Something big, Tucker thought, remembering the massive buck across the lake, watching him, waiting for him . . . "It should do the trick," he assured them.

The old man demonstrated the rifle's bolt design, how to load and unload it. Then he made each man repeat the whole process, several times in fact, until they could operate the gun flawlessly and without stopping to think.

Then it was time to sight in the scopes.

Tucker knelt down and rested the loaded rifle on the

wooden bench, then popped the lens caps off and put an eye to the scope. He took aim on the circular targets down the way. *Crack!* The gunshot echoed across the clearing and on into the woods like ripples of disturbed water, leaving a high-pitched whine in Steven's ears and little else. His hearing returned in time to pick up Tucker saying ". . . pulls a little to the right," as he adjusted the scope. Then he worked the bolt again, expelling the fired casing, and touched off a second round. *Crack.* But this report wasn't nearly as loud, or at least not as startling since Steven had known what to expect this time. He even picked up the soft whump of the bullet striking rotten wood. "Almost there," and another slight adjustment. Another round chambered. Another fired.

Paul Covey peered at the target through his own scope. "In the black that time," he announced.

Tucker nodded. "Naturally. Here, Steven. Your turn."

Wilhoit took the rifle, held it as if it were cast from fine crystal. "What, should I use the bench, or . . ."

"There aren't any benches in the woods," Davejac told him. "Just use the strap as your brace." He quickly showed him how to wind his left arm in the shoulder strap before taking hold of the forestock, so that the tension on the gun increased and the shaking lessened. "Now, work the bolt . . . that's it. Cinch it up tight against your shoulder . . ."

"He can do it, Mr. Davejac," Tucker snapped, irritated that the Indian had usurped his instruction. "Go ahead, Steven. Fire away."

Wilhoit braced the rifle again, the strap wound 'round his left arm just as Barton had suggested, and he tried to peer through the scope. But he just couldn't seem to form a clear picture. His glasses kept getting in the way, and wouldn't let his eye close enough to the lens. The cross hairs and target just wouldn't come together . . .

"C'mon, college boy," Covey complained. "This ain't chess, you know. Sometime today, all right?"

Steven ignored him and, ultimately, the scope as well. Instead he shifted his gaze beneath it, through the ring mounts to the blade sight at the end of the barrel. He could see that well enough. He lined it up with the stump, placed it just under the target.

And pulled the trigger.

The sound was inconsequential this time. In fact, he wasn't sure he'd heard it at all, except for the whine it left in his ear. What had caught his attention most this time was the recoil of the rifle. It gave him a stern jolt and left his shoulder throbbing. "Goddamn," he winced, before remembering that the others were watching. "Did I hit anything?"

Davejac produced a small pair of folding binoculars and inspected the distant target. "Well, Steven," he said, "about a foot too low. But at least you hit the stump."

Covey laughed. "Not bad, pilgrim. For an amateur."

"Then you'll show us how it's done, won't you, Paul?" Tucker said, taking Covey's rifle. The old man took three shots with that gun as well, until the scope was dead-on. Then he returned it.

With a smirk of confidence Covey chambered a new round, raised it to his shoulder, and snapped off a quick shot. But Steven caught the look on his face as he fired, and he knew then that Paul's experience with rifles had been limited to much smaller calibers. Because the recoil took him by surprise as well. There was pain in his pinched expression, at least until he covered it enough to lower the rifle from his face. He wouldn't look at Steven; he kept his eyes downrange as Davejac checked his binoculars.

"In the black," the Indian reported. "The outer edge on the right, but it's still in the kill zone."

"What did I tell you?" Covey bragged, needling the other two. But Wilhoit grinned slyly and rubbed his shoulder, and Paul's horse smile slipped with chagrin. He turned away abruptly, his cheeks flushed to an angry hue.

Andy Church handed up his rifle and waited for the scope to be adjusted. When it was ready, he took his place on the firing line and mimicked Barton's sling hold, drew a bead on the target.

Crack. The recoil was just as harsh as the others had felt, but his extra bulk seemed to absorb it like an airbag. Only his great belly jiggled.

"Bull's-eye," Davejac reported.

"Bullshit," Tucker scoffed. He grabbed away the binoculars and checked for himself. But the eyes did not lie. The target sported a neat hold dead center.

He couldn't deny it. But he could dismiss it. "Beginner's luck."

"Try it again, Andy," Wilhoit urged.

The young man did just that. *Crack*.

Tucker checked the target again, stared at it silently. Then he tossed the binoculars back to the guide, begrudgingly muttered, "Lucky. Again."

"Looks like we've got a natural shooter here." Davejac laughed, clapping Church on the shoulder. "You sure you've never done this before?"

"Nope," Andy said, obviously pleased with himself. "I used to clean my grandpa's rifle sometimes, but he never let me shoot it."

Tucker was still skeptical. "Even two shots can still be luck."

Church bristled at that. "What is it with you?" he asked the old man point-blank. "Is it that unbelievable? How many times do I have to hit it before you're convinced?"

Elton Tucker grinned, and it was less from amusement than a reptilian expression of triumph. Andy knew then that he'd been suckered into a bad place. Right where the old man wanted him. "There's a way to find out," Tucker estimated. "If you can make that shot when the pressure's on, we'll know this isn't some sort of fluke or aberration."

"What do you mean by pressure?" Wilhoit asked.

The grin lengthened. "A wager might do the trick."

Is that all, Andy thought as he immediately began checking his pockets. "You're on, big man," he said, suddenly hot with indignation. "I've got a few bucks here . . ."

"A few bucks?" Tucker shook his head. "No, no, there's

no sport in that. Let's make this worth our while. Say . . . your Christmas bonus. That'll be coming up soon, you know?''

"Go for it, chubby," Paul counseled with the usual subtlety.

"Or even better," the old man continued, "let's say all three of your bonuses." Which brought Covey up short. It caught Steven's attention as well. "If you make the shot, I double each of your bonuses. But if you miss . . . no money at all. Not a penny. Well, Andrew? What'll it be?"

Church glared at him with unconcealed enmity, and that seemed to please Tucker all the more. For it showed that the young man understood what was at stake. If he declined, he would appear weak and unsure, unable to take risks, even away from the office. And if he accepted and lost, it would cost the others just as much as him. The resentment between the three would be thick enough to cut.

Divide and conquer, as Virgil Tucker would have said, though his son had always suspected that he'd lifted that particular wisdom from somewhere else.

"My own bonus, fine," Andy finally told him. "But I ain't playing with their money."

"But that's the bet. Take it or leave it."

"Go ahead, chubs," Covey said. "I think you can do it. Besides, I could use the extra money."

"Do it, Andy, " Wilhoit agreed. Then he added in a whisper, "Make him eat crow."

"But what if I miss?"

Steven looked him in the eye and smiled. "You won't. You can do it."

Church nodded hesitantly, then shot Tucker one last glare and found the old man already gloating. "Get your checkbook out," he tried to sound confident. But when he worked the bolt and raised the rifle again, his hands were shaking.

Slow and steady . . .

The six inches of black on the final unblemished target were still one hundred yards away, but the scope brought them nearer, all but close enough to touch. He tried to center the cross hairs but they wavered before his eyes.

Hold your breath.

The wavering lessened.

Good. Now squeeze.

Like Steven before him, Andy didn't hear the barking report of the Remington. He didn't even feel the buck of the rifle against his shoulder. His senses were tuned to receive only the thud of a bullet drilling into the soft stump, or the sight of rotten wood through a sudden hole in the paper there.

He got both.

"Right on the button!" the Indian exclaimed. He immediately offered the glasses to Tucker for verification but the old man just waved him off. Steven went to congratulate Church but Covey already had him in a headlock, laughing and putting noogies on his scalp with his knuckles. "I love this guy!" he proclaimed, then pulled him up to look him in the eyes. "Andrew, my bank account thanks you, and I thank you." Then he gave Church a big kiss, flush on the mouth, that left the fat man gagging and sputtering. Everyone broke up laughing.

Except for Elton Tucker.

He approached Andy and the others immediately quieted down, waiting for his response. Church himself was unsure how to react to the old man, whether to taunt him and mock his defeat and risk unemployment, or stay modest and silent and lose a rare opportunity to toot his own horn. But before he could do either, Tucker surprised him. He held out his hand and smiled, and there was no trace of the reptile in that expression. It was conciliatory, almost congenial. "Outstanding shot, my boy," he said, shaking a stunned Andy's hand. "I'm impressed."

They all gaped as Andy stammered, "Uh . . . thanks. I guess."

"In fact, you've all done very well," he told them. "I think you're ready to begin. So let's get this show on the road, okay? Get your packs together. Mr. Davejac will show you what to take and what not to.'' He waited for a response but they just stood there, watching him. "Well? Get going. You're burning daylight."

The three men headed for the cabin, with Church still suffering the momentary adoration of his peers. They surely would have hoisted him onto their shoulders had their backs been up to the strain. With such obvious camaraderie between them, a stranger might have mistaken them for old and dear friends.

An observation that wasn't lost on Elton Tucker.

He stood watching after them, his mind racing. You failed, he scolded himself, not realizing that the inner voice sounded remarkably like his father's. You thought you had him all figured out and you failed. Now separating them and making them self-reliant will be that much harder.

He could feel eyes on him, disapproving, reproachful. And they weren't Barton Davejac's. The Indian was looking away at the almost-midday sun, checking its position against his watch. "Excuse me, Mr. Tucker," he said, "but do you really want to leave today? To get to the better hunting grounds we'll have to canoe a good little distance, and we'd be lucky to get there before dark. But if we wait till morning we could get a fresh start and—"

"I said now, mister," Tucker hissed. When he glared up at the younger man, he no longer wore the smiling face of conciliation he had presented for the men. That mask had slipped, uncovering the dark, drawn features of someone accustomed to getting his way, to winning. Until now. "Get them ready," he said in a steely whisper. "Now."

Barton just shrugged a reply and headed after the men. So in turning he didn't see the other expression on Tucker's face, roiling and mingling with the anger there. It might have been frustration. Or confusion. Or outright fear. Because even after the Indian was gone and Tucker was alone, the feeling of being watched did not leave him. He could still feel eyes on him, cold and disparaging. Familiar eyes.

He wouldn't admit it, even to himself. But Chalako Lakes

was beginning to resemble his father's land in Greene County a little too much. More than he cared to remember.

EIGHT

"YOURE TRYING TOO HARD," DAVEJAC CALLED FROM THE stern of the long aluminum canoe. "Work the oar slow and steady, like this." He demonstrated with a smooth stroke of the paddle, one that powered them effortlessly through the water. "Just remember. Slow and steady."

In the bow Steven tried to keep that in mind and mimic the guide's movements, find a stroking rhythm of his own. But he just couldn't seem to grasp the execution of it, and he wasn't sure why. It must have been the excitement that had built up during the day—first shooting the rifles, which had proven rather addictive, and then the much-improved relationship with his fellow hunters. He'd gotten along with Andy Church from the start, except for that paranoid nonsense outside the tavern in Atikokan. But now he found himself rather drawn to Paul Covey as well, despite his outlandish bragging and constant harangues. He reminded Steven of Marmaduke in the comic strips, a gangly dog who would get on your nerves readily enough but eventually ingratiated himself with a big lick on the face (kinda like he gave Andy, Steven thought with a chuckle). For the first time he saw these men not as business competitors but as potential friends. And it wasn't half-bad. He'd heard a lot about male bonding in the past and never put much stock in it. But now it made him want to join a bowling league or something.

Add to all of that a long canoe trip through the unmatched beauty of the Chalako Lakes, and the excitement level of a naive office rodent like Steven Wilhoit went right over the top.

They had left the base camp within an hour of test-firing their rifles for the first time. Steven was in the bow of the lead boat with Davejac at the far end, the middle taken up by their packs and guns and the limp carcasses of the two dozing elkhounds. They were evidently accustomed to such travel. Tucker and the other two men were in a second canoe, lagging behind. They followed the meandering length of Beaver Lake for hours, plowing through the crystalline waters with barely a ripple to mark their passing. It was an enjoyable sojourn marked by scenery every bit as beautiful as that found around the cabin. But it wasn't until they steered into a narrow tributary at the very southwestern tip of the lake and entered the lazy backwaters of Chalako that the anxiousness truly filled him. The forest seemed to swell up around them, and it was all so much more than any *National Geographic* special could have truly captured; it was simply beyond the scope of any magazine photo, or the ratio of a television screen. It had to be witnessed firsthand, from the inside out, where the neck would swivel left and right and tilt on its axis to take in the immense majesty above and below. The trees had grown up all around them, white birch and jack pine taller than they had yet seen, forming a cathedral ceiling of shifting autumnal colors high above the flow. And in the open places, they sometimes found themselves shadowed beneath ragged outcroppings of Precambrian rock, bared and worn by the shifting forces of glaciation. It was a whole other world he was visiting, as alien to him as the moon's pocked surface, and it reawakened the wide-eyed sense of wonder he'd discovered only the night before.

Unfortunately, that was not the only feeling it stirred.

A familiar uneasiness incubated in the pit of Steven's stomach. He had brought it with him on the drive from Atikokan, and felt it most acutely as they plowed deeper into the wilds

of Ontario. Claustrophobia, almost. A stark feeling of isolation. It was strange to even think of home now; it was a
distant world, getting farther away with each stroke of the
paddle. There in the speckled gloom of the trees, in the silence
of the deep woods, he felt as if they were nothing more than
cells in a placid bloodstream, spinning slowly, lazily, through
the arteries of some great sleeping giant, growing darker as
they neared the heart . . .

He checked his watch. Seven P.M., at least in Indiana. It
would be getting dark soon.

The Indian glanced to the rear to check on the other canoe
and found it still lagging behind, though Andy and Paul were
paddling hard to correct it. Tucker, on the other hand, was
sitting in the bow and did not wield an oar himself. In fact,
he did nothing; just sat there, an imitation Washington crossing the Delaware, rifle laid in the crook of an arm and ready
for the barest glimpse of a game animal. "What a dick,"
Davejac muttered. "Steven, tell me the truth. Is your boss
always nuts, or is this trip just a special occasion?"

"Oh, he's not nuts," Wilhoit corrected. "Poor people are
nuts. Rich people are just eccentric." He self-consciously
looked back for the other boat, to make sure it wasn't within
earshot. "He acts a little irrational at times, but he can afford
it. Why, what's wrong?"

"I don't know. The way he acts is so damn odd. He
changes moods like we change a shirt—one minute he's
smiling and jolly, and the next he's crawling down your
throat. It's sorta schizo."

Steven nodded knowingly. "That's the boss, all right."

"If you ask me, the guy's about three bricks shy of a load.
And the idea of him carrying a rifle out here doesn't sit too
well with me."

Steven shrugged. "What are you gonna do . . . it's his
dime."

It was getting dark now. The trees were just a wall of
ragged shadow around them. Wilhoit took out a flashlight

and used it to point much of the way. Behind them a second light blinked on. The others were doing the same.

The canoe was just passing beneath a shadowy outcropping of rock. Steven played his light along the rough grey surface and spotted something there, low, just above the waterline. A stick figure painted in red, four-legged, with other bipedal figures behind it. Intrigued, Steven leaned closer as they passed, actually reached out and dragged his fingers across the stone. "What is that?"

"A pictograph," Davejac told him. "Rock paintings. You'll find them all through Chalako, and in Quetico too."

"Who painted them?"

"I don't know," Barton shrugged. "These things are pretty old, and my people weren't the first ones in the area. There were the Forest Sioux, then the Cree, then the Ojibwa, and those are just the ones I know of. Some say they were painted by the manitos themselves, the spirits who were here before us."

Steven followed the painting till it was beyond his sight. The mystery intrigued him, awakened that educated side that thrived in the classroom, especially the folklore and anthropology courses back at IU. "Do they mean anything?"

"Not to me. Except when it's really obvious. Like that one back there. The animal looks like a deer, and the men chasing it are probably hunters. And since I've always had pretty good luck around here, I figure it's a signpost that means the game's good. At least it's logical, eh? Myself, I use it as a marker. When I see it, I know it's time to put in. See here?" He gave one more powerful stroke, just enough to carry them around the rocky ledge, and pointed his own flashlight to a bare spot along the weedy bank. A small footpath there wound back into the trees. "Steer for that," he told Steven, then motioned with his light for the others to follow.

After canoeing for much of the day, Steven was relieved to finally set foot on firm land again. He was barely out of the canoe and rubbing the kinks from his numb legs when Yogi and Boo-Boo bounded past him and down the trail playfully, obviously familiar with the surroundings. Then he and Davejac dragged the craft out of the water and unloaded their gear. They were packed and ready to move by the time the others caught up.

"This is it?" Elton Tucker asked as he climbed from their canoe and looked around, wholly unimpressed.

"This is just where we put in," Davejac explained. "We leave the canoes here and start the hunt on foot." Then he added, "In the morning," in case Tucker had other ideas. But the old man said nothing, just nodded.

Once the second boat was grounded and empty, Barton led the men into the forest. Dusk was finally sifting through the trees, quickly becoming night. Shadows hung from the limbs like cobwebs, growing steadily thicker, blacker. But then they were through it and out the other side, at least for the moment. They found themselves in a small clearing ringed by white oak, with a shallow stone-lined fire pit in its center and two stout dogs wrestling in the dirt beside it. This place had known its share of Davejac odysseys, that much was certain. He went back into the trees and gathered wood for the fire while the men got settled for the night.

Elton Tucker unlashed a small one-man dome tent from his pack and erected it with experienced ease. But the other men did not fare so well. Their tent was much larger, more intricate, and for professional men, their problem-solving skills were woefully inadequate. It took three tries before it would even stand on its own, and as for sturdiness, all they could do was pray for a windless night.

Before long Davejac had a good fire going in the pit, and that signaled one thing to Church. Suppertime. He was already digging through the bagged meals in his pack.

Each of them carried three such meals. There was no reason to take more than that, Davejac had told them. If they found game, the packets wouldn't be needed at all. And if they did use all three, it would mean the area was barren, and it was time to turn back to the base camp and redirect their hunt.

The men silently gathered around the campfire with their processed food, such trail standards as marinara beef and chicken teriyaki. But somehow the taste never quite matched the labels. They ate with sour expressions and each made a silent vow to kill something the next day. A deer, a bear, anything that didn't come in a brown bag.

As he finished his meal, Barton Davejac took a pipe and small pouch of tobacco from an inner packet of his coat. He also produced a small square of fabric, cut from old T-shirt material from the looks of it, and laid it on the ground before him. Once he'd filled his bowl, he up-ended the pouch and tapped a small hillock of tobacco out onto the swatch. "What the hell are you doing?" Church wanted to know, but the Indian was too involved to answer just then. He had taken some foil from his pocket and unwrapped it to reveal a little less than half of a Hershey bar. He broke off a corner of the chocolate and laid it next to the tobacco before folding the corners of the square in and tying off the little bundle with a piece of string. "It's an old superstition," he explained as he stood and walked to the edge of the clearing and hung it on a low tree limb. "All hunters leave an offering of tobacco and candy for the baguck. That's a small birdlike spirit. If the offering is accepted, it means you will have a successful hunt."

Tucker laughed. "You actually believe that? Or is it just a show for us tourists?"

Barton managed a smile, a shrugged excuse. "Maybe a little of both. I'm not that superstitious myself, but this is my heritage we're talking about. That's something I don't take lightly. If nobody remembers these rituals or practices them, how will our grandchildren know about their roots? Besides" —his smile widened—"it doesn't hurt to play it safe."

"What a load of horseshit," Covey guffawed.

"Don't be too quick to judge," teased Steven. "You don't want to piss off the spirits. Not around here."

"Say what?"

"Didn't you know?" He leaned forward and whispered, "These woods are haunted."

"Oh, man," Davejac sighed with exasperation.

"What? Was it a secret or something? Go on, tell 'em about the windigo."

"The whaty-go?"

"Windigo," the Indian corrected. "C'mon, you guys don't want to hear all this stuff, do you? It's just Indian myth and superstition."

"Sure we do," Andy Church said, his curiosity piqued. "What's a good campfire without a few ghost stories, right?"

Even Elton Tucker was mildly interested by now. "Go ahead, Mr. Davejac. It's too early to turn in, and there's nothing else to entertain us."

Barton finally relented with a nod, though not without shooting Steven another irritated glance. "The original pronunciation was *witiko*, also called He-Who-Lives-Alone by the Cree. The demon has many names. It's a giant cannibal, a spirit of madness that wanders the deep woods of the north like the Flying Dutchman, looking for lost hunters and any who should trespass there. The lucky ones would be consumed. But the others would suffer a far worse fate."

Boo-Boo, who was lying half on Davejac's lap and half off, woofed softly and then growled for no reason. "Hey," the guide warned, tapping him lightly on the noggin, "I'm talking here, okay? Now, where was I? Oh, yeah. The legend goes that if a man hears the windigo call his name, he is destined for madness. And if he should feel its icy touch, then forget it. He's cursed. For he'll soon know the hunger for human flesh himself, and he'll turn windigo. Doomed to wander the forest for eternity."

"Jeez," Covey said, chuckling. But the others were listening intently. They waited like anxious children, hoping the story would have a happy ending and let them off the hook. There was no sound except the pop and crackle of the fire, and when Boo-Boo raised his head and growled again, it startled Steven and Andy visibly. They had to laugh off their embarrassment.

"What is it, Boo?" Barton said, patting the dog's haunch and scratching his neck. The growling stopped but the elk-hound did not lay back down. His head and ears stayed alert, watching the camp, the forest around it.

"Those darn windigos," Paul chided them. "They'd do well in the business world. Same rules, right, Mr. Tucker? Eat or be eaten?" That drew a smile from the old man.

"Yeah, it's funny now," Barton agreed. "But in harder times, this was serious stuff. My people actually feared the windigo, and for someone who depends on the forest for shelter and food, that was a very palpable thing. Like I told Steven, you have to consider the time and circumstances surrounding these old legends. The winters can be hard on people up here, even today. But in the past they were especially bad. Game would grow scarce, and a hunter could be snowed in for an entire season, separated from the rest of the world. The isolation drove some men insane, and others even further. When starvation is imminent, sometimes cannibalism is the only alternative. Just like your Donner party, or those plane crash survivors in the Andes sometime back. If the situation's drastic enough . . . Well, most societies won't condone cannibalism, even relatively uneducated ones. So the Ojibwa needed something to explain why a member of the tribe might have eaten his mother-in-law during the winter. And that leads us to the windigo. Blaming the evil spirit was like saying 'the Devil made me do it.' And once that was established, it became an all-purpose devil. Didn't like somebody? Say they're a windigo in disguise, tell the village elders that he tried to eat you."

"Sounds like the Salem witch trials." Steven nodded.

"Same principle. And it also served as a bogeyman, to keep the little kids in line. Go right to sleep, boys and girls, or you'll hear the windigo call your name . . ."

Boo-Boo suddenly raised up, growling yet again. Only this time no amount of neck scratching could silence him. On the contrary; Barton touched his pelt and found his stiff guard hairs at full attention, rippling all along his spine. Even good-natured Yogi, who was napping beside her master, roused at the sound and then she chimed in with a throaty growl of her own. Both dogs were looking away from the river, into the depths of the forest.

"What is it?" Barton whispered to the dogs.

As if in reply their growls changed, slid deeper into their throats and became exhalations that seemed to shake each dog's entire frame. Especially the male. Boo-Boo came off his master's lap in a slinking crouch, his bull-like neck extended and taut as a cable, his grey fur bristling and the ears laid back against his broad skull. He stalked just to his sister's side and no farther. Both dogs watched the woods balefully. But neither was eager to approach the darkness there.

The other men looked around, stymied. They didn't know what to make of these developments. Steven felt the hackles raise on his neck. Just the tone of those growls, the threat they conveyed . . . What could be wringing such a response from them?

"I get it," Paul Covey gave a nervous laugh. "It's a gag, right? Don't you guys see? He's making 'em growl—to scare us. It's part of the ghost story, right? Am I right?"

Davejac spared them little more than a glance as he concentrated his eyes and flashlight on the forest along with the dogs. But his one quick look told them otherwise. The Indian's normally stony expression was knitted with confusion. Maybe even alarm. In a smooth steady movement he reached to his pack and slid his rifle out of its scabbard for the first time. It was a well-worn Marlin cowboy gun, thirty-thirty caliber. He worked the lever to chamber a round and rose up on one knee, shifted his weight expectantly.

Over the throaty rumblings of the elkhounds, each man heard a distinct sound out there in the darkness. Rustling. Movement through the leaves. It was there for an instant, then silence. Then again, just in front of them. Just beyond the trees.

"What is it?" Steven whispered, growing anxious. But no one volunteered an answer.

Elton Tucker reached for his own rifle. "What are we waiting for? We can outflank it, whatever it is. Church, you and Steven and Andy head in on the left, and we'll—"

"Don't move," the guide ordered in a steel-edged whisper, and it was startling enough in its own right to stifle any further response. They stayed right where they were, only now each man clutched a weapon. And they waited.

The sounds from the darkness did not come again. After a long tense moment the timbre of the dogs' voices changed, dropped off to whimpers of confusion. The alarm was over; they slunk back to Davejac's side and sat down quietly, licked at his hand to ask for some ear scratching. But the episode was not so readily forgotten. The fur along each dog's spine was still standing straight up.

Andy finally found his voice. "Is it gone?" he asked.

The guide lowered the hammer on his rifle and laid it aside. "Looks like it."

"What was it?"

He shrugged, his expression once again calm and inscrutable. "Could've been anything. A bear maybe, or a moose. Maybe one the tourists have been feeding along the road— they lose their fear of man that way. Animals are naturally curious, you know. And sometimes when they see a fire or hear voices, it tends to override their natural sense of self-preservation."

"You shouldn't have stopped me then," Tucker said, annoyed.

"You don't chase game in the dark," Davejac told him flat-out. "Especially not in these woods. If you didn't trip and break your neck or hang yourself on a low limb, you could still fall into a sucking place and then it's bye-bye, baby."

"What's a sucking place?"

"A sump hole, a weak spot in the bedrock, beneath the soil. The natives called them sucking places because that's what they do. The earth just seems to suck you in. I've seen several through the property. Almost fell in one once. So we only travel in daylight around here, clear? And you stay alert, even then."

"A wonderful place," Andy sighed sarcastically. "When is the next bus back home?" Then he looked to Tucker and emphasized, "Just kidding."

"We'd better turn in," the old man instructed. "I want to be moving at first light."

"But what about that . . . thing?" Church asked. "What if that bear or whatever it was comes back during the night?"

"The dogs will know it," the Indian assured them. "If it'll make you feel any better, one of them can sleep in your tent tonight." He motioned the dogs to stand still at his side for inspection. "Which'll it be? Yogi or Boo-Boo?"

Andy drew back from the glaring male dog. "Do you really have to ask?" he said, then patted his leg and gave a slight whistle. "C'mon, girl. We're having a few friends over to the bungalow. Nothing special, just a little wine and cheese. Dress casually, all right?"

The dog's tail wagged excitedly and she wriggled in anticipation, but she wouldn't move from Barton's side. Not until he nodded that it was okay. Only then did the elkhound jump on Andy and bowl him over, licking his face and urging a chuckle from all present.

"If you people will excuse me," Davejac said, rising, "I have to water the plants before bedtime. So get some sleep, and I'll see you in the morning." He walked away from the fire, back toward the river and stood at the very periphery of the clearing, fumbling with his zipper while the other travelers crawled into their tents.

Almost all of them.

Barton was in mid-stream when Boo-Boo growled again. But this was not as frantic as before. He was pointed not into the woods but at the approaching Wilhoit. The guide snapped at the dog and he fell begrudgingly silent. "It's not nice to sneak up on a peeing man, Steven," he said with a smile. "Your bladder full too?"

"After that little episode? You bet," the American exclaimed, making use of the natural facilities himself. But he was noticeably leery so close to the woods with the myriad shadows there, and he finished his business with amazing speed. Then he cast one more look into the darkness around them and, in a low voice, asked, "What do you really think it was out there?"

"I told you, Steve—"

"It wasn't a bear or a moose, my friend, and you know it. These dogs of yours are hunters, right? I don't think they'd back down from a game animal so easily. But they weren't budging this time. Besides, I saw the look on your face. Not afterward—you hid that pretty well. But while it was happening. You were just as nervous as the rest of us."

Davejac smiled knowingly. "A Sherlock Holmes fan, huh? Well, your powers of observation are keen, Steve, but you'd better work on the deduction bit. It surprised me, that's all. No, I'm not sure what it was out there. But there's a rational explanation. And I wasn't nervous. Or scared. And you shouldn't be either." He sighed. "Man, I knew I should never have opened my mouth to you about that haunted land jazz. I'll be up every night with you guys, holding your hands for the rest of the trip."

"Don't worry," Steven snapped right back at him. "I think we'll be just fine on our own." He turned and stalked back across the clearing, disappeared into the three-man-and-one-dog tent, leaving Davejac alone in the night.

City boys, the Indian smirked. Let them hear a few strange noises and they go to pieces. He knelt down by Boo-Boo and stroked the dog's bristly fur. "Just an animal out there, right, boy?" he said, half statement and half question. But neither with complete conviction. And the elkhound wasn't offering to elaborate. "Sure it was," he finally answered himself. Then he headed for his own tent, dog in tow, and picked up his rifle on the way. Taking the gun to bed with him was a completely normal practice, one he generally repeated automatically without really giving it much thought. But tonight it was different. It was all he thought about as he crossed the deserted clearing, and it certainly quickened his steps.

And that worried him.

"Just an animal," he repeated softly. But he himself was a more skeptical audience than Steven Wilhoit could have ever been.

Under the gaze of the night Tucker crouched down beside the campfire that still burned brightly and set the coffeepot on the ground beside him. He was preparing for his favorite ritual once again, just as he had back at the cabin, but . . . Something was missing. The nostalgic smile was gone from his face. Now there was only a frown of anxiety, and a nagging unease that he couldn't explain. His hands were even shaking as he scooped the coffee from its can and into the pot, not the new one with the blue-flecked enamel but a much older piece, familiar and dented, scorched black over many a fire. He filled the pot and set it on a simple metal grill over the flame. Then he held his hand before his face and stared at it, at the darkening liver spots and grey fuzz across the knuckles. And he told it to stop shaking. Stop right now . . .

"Elroy? I want my coffee, boy. And it better be right."

The voice came from behind him, deep and guttural as it echoed across the clearing and through the Greene County forest. And the very sound of it made his heart tighten and his lungs refuse to take a breath. No, he thought, it can't be him . . . But there was no denying that belligerent tone or the despised nickname that had haunted him for most of his life. Already Elton was stammering out an answer. "Almost . . . almost done," he called, in reflex, his throat suddenly dry, his voice cracking. He reached for the coffeepot and almost burned himself before thinking to wrap a hankie around his hand. He did so quickly, much too fast to notice the change that had taken place. His hands were different from before; no more wrinkles, no more spots. They were slender and white and only ten years old again.

Ten years old . . .

"Elroy!"

"Coming, Dad."

He turned with the coffeepot and found the night around him complete, no stars or moonlight to penetrate its totality. The flames left him in a fluttering spotlight that threatened to collapse from the weight of the blackness around it. He was alone in that light except for an old oak stump nearly as tall as he, and for the imposing figure that leaned against it. The man was not especially large but seemed so, even seated. Always had. In the ten years since his son's birth, since he left the Marine Corps, Virgil Tucker had started a downhill slide of physical change. His barrel chest was still impressively broad, straining his hunting jacket, but it was offset by the growing ring around his middle. Likewise his face was no longer as angular and severe as it once was, not since the jawline had softened with added weight and his chin had become plural in nature. In fact, he was now a friendly looking man, his smile broad and ever present. But in the harsh glare of the campfire, as few but his son Elton had ever seen him, that buttery countenance reverted to an earlier incarnation. The soft features grew hard and the pig eyes gleamed and the smile became cruel and threatening. Just as it was now.

He held out his tin cup and fixed the boy with a glare. "Get a move on," he ordered in a low growl.

Elton hurried to pour the coffee, his breath coming fast and his heart fluttering as he tried not to spill any, no, not a drop. That would only make things worse. So carefully he poured the steaming liquid, nearly to the top, then quickly stepped away before Dad could tip the cup and blame it on him. No spills, he sighed. So far, so good. But the relief was short-lived, for his father had yet to taste the coffee. Maybe I got it right this time, he thought hopefully. I was sure to follow his instructions, right to the letter, and my hand's just now getting better and he just can't make me put it out again, he can't . . .

Elton bit his lip, crossed his fingers. Waited.

Virgil Tucker sniffed the steaming cup, waved it under his nose as if admiring the bouquet. He looked at his son, then sniffed again. Looked. Sniffed. Prolonging it.

Taste it already, for God's sake!

But the man did not. He lowered the cup to his knee and fixed Elton with a stern glare. "I'm disappointed in you, boy."

Oh, no . . . "But . . . but you haven't even tasted—"

"You let it go."

"Let what go, Dad?"

His father's eyes drilled into him. "The buck," Virgil told him. "The sixteen-pointer. The one across the lake this morning. Remember?" He reached behind the stump and lifted the Weatherby into view with one big hand. "Your old man never had a fancy gun like yours, Elroy. That's for sure. You should be able to hit anything with this." He laid it down, once again fixed Elton with the same glare. "I tried to help you. I tried to talk you through it. But you wouldn't listen, would you?" He was getting angry now. Gritting his teeth. "No, not you. You Just. Wouldn't. Listen!"

"Dad, I—"

"You failed," Virgil decreed. "And what is it we can't tolerate?"

"I, uh . . . it's just . . ."

"What is it!"

His lip began to quiver as tears welled in the corners of his eyes. The first of many to come. "Failure," he said weakly. "We won't tolerate failure."

Virgil couldn't keep the smirk off his face as he sat down his coffee cup and reached beneath his gut, pulled the dreaded leather belt out with a taunting slowness. "You know it's for your own good," he said as he had all the times in the past. "Once you learn that failing can hurt, you'll never let it happen again. Trust me. I learned it from my dad, and you will too. And you'll thank me, Elroy. You will. Because it'll make you a better man.'' But even as he spoke those words, his expression betrayed them. The growing leer was reason enough.

He enjoyed it.

"I'm sorry, I'm sorry," Elton cried, shrinking away as he stared at that heavy leather strap, the cutting edges of the metal buckle. He'd felt them both before, so many times . . . "I'll do better," he pleaded. "I promise. I'll get a buck tomorrow. I'll get one for you, Dad. Please . . ."

The glare did not lessen. But finally Virgil lowered the belt, started threading it back through the loops of his jeans. The cruel smile remained. "You'd better do just that, Elroy," he said, picking up the Weatherby, holding it out. "I'd better see a trophy. 'Cause you promised."

Elton wiped away tears of relief. "I will, Dad," he said, reaching for the rifle with hands once again large and wrinkled, spotted with age. "I'll get you one, I promise." He actually felt himself smiling. He was just so relieved to escape his punishment, even if he did deserve it, even . . .

Oh, no.

His father was picking up the tin cup again.

"I hope you made it right this time," Virgil warned, a twinkle in his small black eyes as he blew into the steaming cup, cooling it enough for a sip. He tasted it tentatively, rolled it around his mouth . . .

And spat it out.

No, no, no . . .

"Come here, Elroy. Did you hear me? Come. Here."

Elton stepped closer. The tears were coming freely now, expectantly. "I'm sorry, I'm sorry . . ."

"You were close this time"—his father grinned— "but it still ain't right. So put it out. You hear? I said, *Put it out*!"

Whimpering, the boy bowed his head and extended his left hand, same as last time, always the left. Because Elton was right-handed and he couldn't let it happen to that one, then he couldn't cook supper or clean Dad's rifle or anything else and then he'd get it doubly bad. He put it out and squeezed his eyes shut and he could still see his father's face, his grinning face as he held the still-hot coffee overhead, and he could hear him giggling under his breath as he tipped the cup and the pain—

Woke him.

Tucker sat up with a jerk, his ears filled with the hammering of his own heart, his eyes with an orange haze that he finally recognized as the color of the tent around him. Just another dream, he tried to assure himself, though he couldn't exactly remember what it had been about. Nor did he know why he was panting so hard and sucking on the back of his left hand when there was nothing wrong with it.

Or why he was trembling.

He thought about climbing out of the tent, of seeking the warmth and reassurance of the campfire. But he couldn't will himself to move. It was a flash of mortal fear at first—an unexplainable dread of what he might find there, as if whatever specters that haunted his dreams might still be lurking nearby. But then the Tucker pride offered a more acceptable explanation. The others can't see me like this, he fretted. Not like this. So he settled back in his bedroll and thought about other things, about the business and production schedules and board meetings and quarterly earnings and other dreary details steeped in reality. And the trembling finally eased. After an hour or so he even became drowsy again and slowly slipped into a muted half sleep, but no further.

And just before he drifted off, he muttered softly, unconsciously, over and over, "I'll get one for you, Dad. I'll get one . . ."

NINE

MORNING CAME LATE TO THE FOREST. EVEN AFTER THE SUN boldly climbed over the horizon and announced the day begun, its rays had yet to penetrate the natural roof of leaves and branches. The twilight gloom remained in place, and a cool fog clung to the trunks of the trees. *Plop, plop* was the only sound, pearls of dew dripping from the higher vegetation to the leafy floor below. The clearing remained in twilight as well, and the contrasted brightness of the sky high above seemed like the mouth of a deep pit, as seen from the inside.

Davejac was up at first light, even if it didn't reach down there to greet him. His internal clock was that well set. He slipped into his clothes and a down vest, pulled the toboggan onto his head, and climbed out of the tent, sucking in a lungful of crisp morning air. Boo-Boo stood right at his side and stretched catlike, gave a long yawn and then sneezed the dampness from his nose. The sound must have alerted his sister, because just then Yogi came wriggling through the flap opening of the three-man tent and joined them. She greeted her master with a tail wag and an affectionate lick on the hand, the other dog with a thorough hiney-sniff. Then they both looked at Barton with a questioning stare.

"Play in a minute," he told them. "First we take a look around."

That episode from the previous night was still on his mind. It was the primary reason he'd gotten little sleep; even with an alert elkhound in his tent, he couldn't shake the feeling of wrongness that pervaded that scene. Steven had been right—the dogs were hunters, and normally they would have been bristling for him to give the nod, to send them into the brush to bay whatever was out there. But they didn't move, not at all. And he'd never seen that, not in the six years he'd hunted with them.

Damned odd's what it was. Even a little scary.

Nothing to be scared of, you panty waist. He looked around the clearing, through the netting of drying limbs and creeping brambles that surrounded them, less solid and intimidating in the light of day. What had raised the fine hairs on his nape the night before now made him chagrined for being unduly alarmed. Still, he was a thorough man and took nothing for granted. So he fetched his rifle from the tent before venturing into the trees. The dogs obeyed his unspoken command, staying close by his side.

He watched the elkhounds from the corner of his eye, waited for a repeat performance to tell him whatever had alarmed them was still nearby. He would have caught any little change in behavior, a curious turn of the head or ears upright, alert for any little sign of their visitor. But the dogs were oblivious this morning. In fact, they seemed to be waiting on him for the next move. He finally scoured the area himself, searching for any little clues, no matter how subtle. Davejac was an experienced hunter and tracker, and as such he had trained himself not to dismiss any little detail. Not just tracks, though that was the most obvious. Disturbed areas in the mulchy compost of leaves that made up the forest floor. A tuft of fur caught on a rough section of bark. A bit of refuse dropped along the way. But there was nothing to be found in that area. It was as if a phantom . . .

Now don't start that again.

The dogs were mewling now, prancing in their restlessness. They looked at him again, imploring.

"All right," he said, grinning. "Go play. I'll call you when the chow's on."

Whether from his words or his expression, the dogs understood the command. They raced off into the woods, chasing each other and seeming to alternate the pursuer role every few strides.

Barton walked back into camp, and in bending the underbrush aside to make way for himself, he knocked the small bundle of tobacco and candy from the limb where he'd hung it. So the baguck didn't come, he said to himself with a wry and knowing smirk. As if he'd expected it in the first place. Of all the times he'd hunted Chalako Lakes, that he'd left the offering and asked the spirit for a good hunt, the pouch had only been taken twice. And even then he dismissed it as inquisitive squirrels. After all, that was a more reasonable answer, wasn't it? Certainly more so than some hoary old superstition.

But didn't you bring down game on those two trips? A moose one day, and black bear the other?

Yes, he admitted. But he'd been successful on other trips as well, when the pouch was left hanging right where he'd put it. It was coincidence, that's all. Pure coincidence.

Then why do you do it? Why continue the charade?

He did feel a little guilty at times, repeating rituals that held no meaning for him beyond what George Wilson had told him. But it was all he could do. It was as he'd told the Americans, he wanted to keep his heritage, to value it. After all, it was something he'd been cheated out of, being brought up almost white in a moderate income family near Toronto. That was why he was out here in the first place, to try to recapture at least a hint of that past, to see where his forefathers walked and hunted and try to fill their footsteps. And even if he couldn't accept all of their beliefs and customs, at least he could offer his respect for them by repeating the rituals, keeping that much alive.

He was sure that they would have understood.

He retrieved the pouch off the limb and stuck it into his pocket. No sense letting the others know. Let them believe for a while that the stories could be real, that their hunt has been blessed by the spirits. Hell, let 'em believe in the windigo while they're at it. Maybe they'll be a little more careful out there.

He went to the fire pit and pulled his rain jacket from over the kindling pile, then took out his magnesium fire-starter (wouldn't the ol' ancestors have loved a few of these!). He used a knife to scrape the tool and dropped the shavings into the pile. Then he struck a spark there. The magnesium caught quickly, and soon he had a fire going again, weak at first but growing as he added more sticks for fuel. Then he raided the mess pack for Tucker's coffeepot and some other supplies, and heated up some pseudo-egg material from one of the brown bags.

Elton Tucker was the first one up. "Good morning, Mr. Davejac," he said with his usual bluster. He took an exaggerated inhalation, "ahhh"ed with gusto. "Great day for a hunt, aye?"

"Looks like it," Barton said, pouring a cup of coffee. He held it out for the old man.

But when Tucker saw it, he flinched.

"Something wrong?"

Tucker blinked at him for a moment, confused and unconsciously rubbing his left hand. Barton noticed for the first time that the old man's eyes were bleary and red-rimmed, as if rest had eluded him for most of the night. Then he shook it off and smiled and reached for the cup. "Why not?" He laughed uncertainly.

"Are you okay, Mr. Tucker?" Davejac asked. "If you're not feeling well, we don't have to leave right away. We're in no hurry, you know. We can hold off if you're not up to it . . ."

"Not on your life," Tucker snapped, his eyes flaring. From his agitation, it was readily apparent that he took this hunt seriously. Dead serious. "This is what I came up here for. It's why I brought them up here. We can't disappoint them, can we?"

"No, sir."

Tucker sat down across from him, sipping his coffee and

staring into the flames with a faraway look, making Davejac feel very uncomfortable with his presence. Thankfully the others started rousing about then so he didn't have to be alone with the boss for long. Andy Church came out of the tent immediately in his coat and a pair of sweatpants he'd been sleeping in, drawn by the smell of coffee and food on the griddle. Covey and Wilhoit were a little longer in appearing, and when they did so they were fully dressed for the hunt. They wore the orange vests and hats Tucker had provided for them (good, Davejac thought, they'll be less likely to shoot each other) and carried their rifles in the crook of their arms, just as they'd been taught. "Pip pip and tally-ho, gents," Covey said, his Hoosier twang hard to mistake for British. "Are we ready to go or what?"

"After you eat," Davejac told them. "C'mon, boys, dig in. Get it while it's hot."

"I notice your little spirit offering is gone," Tucker observed.

They all looked to the tree limb, now empty. "Aw, he just took it down," Covey said. "Didn't you, chief?"

Davejac wore his best poker face and shrugged. He turned his attention to Wilhoit, who was surprisingly wolfing down the egg stuff with gusto. "You're a little eager, aren't you?"

Steven grinned like a mischievous child. "Actually I am, and I don't even know why. I'm not sure I'll even be able to shoot a deer if we come across one. A target's one thing, but a living thing . . ."

"There ain't no difference, Steve." Barton shrugged. "That comes afterward, when you've gotta look at what you've shot. Look at it and live with it."

Wilhoit looked sheepish. "Do you think I'll be able to do it?"

"Sure. But just remember—you dress what you kill. And that, my friend, is a whole different story."

"Dress?" Steven asked, looking to the others. "What the hell is dress?" He got out his *Complete Survivor* manual, started looking it up.

"Clean it," Covey explained. "Tie off the bung hole and cut off the genitals before you gut it. You know, the good stuff." Then he laughed when the other man apparently found pictures in his paperback and halted in midchew. "Don't worry about it. I'll help you out. If you bring one down." Then, muttered, "And that's a big if."

Andy Church finished two helpings of breakfast and hurried to his tent to get ready, showing just as much enthusiasm as Wilhoit had. Davejac was taken off-guard by it and immediately looked to Tucker for some reaction, to see if the men were betraying his expectations as well. But the old man did not seem to notice. He was too busy slurping down his coffee and looking impatiently to his watch, counting the minutes. "Hurry up, Church," he snapped testily. Then he poured out the remaining brew and went to take down his tent.

Covey and Wilhoit took up their stakes as well, as much to irritate the half-dressed Church as to ready their gear, while Davejac put out the remaining food for the dogs and started packing away his belongings. A whistle brought the elk-hounds running. Once they were done eating and Andy was suitably prepared, Davejac stepped back and surveyed his troops. At least they looked the part, he allowed. "Let's move out," he called and set off through the trees, following the southwestern route he had traveled so many times before. The dogs moved out ahead, and the others fell quickly into step behind him.

He heard Steven chuckle, unable to hold in his excitement. To play it safe, Davejac called back for him to check his rifle and make sure the safety was on.

Just in case.

They saw their first wildlife somewhere around noon. Covey spied two squirrels playing in the branches overhead, scampering back and forth and chasing each other. And he was convinced he could hit one of them, even on the run. He bet Andy a ten-spot and readied his weapon. But Davejac told him not to.

"A 30.06 shell will just vaporize the little shit."

"So?" Covey looked at him blankly.

"So we hunt for meat," Davejac told them, "or we hunt for trophies. But we never hunt just to kill."

"It's only a squirrel," the man offered.

"Oh, let him have it," Tucker told the guide. "It'll be good target practice."

"Okay," Davejac sighed in surrender. "It's your nickel. But keep in mind that your target practice will probably scare away any other game in the area."

That thought obviously hadn't occurred to them. Covey reshouldered his rifle on second thought and they continued their trek.

The monotony began to wear on them by midafternoon. There had been no game sighted yet, only two more squirrels and some birds in the upper branches of the trees. Rifles were no longer carried at the ready, for their sense of expectation had been dampened by the drudgery of walking. Andy Church kept himself occupied by raiding the cache of junk food that he'd liberated from the Tom Boy grocery in town. They could hear him at the back of the line, crunching Pringles chips with gusto. Paul Covey sang country songs to pass the time, Ricky Skaggs and Ronnie Milsap, until he got too loud and Tucker barked at him to stop.

Where Andy snacked and Paul now hummed softly to himself, Wilhoit just complained. A stinging pain had asserted itself around the heel and Achilles tendon of his left foot, and when he paused on a stump and peeled off his sock, he found two angry blisters staring back at him.

"What'd you expect, college boy?" Covey smirked. "Any boob knows not to wear new boots hiking. Not right away."

"But they said these were really good boots . . ."

"They probably are," Davejac said, a little more understanding. "But everything needs to be broken in. Can you walk, or should we turn back?"

Wilhoit caught the old man's angry glare. "Keep going," he said, knowing it was the only answer Tucker would have tolerated. Just grin and bear it, he told himself. You've got to expect a few blisters on the road to success.

But after another hour of walking, such platitudes were meaningless. He began to limp. And then it was him bringing up the rear instead of Church.

Just before dusk it started to rain. Not a downpour by any means, but a light grey drizzle that seemed the perfect capper for such an empty day. They each broke out a rainsuit, except for Church, who'd brought an Army poncho instead. He spent the next hour trying to keep it from snagging on the underbrush.

They camped for the night beneath a tall rocky shelf so the overhang would keep the rain off of them. There wasn't much talk; they were too tired for that. They ate their precooked meals and turned in, assuring themselves that tomorrow would be the day . . .

Elton Tucker sat by the fire, alone, for most of the night. It wasn't that he couldn't sleep. He just wouldn't allow it.

The second day proved little better than the first.

Barton Davejac knew the luck and misfortune of the hunt, and he'd taught himself the patience required. But even he was surprised and more than a little chagrined by the lack of sightings on this trip. To be precise, they had seen absolutely nothing. Not just an absence of game animals, but of *all* animals. A few minutes after starting that morning they had scared up a covey of quail while crossing a shallow meadow, but since then . . . It was almost eerie. Even the birds seemed to avoid them; their songs could still be heard in the distance, but the forest directly around them was unsettlingly quiet.

"I just don't get it," he muttered yet again, as much to himself as the ragged men following behind. "We should have found something by now."

A wheezing groan was his only answer at first. Andy Church was still next in line, red-faced and exhausted, his breathing now a rattle that made Barton cringe when he heard it. He'd tried to hold up the pace a bit to suit the fat man, but Andy still looked ready to pass out at any moment. And despite his poor condition, he refused to give up or take a long break. Davejac had to give him credit for stubbornness if not common sense. "We'll stop here for a few minutes," the guide told them. And this time he wouldn't take no for an answer.

Church looked defensive. "Not on my account," he huffed.

"Not you, Andy. I just need some rest."

The fat man nodded affirmative and looked relieved. He leaned against a tree and almost slid to the ground.

"What are you stopping for?" Tucker wanted to know as he pushed past an equally tired Paul Covey. "Have you seen something?" He brought up his rifle, looked about excitedly. Tucker was haggard; the red-rimmed eyes had become bagged and shadowy as if he hadn't slept in days, and his face was drawn with fatigue and something else . . .

"There's nothing," Barton told him. "We're just resting."

"Resting?" the old man asked, as if the term had no meaning for him. He looked up through the trees to the sky beyond, checked the position of the sun. "We've got a few hours till dusk. If we keep at it we can get a few more miles . . ."

"This isn't a race," Church snapped angrily.

Tucker looked at him as if he'd just committed heresy. "We might find better ground," he said weakly. "The white-tail have to be around here somewhere. They have to."

"I've tried to tell you, Mr. Tucker," Davejac said, slowly now so the logic of his words might sink in this time. "This area is tapped out. I don't know why, but the animals have moved on. We've gone far enough to see that, okay? Now it's time to turn back."

"No."

"But it's time," he continued. "We're almost out of food—we each have one more bagged meal left—and there's no game to live on. If we turn back now, we'll get to the base camp with a few days to spare. We can stock up and go back out, take another direction next time. We might still find something."

"I said no," Tucker said vehemently. "You want me to fail, don't you? You want me to say it. But I won't. Because we can't tolerate failure. We won't."

"What are you talking about? It's not failure if . . ." But the old man was adamant. Barton finally shrugged and gave in. Remember, you acquiesce with the best. But that was a rule he was finding hard to live up to this time out. "All right, boss. It's your call. Stay together back there, okay, and . . . wait a minute." He counted heads, looked around. Only three men. "Where's Steven?" He glared at Tucker. "You were looking after him. Where is he?"

"Back there somewhere," Tucker spat with disdain. "He kept sitting down on me. So I left him. We don't need the dead weight."

Davejac just stared at the man, incredulous. "You what? You just left him? Didn't you know he could get lost?"

"He won't get lost," the old man sniffed. "He's not that far back. Besides, it might put the fear o' God into him. Maybe he'll pick up the pace, quit being such a mamby-pamby."

Barton massaged his temples. He could feel a headache coming on. "Wait here," he sighed. "I'll go back and find him."

"We're not waiting," Tucker told him outright. "If you want to baby-sit Wilhoit, fine. But you'll do the catching up. Got it?"

The Indian glared back at him. "Go ahead. I'll find you. Even if you get lost." He gave a sharp whistle and the dogs came running, followed him back along the impromptu trail they'd blazed this far. They were out of the men's sight within sixty yards.

Where to start, Barton wondered, surveying the grey thicket of trees and brambles that lay in any given direction. Wilhoit had to have stopped within the last twenty minutes

—it was the last time Davejac had seen him, readjusting the new boots that were still giving him fits. Well, better get moving, before he takes a wrong turn and gets himself lost good and proper.

He retraced their steps for the past mile, through dense timber and over hillsides of loose shale, all the way back to the weed-grown gully where he'd last seen the man massaging his blistered feet. But there was no sign of him, at least to the naked eye. Damn, he cussed. This might be harder than he expected. He motioned for the dogs to scour the area and he followed close behind.

They found his trail not more than ten minutes from the gully. Boo-Boo, the sharper of the two elkhounds, sniffed the air and turned in the direction of an open notch in the terrain, leading off to the left. A more inviting path to the eyes of a novice, Davejac wagered, though he wanted more proof before setting out in that direction. He dropped down into a crouch, sifted through the sodden leaves and soil at his feet. Nothing . . . no, there. A wadded Wrigley's wrapper. And the foil was discarded a foot or two away. In the direction of the notch.

"Good job, Boo," he said, cuffing the dog affectionately behind the ear. "Go on now. Get after him." The elkhound woofed softly in reply and set out in the new direction, his sister right on his heels. The guide had to hurry to keep up.

Wilhoit must have panicked, he decided. It explained not only the deviation in course but the ground he'd covered as well. For though Barton had expected to find him right away, he soon found that was not the case. Not for a quarter mile, then a half. Then a mile and more. The man must have been running by now, or he couldn't have gone so far so fast. Running and scared, not knowing which direction to turn, not knowing where to go. "Steven!" Barton started to yell in earnest now, hoping for a sign. But there was only the distended resonation of his own voice in the distance. He started to get a sick feeling deep in his gut. I knew this was going to happen, he fumed inwardly. *I should have seen it coming, the damn amateurs, I should have held their hands all the way* . . .

He came up over the crest of a hill and slid to a stop, right behind the two elkhounds. They were standing stark still beneath the arms of a leaning oak, at the edge of a depression in the earth about ten feet across and a foot or so deep. Unlike the rest of the forest floor, this large spot was not covered in brown-to-blackening leaves. Only the dark soil showed here, as well as a few tendrils of the oak's now-exposed roots, and it made that sick feeling in Barton's gut flare into a full-sized ache. For he'd seen such things before. To be sure, he reached out with a boot and stepped on the edge of the hollow. Immediately the dirt there moved under his heel; it gave and slid farther into the concavity and was swallowed up. Just like whatever had traversed this trail before him. "Jesus," he whispered. "Steven . . ."

Yogi was whining now, trying to tell him something. But Barton wasn't paying attention. Not until the voice startled him. "So that's a sucking place, huh?"

Davejac looked up at Wilhoit numbly, not registering him at first. Steven was sitting on the far side of the oak tree, vigorously brushing at the dark soil that stained his clothes from the waist down. "That stuff's like quicksand," he said with an unsteady smile. "I had a helluva time getting out. Guess I was screaming like a woman, wasn't I?"

"I don't know," Davejac said with a shrug. "I never heard you. We were probably too far away. Are you all right?"

"I suppose so. I saved my stuff," he said, holding up his dirty backpack like a trophy. "But I lost my rifle in there. Any chance of getting it back?"

"I doubt it. These holes can go pretty deep." He picked up a long broken tree limb from the underbrush and used it to probe down into the center of the hole. It disappeared into the sinking soil as far as he could reach, and surely would have slid beyond sight had it sufficient weight to drag it down.

He turned back to Wilhoit. "You'd better thank your stars, my friend. You're lucky to be alive."

"Yeah, that's what I figured. If it wasn't for that branch up there." He motioned to the lowest limb of the oak, extending just over the hole. "I was about chest deep when I used my backpack strap and looped it over that branch, hung on for dear life. I yelled my ass off. But when nobody came I finally decided, Hey, it's up to you, kid. So I gritted my teeth and pulled myself out." He sighed wearily. "This trip really isn't much fun anymore. I hope you know that."

Barton skirted the hole, testing the ground with a boot before each step, and helped the exhausted man to his feet. "Don't worry about it. I've already told your boss it's time to call it quits. I think this proves it."

"Amen."

"Now we've just gotta catch up with the others."

Steven laughed. "You know, after this little adventure, I don't even feel my blisters anymore. Lead on, McDuff. This time I'll stay right behind you."

"Good." The Indian surveyed their location and then checked the small compass on his belt. "It's this way," he said, pointing to the west. Then he added, "I think."

Steven wasn't laughing now. "What do you mean, you think? You mean you're not sure?"

"You remember when we talked that night by the lake? You asked me if I knew Chalako Lakes and I said I'd seen at least ninety percent of it? Well, welcome to the other ten percent. I haven't been back this far before."

"You're kidding."

"Afraid not." Then he saw Wilhoit's worried expression and tried to reassure him with a smile. "Don't worry. Just because I'm not familiar with it, doesn't mean we can't find our way. That's what you people are paying me for, remember?" He gave the dogs a hand signal and showed them what direction to go, then the two men followed after them. They couldn't tell just how high the sun was above the horizon, but the gloom settling around them bespoke a late hour. Davejac set a quick pace and didn't ask if Steven could match it. He had to. It was getting dark already.

They made it back to the others' trail within the hour and found the place where Barton had turned back. But they were no longer there. True to Tucker's word, they had not waited around. "That sonuvabitch," Barton said under his breath.

"Are they lost?" Steven asked.

"They will be, if we don't find them before dark. C'mon."

They followed the slope of a hill until the tangle of undergrowth lessened and they found themselves on the top of a tall escarpment, at least as high as the glacier-smoothed landscape of Chalako normally reached. The vegetation broke along the ragged promontory of shale and bedrock, giving them an unrestricted view of the surrounding countryside. It was a coniferous ocean of green that spread before them, its pine limbs and saplings waving in the breeze like swells of lazy water. Beyond a second spine of land to the west, this one whiskered with scrub and briers, they could make out the reflection of waning sunlight in a tranquil lake, and even more water scattered beyond that, into the distance and well beyond their sight.

Steven paused to take in the sweeping vista, at once heartened at the scenic beauty and yet overpowered by its sheer size, while Davejac concentrated on the trail of the others. He had noted the position of the sun and knew there was little time left. He was scouring the rocky area when Steven called to him.

"What is that out there?" Wilhoit was shielding his eyes with one hand, pointing to the southwest with the other. "I saw something, in that dark open patch between the trees."

Davejac took out his binoculars. "What was it?"

"It looked like headlights . . . there! Did you see it? There it is again!"

Barton caught the flash of light this time and centered on it as he brought the glasses to his eyes, focused them. He got one good look before it disappeared into the trees, but it was enough. "A four-wheel drive," he said, puzzled himself. "Who the hell would be this far out?"

"A logging company maybe?"

"I guess it's possible. We might be near the border of Chalako so it could be an Ati-Kut Timber camp." Then his brow furrowed. "Or they could be trespassing, harvesting wood without permission. That's been happening a lot lately."

"You mean there's a camp near here?" Steven brightened. "Other people? Civilized people? You mean that —" Then he noticed that Davejac was no longer standing beside him with binoculars in hand. He had returned to scouring the trail. "What are you looking for?"

"A reason why those dickheads took off so fast," Barton replied. "And I think I've found it. Take a look at this."

Steven found him crouched over a dimple in the dirt trail. He had to lean closer himself before he saw that the indentation was split into two halves, and that there was another a foot or so away. Hoof tracks. "A deer," the Indian identified it. "It's dried—could be a day old, could be a week or more. But Tucker's so hot to bag something, he probably saw it and went apeshit. My hunch is that if we follow these tracks, we'll find your friends . . ."

A shot rang out. It was distinct, easily separated from its own reverberations. To the south.

"That must be them."

Barton was looking around. "Where are the dogs?"

Steven noticed for the first time that the elkhounds were nowhere to be seen. "They were here just a second ago . . . oh, shit. You don't think . . ." But Davejac was already moving. The big Indian ran along the rock-strewn ridge with an agility that his size belied, then dashed back into the woods at a deadrun. Steven cursed his own slowness and blistered feet and hobbled after him as fast as he could, determined not to be left behind for a second time.

The Indian swept through the woods with dizzying speed, dodging limbs and slipping through nets of sticking brambles with amazing dexterity. His ears were still primed and sifted through the gunshot's distracting echoes to center only on the source of the sound, the direction, the distance . . . "Stop shooting!" he yelled his loudest, even before he saw the standing shadows through the trees, before he broke into the clearing where the men now stood.

"What the hell are you doing, you fucking fool!" Tucker hissed at him as he stood poised with the Weatherby at his shoulder. "Are you trying to scare it off?"

"Scare what off?" Barton asked between gasps.

"The whitetail we're following," Covey reported in a low whisper. "The boss just saw it."

"Are you sure it wasn't one of my dogs?" the Indian snapped. Andy's and Paul's features slackened with the suggestion. Davejac turned to Tucker. "Are you sure?"

The old man hesitated at first, but he covered it well. "Well . . . yes, I'm sure. I can tell the difference between a deer and a goddamn dog, you know."

"You'd better be able to," the guide said in a low and threatening tone. "Because if you've shot one of my dogs . . ." He continued to glare at the old man as he gave a shrill whistle once, twice. Then he waited. Soon there came a thrashing through the bushes but it was only Steven catching up, wheezing and limping. The other hunters helped him to sit down and started to ask him what had happened but Barton shushed them, whistled again. Silence.

Then a dog barked.

Yogi came bounding through the underbrush and went right to her master's side, panting and licking at his hand. But no Boo-Boo. Barton's throat constricted with the intimation.

Andy turned to Tucker. "Could it have been a dog?"

The old man said nothing.

Barton started back into the trees to find out. But before he could get there the missing elkhound came slinking into view. He went to Davejac with his tail tucked between his legs, leaned against him, and begged forgiveness for not coming faster.

"See there?" Tucker said after a sigh of relief. "I told you it wasn't a dog."

"It could've been," the Indian said then. "You could've missed your deer and hit my dogs."

"I don't miss."

"Oh, yeah? Then where's the buck? Show it to me."

The old man glowered at him, the veins in his temples standing at attention. "One shot wouldn't stop it. It's huge, you should see the size of the tracks—"

"The tracks are old," Davejac interjected. "The buck that made them could have left this area weeks ago."

"You don't know that."

"Look, Mr. Tucker. It's time to call this quits. I told you earlier that we're damned low on food—probably enough for tonight, maybe breakfast if we make things stretch. As it is, we'll still be damned hungry by the time we get back to camp. But now it's getting dangerous out here. You abandoned Steven back there, and it almost got him killed. And now you're shooting into the woods at random. Hell, that could've been the dogs, or me, or Steven out there. The stakes are too high now. I say we turn back."

Andy and Paul stepped back, wide-eyed, as if someone had just been foolhardy enough to insult the school bully. But Steven did not join them. "He's right, Mr. Tucker," he said, surprising the others and even himself. "Look around—there are no animals here. And if you come across one of those sucking places the way I did, you might not be as lucky. C'mon, you've had your fun, you've run us around and made us look like dicks. Now it's time to call it off."

Tucker glared at the both of them, his dark and sleepless eyes not even blinking. But then he grinned. His driven expression of the last few days was temporarily displaced by a more familiar smugness. "I am footing the bill here, you know," he reminded them, "and I could just say, Fuck the both of you, we're staying. But I am a thoughtful man, and an admirer of the democratic process. So I will let you put it to a vote. The majority rules.'' The grin slid away. ''I vote we stay.''

''I say we leave,'' Davejac countered.

Steven nodded. ''Leave,'' he said, and noted the frown on his boss's face.

They turned to Covey. But only when Tucker was looking did he flash that patented horse grin. ''I'm with the boss,'' he said, putting an arm around the old man's shoulders. ''I say stay.''

''You don't have to brown-nose anymore, Paul . . .''

''Hey, fuck you, Wilhoit. Just because you can't take it.'' He saw Steven's face cloud with anger, so he stepped away from the old man and balled up his fists threateningly. ''You want to say something, punk? Huh? C'mon, say it!''

The muscular Davejac blocked his path. ''You start something, mister,'' he said in a low even tone, ''you be prepared for me to finish it, eh?'' And he remained there, expressionless, until Covey dropped his fists and backed away. Then the Indian turned to the only one who hadn't voted. ''Well, what's it gonna be?''

Andy Church was still red-faced from the day's hiking, and his breath was just now catching up to him. The rifle on his shoulder obviously weighed three times its normal weight and his pack was loaded with rocks the size of basketballs. If any one of them didn't belong in the woods, it was him. But when he looked to Steven, it was sheepishly, apologetic. ''I told you why I came, Steve,'' he said simply. Then, to the others, ''We stay.''

Wilhoit sighed in disgust.

''Okay,'' the guide begrudgingly surrendered. ''We stay. For now. But when the food's gone and your stomachs start to burn for something to eat, don't complain to me. Talk to your boss.'' He looked around the trail, now cast in dusky twilight, and fished the flashlight from the loop on his pack's shoulder strap. ''Too dark to go much farther. First clearing we come to, we'll bed down there.'' He saw the mocking grin on Tucker's face. "Is that all right with you, boss?"

The smirk widened. "Whatever you say, Mr. Davejac. You're the guide."

They walked another fifteen minutes, until the evening chill stung the skin and the shadows of the trees lengthened and widened and closed in around them. In the glow of the flashlights they came upon no real clearings, just spread out places where the trees did not grow so close together. That was where they finally pitched their camp for the night. The tents were erected, close together since space was limited, and then the men gathered around Barton's small fire and finished the last of their plastic-bag meals. No one spoke. The silence of the forest seemed to infiltrate the circle of men, and only the distant birdsongs and the sounds of their eating were discernible.

It was during the meal that the winning smirk slowly left Elton Tucker's face. Especially as the other men, one by one, turned in for the night. First Church disappeared into the big tent, then Covey. Wilhoit chanced the morning dampness and threw his sleeping bag out a few feet from the fire, where Yogi decided to sleep as well. Within just a few minutes fatigue caught up to both he and the dog and soon they were both softly snoring. That's when Davejac poured out the remainder of his coffee and retired to his tent as well, taking the other dog and leaving Tucker alone.

By then the smirk was a memory. And in its place, a drawn look. Confusion.

Fear.

But why, he wondered. Why did he fear the slumber that he'd eluded the night before, that he so desperately needed now? Was it the nightmares again? Surely they could not be so bad as that . . .

Could they?

Nonsense, he brushed it off as he stood and stretched and went into the little orange tent, slid into the quilted warmth of the sleeping bag. What could a nightmare do to him? It was just like Father used to say . . .

Strange. For some reason he just couldn't think of the quote.

He laid there and relaxed and told himself that sleep would be blissful tonight. He'd already made up his mind. And when Elton Tucker makes up his mind . . . But his thoughts dwelt on business just the same, vagaries and details, till even that would no longer stave off the arms of slumber.

And the other who waited with it.

Elroy . . .
Elroy . . .

Tucker jolted awake, a fist jammed between his teeth to keep from screaming.

Because this time he *knew*.

He knew exactly where he was—it took no time to dawn on him, to get his breath and recognize the tent or his belongings. He was minutely aware of them, because it was exactly where he'd been trying so hard to get to, running and running until his sides split and his lungs threatened to blow. For he knew it was the only place he could be safe from *him*.

Calling his name that way . . . Dad's voice still rang in his ears.

He'd been in a forest. At first he'd been sure it was Greene County, straight from his memory. But then the trees had twisted and gnarled themselves as no Indiana forest had ever done, and he realized that he was not ten years old there but as he was now, a grown man, old, older even than that grinning specter of Virgil Tucker.

"You promised me, Elroy," he'd called, brandishing the belt. "You promised me a kill." The buckle whistling in the cold night air . . . *Whack!*

"Promised . . ."
Whack!
"Can't tolerate . . ."
Whack!

"Your own good . . . ."

His back and face still stung from the blows. His skin was warm and moist with blood that hadn't flowed in fifty years.

That's when he ran. Deep into the forest, into a primal night, a darkness whose profundity was absolute. Unseen branches tore his naked flesh, raked it raw, grabbed for him and sought to hold him for that voice that still followed behind, closer and closer . . .

Elton Tucker began to cry. For the memories were all around him now. They poured like brackish water from all the hiding places where he'd carefully stowed them years ago, and they overwhelmed him. They tore at the carefully conceived image he held so dear, bringing down wise old Virgil Tucker and replacing that empty vessel with a more accurate rendition, a bitter man with a twisted leer and a taste for pain . . .

A cigarette sizzled against bare skin.

A steaming cup of coffee. A wide grin. "I hope it's right, Elroy. For your sake." And a high girlish giggle when it wasn't.

Tucker squeezed the tears from his eyes. How I hate you, he thought. How I despise your memory . . .

"El-roy . . ."

The word, the tone, hit Tucker like a slap in the face. It echoed from a distance, from beyond the tent, and it hung in his ears like the tolling of a great bell. It was deep and hollow, not Dad's voice at all. But Elton knew it was Virgil Tucker just the same. Trying to trick him. You can't touch me here, he wanted to yell. You're dead and I'm awake and you can't touch me! It's still the dream, he told himself. That's it. The dream's still trying to hurt you. And you know how to make them stop. You can do it. You can make them go away, if you put your mind to it, because Father always said, you can do anything if you try and he was right, yes, he was always right.

He laid back down, calming himself, and he forced the black memories and corrupt dreams back behind their tidal wall, just as he had all the times in the past when there had been a crack that threatened his fragile world. He pushed them back with a dogged tenacity and he worked until not a shred remained, not a ravel of bitterness to remember.

Nothing to remember . . .

Tucker lay facing the rear of the tent, so he didn't see the zipper loosen halfway up and Steven poke his head inside. He looked at the man hunkered in the sleeping bag, surveyed the inside of the tent, then retreated.

Wilhoit stood there in the darkness for a moment, an alert Yogi at his side. Then he went to the bigger tent and checked on Covey and Church next, found them both sound asleep, and then to the guide's as well. Davejac was snoozing fitfully, though Boo-Boo was sitting wide awake. The dog growled at the intruder, at least until Yogi poked her nose into the tent. Steven let her go inside and then pulled the flap closed after her.

He went back to his bed and fed the dying fire a few more sticks. But its warmth couldn't chase the chill from the back of his neck. The men were all in their tents. But he could've sworn he heard someone yell out there in the woods. And he was sure the elkhound had heard it as well.

He looked into the solid wall of blackness beyond the reach of the meager fire.

Go to sleep, Steven, or you'll hear the windigo call your name . . .

He chuckled to himself—very funny, Wilhoit—but it sounded hollow in the silence.

Something brushed against his arm. Yogi had come back. And to Steven's surprise, the male had come with her. Boo-Boo walked over beside him and grumbled something before lying down, right up against him. Yogi curled up on his other side, nuzzling his leg.

He smiled and patted them appreciatively. But that's when he noticed that, despite their lax position, the guard hairs on both animals were standing up.

He laid back between them and cursed himself for losing that rifle.

TEN

"I WAS WONDERING WHERE THOSE GUYS WENT."

Steven awoke to those words, blinked the sleep from his eyes to find Barton kneeling nearby. He was uncovering the dry kindling to restart the campfire. Gloom hung heavy around the trail. It was barely past dawn.

"What did you say?"

"These guys," Barton repeated, referring to the two mounds of grey fur still flanking Steven's sleeping bag, just rousing themselves. The elkhounds yawned and sneezed and scratched, then saw their master and went to him with tails wagging. "They've never taken up with anyone else," he reported. "Looks like you've been adopted."

"Maybe," said Steven. "But they didn't come out here to get warm. They were keeping an eye on me. Barton, you didn't hear anything last night, did you?"

"Like what?"

Wilhoit shrugged. "I don't know . . . like someone yelling, off in the woods?" He could tell the answer from the other's suspicious expression. "Aw, maybe I just dreamed it or something. But it was so real . . ." Real enough for the idea alone to bring a shiver to his skin. He pulled the sleeping bag closer around him. "This whole place kinda gives me the creeps. Listen." He paused. "You hear that? There's not a bird or a cricket or anything in the whole area. I noticed that last night. Damned weird, isn't it?''

"Aw, pay it no mind," Davejac said, dismissing the other's worries. But his expression refused to back up his words. Barton's patented poker face just didn't seem to be working today. Steven could see the lines of discomfiture etched around his eyes. Something about this place was bothering him too. Was it just its unfamiliarity, or the birds? Or something else . . .

Elton Tucker came out of his tent just then and greeted them with a cheery good morning, taking both men by surprise. This was not the same displaced soul they'd traveled with the last two days, stark-eyed and quiet, his attention straying no farther than the confines of the hunting trail. The night had brought a remarkable transformation. It had returned him to the high-spirited, enthusiastic man who had initiated the trip in the first place. He was once again in control.

Barton and Steven looked at each other, both mystified by the man's schizophrenic shifting. "How are you feeling, Mr. Tucker?" the guide asked.

"Never better." He laughed, sitting down cross-legged beside Wilhoit and the fire. "Never better. Nothing like a good night's sleep." He looked at Steven with a lopsided grin, as if waiting for him to contend the statement. But the younger man just nodded in agreement. "That reminds me, Wilhoit," Tucker continued, "I just wanted you to know that I bear you no ill will after last night—you know, the dissenting vote. I understand you'd been through quite a struggle out there in the woods alone, and that you might have been a bit testy under the circumstances. No harm, no foul, aye? And you did remarkably well to save yourself from that sump hole, with no one else to turn to. That's thinking on your feet. I admire that. So we'll just sweep the slate clean, start over. What do you say?"

If the old man was expecting a gush of appreciation for his magnanimity, he did not get it. Instead Steven just looked at him, a wan smile barely turning his lip, a mixture of amusement and irritation. "I say that's very big of you. But I feel just like I did last night. We're out of food, we're chasing game that isn't here, and I almost got killed yesterday. It's time to go home, whether you believe it or not. I just hope you come to your senses before somebody gets hurt."

Barton was surprised by the response, and so was Steven himself. The words just poured out of him, and he made no attempt to stop the flow. Janet had been right—they came up here for all the wrong reasons. It wasn't just a hunting trip anymore, not after that sump hole incident. This was serious stuff. Serious enough for him to finally say fuck the job, fuck these men, fuck it all. None of it was worth risking his life, or anyone else's for that matter.

Tucker just sat there, looking at him. Smiling without meaning. And Steven saw the flickering of uncertainty behind his eyes. He knew then that it was a facade; the old man hadn't regained his composure after all. This was a carefully orchestrated act, a charade for their benefit, maybe even for his own. And it was in that moment that Steven knew the boss wasn't just eccentric. He was slipping away, little by little. Maybe he'd been walking the tightrope for years now and this trip was simply the catalyst for that one bad step off the line.

Maybe he'd gone too far already.

Tucker didn't say a word after Steven's reply. He simply turned around and walked back to his tent, disappeared inside.

"He's getting weirder," Davejac said. "I think the time for voting is past. Tell your friends to pack their stuff and we'll—"

Tucker came back out of his tent. Carrying his rifle.

Barton and Steven sat stark still, unsure of what he had in mind or whether any little flinch on their part might provoke him. Only the dogs moved. Yogi and Boo-Boo raised into a half crouch, growled in warning. That seemed to take Tucker by surprise. "What's the matter with them?" he wondered.

"Why the rifle, boss?" Davejac asked in return.

"I was just going to suggest we get this hunt under way, so we can get Wilhoit home, as he seems to want. That's all." The dogs growled deeper in their throats, took a slinking step in his direction. "Call them back, mister," Tucker said in apprehension. He chambered a round into the Weatherby, held it at the ready. "Call them off, or so help me . . ."

"No, listen!" Wilhoit held out a hand to both men, so that only the raspy snarls were heard. Then he motioned to Tucker. "Move to the side," he whispered, "slowly."

The old man did just as he asked, sidestepping the ire of the elkhounds. But their attention did not waver. They continued to point in the same direction, even after Tucker was removed from their path.

Just like the first night they camped.

"Is there something out there?" Davejac said softly to the dogs, moving over alongside them, whispering into their ears like a track coach. "Do you see something, huh? Smell it? Then go get it!" He clapped his hands. "Go on!"

But the dogs would not move.

Steven stared into the woods, into the gloom that the new sun had yet to penetrate, and his flesh prickled with what he couldn't see. "What is it?"

Tucker brought up his rifle. "Only one way to find out," he said and started into the woods.

"Don't go alone!" Davejac yelled, heading for his tent and rifle. "Wait . . ."

But the old man had already disappeared into the trees.

The snarling of the dogs faded behind Elton Tucker as he waded deeper into the undergrowth, away from the trail, away from the others. The silence enshrouded him as quickly and readily as the forest and its shadows. Within just a few more steps he was isolated entirely. And he suddenly realized he wasn't sure which way he'd come.

Don't worry about that, he cautioned. Find whatever's out here. Find it and . . .

Kill it.

You promised me a kill, Elroy . . .

Where did that come from, he wondered with a queasy feeling. Then he told himself he couldn't remember.

Branches moved just ahead, swaying gently about twenty feet, maybe more.

He thumbed off the Weatherby's safety and held it at the ready as he stalked forward, ignoring the squelch of his boots in the dew-laden leaves. Whatever was there would not be scared off by the sound, else the growling of the dogs would have sent it packing long ago. No, this thing was intent on stalking them. And now it was time to turn the tables.

The branches were not yet still when he reached them. His breath was coming short and fast and his hands were slick on the polished stock and the adrenaline was pumping, thundering like a locomotive. But he still heard the voice, buzzing in his ear.

Slow, boy. Steady. Just like I told you . . .

Shut up. This is my game.

He swept the branches aside with the rifle and quickly brought it back into position as he charged forward, but . . . There was nothing there. More trees, the continued maze of leafy limbs and pine needles.

Damn.

But you promised, Elroy . . .

I SAID SHUT UP!

The heavy rifle sagged in his arms as he turned back toward camp (at least where he assumed camp to be). But there was someone in his way.

Some*thing*.

His gaze was lowered, so all he saw at first were the hooves, unmoving there in the thick soup of leaves. He gulped. They were huge, nearly as big as his own feet. He moved slowly, his eyes traveling up the muscular legs, nearly five feet to the withers, then across the wide silvered chest and shoulders and up the thick neck. The head was immobile, as was its magnificent crown of antlers. The bony rack of horns was overpowering, spreading out like brown skeletal hands from its skull, counting sixteen, no, more than that . . .

Eighteen points?

He could count each one, for the massive whitetail did not move, hadn't since confronting him. Not even the softly pointed ears, which should have been swiveling left and right in alarm. Only the occasional blink of an eye evidenced any life at all.

The photo. The lake. Could it be the same one . . .

The big deer craned its neck just slightly, looked at him with a wide black eye, so close that he could see his own reflection. But beyond that mirror image was a blackness whose depth invited him to look deep, to try to find something there.

And he told himself he had.

This animal was for him—he knew that intimately, without doubt. It was as if it had spoken as much to him, the thought was so clear and intentional. This buck had been born to the task and lived just for him, had eluded other predators and grown huge and strong for this moment alone. When he would come after it. It was predestined. And he had known it as well, from the moment he saw that photograph, perhaps even before.

Dad never took such an animal. He never even dreamed of it. *If I take it, I'll be the better hunter. The better man. And I'll be free.*

You promised me a kill . . .

Fuck you, he thought with relish. This ain't for you, old man. This one's for me. And then you'll go away.

He smiled and mouthed the words "thank you" as he started to raise the Weatherby.

Then the deer bolted.

It leaped right past him, almost knocking him down with the wind alone. He dropped the rifle and cursed himself, groped for it in the leaves and finally grabbed it and pulled it back to his shoulder. But the buck was already twenty yards away and dodging through the heavy bracken, too thick for a good shot.

Dammit! He lowered the rifle, fuming as he watched his prey escape into the wild. But then, just before it disappeared from sight, it turned as it loped away and looked over its shoulder at him. Inviting him. Daring him.

He knew then. It wasn't enough to just bring it down. No, it had to be a hunt. He had to earn this.

The voices of the others were coming closer then; if he'd listened, he could have heard them, calling his name. But he was oblivious to that now. Only one thing mattered. ''I'm coming,'' he said as he set off through the woods, unable to keep the giggle of anticipation from his voice.

The other hunters searched for Tucker for three hours. And with each step they took, they plunged deeper into an area that few people had ever seen. Including Davejac.

The landscape was more varied here than the flatlands and waterways they were used to. Rocky ridges were more prevalent than anywhere else in Chalako, and to forge a meandering gully every half kilometer or so slowed their progress even more. It was as if the massive glaciers had failed to touch this isolated section of earth, leaving its hills and valleys resolute, its sanctity intact.

Steven's feelings went much further than that, however. To him it was as if nothing had ever touched this place—no animal, no human foot, nothing. He felt alien here, an invader, and at times his skin crawled as if the forest were glaring at him angrily for his sacrilege. Even the dogs seemed ill at ease; Barton had to put a lead on the collar of each dog, just to keep them in line. They now prowled along silently but showed no interest in playing in the woods as usual. They stayed close to their master's side.

At midmorning they came out of the forest to find a slight ridge and, beyond that, a valley that snaked lazily through the land. It was perhaps two miles across at its widest and three or four long, though it was hard to tell the distance.

Only its undulating shape could be made out. As for the interior of the rift, that was anyone's guess. Despite the sun's presence, the morning mist had yet to dissipate and now lay before them like a fallen cloud, only the tops of the trees piercing through from below.

And on the lip of that misty lowland stood Elton Tucker.

"It's about time you showed up," he snapped testily at them, without looking up. His eyes were still centered on a natural stairway of loose shale and bedrock that led down into the valley, beneath the canopy of white.

Davejac's anger had been building for several hours, and he wasn't about to hold it back. "Mister, that was the stupidest thing I've ever seen anyone do. I thought you were supposed to be experienced in the outdoors, but you sure don't show it. Even a rank amateur wouldn't run off and leave the party, especially in unfamiliar terrain. Hell, I don't even know my way around these woods. You're lucky we found you at all . . ."

"Are you about finished?" the old man was impatient.

"Ooh, I haven't even started yet."

"Then it will just have to wait." He pointed down that steep grade, into the gorge. "It went down there, just a few minutes ago. I think I've cornered it."

"What is 'it'?" Covey wanted to know.

"A buck, the biggest whitetail you've ever laid eyes on. That's what the dogs were barking at. It's the one I saw near the base camp, the one we've been following all along. And it's down there."

Church peered down into the valley. "Cornered? How do you know it hasn't gone out the other end?"

Tucker glared at him. "I just know, all right? Now, let's get moving—"

"Just a minute, bub," Barton ordered. He went over and looked down the grade himself. And immediately the dogs reacted: they shrank away from the valley, snarling under their breath, showing white teeth beneath curled black lips.

Their neck hair stood straight out like a lion's mane. "What is it?" he asked them. But they continued to act erratically, till Steven had to take their leads and pull them back from the ridge. Barton inspected the grade again, and found it didn't look safe. The loose shale alone made it dangerous, and not a one of them could be considered nimble by any stretch of the imagination. Broken legs would be a prohibitive bitch to remove from these woods. And aside from that, there was something else about the valley that he didn't like, something he just couldn't put a finger on. It crawled across the back of his neck on spider legs and prickled his senses. "I ain't going down there," he told them flat-out.

"What is it?" Steven asked.

"I don't know. I just don't like this place. We're not going down there."

"Sez you," Tucker dismissed him. "I'm not paying you to tell me where you will and won't go. I said I want that buck. Now you guide us down there. Or you're fired."

Davejac looked into the valley again, heard the dogs. Felt the spider legs crawling. "I guess I'm fired," he finally said.

"Your choice," Tucker told him. "But you'll stay up here and wait for us if you want severance pay. You abandon us, and I'll have your guide's license in a heartbeat." He turned to the other three. "Well? Follow me." Then he slung the rifle over his shoulder and started down the steep hillside.

"You heard the man," Covey said, following close behind him. Andy Church was a bit less enthusiastic; in fact, his face had gone white at the idea of climbing down the incline. But he gave Steven a sheepish glance and went after them nonetheless.

"You aren't going, are you?" Davejac asked Wilhoit when he saw the look of indecision in his eyes. "I thought you were through with the man's games."

"I am," Steven told him. "But you won't be there, and somebody's got to watch out for the other two. They're okay, if you can get 'em out from under his thumb for two minutes.

They're the ones I'm worried about. And sooner or later they'll come to their senses. That's when I've got to be there. To keep him from shooting them.''

Davejac held out his rifle. ''Here, you might need this . . .''

''No, you keep it. I can always get Andy's if I need one.'' He stepped toward the edge, then called back over his shoulder, ''If there's any trouble, I'll signal you. Four shots, in succession?''

And what, Barton thought. I'll come running? Into that place? The spiders moved again, skittering like mad, making his flesh crawl. But he still managed to say, ''Okay, Steve. Four shots. And be careful down there.''

Wilhoit tried to smile confidently, but it slid off his face as he descended into the valley, leaving Barton and the dogs in the forest world above.

ELEVEN

STEVEN ALMOST FELL TWICE AS HE NAVIGATED THE STEEP grade, wincing at the lack of footing and the strain it put on his still-painful blisters. The rocky slope was overgrown with scrub and vines that hid the looseness of the shale beneath, so he had to be extremely careful. He paused halfway down, already winded and wondering whether the others had made it all the way without an accident. But by then he was within easy sight of the bottom and could make out the rest of the hunting party, and vice versa. They were resting at the foot with their packs off. Tucker was watching the woods directly ahead of them while the others had noticed Wilhoit's approach and not without a fair amount of surprise. He caught his breath and climbed the rest of the way down.

"I didn't think you were coming," Andy said.

He just shrugged. "Neither did I."

"Aw, he's not here to hunt, Andy boy," commented Covey, directing it at the new arrival. "He's just realized he shit in his mess gear up there and now it's time to suck up to the boss again."

Steven shot him a disgusted glance. "No, that's your job, Covey. I guess mine is looking out for you'uns."

Covey laughed. "Looking out for us, huh? Ooh, I feel safer already, don't you, Andy?"

Church was less mocking. "I won't turn down the company, I'll tell you that. The more the merrier. 'Specially around here." He looked at their surroundings sheepishly, rubbed the sudden chill from his arms as he whispered, "This place is damned spooky."

Steven surveyed the valley himself, and he had to concur with the younger man's evaluation. It was densely forested, the same kind of landscape they'd fought to conquer all day long. There was a narrow corridor of open ground directly before them, littered with leaves and pine needles. But the rest was all trees and nothing but, so thick they completely obscured any view of the valley's other slopes. It was hard to tell they were in a lowland at all. From this new vantage point, the early fog seemed to cling in the upper limbs of the trees like cottony hair, and was not nearly so opaque as it had appeared from above. It was thinning in places as the day warmed up, letting random beams of sunlight through to shine here and there in the murk of the forest like winks of faerie glow. It might have made a good illustration for one of Janet's children's books, he thought, but it was less inspiring to witness in person. It sent a chill of unease slithering beneath his skin.

He looked back up to the ridge. But the Indian was no longer in view. A flash of panic went through him. *Barton, if you've left us here, so help me God . . .*

"Get off your asses," Tucker snapped anxiously without turning. The remark must have been meant for Andy, because he was the only one seated. "Let's get moving." Holding the Weatherby at the ready, the old man stalked into the narrow clearing and they followed behind. His eyes were on the trees, so he didn't notice the slight indentation ahead where the ground dipped . . .

Dipped?

The creeping familiarity caught Steven's attention, and his alarms went off all at once. He shouldered Andy and Paul aside, grabbed Elton Tucker by the collar, and jerked him backward. The old man was off-balance to begin with and would have sprawled flat on his back had Steven not held him upright. But when he finally recovered his footing, he jerked himself from the young employee's grasp and fumed angrily. "Goddammit! This isn't some street-corner mugging, you know! What's your problem?!"

"Yeah, Wilhoit," Covey challenged, stepping closer as if to protect the boss. "What's up your ass?"

Steven pointed to the open depression facing them. "That's what I'm talking about. It looks just like the sucking place I fell into yesterday."

Andy came forward. "Are you sure, Steve?" He tested the edge with his foot, sliding it through the leaves there until Covey grabbed his arm to startle him. The young man lost his balance and almost stepped into the clearing, but he caught himself and shot the laughing Paul a withering glance.

"I'm not sure of anything, Andy. I just know this looks the same. Kinda."

"Kinda, huh?" Covey said skeptically. He reached out, prodded the ground with his rifle butt. "I don't know, Wilhoit. Feels pretty firm to me."

"Then step out there, Paul. Test it for us."

Covey met Steven's gaze, held it. Then, with a smile, he

took him up on the dare. Before the others could shout a warning or call him back, he walked down into the middle of the depression. "You stupid ass!" Steven cringed, prepared to see the man's feet and legs disappear into the dirt at any moment. But to his surprise and ultimate chagrin, nothing happened. Covey just stood there, smirking at him, even jumped up and down in the nadir of the hollow to prove his point. "I'm sure glad you decided to come along, college boy," the man mocked. "We might have died in here if it weren't for you."

"Knock it off," Tucker snapped as he walked through the depression himself and out the other side, into the thick of the trees that confronted them. It was just a moment before the others followed after him. "Hurry up now," he chided and picked up his pace even more. He was irritated with all of them. It wasn't the noise they made that concerned him, for he knew they could not frighten his quarry away. It was waiting for him. It was preordained. But they were holding him up with their childishness, delaying his kill, and he felt tempted to leave them behind, head deeper into the forest without them. But that would lessen the hunt, he told himself. It would rob him of some of his glory. For bringing down the buck was not enough of a culmination to this pursuit. They had to see him take it. They had to know it was not by some fluke that he took such a prize. Dad was always doing that, after all, minimizing his achievements, saying the rabbit he caught was lame and slow or that it was dead when he found it and he was lying about it now. And you know what you get for lying . . .

He brought himself up short, surprised by the memory's presence and how it had slipped out from behind his barriers with little or no effort. You can't hide them forever, he told himself. There are too many of them now. But calmly, more so than he'd ever thought he could muster, he accepted their existence. For the moment, anyway. They were no longer of consequence, he told himself, because in a few minutes he would have his trophy, an animal Virgil Tucker had never even seen the likes of, and there would be no question then who was the failure and who wasn't. And then he could rub it in that specter's leering face and those damn dreams would go away once and for all . . .

Anxiousness seeped into his ambling gait, tightening his already white-knuckled grip on the gun as he peered through the dull lattice of the forest. Greying branches and tanglevine stretched from tree to tree like the petrified strands of a monstrous spiderweb, slowing his advance and feeding his impatience. And with each minute that ticked by uneventfully, the knowing, mocking laughter became more audible in his ears and his alone. Come on, he urged his unseen quarry silently. You've led us a merry chase but we've kept after you. The game is up already. Show yourself.

The laughter grew louder.

His plea became strained, plaintive. Please . . .

A gasp sounded close by. It was Andy Church, standing right behind him. "Jesus," the man said breathlessly, and, unable to elaborate, said it again. "Jesus . . ." He pointed past Tucker, off to the left.

Through the trees about fifty yards away was a shallow thicket, clogged with sticker bushes and angry brambles that looked even less hospitable than the path they'd traversed so far. There was something standing at the far edge of the brake, steeped in shadow at first but becoming more visible as the fog shifted and pinpoints of sunlight snuck through. The illumination was actually well beyond that place but it served to silhouette the figure there, the wide shoulders and powerful flanks, the awesome rack of antlers. The buck just stood, barely moving at all, an ear flip here, a shift in weight there. Just enough to convince them that it was indeed a living, breathing thing and not some trick of the ambient light. It remained little more than an outline, its features lost in the gloom. But to a man they could tell it was watching them. Staring, in fact, with an unnatural intensity.

Tucker's breath caught in anticipation. The moment of

truth, Dad would have said, at least the revered and beneficent version he had so carefully built up over the years. He caught the animal's unseen gaze and held it, and he was sure that something passed between them, something beyond words or even meaning but which left a chill along the back of his neck all the same. It was just he and his quarry, and the silence closed in around them, and the world had been created just to witness this moment . . .

"Nobody move," he suddenly heard someone say behind him, and immediately after that the click of a safety switched off. Church's rifle barrel extended just past his shoulder. He was going to take a shot, the old man realized. At my deer.

My deer!

He turned and drove the buttstock of the Weatherby into the boy's side, just below the rib cage and a lot harder than necessary. Church let out a pitiful gasp of surprise and pain as he dropped his gun and staggered back a step or two before falling. Steven tried to catch him but the younger man's superior weight dragged them both down. Covey just stood there gaping in surprise as Tucker towered over the other two, his face lit with a look of betrayal and rage. "Who the hell are you?" he demanded in a sharp hiss, barely controlling his tone. "Who said you could shoot first? Huh? This is mine, you hear? Mine!"

"Then shoot the fucking thing," Steven snapped back at him as he tried to stand and pull up the still-groaning Andy. "Get it over with."

"Jeez, be quiet!" Covey warned all of them. "You're gonna scare the—" But when he looked, even after all the shouting, the buck was still standing exactly where it had been. "That's weird," he whispered, unable to comprehend its stoic presence. "Why hasn't it moved?"

Tucker turned on the animal and raised the Weatherby to his shoulder. The cross hair centered on the deer's shape in the brake, right on the chest and heart.

If you miss this, boy . . .

He ignored the threats. He took his time, breathed in and held it, eased the safety off with a fingertip before caressing the trigger. One smooth squeeze . . .

The report was magnified through the tubelike silence of the valley and, unable to breach the geographical confines, ricocheted around them with deafening intensity. The other three men shielded their ears from the onslaught. Even the deer seemed jolted by it. It started a bit, shifted its weight from leg to leg. Then it froze again, staring. Did not fall.

No . . .

Church was not afraid to say it. In fact, he took a great deal of satisfaction in wheezing, "You missed, you . . . old cockbite."

Tucker's face went slack as he lowered the scope from his eye, unable to comprehend a target still standing. "It can't be . . ." He heard his own voice as a pitiful whine while the jeering laughter echoed in his mind. "I know I hit it. Dead center, I know it." He snarled with impotent rage as he chambered another round and raised the rifle, took aim again. Fired. New thunder shook the valley even before the reverberations of the first shot had entirely died.

The men watched the deer. The deer watched the men. Nothing changed.

The three watchers behind Tucker gaped in confusion, so unsure of what they were witnessing that they could not even pull their eyes away to exchange baffled glances. Whether the shots had been on target was beside the point, though even Wilhoit could've hit it at that distance. The sound of the shots alone should have sent the animal careening through the bush in terror. But it was still there. Its continued presence unsettled them.

Such observations were lost on Elton Tucker. He was panting now, almost whining as he chambered another round and fired and worked the bolt again and fired and still found his target upright, watching him with eyes he couldn't see. And in the back of his mind was that laughter, growing louder, basking in each failed attempt . . .

A heavy belt buckle jingled nearby. The sigh of the heavy strap leaving the belt loops.

"Fall, damn it!" he muttered, peering through the tear-stained lens of the scope and placing its cross hairs on the head of the animal's outline this time, just below the antlers. He aimed at where the eyes would be, where he felt that unblinking gaze that mocked him as readily as the voices in his head. His digit tensed on the trigger, ready to blow out the back of its head. But that's when the deer finally moved. The head tilted to the side and he could see that the mouth was open and the neck was dipping drunkenly, beyond muscular control. It disappeared from the frame of his scope, and when he lowered the rifle he found it staggering sideways for a step, maybe two. Then with a shudder the legs buckled under its weight and the massive animal dropped straight to the ground.

One last shudder. Then stillness.

The echoes of the gunshots finally moved away to the far end of the valley and died there, leaving the hunters immersed in a dread and oppressive silence. They hesitantly looked from one to another, each unsure of what he'd seen, whether individual imagination or something experienced by all. And they did not dare move, not until things started making sense again. But Tucker showed no such reluctance. "Yes!" he yelled in triumph, dropping his rifle and holding his arms up to the audience of birch and spruce, accepting their silent applause. He danced a demented jig there in the leaves and the silence, unmindful of the stares of his employees. "Take that, you old bastard!" he yelled with relish. "Did I do it right, old man? Huh? Did I? You sure couldn't've done it, isn't that the truth!"

Church, still holding his aching ribs, asked who the old man was talking to. But Tucker didn't hear the remark. For he was already wading into the overgrown brake, seemingly oblivious to the stickers that picked at his clothing, tore the skin of his hands. And when he fought far enough through the bosk to reach his kill, he saw just how massive the fallen buck was and he whooped with triumph yet again. The animal was half on its side with its long legs splayed out to the four winds, its head and horns pointed away from him. But the size of it . . . Were it not for the horns, it might easily have been mistaken for a draft horse. It was fully twice as large as any he'd ever seen before, especially in Greene County.

Are you listening, Dad? Are you watching?

Tucker was still caught in his reverie and dancing another jig when he noticed the other three hunters standing just beyond the carcass, having skirted the thorny break and approached from the other side. "Well, what do you think?" he called to them proudly. "A beauty, right? Have you ever seen a bastard that big before?"

No one answered him right away. Andy Church was holding a handkerchief over his mouth for some reason, and it took Tucker a moment to remember hitting him. Maybe a little bit too hard, he decided, if he was puking up now. Oh, well, I'll make it up to the boy, he promised. As for the other two, they appeared discomfited as well. Covey and Wilhoit stood there, the latter carrying the discarded Weatherby, and they looked hesitantly from Tucker to the deer and back again, their brows knitted, their expressions confused, troubling. At least until the old man deciphered their meanings. "Oh, come now," he said with a laugh. "No need for jealousy. I got lucky, what can I say? You might get a shot at one yet, though I doubt we'll see another this size." He looked the deer over again, couldn't control his giddy laughter. "They'll never believe this back home." He shook his head. And that gave him an idea. He slipped off his backpack, dug through the outer pouch until he found the Polaroid camera, and unfolded it. "Here," he said, holding it out to the men. "Take a picture of me with it."

Not one of them moved for the camera. Instead they exchanged unsettled glances, shifted about restlessly. "Well?" the old man said with customary impatience. "What's the matter with you? I just want a picture, is that so damn strange? Come on, one of you . . ." But still no volunteers. He pursed

his lips in frustration, motioned to Covey with the camera.
"You do it, Paul."

The lanky man seemed unsure at first, looked for support
from the other two, but they just shrugged in answer. "Uh
. . . yeah, sure," he said, forcing a smile as he took the
Polaroid. "What kind of picture, Mr. Tucker?"

"I'm not sure . . ." the boss muttered as he stepped back
and surveyed the great animal. Then his eyes centered on that
massive rack of antlers. "That's it! Paul, move over in front
of it," he instructed as he straddled the buck's bull-like neck
and got a good grip on the horns where they sprouted just
above the skull. With considerable effort he lifted the massive
head off the ground. "I could use some help," he wheezed
from the strain. But no one moved to lend a hand. Finally
he wrestled the head around so that it was facing the cam-
eraman, and he leaned down above it and gave a big cheesy
smile. "Okay, Paul," he said nodding. "This will do."

Covey just stood there with a blank look on his face, unable
to move, kept glancing at Wilhoit and Church for help.
"Dammit, Covey!" Tucker barked. "Take the fucking picture already!" It was enough to jolt the salesman into movement, and as soon as the flash went off and the camera spewed
the developing photo out the slot with an electronic whine,
he turned and shoved camera and picture into Church's hands,
just to be rid of them.

Tucker frowned, dropped the buck's dead weight with a
thud. He was growing more and more irritated with the men's
rude behavior, their tight-lipped manner. *Fucking amateurs,*
he fumed. *If they can't accept my natural ability, that's tough.
I won't put up with any more pouting just because they can't
make the grade . . .*

He decided to ignore them for the moment, turned his
attention to the task at hand, and took the stout utility knife
from his belt. That finally brought a response from Steven.
"What are you going to do with that?" he asked.

"What do you think I'm gonna do, Wilhoit? It's time to
dress the meat." At that the three men grimaced. Tucker

sighed knowingly. He had expected it of that wimp Wilhoit, maybe even the boy. But he'd thought Covey was made of stouter material. "If it's going to bother you, turn the other way," he said, kneeling down by the rump of the carcass.

"Jesus, he's off his nut," Church said to the others, his words muffled through the handkerchief.

"I don't think you want to be doing this, Mr. Tucker," Paul Covey said in a slow, soothing voice, taking a step closer.

"Nonsense, my boy," Tucker dismissed him as he lifted the silvery white tail and made his first cut around the deer's anus. Covey swallowed hard, backed away again. "Oh, come on, Paul. I thought you'd hunted before. I didn't know you'd be this squeamish. It's like my father used to say . . ." He paused a moment, considering what had almost flowed from his mouth without conscious thought. "No, my father didn't say that," he observed. Then, satisfied with the confession, he went back to work. He cut all around the anus until he could separate it and then tied it off with a bit of string so no waste would leak out and foul the meat. "To be quite honest," he continued, "my father didn't say much of anything. Ever. He was a small, hateful man now that I think of it."

"Mr. Tucker . . ." Covey started again, but he couldn't decide how to continue and just trailed off. Andy Church finally took up the slack and stepped closer to the animal, grasping the hankie tighter over his mouth and nose as he went.

"How does this—this animal look to you, old man?" he said, flecks of anger in his voice from the pain in his side.

"What do you mean, how does it look?" Tucker laughed as he pulled the rear legs apart to expose the buck's lower abdomen and groin. "What kind of question's that?" He shook his head with exasperation—kids these days!—and busied himself with cutting out the genitals, ignoring the way they all but came off in his hand even before the knife had finished its work. "You know what your problem is?" he said, waving the knife at Church, who stepped away when he saw it was littered with crawling flecks of white. "You just don't know anything about hunting. I was hoping I could teach you something up here but, well, maybe I bit off a little too much . . ."

He slid the knife back into the upper part of the groin cut and started up the abdomen, headed for the sternum. He expected hard going; on an animal that size, overdeveloped muscle and tendon would probably fight him all the way. So he put his weight behind that long cut, and he was caught off-guard when the blade found little resistance. It slid effortlessly through soft spongy tissue that seemed incapable of carrying a burden of muscle and entrail. The flesh peeled back almost of its own accord and a gust of fetid gas came bubbling out of the incision like a dark cloud, catching Tucker full in the face. His gag reflex triggered with violent immediacy, but he was too stunned to give it full reign; he just choked it down and stared through the buzzing black flies, into the carcass that gaped before him. The putrescent smell did not do the sight justice; the inner lining of the abdomen was a bright grey-green with rot, and the entrails were bloated from decomposition, except for the loose and noisome folds he'd already deflated with the knife. It was that latter tissue that now undulated before his eyes as handfuls of maggots came roiling out of the ruined intestines and fell into the abdominal cavity in a living cascade, all pasty white and wriggling.

The queasiness came over him in a wave and he suddenly couldn't breathe, began to gasp. Even the air around him seemed to have a wormy texture now, the taste of decay, and he began to retch in earnest. He crawled away from the carcass, bringing up what little his stomach still held, gagging dryly when there was no more to give.

"Are you okay, Mr. Tucker?" Paul asked in concern. He was holding a rag over his face now as well, trying in vain to block that overpowering stench.

The old man stayed there on all fours until the tremors left

him and he could once again breathe without gagging. He
put the sleeve of his jacket to his nose and turned to look at
the carcass. And this time he truly saw it. The animal was
massive to be sure, just as large as he'd first realized. In life
it must have been a sight to behold. But that had been sometime back, if its present state was any clue. The trunk of the
beast was bloated from the gases of putrefaction, though a
bit less now that he'd vented some into the chilled air of the
forest. The limbs and neck had withered away to nothing,
simply bones wrapped in brittle sheafs of dead flesh. He was
still to the rear of the animal, so he couldn't see the head.
But it was enough.

Tucker turned away, breathing long and slow to quell the
dry heaves he felt coming. "That . . . that isn't what I shot,"
he said, trying to sound convinced. "That deer, my deer, it's
still around . . . got to find it . . ." But it was all rambling
without conviction; he couldn't even hear his own voice, not
over the others that echoed through his mind.

You failed, Virgil said with a high giggle. *Come to Daddy*.

Elton Tucker was sitting on his knees, looking away from
the stinking carcass he'd all but caressed moments before,
and all he could do was mutter mindlessly, "Gotta find the
deer. Gotta find it . . ."

"You don't have to look far, you fucking psycho," Church
said cynically. "This is your baby right here. You were right
the first time."

"You're not helping, kid," Covey snapped at him.
"Something's wrong with this man—"

"Yeah, he's blown a fucking gasket."

"—and your bullshit'll only add to his problems. This
isn't the deer he shot at. It can't be. This thing's been dead
for weeks."

"Then where's the real deer?"

Covey looked around hopefully as if to find it hiding
nearby. "I don't know." He finally shrugged. "I guess it
crawled off before we got here."

Andy scoffed. "That's bullshit and you know it. We'd have seen something that big—the underbrush isn't that dense here. And I'm telling you, once he started shooting, I never took my eyes off that thing. Not once."

"What are you saying? That we've been tracking a dead deer all morning? C'mon, get serious!"

The boy shrugged and nodded, swayed by the logic of the moment. But what had he seen then? There was just enough doubt there to spur him further. He found a stout stick nearby and worked up his constitution, took a deep breath and stepped around the animal for a closer look. He prodded at its broad chest, inspected the moldering hide for unusual tears or punctures. Just above the shoulder, in the heart-lung kill zone, were four distinct holes, none more than two inches from the other. "How many shots did Tucker take?"

"Three," Covey said.

"No," Steven corrected. "It was four. Why?"

"Bingo." He stood, looked at the other men. "Jesus, this is getting pretty fucking weird . . ."

"That's not my buck," Tucker said abruptly. They all turned as he stood and walked over beside them, more composed than before, as if he'd just shaken off the last vestiges of a long sleep. "Somehow we missed it, didn't we? But we'll get it yet. We have to." He turned to Steven, motioned to the Weatherby. "I'll take my rifle now."

"I don't think so."

Tucker looked at him blankly. But once he realized the younger man's intent, his face began to change, first grew livid with rage and then became indifferent and just as quickly shifted to plaintive and pleading. "I have to get that deer," he whispered as if in explanation, his voice cracking. And in his eyes Steven saw not a shred of rational thought lingering. The man was as mad as a hatter.

"I promised, you know," the old man continued to ramble. "I promised, and you know what we can't tolerate, don't you? Failure. No, we can't, *so give me my gun now*!" He grabbed the stock of the Weatherby and tried to wrestle it away, but Steven jerked it out of his grasp and backed up a few steps.

"Sorry, Mr. Tucker. But it's time to go. We're leaving."

"No . . . *No!*" The boss looked at the others, his face stretched into a rictus of dread. "Not now! You can't! I . . . I'll fire you! I mean it. It's my company and I'll fire whoever I want and it's my way or the highway. I mean it!"

Andy Church stepped up to Tucker, said it right in his face. "Stick your job up your ass, old man. I'm with Steve."

Wilhoit looked to Covey. "What about you, Paul?"

The lanky salesman fidgeted a moment, especially when caught in the old man's stark gaze. "You go on ahead, Wilhoit," he said, giving Tucker a smile of support. "I'll stay with him."

"Are you crazy?" Church cried out, dumbstruck. "Why don't you pull your nose out of his ass once in a while and look around you. This isn't about a fucking job anymore." He held out the Polaroid photo. "Is this guy gonna be the one to promote you, Paul? Is he the one to give you the cushy office job? Dammit, look at it!" He thrust the picture under the other's nose where Covey couldn't avoid the image. The dead animal stared out at him vacantly, for its eye sockets had rotted empty long before. The surrounding flesh had dried and cracked and was peeling away along the base of the antlers, letting calcium white peek through. Its mouth was open and crooked, upper jaw one direction, lower the other, and it seemed to have a rotten apple clamped between the two. But then Covey recognized it as a tongue, all bloated and discolored and splitting down the middle, filled with whiteness that seemed to writhe before his eyes. And poised just above that visage of decay was Elton Tucker, a mindless grin etched into his features. "You want to placate this bent rim?" Andy asked. "If you do, you're as nuts as he is."

"You're just a coward, Church," Tucker grumbled through clenched teeth. "A fat lard-ass coward."

Andy laughed at that. "You know something, old man? You're right for once. Right now I'm shaking in my fucking boots because something's seriously wrong here. I can feel it. But at least I'll admit when I'm scared. Not like you, Mister Big Adventurer, Mister High and Mighty who lays in his tent at night and cries and whimpers like a goddamn baby.''

Tucker flinched as if hit. "I never . . ." he stammered, his eyes widening. But from what emotion Wilhoit couldn't tell. And that's what scared him.

"Lay off, Andy," he warned.

"Why, Steve?" the boy smirked. "I'm just getting started. What's the matter, old man? Didn't think anyone was listening in the night? 'No, Dad, I'm sorry, Dad, I'm sorry . . .' Isn't that right . . . Elroy?"

"Shut up!" Tucker growled, throwing a haymaker that caught the boy flush on the jaw and spun him around completely, took him right off his feet. But Andy Church was back up immediately, wearing a grin of satisfaction. "That's all I wanted to hear," he said and launched himself at the bigger man like a wolverine. He drove his forehead straight into Tucker's chest, hard enough to stun him, then dug a fist into his stomach with all he could gather. Tucker went down with Church on top of him, wailing away, not letting up for a minute. Paul Covey waded into the fray and pulled the younger man off, even held him there while Tucker took a few pokes at him, though it was unclear to Steven whether the salesman meant to do that or not. But in another minute Church had thrashed loose again and was back on his exboss, punching and kicking, making up for the shot in the ribs and much more. It took Paul and Steven both to drag him away this time, struggling all the way. Tucker made no move to retaliate. He was curled on the ground in a fetal position, covering his head from Andy's blows and whimpering pitifully. It wasn't until they got the other man settled down that they could make out the old man's words.

"Don't hit me, Dad, I'm sorry, I'm sorry . . ." Over and over. Sobbing.

They all listened in silence. Especially Church, who turned

away, still angry but mortified at the same time. "He asked for it," he tried to justify, more to himself than the others. "He just kept pushing, kept asking for it . . ."

Steven listened to the pitiful whimpers echoing softly in the silence of the valley. And he suspected such pleas would find no solace in this place.

"Help him up," he said softly. "We're getting out of here."

TWELVE

"HOLD UP, STEVE," ANDY CALLED HIS VOICE THICK WITH exhaustion. "I've gotta rest." He sagged against a nearby spruce and sank onto his rear end, wiping a cool sheen of sweat from his face with a coat sleeve. "How far have we walked, anyway?"

"Seems like five miles," Covey said, slipping off his backpack with an audible sigh before dropping to the ground himself. "My back's killing me. How are you doing, boss?"

Tucker stood off to one side in brooding silence, head down and hands buried in his coat pockets. He'd been that way for hours, ever since they'd pried him from that fetal curl and made him walk under his own power. He looked bad; his fight with Church had left his face a mottled combination of black and blue hues, and his lower lip was already swollen twice its size, giving him the pouting expression of a lost child. Which was an apt description in a way. The old man did look lost. Especially in his eyes.

"Mr. Tucker?" Covey tried again. But he still wouldn't respond.

"Why are you so worried about him?" Andy wanted to know. "It can't be the promotion thing anymore . . ."

"Aw, I don't know," the lanky man said with a shrug. "I guess I just feel sorry for him, that's all."

"Well, feel sorry for yourself awhile," the young man said. "Feel sorry for all of us. 'Cause at this rate we're never gonna get out of this valley."

"Don't be so pessimistic, Andy—"

"No, I mean it, Steve." Church sounded solemn. More than a little frightened. "This place is evil, no two ways about that. You know it, I know it. You can feel it, right? Am I right?"

The others scoffed and grumbled but did not dispute him.

"It wanted us. It lured us here. And now it won't let us go."

Covey forced a laugh. "Sounds like you've been watching a little too much TV, Junior."

"Oh, yeah? Then how do you explain the dead buck walking around back there, decomposing on the hoof? How do you explain walking five miles through a two-mile valley and never reaching the far side? We should've been out of here hours ago."

"There's got to be an explanation for that. Maybe we're going in circles."

Church pointed to the hatchet on Steven's belt, the one he'd scavenged from Tucker's pack hours before. "He's been marking the trees as we go, Paul, remember? And so far we haven't come across a single mark he's made." Then he waited for the next explanation.

"I don't know!" Covey blurted, irritated both with the boy's insistence and his own inability to answer. "I do know there's weird shit going on here. But I'm not about to start seeing ghosts or saying the place is haunted. That's crazy talk." He lowered his voice to a whisper. "Keep it up and you'll be just like him," and he pointed to Tucker, who was shuffling around aimlessly nearby.

Steven tried to call a truce. "Maybe we should try signaling Barton again," he suggested. But Andy cut him off with an exasperated shake of the head.

"It won't work now any better than it did before. He said four shots, right? Then he should have come a'running when Tucker shot at the deer—that was four, remember? But no sign of the Indian. Not even when I tried it a few hours ago."

"I'll agree with him there," Paul said. "Don't count on that guide. The way we turned our backs on him, I'd say he's long gone by now."

"Barton wouldn't leave." Steven was adamant. "I feel like I know the guy. He said he'd stay, and I believe him."

"Then why didn't he come?"

Andy volunteered an answer. "Maybe he didn't hear the shots—maybe this place wouldn't let him. Or he did come, and it took him out before he could reach us . . ."

"That does it!" the salesman blustered, getting to his feet and jerking his pack back on, reaching for his rifle. "I'm getting pretty fucking fed up with this butthole's spook stories. The quicker we get moving, the quicker I'll be rid of him. Go on, Wilhoit, mark your tree so we can leave."

Tucker looked up about that time, finally broke his self-imposed silence. "I'm hungry," he croaked.

"Yeah, who isn't," spat Church bitterly.

"We'll try to dig something up before long, boss," Paul tried to comfort the old man. "Just be patient and—"

"I'm hungry!" he barked, wearing the wide-eyed face of a lunatic. He started howling the word at the top of his lungs, sending it through the forest. "Hungry! Hungry! Hungry!"

"Shut him up," Wilhoit snapped, then saw Church chambering a round into his Remington. He jumped forward and grabbed the boy's arm.

"I wasn't gonna shoot him," Andy said. "Just scare him a little. That's all."

By that time the old man's siren was winding down. He

stopped and stared, listening to his own strident echo as if waiting for an answer.

Steven finally forced down his discomfiture. The wails of the unbalanced were ever unsettling to him, but in this dread silence it was positively frightful. Covey seemed just as unnerved; all he could manage was a breathless "Fuck me blind." Then he turned to Steven, more impatient than ever. "Can we go now? Huh?"

"Sure," he replied, taking the hatchet from his belt. "I'll be finished in a second."

He scanned the immediate area, tried to decide which of the look-alike Stepford trees would stand out the most were they to inadvertently pass this way again. It was a hard decision; one was as tall yet visually unimpressive as the next. Finally a few yards ahead he found a spruce with an odd-shaped knothole, three circles that seemed to interconnect in a way that, at first glance, made them look like . . .

Wait a minute, he thought. What is this, déjà vu?

He stooped, took a closer look. It really did look like Mickey Mouse in profile, the ears and everything. But so did a tree he'd marked several hours ago. Exactly like it. He ran his hands along the thick bough of the tree, searched for the hash mark he had cut earlier. It was not there. The bark was unblemished.

But what were the chances of two sets of knotholes looking exactly the same?

He caught himself. Don't be stupid. You're starting to sound as gullible as Church. Trees don't just heal themselves, you know. The cut you made couldn't have sealed over in a few hours.

Could it?

He swung the hatchet with a fearful strength, half expecting the spruce to cry out in pain. But there was only silence beyond the thud of metal sinking into soft wood. He chopped at angles, deeper and wider than before until he'd excised a wedge of the trunk a bit larger than his fist. "Let's see you cover that up, bub," he whispered.

"Which way now, Steven?"

He rejoined the others as he slipped the hatchet back into his belt, shouldered the Weatherby. "We've come this far, so let's keep heading northeast. We're bound to hit something sooner or later."

They started their hike again, groping through the dense underbrush and cursing the way it fought them. The battle was just as exhausting as before, and within ten minutes it was as if they had not stopped to rest at all, had only dreamed that brief respite as their minds wandered from the trudging monotony. Which suited Steven fine; that way he could put little significance in the Mickey Mouse knothole that still clung tenaciously to his subconscious and refused to be dislodged.

It's nothing, he told himself. Just let it go. But he couldn't. It stayed behind his eyes and tormented him, forced him to scour each tree that he came to, no longer content to search for hash marks alone. Exposed roots, peeling bark, the odd crook of a branch—any little detail that he might recognize, that would tell him that he'd been this way before. It was more than a little paranoid, he realized. But after this day's events, he did not dismiss anything.

"Hold up a second," Church called from the rear of the line. He had stopped a few yards back and cocked his head to one side, straining to listen. He held a finger to his lips and the others complied, froze in their tracks. The faint reverberations of their movement died away and the valley's silence resettled around them with startling speed, as if it had been waiting for just such a chance. It made Steven nervous, standing there like a statue, hearing his own heart thrum in his ears.

"What is it?" he whispered.

Church hung on for another full minute, then shook his head in stymied surrender. "I'm not sure. I just thought I heard something out there . . ." He pointed to the west, where the mist and dense undergrowth limited their vision to no more than fifty yards. "In that direction, I think."

"Probably just an animal."

Covey laughed humorlessly. "An animal . . . are you kidding? In this valley? Not too damn likely, I'd say."

Just then a sound did issue from the deep woods where Church had pointed. It was the barest of echoes, the edges worn down by its pinball-like travel through the trees until few distinguishing features remained. It reached them indistinct and unrecognizable; disrupting the utter silence was its only effect.

"There!" Church whispered, vindicated. "Did you hear that?" But before the others could reply, it came again. Only this time it was imperceptively louder, a fraction more distinct. Mostly the shushing of disturbed leaves, intermixed with the popping of brittle twigs. A subtle noise yet alarming given the surroundings. Steven thought it was at least as scary now as when he'd first heard it, standing in the darkness and staring across Beaver Lake . . .

"That's it!" he sighed as recognition set in. "It's just that freaky wind. Barton said it blows through Chalako all the time, from any direction, and—"

Crack!

A branch snapped, a very heavy one from the sound, and was followed by the thud of it hitting the ground. Then another one went just after that. And before the echoes could die, another.

"Helluva wind," Church whispered.

Paul Covey tensed, took a better grip on his rifle. "That ain't no wind," he told them, adamant. "And whatever it is, it's coming this way."

"How do you know?"

"Just listen to it."

A startling crash rang out. Shards of noise ricocheted off the trees around them like auditory shrapnel. And even before they recovered from that, the groan of another teetering titan reached their ears. Its thunderous landing somehow eclipsed the first.

Because it was closer?

"Oh, jeez," Andy muttered under his breath. "Oh jeez oh jeez . . ."

Steven felt his mouth go dry, his throat constrict, his spine numb. It's coming, he realized, whatever it is . . . And it *was* something; not the wind, not some trick of the ear. He was sure of that. Because through those sounds he could feel a palpable presence, feel it as readily as if someone had stood right behind him, belly to back, their breath bristling the hair on his neck. To feel that nearness, yet not know what it was or what it wanted . . . That frightened him. Clear to the bone.

It's coming, and soon the thrashing sounds won't be enough. Soon the trees will part and something will loom through the mist and you'll look upon the owner of that presence.

Oh jeez is right. Run. Run now.

But he didn't. And neither did the others.

They all crouched down behind the nearest tree and worked the bolts on their rifles, braced them against the sturdy boughs. Covey tried to get Elton Tucker to take cover but the old man ignored him, preferring to stand in plain view and stare into the forest with a child's unabashed curiosity.

The air grew tense, thick with fear, as the hunters waited. They winced as the clamor continued to grow around them, would have covered their ears had their hands not been grafted to the stocks of their weapons. And then as the thrashing reached its zenith and the whole valley seemed to quake with the sound, it . . .

Stopped.

A tentative silence returned.

Andy looked around in confusion. "What the hell?"

Steven rose slowly, listening with every fiber of his being. "Where did it go?" he wondered. "It can't be gone that fast. Can it?"

"Whatever 'it' is," Covey muttered.

"It's there," someone else proclaimed. It was Tucker standing several yards away, staring into space and nodding, a wan smile on an otherwise blank face. "It's there all right."

"Who put a nickel in him?" Church started to comment, but was drowned out by the resurgence of the unseen cacophony, of dried leaves whispering and heavy branches snapping like pencils. Only now it came from off to the right, as if traveling a parallel path. All three men shifted their positions, swiveled their rifles to cover the new area. And they followed it all the way along until the clamor began to fade into the distance.

"It's leaving!" Covey exclaimed. His voice echoed overly loud and the others shot him vehement glares, afraid his outburst might lure it back. But the sounds continued to lessen, steadily, until the men finally dared to sigh in relief.

At least most of them.

"No . . ." Tucker whispered. His breathing was suddenly shallow and rushed, his eyes wide with disbelief. And the whisper became a frantic cry. *"No!"* With no explanation or warning, the old man bolted through the trees, across their field of vision and in the direction of the fading sounds.

"What the hell is he doing—"

"Mr. Tucker!" Covey yelled, jumping to his feet. He raced past the others in pursuit, called back to them, "Don't worry. I'll get him."

"Paul, wait—" Steven started, but the salesman was already gone, vanished into the mist-shrouded undergrowth. "Dammit, we can't split up! Come back!"

His words rang hollow and unheard.

"What do we do now?" Church asked. But deep down he already knew the answer. There wasn't anything else to do but go after them. And Wilhoit's expression showed that he knew it too. "Fuckin' A," the young man grumbled as they both started through the obscuring fog at a quick but wary run.

The thrashing was gone now, died away. All that met their ears was the echo of their own movements through the brush. Steven no longer worried about hash marks or distinguishing features on the trees, for the landscape itself told him they had not been this way before. The ground wasn't as flat here, instead undulated in wavelike ridges and shallow ravines. The latter, though clogged with weeds and briers, was still easier to navigate than climbing one rise after another. But the low paths badly limited their field of view, so more than once Steven had to clamber up a ridge for a better vantage point.

"See anything?"

"Nothing," he complained bitterly from higher up. "Too many fucking trees . . . Paul! Can you here me?"

A faint answer from the distance, the last generation of a fading echo. "Over here."

"How the hell did he get so far away?" Steven muttered aloud as he tried to get a bearing on the voice, settled for a western direction and communicated that to Church below. Then he paused to survey the terrain that lay ahead. The ravine they had been following did not break to the west anytime soon; they'd have to travel the highlands for a while. Church agreed and clambered up the ridge himself, crested the top panting and out of breath. But he refused to slow down or rest. "Which . . . way now?" he managed to stammer.

Crack!

The two men froze, listening to the reverberations, trying to decide whether it had been a gunshot or not. But another came soon afterward. A branch breaking, and then the groan of a smaller tree toppling to earth. After that, silence.

"Paul?" Church said softly, tentatively, as if testing the integrity of the quiet. Then he yelled it. "Paul!"

The answer was again weak, distant. Fearful. "Did you guys hear that?"

"Yes!"

"Can you see it?"

"No! Can you?"

There was a pause, and in that time several smaller branches fell through the canopy of the forest out there somewhere, made a snickering sound as they caromed through the other limbs before making it to the ground. Andy and Steven tensed, fearing they wouldn't hear the other man's voice again. But then it came, high and frantic, terrified. "Hurry! Something's coming . . ."

Crack!

A groan to a crash. Something large was moving.

" . . . goddammit, *hurry*!"

The men ran then, down the serpentine crest of land to the next ridge, one which curled back to the west. They were just turning in that direction when the gunshot rang out.

All sound stopped in the forest. All movement. Steven felt his heart rising into his throat, climbing as if it had grown arms and legs of its own. It kept him from calling out or even breathing. His mouth was suddenly dry and his pants wet and for an instant it seemed as if the forest was spinning madly around him. Don't you faint, you candy ass. Don't you even fucking think about it. Not when those men are counting on you. "Come on," he whispered, his voice cracking. He pulled an equally stunned Church along after him.

He had taken three or four steps, was just regaining his bearings when Paul Covey's voice sifted from the bowels of the forest. But it was not a yell or an anguished cry this time. It was a softer sound. A gasp. "Jesus . . ." The echoes whispered in a bleak, despairing tone. "Oh, sweet fucking Jesus . . ."

Another gunshot, like rolling thunder. Then the reverberations were drowned out by the silence, and all was still.

Minutes seemed to tick by in the aftermath, or maybe it was hours; Steven could not be sure. Maybe time did not pass at all. In that unnatural quiet the world did seem to have ground to a halt, if only to extend the two men's torment. Neither could move a muscle. It was as if that last plaintive voice had stolen their strength and will and left a numbing-cold fear in their place. It wasn't until a branch suddenly snapped just overhead, shattering the crystalline silence, that the two were startled enough to move. They dove for cover as bits of wood rained down around them.

A long, thin piece struck ground right next to Church's

head, not six inches away. The impact was so hard, it had a
metallic ring to it.

Wait a minute . . . Metallic?

Andy fished through the leaves for it and held the piece
up in both hands. Tubular steel, the front sight still in place
. . . It was the end of a rifle barrel, broken just ahead of the
receiver. The latter part of the Remington name was still
visible. "Oh, God," he muttered, turning to Steven just as
the other man held up two more pieces, a broken buttstock
in one hand, a shattered Redfield scope in the other.

Neither man asked whose. They knew that already. What
they didn't know was "How? How did it get here?"

Their eyes climbed the nearest tree to where they'd heard
the "branch" shatter. But there were no broken limbs there.
Only a bare place in the bark about fifteen feet up, where the
rifle had struck. After being thrown.

Wilhoit felt the nausea building in him, filling his throat
and flooding his nostrils. The forest started to spin again and
this time he wasn't so sure he could fight it. He turned to
Church and found the boy still holding the broken rifle barrel
in his hands, turning it over and over. His whole frame was
shaking. But this wasn't a tremor of fear like that which
gripped Steven's stomach so mercilessly. Andy was assim-
ilating his shock in a different way entirely. He was getting
angry, just as he had with Tucker. Stoking the flames until
they were white-hot. "Bastards," he sneered, finally tossing
the barrel aside and reaching for his own rifle. And without
another word he charged ahead like an enraged bull.

"Andy, wait!" but Steven's words were in vain. Church
was already disappearing into the trees, leaving him with a
hapless decision. Rush into the woods, where the cause of
his fear lay just waiting to be discovered. Or stay here. Alone.

Not much of a choice at all. He broke into a sprint, determined not to let the boy out of his sight.

The ridge and ravine topography flattened out as they went
and they soon found themselves back in the forest proper, in
the maze of identical trees where every direction seemed the

same. For all they knew, they could have gone in circles and come out just where they started. But the possibility didn't occur to Andy Church. He was operating on a lower, more primal level now, ignoring what he saw and heard in favor of what he felt. And now Steven knew why. Because he felt it too. The presence again. It was there, silent and watching, looming out of the forest like some unseen colossus. Its tangibility made his skin crawl, for there was no questioning the malevolence there. A numbing chill clutched at his heart and if he'd stopped to consider his actions, he'd have curled into a fetal ball and hid his head in fear. But instead he took Andy's example, cursed under his breath and gritted his teeth, and almost passed the boy in his angry charge.

Broken branches littered the forest floor before them. A towering spruce had been leveled, pulling down a netting of limbs from the surrounding trees as well. The two did not stop, only noted it as evidence that they were on the right trail. Then they fought their way over the obstructions and kept going. More fallen titans lay ahead—a sturdy oak leaning against its brethren with roots pulled from the soil, a host of jack pine broken to kindling as if pressed beneath the palm of God. What could have done this? Steven wondered. Or more to the point, what could a hunting rifle do against it?

You'll find out soon enough, he thought. Because the presence was growing more palpable. More threatening. There, just beyond those trees ahead, where daylight peaked tentatively through into their forest. A clearing.

It's in the open . . .

His knuckles whitened on the Weatherby. Not much farther.

Church must have felt it as well, for despite his gasps and wheezes, he actually picked up speed as they approached the tree line. But then, suddenly, the presence . . . simply wasn't. It was gone, suddenly, jarringly, and the void it left behind startled them. They slowed their charge in confusion. But only for a moment. Andy was too angry to accept it. With a renewed battlecry—"Banzai, fuckers!"—he burst through the groping limbs and curtain of pine needles, his Remington leveled at the hip. And Wilhoit was right behind him.

The dusky sky was still filtered through a lingering layer of fog. But compared to the gloom of the deep woods, the light they stepped into was glaring and bright, enough to bring the two up short and make their vision swim. Steven shielded his eyes with an upraised arm and managed to look around warily.

They were standing at the edge of a clearing some fifty feet across, and it had not been there long. The trees that had stood in that spot until today were now splintered and in pieces, littering the open ground. It looked like a battle zone after the armies had moved on, as the perpetrator must have done. For there was no sign of it here now, or of Covey for that matter. The clearing was empty.

But it could come back. They stayed tensed and cautious.

"What now?" Steven whispered.

Andy didn't answer right away. His head was cocked to the side again, just like before. Listening. "Don't you hear that?" he said, creeping into the clearing.

"I don't hear anything," Steven replied. But he followed along just the same.

They threaded their way through the devastation, covering each other like trained soldiers on patrol. Steven noticed that the young man was beginning to pick up speed. But then, an instant later, he heard the soft sound that had drawn Andy's attention.

Humming. Someone was carrying on a strange tune, curiously devoid of any sort of melody.

They tracked it through the fractured vegetation, past jagged remnants of a great oak that had been torn asunder. Just beyond it lay a battered and twisted carcass, flat on its back, the legs splayed in different directions. It was bare-skinned, its clothes having been cut away. And that wasn't all. The genitals were missing as well. Only a ragged hole remained in the loins, allowing pink layers of muscle to bulge through.

There was a man there crouched over the body, humming to himself. His back was to them and he seemed unmindful of their presence. And as they watched, he slipped a knife into that hole and made a strong upward cut, from stomach to sternum. The abdomen opened like a blooming flower, its warmth spilling out in a breathy gush of steam.

"My God . . ." Church gasped.

The man stopped humming, turned to look at them. Elton Tucker's face was drained and colorless, his hair standing away from his head in a tangle. He was gaunt and hollow-cheeked, his eyes wide, bulging. And his mouth was smeared with blood. "I got it," he said, pointing to the butchered corpse. "I told you I would. And it's a fine animal, isn't it?" He reached behind him and picked up something, held it out for their appraisal. Paul Covey's head was no longer attached; the neck appeared twisted and tapering, as if it had been screwed off his shoulders. That explained the look of horror etched into his features. The eyes squinted in agony. The mouth frozen midscream. "Well, what do you think?" Tucker said proudly. "Won't it look good on my office wall?" He looked past them, all around the clearing as if searching for someone. "Covey!" he called. "Bring the camera! I want a picture of this." Then he held his trophy up beside his own face and posed, smiling broadly. Madly.

Both the men were struck dumb, mortified by the sight before them. But Church willed himself to move. He raised his rifle slowly. Pointed it toward the head that grinned . . .

A gust of wind came howling out of the forest then and into the clearing like a tempest, its swirls darkened by the leaves and sticks and pine needles it carried. Its sudden appearance took the men by surprise; it was on them in an instant, buffeting their clothes, blinding them with debris. Freezing them to the bone. Steven knew intuitively that this was the cold wind he'd watched from across Beaver Lake, the same freakish wind Davejac said came at any time and from nowhere. And in that same instant, as its unnatural chill cut into him, he was suddenly aware of its origin. He wasn't sure just how, whether a wild hunch or the wind itself whispering in his ear. But he knew.

It came from here, in this valley. This damnable valley.

Someone else was listening as well. Elton Tucker heard its voice of rushing air in his ear and he began to laugh. It was a mad and capering sound, and the wind carried it deep into the forest.

THIRTEEN

THE MOON LANGUISHED JUST ABOVE THE WESTERN TREETOPS, having all but completed its nightly sojourn across a star-flecked sky. But its brightness was not diminished by such efforts; it still cast the landscape in startling monochrome, either cold silver or shadow black. Along the rocky treeless ridge where Davejac still sat, the former held sway. But below, in the valley . . . That was another matter.

He looked down the scrubby almost-trail that Wilhoit and the others had descended some eighteen hours before, peered into the inky dark that lapped against the loose shale and weeds and separated the world above from that below. And his discomfort grew. "Anytime now, guys," he muttered softly, then immediately questioned his reticence to speak it aloud. Why not? Who would you disturb? "Did you get that down there?" he yelled, this time hearing his words ripple across the treetops of the gorge like a dark ocean. "I said anytime now. I'm still waiting, you know?" But his only answer was that same mocking echo.

Go on, get it over with. Go down after them . . .

Boo-Boo mewled softly beside him, roused by his yelling. Both dogs were still right with him, curled on either side like overprotective bookends, and they refused to stray any farther than that. They seemed to have gotten over their initial anxiousness upon reaching this place, but Barton had only to reach down and scratch one's neck to realize how alarmed they still were. Their fur bristled like taut wire against his palm, and the muscles beneath were hard, bunched, ready for any sudden movement. Their wariness did little to allay his own fears.

Fears? You aren't afraid, are you, boy? Not the big woodsman, the hunter and guide . . . I thought you said those old natives were the frightened ones, with their legends and superstitions. Not an educated man like you—

Shut up.

There's nothing to be afraid of here, he assured himself. No reason to be worried. So they haven't come back yet . . . big deal. There haven't been any four-shot alarms signaled. In fact, no shots at all. Period. Just the silence, and all that means is they haven't found Tucker's deer yet. They're probably still tracking it, running around in circles like a bunch of boobs. But Wilhoit's got a good head on his shoulders. Before long he'll lead 'em out of there, tired and ragged and ready to go home. Even Tucker. So stop worrying.

I'm not worrying. It just better be soon, that's all. 'Cause there isn't any food around here and we've all been a full day without it now. And it's a long walk back on an empty stomach.

That voice in his head considered his words, came back with the same sly suggestion as before. If it's bothering you that much, it told him, then go down and get 'em. You're the guide here, quit "acquiescing" and put your foot down for once. After all, they're your responsibility, right?

Right.

Then go after them.

Davejac looked down into the darkness again, felt himself tremble.

What's the matter? You aren't afraid, are you?

I said, *Shut up*!

He got up to pace again, to keep busy, anything but argue with a conscience whose pragmatism he did not need at the moment. But aimless walking was out of the question; the elkhounds stood right with him, and their determined closeness tied up his feet and made it too much of a struggle. Instead he went the short distance back to his impromptu camp along the tree line, where the tent was erected and a small fire still flickered. "Well, fellas," he said, scruffing the ears of Yogi much to her delight, "should we try turning in again?" But then he looked into the open tent and found it no more inviting than before. He knew he wouldn't sleep, and he had no desire to lay there awake, thinking . . . Nope, that would be the wrong thing to do entirely. Keep moving, he counseled. Keep your mind on something else. "We've been setting around here long enough," he finally decided. "What do you say we get a little exercise." He looked back at the valley. "If we move along this ridge and circle around, maybe we can find a better vantage point, maybe even see a campfire or something. Maybe I could even get a shot at one or two of them." The dogs regarded him solemnly. "Hey, lighten up." He shrugged. "I'm just kidding. Besides . . . I wouldn't aim for anything vital."

He kicked dirt into the fire to smother it, then left everything else in camp as it was. All they'd need for this little hike was his rifle and flashlight, though on second thought he picked up the dogs' wound-up leads and stuck them in his coat pocket. If they decided to get out of hand again, he'd need a sure way to restrain them. With that taken care of, they were ready to go. He gave a hand signal and started for the trail.

Yogi was immediately hesitant, whining and acting skittish. But once it was apparent that they would be skirting the valley and not going down into it, she settled down to a silent canter, just like her stoic brother.

The high trail was not easy traveling, especially at night.

In the open areas the loose shale proved unstable under his weight and the bared bedrock was dew-soaked and slippery. But he was nimble for his size and could take bad footing in stride. What he didn't like were the narrow areas, where the soil held right down to the valley edge and allowed trees to grow there, some with roots that poked through the slope beyond. Those places bothered him; not only did they force the three to move single file rather than three abreast as the dogs insisted, but it also limited the moonlight. With those trees so close and shading the ground, it was as if the shadows of the forest and valley were coming together there, joining forces and just daring him to try to breach their solidarity. His flashlight was little solace in such instances, for its battery power simply could not fend off such an overpowering veil of darkness. And in those moments when he had to walk without the moon, when his breath caught and he quickened his pace just to be free of the dark, he heard that smug voice within him asking, Why? Why do you hurry? Why do you run? And this time, away from the campfire and the rational anchor it represented, he could finally admit it to himself.

He was afraid after all.

It was not a normal kind of fear, like being tired and hungry and miles away from any apparent food. This was a much more primal dread, deep down, and there was an unsettling familiarity to it. It reminded him that he had not always been so at home in the forest. Not when a Toronto-raised teenager came to the backwoods with his grandfather for the first time. There was always that fear in the beginning, that lack of knowledge that makes things strange and unfamiliar seem supernatural, almost malevolent in nature. There was inevitably a time on each trip when Grandpa George would go into the brush to gather wood or relieve himself and Barton would be left alone, and in that instant the forest would change its face. It would watch him and listen to him with unerring interest, and he was sure that beyond the birds and the animals that lived there, the woods had a special life of its own . . .

A chill slid along his spine, and he dismissed the notion

out of hand. "That's enough of that," he said, letting the memory slip away. After all, this wasn't exactly the time and place to examine old fears. Instead, he turned his attention to the valley, searched for the glow of a distant fire, for any sign of movement or life down there. But there was only the unreckoning darkness, darker even than the shadowy forest behind him . . .

That fear of the unknown made a grab for his spine again, but he shook its cold grasp and urged the dogs onward. If I can't fight it, he figured, maybe I can outdistance it.

It was just a few minutes afterward that he came to the rock.

A massive piece of the Precambrian Shield jutted through the soil directly ahead like a great petrified tumor, over-powering the ridge, looming out over the steep valley wall. If they were to continue, Barton decided, it would involve a fair degree of climbing. And so far, the results did not justify the effort. They had gone well beyond sight of their original position and camp, yet had seen nothing new in the valley, not even the dancing dot of a flashlight.

"Looks like the end of the line, kids," he said to the dogs, "unless you feel like climbing."

Apparently not. Yogi and Boo-Boo lay down a few feet away, resting lightly but still keeping a wary eye on him.

Davejac looked around for the least-damp place to sit and rest, and as his flashlight beam swept across the pocked and cracking surface of the great rock, he caught a glimpse of something there—dark lines, incongruous with the other natural markings. This time he trained the light on the stone dead-on, adjusting the lens ring to widen the field of coverage. And in so doing, he saw the figures emblazoned there, the natural dye weathered and fading but still easily discerned. "Pictographs?" he marveled. "But they're usually around water. What are these doing way up here?"

His curiosity piqued, he moved closer, stooping down to see them more clearly. And the glow of his light proved that location was not the only thing strange about these paintings.

They were abstract and distorted, not at all like the rather simplistic deer that marked his favorite river portage. The figures were greater in number here, like an army of miniature shadows, and their sizes and shapes all but defied translation. Many had heads that were oddly placed or shaped or sported multiple pairs of arms and legs, while others seemed a curious amalgam of human and animal parts, lizard tails and bird wings and serpentine necks. The only figure among them even partially identifiable to him was another deer, marked as such by its tremendous rack of antlers. But that was the only similarity. This one pictured the animal grazing, only it had no skin; the skeletal aspect was unmistakable since each bare rib bone had been carefully drawn in place, each ridge along the spinal column. There was even a dot of unpainted stone to mark the eye socket. A deer, all right. But a dead one.

He stood back and surveyed the rock as a whole, took in all the mottled, mutable characters there. Their demented aspect intrigued him. What could the artist have been thinking of when he painted it? A nightmare?

Worry about it later, a pragmatic voice reminded. You've got men missing, remember? Keep your mind on the job.

They're not missing, he growled to himself as he stalked to the edge and peered into that shadowy rift below. They'll hear me this time. You watch. "Wilhoit!" he yelled his loudest. "Tucker!"

But only the echoes returned.

"Dammit, answer me!"

Still nothing.

You'll have to go down after them.

Barton's flesh crawled at the suggestion and he wasn't sure just why. He only knew he wasn't going down there, and that was that. He sank back into the umbrage of the great stone and leaned against it, wishing he could draw some sort of strength from its agelessness. But there was none there, only a damp cold he could feel right through his coat that made him tremble all the more. He stared numbly into the valley and tried hard to ignore the voice in his head.

Why don't you go down there?

I . . . I just can't.

But why? Because you're afraid? But you said it yourself, there's nothing down there to be afraid of.

It's more than that, dammit. This place . . . it just doesn't feel right.

Oh, come on. This trip hasn't felt right for the past two days, so it can't be just that. Cut the shit, eh? Why don't you go down into the valley? Why—

Because I can't, okay? I can't 'cause if I go down there I'll . . .

I'll die?

He just sat there, stunned and silent. The voice in his head no longer chided him, for its goal had been realized. He'd finally admitted it, faced his fear and looked upon it. And now he saw that it wasn't some childish dread bubbling from his subconscious. This was fresh, as new as the morning before, and it took on life the moment they stepped from the forest and looked into this valley for the first time. A single thought had filled his mind then, though not in words or pictures, nothing that concrete. Perhaps it was more a premonition. But it was clear and complete and did not leave any doubt as to its message.

Go into the valley, and you will never come out.

Superstition, he tried to scoff. There's nothing in these woods, in that valley, to be scared of. You know better than that. But no amount of rationalizing could pry that dread warning from his mind.

As he wrestled his fear, he looked from the corner of his eye, and for an instant, he saw the pictographs move. They stretched their shadowy limbs, tried to peel themselves from the rock itself. He knew it was not real, and when he blinked the paintings were suddenly just that again, stick figures on a field of stone. But the thought of their movement . . .

somehow it did not seem all that implausible. He looked at them and had the odd feeling that they had moved before, if not on the rock then in life, as models for these same paintings. And he no longer questioned what the artist was thinking. What was he looking at?

Barton's eyes strayed from the stone to the valley below, and he looked out upon it from the same vantage point the ancient artist had. And the allusion made his blood run cold.

The silence was being overruled, at least in Barton's ears, by the pounding of his own heart, the quickening of his breath. He thumbed back the hammer on the Marlin and stood slowly, stepped away from the wall of rock and didn't dare look back at it, not once. For he knew that the freakish things painted there would be moving again, and he wasn't so sure they would stop with a simple blink this time. He wanted only to get out of this place, out of these woods, and never look upon them again. But you can't travel at night, he reminded himself. You'll break your leg or fall in a sump hole like Wilhoit or you might even get lost in these unfamiliar woods. Just make it back to the camp for now. And at first light, you get the hell out whether they're back or not.

As soon as he was on his feet, the dogs were right with him again, taking up their guardian positions on either flank. And the three of them set out at a brisker pace than before along the lip of the valley. This time there was a noticeable urgency in the Indian's stride, a certain fear in his step. The dogs had to break into a lope just to keep up.

The beam of the flashlight jumped and bounced erratically through the darkness as he used it to bat aside low limbs and sticker bushes, not daring to take his other hand away from his side where it kept the rifle ever ready. He was making much better time than before. Shouldn't be much farther . . .

The cold moonlight lit the way, except for those areas where the encroaching shadows made the flashlight necessary. He slowed down for those, stalked through them with his eyes alert and his heart crowding his Adam's apple until he made it to the light again. Then he'd stoke up his fire once more and sprint across the open ridge, the dogs running silently beside him.

He was moving out of the third eclipse and just breaking back into the light, just picking up speed, when his toe caught on a rock and the momentum sent him sprawling. Reflexively he curled himself around the still-cocked rifle, shielding it from an impact that might make it discharge and hit one of his dogs. So he landed hard and with little grace. His elbows were stone-bruised and his knees skinned bloody. But Barton didn't even notice. He was watching in stunned silence as the flashlight he'd discarded in favor of the rifle went spinning across a long flat shelf of rock, right toward the valley. It came to rest on the edge and teetered there for an instant, its bright eye turned back toward him for a last plaintive look. Then it dropped over and was gone.

The Indian laid there on the rocks, gaping in disbelief. "Stupid," he grumbled, slinging stones away from him. "How could you be so fucking stupid!" He grabbed up anything within reach, hurled rocks and sticks over the edge in a fit of rage.

Yogi was suddenly there beside him, pushing her way past his arms to lick his face diligently. If it was a canine attempt at diverting his attention, it worked. He was suddenly too busy fending her off to complain about anything. "Okay, girl, okay," he surrendered, pushing her away. "I get the message."

Satisfied, she rejoined her stoic sibling, who was sitting close at hand, keeping a watchful eye on the forest around them.

Barton picked himself up slowly, hissing from the pain in his knees. He was still disgusted with himself but had determined to get over it. "Well . . . at least we've got the moonlight," he sighed, then pointed along the ridge ahead. "And look over there. I think I can see where we camped. It isn't that much farther. C'mon, stay close."

They resumed their trek, albeit at a slower, more cautious

pace. And that was all that saved the Indian from going down for a second time. They had traveled no more than thirty feet when the dogs suddenly veered inward toward each other, across their master's path, and he had to stop suddenly or go flying again. "You stupid goddamn . . ." was the curse that started for his lips, but it never got all the way out. For he could tell it had not been a playful prank by the two. Yogi and Boo-Boo were still blocking his path, staring straight ahead into the shadows of a small stand of jack pine. And their bodies were rigid with alarm. "What is it?" he whispered, bringing the rifle to his shoulder, wishing he still had that damn flashlight.

The dogs answered deep in their throats as they lowered into predatory crouches, coiled and ready.

The object of their unease was just coming into view.

"Lord Almighty," Barton whispered breathlessly upon seeing the dark figure that stepped from the shadows some forty feet ahead, now silhouetted in the moonlight. He blinked his eyes once, twice, squeezed them tight for a full three count and prayed it would go away, return to its stone with the others just like the last time. But when he looked again, the thing remained. Motionless. Watching him. It looked like one of the rock paintings had come to life—black as pitch and twice as wide as Barton, with no head in sight. But its most alarming features were the three or more arms and four legs and the shuffling gait that had carried it this far. And as he watched, the strange creature took another step, dragged more than one leg, staggered a bit. Another step. Drag. Another.

The dogs tensed, ready to charge. But Barton's whispered "Stay" kept them in their place. He didn't want anything getting into his line of fire. The rifle barrel was trained on the thing's center of mass, chest level, and his finger tightened on the trigger . . .

But then it stopped.

He didn't fire. He just watched as the thing seemed to tremble a moment, lean to both sides at the same time. Then, before his eyes, it just split down the middle, right in two like some giant amoeba. Part of it fell to the ground with a dull thud. But the rest was still standing, wavering unsteadily. Barton suddenly found himself staring down the Marlin's iron sights at the shape of a man.

"What the hell . . ." He looked at the discarded mass on the ground, writhing there, and found it human as well. And he realized then just how badly the moonlight and his own fear had fooled him. It had never been a multilimbed monster. Only one man carrying another, an arm around his shoulder and dragging him as he came.

The hunters? But . . . which ones?

He motioned for the still-growling dogs to stay, did it twice to make sure they understood. Then he crept cautiously toward the figures out there, his rifle ready and leveled at the hip.

He was not yet halfway to them when he saw the condition of the fallen man, the torn coat and the dark stains spreading from his shoulder, the harsh moonlight turning red to black. And when he rolled over onto his back, moaning and clutching himself in pain, Barton could see it was Andy Church. His face was frozen in a rictus of agony and terror, and spots of blood freckled one side of his face.

The Indian looked to the other man, whose features were still hidden by the lunar backlight. He didn't move. Barton took a few more steps forward, unsure of what to do, whether to rush in and see if he was hurt or keep the rifle on him, just in case. But at least this close, he could surmise his identity. Not tall enough to be Covey. Nor as stout as the old man. "Steve?" he whispered tentatively. "Is that you?"

The shadowy man took a few shambling steps forward, and Barton instinctively backpedaled. But then he reconsidered and slowly circled the man, as wide as the ridge allowed, until the moon was at his back and the other man was turning, into the light.

It was Wilhoit, all right. But not as the Indian knew him. The glasses were gone and his hair was standing spiky and erect like the fur along the dogs' backs. His features were drawn tight, frozen, as if in the act of screaming, and his eyes nearly bulged from their sockets. It was a maniacal look, one of either fear or madness, and the color of his skin did not help. Both he and Church looked pasty, almost cadaverous.

Steven looked at Davejac, stared at him without a single blink, and his mouth moved soundlessly.

"What is it?" the Indian called. "My God, what the hell happened to you?"

Wilhoit reached out, took a single staggering step, and then collapsed into Davejac's arms. He was deep in shock, his glassy stare fixed on empty space overhead, and his mouth kept moving, kept muttering softly. It was a bare whisper. Barton had to lean closer, put his ear to those quivering white lips to make it out.

"Wind," the man stammered over and over. "Wind . . . wind . . ."

FOURTEEN

"COVEY! TUCKER! ANSWER ME!"

But the echoes broke on the far shore of the valley without response.

"They're dead, aren't they?" Davejac said aloud. "They're dead and I'm stuck in the middle of nowhere with two injured men. What the hell do I do now?"

No one offered answers. Not the still-skittish dogs. Not the two men on the ridge with him, enveloped in the folds

of catatonia. In fact, their silence only drove home the help-
lessness he felt.

No, he thought defiantly. I'm not helpless. We'll make it
out of here if I just calm down, take things one step at a
time. First, take care of the men . . .

He pushed his fear aside as he inspected each man's condition. Neither fought him; they were barely lucid as it was.
He found only superficial cuts and bruises on Steven. But
when he peeled back the shredded and bloody yoke of Andy
Church's jacket and shirt, Barton gasped in spite of himself.
A big chunk of flesh had been torn from the young man's
deltoid. Blood was still bubbling from the horrendous wound,
though remarkably little considering its severity. The Indian
took off his flannel shirt just long enough to skin out of his
thermal underwear. Then he used his knife to cut the latter
into long strips, which he wrapped around the shoulder tightly
to put pressure on the wound. Finally, he tied the arm to the
man's midsection, just to keep it immobilized.

Barton sat back and took stock of his situation. The two
couldn't walk, that much was obvious. And even if they
could, it was too far back to the base camp anyway. They
would have to be airlifted out of there, something the dense
forest in the immediate vicinity precluded. Get them to a
clearing, he decided, where a chopper can touch down. That's
step one. Get that done and then take it from there.

He thought back along the trail they had blazed this far
and remembered a suitable clearing about a kilometer back,
maybe a little farther. There was no easy way around it; to
get there, he would have to carry them, one at a time. There
was nothing else to do. So he picked up Andy Church and
hauled him all the way back to the tent, where he wrapped
him in a sleeping bag and told the elkhounds to stay and
stand guard. They didn't seem to like it but they obeyed
nonetheless. He retrieved his rope, then went back for Steven
and draped him over a shoulder.

Without a flashlight to show the way, it took them more
than an hour to locate the clearing he remembered, a rock

field strewn with some boulder-sized fragments but not so many as to prevent a helicopter from coming in. At the edge of the field he sat Wilhoit down beside a tall rock and tried to talk to him, told him to stay right there, that he'd be back with Andy. But the man was stuporous; his eyes had glazed over and his mumblings were no longer even audible. That's why Barton had brought the rope; he uncoiled it and tied him to the rock to keep him from wandering off. Then he went back for Church.

The other man was still unconscious when Davejac returned to the camp. Barton was not looking forward to the strain of carrying such a large load. But once he wrestled the fat man into a fireman's carry position over both shoulders, he was surprised to find him lighter than he'd expected. Maybe his adrenaline blinded him to Church's true weight. But whatever the reason, Barton didn't question it further. He simply staggered into the woods as fast as his burden allowed, and the dogs followed close on his heels.

The morning sun was just coming up, stabbing its rays into the thick forest, when he made it to the clearing, wheezing and exhausted. Wilhoit was still there, trussed to his natural anchor and gibbering soundlessly, just as Barton had left him. The Indian put Church down right next to him and used the remaining coils of the rope to secure him as well. As the sunlight beamed brighter over the high horizon of the trees, he began to see the seriousness of their conditions, especially the stricken pallor of each man's face. He had seen exposure before, some bad cases of frostbite. But these two looked even worse. He knew then he had to get them help quickly. But how? It would take him at least two days to reach the base camp, even if he'd been rested and traveling on a full stomach instead of bone-tired and half-starved. How . . .

Wait a minute. He remembered standing on a rocky escarpment with Steven at dusk a few days past, watching a pair of headlights blink through the trees in the distance. The timber camp! They're bound to have a radio! He estimated the distance from memory—let's see, we left the rocks after

Tucker's gunshot, maybe a kilometer to where we met up with the others and camped. Then Tucker ran off in the morning and we followed for another three klicks . . . You can make that in about three hours, he told himself. If you can will those tired legs to move, that is.

Oh, I can make it. Don't you worry.

He sat down with the dogs and wrestled them affectionately, feeling guilty for making them stay behind again. But this time they took the order with little complaint, seeming satisfied just to be away from that tainted valley. They took up vigils around the two men, keeping a wary distance but nonetheless standing their posts. And they watched as their master disappeared into the woods once again.

The daylight filtering through the trees now made traveling much easier. But then, so did not carrying someone. The adrenaline was still pumping—Davejac felt as nimble as a jackrabbit, and his breathing wasn't nearly as labored as it had been back at the clearing. But maybe, like the dogs, it was just the idea of escaping, of putting distance between himself and that valley. He quickly retraced the trail they had tramped down previously, passed their old campsite, and kept going until he came out of the trees and found himself on the same rocky rise as before.

He paused there, wheezing, as he looked out over the green expanses and searched for some sign of the timber camp. There were no lights to lead the eye this time, and the road he had wagered on was nowhere to be seen. Nothing but forest and a few small lakes off in the distance. But when he had quieted down, when he stopped his rattling breath and held it, he could make out misplaced noises in the distance . . .

The buzz of saws. The clanking engines of harvester machines and log sleds pulling the felled materials out of the woods.

He'd been right after all. Barton sighed with relief. Hang on, guys. Help's on the way.

Davejac redoubled his efforts now that his objective was

at least within hearing range. As soon as he had his bearings, he skirted the cliff and looked for the first gradual slope, found it and went down half running, half sliding to the forest floor below.

He ran for another ten minutes before he came to the logging road. It was fresh-cut within the last month or so and not nearly as maintained as those that led into Chalako Lakes. But for a new road it was already deeply rutted from the heavy trucks. Its presence surprised him. He had not heard about any cutting this far back, and he couldn't even guess where the road came out. Surely it didn't circumvent the entire Chalako area. More than likely an offshoot of some other timber network farther to the south. But besides all that, the road simply seemed misplaced. After three days in the forest, much of it previously unseen even by him, he'd begun to think of this region as a world unto itself, wholly apart from that which bore them. The mark of man in this harsh untamed landscape was alien to his eyes. Alien, but in this case reassuring. He began to follow the dirt road at a steady jog, toward the distant lakes and the motor sounds that grew steadily louder. And as he ran, he saw where the woods had been thinned by the axe and the saw. He even glimpsed the cutters off through the trees, wraiths in heavy flannel shirts and yellow helmuts. But he ignored them and kept running and the road took him straight into the center of the timber camp.

There were two log haulers directly ahead, their flatbeds partially loaded with trees ready for the market. They were parked by a third vehicle, a tank truck used for refueling. Beyond that was a small mobile home with OFFICE above the door, and farther on were pickup trucks and small campers, ostensibly for the employees who stayed on-site until the job was completed. Davejac knew at a glance that these were independent cutters. The trucks were too archaic for one of the big firms like Ati-Kut Timber—the prediesel rigs were lucky to still be operating. The lack of a company logo on the driver's door was also conspicuous. Nothing, not even the simple stenciling of the family name to advertise their trade. There was no identification on the office trailer either. He knew then that these people were harvesting illegally on Chalako land. It was probably close to the boundary line so they could plead accidental cutting if caught, but he was sure they knew exactly what they were doing. This went on now and again in the backcountry, where timber was filched from private and provincial land, sometimes from Quetico Park itself, and sold to manufacturing firms in Ontario and the U.S., with both parties profiting handsomely. They would move in on an area and pick out the best trees, load their wood and be gone before they were ever found. But this operation seemed to be holding out much longer than usual. The well-rutted roads pointed to many hauls already, yet they were still here. And would be, he estimated. As long as the money kept coming in. As long as they didn't get caught.

Well, your secret's safe with me, Barton thought. All I want is some help.

The workers were all apparently afield. Barton headed to the office with rifle in hand and went right in, surprising the man he found seated at the desk there. "I've got two men hurt out in the woods," he told him, "about six kilometers from here. And two men are still missing. I need your radio."

The camp boss, a wiry man more fitted for paperwork than logging, just sat there and stared at him. He was obviously surprised by the Indian's sudden appearance and more than a little chagrined at being caught harvesting on private property. He didn't move or say a word, and for a minute Davejac thought he'd have to put the barrel of the Marlin under his nose to get a response. But then his words began to sink in —two hurt, two missing—and the man immediately led him to the radio. It was the way of the northern woods, to pitch in when anyone was lost or hurt, and the camp boss was no exception. He put the call through himself, though not to the police, which was understandable given his profession. "There's a helicopter that's closer," he assured, calling into the microphone again.

After a crackle of static, a woman's voice issued over the speaker in response. She called him by name, Walter, but did not identify herself. Still, the voice was already familiar to Barton. He recognized it right off. Bailey, the helicopter pilot who had playfully strafed the Rover on their way to Chalako. "Tell her to come quick," he instructed Walter. "Tell her Barton Davejac needs her help."

The camp boss transmitted the message verbatim. There was a pause, and then the response came, short and sweet. "I'm on my way. Out." And that was all.

She knew the boss by name, Barton noted. And she didn't ask for directions, which meant she had more than a passing familiarity with the locale. Guilt by association—she worked for Ati-Kut Timber, so it was safe for him to assume that Ati-Kut was buying all the unauthorized lumber. Not that he really gave a damn. Just as long as she got there and fast. He couldn't stop thinking about Wilhoit and Church in that clearing . . .

Walter was relatively hospitable while he waited, getting him coffee and some eggs and sausage left over from breakfast. He also offered the help of his crew if they were needed in any kind of search party. But Barton doubted his sincerity; he got the distinct impression that the man was just currying favor in hopes of averting any lawsuits now that their operation had been found out. The guide tired of him quickly and went outside to wait for the helicopter's arrival.

It was almost noon when the *whup-whup-whup* of rotor blades reached his ears. *Fannie Mae* came swooping in over the trees. It sat down at the end of the camp, which appeared to have been cleared away for just that purpose. The imposing figure of Bailey was at the helm, alone, and she motioned for Barton to climb aboard. He quickly explained the situation, gave her rough directions as to the location of the clearing where he left the men.

"That's in Chalako Lakes," the big woman said warily.

"I hate to tell you, sister, but you're in Chalako right here."

"Maybe," she said, very cagey. "But this close to the boundary, you don't get those crazy damn winds as much."

"Well, I guess we'll just have to chance it," he said, buckling himself right in. "Won't we, darlin'?"

Bailey gave him a labored smile and eased back on the stick, taking the craft nearly straight up. Then she veered back toward the escarpment where Barton had stood only a few hours before, and they sailed out over the ocean of prickly green.

He guided her toward the clearing as best he could, though it wasn't easy to remember the way from this new and precarious perspective. He could feel Bailey tense up beside him, fighting her urge to go higher where those sudden winds seldom reached. But when he recognized the rock field and pointed it out, she did not hesitate; she leaned on the stick and dipped right into the opening, sat down as close to the dogs and men as possible.

The wind did not come. Yet.

Davejac found both men unconscious. He untied them and carried each to the Bell, loaded them into the backseats and strapped them in. Then he told Bailey to take off.

"Aren't you coming?" she asked.

"No room for the dogs. Besides, I have to keep looking for the other two."

"I'll call some help in for you," she told him, allaying any fears he might've had that she would keep this quiet to avoid incrimination in the illegal timber camp. But she need not have worried. Barton had no such fears. They had known each other for many years, and he trusted her to do the right thing.

He cleared away from the Bell as it lifted off. There was a gnawing fear in his mind that the freakish wind would come howling out of the trees then and dash the craft back to the ground like a child's toy. So he held his breath. Up it went, past the treetops, farther, and then he finally exhaled. It was beyond Chalako's reach and turning back toward Atikokan. The *whupping* of the blades faded to an echo and then to nothing at all, returning him to the silence of the forest that he had escaped, if only for a little while.

Barton kneeled down beside Yogi and Boo-Boo, playfully scruffed their ears and patted those bull-like necks. But the dogs seemed to know what was on his mind; their eyes implored him as they fidgeted and pawed the ground nervously. "We've got to go back there," he told them. "Sorry, guys. I don't like it any better than you do. They're probably dead, I know. But if there's a chance . . . We can't just leave 'em there." Of course, the dogs did not need the rationalizing. He gave it voice only to soothe his own nerves. But it did not. His stomach was still rolling with trepidation as he went back into the woods, heading in the direction of the valley, and the dogs begrudgingly prowled along behind him.

When they were deep into the trees, out of sight of the rock field, he stopped. There was a soft whistling sound from back behind them . . . The wind. It was blowing through the clearing, right where he'd been standing only a few minutes before, as if to taunt him and whisper *I am here now and I could have been before. I could have . . .*

Stop it. It's just the breeze.

Yeah, sure it is.

He kept moving, but he just couldn't convince himself to hurry. No matter how bloody or helpless he imagined Tucker and Covey, the image could not breach the wall of wariness he was constructing around himself. But in the end, despite his hesitation, he finally arrived at that valley he'd grown to hate in the short time he'd known it. And as soon as he stepped out onto that ridge once again and he peered into that wooded cleft, a familiar inkling came to him, whether dredged from memory or visited on him anew.

Go into the valley, and you won't come back.

But what about the men, he argued. They're still down there. How do I help them if I can't go down?

No more warnings came in reply. But the original still echoed in his mind, whispering and adamant. *Won't come back. Won't come back . . .*

No sense pushing your luck, he decided. So he tried everything he could to avoid the matter altogether. He stood on
the ridge and yelled the men's names until he was hoarse
from the strain. No response. Then he walked all along the
rim of the valley, this time the side opposite the pictographic
rock with its warped and unsettling figures. He called the
names all along the way, repeated them all the way back.
Still nothing. The echoes of his raspy voice melted away and
left him draped in silence, back where he started, staring
down the rock-and-weed-choked grade.

I can't just leave them down there . . .

. . . you won't come back.

The struggle between rationality and instincts raged within
him, back and forth, as he stood frozen to the spot, staring
unconsciously into the valley. He was there a long time, but
he did not realize it. So total was his concentration. The dogs
could not gain his attention, no matter how much they whined
or nuzzled his leg as if pleading to leave. Not even the drone
of airplane engines, growing louder, could disturb him. They
passed directly overhead but their flight went unheeded; long
after the sounds had faded into the distant corners of the
forest, he still stood there. Mannequinlike. Slack-jawed.
Somehow transfixed by that dread stillness awaiting him down
below . . .

He was still standing there, staring, when a hand abruptly
touched his shoulder.

Barton gave a startled cry in response, and that brought
the dogs to his side with a protective snarl, though they had
not been growling before then. He staggered a few steps
forward, off-balance, then righted himself enough to whirl
on his assailant with the Marlin leveled at the hip. He found
he was staring at nine different figures who had seemingly
stepped from the woods at a moment's notice. The beefy man
in the lead wore an Ontario Provincial Police uniform beneath
his light parka, and the zipper was open just enough to see
the name tag BULTMAN over the breast pocket. There were
two other OPP officers there whose names weren't so ap-

parent, carrying packs and ropes and other rescue gear. There was at least one other familiar face present. Cooper Smith, a rival hunting guide, was there with his much-revered Bouvier des Flandres tracking hounds. It was a hearty breed of dog, noted for a thickly curled pelt that seemed a cross of sheep's wool and Bob Marley's rasta-locks. Smith was having a hard time keeping the big dogs under control. Their skittishness was not due to the elkhounds, who had ceased growling by then. Rather, they were reacting to the geography itself, just as Yogi and Boo-Boo had before them. The other men present, dressed in coveralls and assorted work clothes and wearing yellow hardhats, must have been the timber cutters he'd heard at work earlier in the day. And he was proven correct when he recognized the small man in the rear as Walter the camp boss.

"Are you Davejac?" Officer Bultman asked in a clipped no-nonsense tone.

Barton just gaped at them stupidly. "Where the hell'd you people come from?"

"Where do you think, Tonto?" Cooper Smith snapped, irritated from wrestling with his dogs. "Didn't you hear the float planes? We flew into those lakes over by the bush camp a coupla hours ago. Then we hauled ass to get back to that clearing where Bailey said she dropped you off. You should've stuck around and waited for us, Davejac. We didn't even know which way to go once we got there. Good thing my babies were along to lead us." He reached down and patted one of the big dogs as it tried anxiously to hide behind his legs.

"I don't understand," Barton continued to stammer. "How did you get here so quick, I just don't . . ." He trailed away when he glanced at his watch. Almost five o'clock. He'd been standing there on the ridge, arguing with himself, for nearly three hours.

"Well?" Bultman said impatiently. "Aren't you gonna fill us in on what the hell's gone wrong here?"

Barton told them what he could, recounting the events of

the past few days. He did not color the story to make himself look better, not even when their brows furrowed with disapproval at his admission of staying behind and letting the four go on without him. He didn't skimp on the details because he wasn't so sure he understood them himself, and he was desperately hoping someone might decipher the whole mess and explain it to him. When he finished his story, there was an extended pause as the men just glared at him. Especially Bultman.

"Let me get this straight," the officer said. "You haven't even gone down there to look for them yet?"

Barton shrunk under the accusation in their eyes. "No. But you don't understand . . ."

The searchers ignored him from there on. They went straight to the lip of the valley and started down, all except Cooper Smith, who was still fighting his dogs and cursing their obstreperous behavior. He finally tied their leads to a tree away from the edge where they would at least settle down, and then he went to follow the others. But not before a parting shot in Davejac's direction. "I hope you like sacking groceries at Foodland, Tonto," he sneered. " 'Cause once word gets out, it's the only job you'll get in these parts. I guarantee, you'll not work the woods again." Then he started down the grade, almost falling in his haste to catch up. Barton and the dogs were left alone on the ridge.

An hour passed. Two. He heard no sound in that time, saw no sign of movement through the trees below. The search party had vanished as readily as the Americans before them, and Barton began to feel as if this were a nightmare he would never awaken from.

Boo-Boo was standing a few feet away, near the lip of the grade, which was odd since the dogs usually avoided it like the plague. But then the elkhound stiffened, his eyes searching the trees below, and Barton knew then that he'd seen something. Tucker and Covey? The search party? Or something else . . .

That last notion almost stopped him from looking himself.

He couldn't make out anything at first. Just the same tree-thick void, eminently silent. But then right near the edge where his vision penetrated, a shadow slipped from hiding, moved from one concealing trunk to the next. Another stepped into the open, a different one, and this time it stayed there. Another figure joined it. Another. Coming toward the grade. Barton could make out too few details, so he turned to Boo-Boo, who was watching the scene below with equal persistence. He gauged his pet for a reaction, any sign of danger. Or worse. But the dog did not seem especially alarmed. Only alert.

It's the search party, of course. Lord, what'd you think it would be?

Don't answer that. Just don't even try.

Five of the men came out of the trees and trudged wearily up the slope. Bultman was again in the lead, with Cooper Smith behind him and three of the tree cutters bringing up the rear. The other four in the party, including Walter, were nowhere to be seen.

"Where are the rest of your men?" Barton asked as soon as the OPP officer mounted the ridge.

"The other end of the valley," he replied. "They're covering the forest beyond in case your hunters wandered out of there. We'll circle around the sides with the dogs and rejoin them."

"So . . . you didn't find anything then?"

"Oh, we found things, all right." Bultman motioned to the timber men bringing up the rear, just being pulled to the crest of the slope by Cooper Smith. They carried extra gear—packs, sleeping rolls, a bundled tent—that belonged to all four men. The cutters also carried two rifles, the Weatherby and one Remington, with pieces of a second sticking from the top of one of the backpacks. They even had the flashlight Barton had dropped from the rim of the valley, along with Steven's dirt-stained copy of *The Complete Survivor*. "The gear was strewn all over the place, here and there. But no sign of the men. It's like the place just swallowed 'em up and spit out their belongings.'' Bultman looked back down into the valley, peered into its depths as if to somehow intuit its secrets. "Strange place," he mused darkly, concealing a shiver from all eyes but Davejac's. "There's a lot of downed trees in there. Must've been some storms in this area recently.''

A logical rationale. But the look on his face showed that even he didn't buy it. Not for a minute.

"There's some sump holes down there too,'' Cooper Smith injected as he knelt down and hugged his relieved but still antsy dogs. "I felt the soil shift a couple of times—you gotta watch it around those things, you know. That might be where your hunters disappeared to. And if so, just kiss 'em off, I say. We might never find 'em. This part of the country's shot through with caverns and weak spots in the bedrock. They can go plenty deep too. The only way we're likely to see 'em again is if they hit an underground river or stream. Then they might come afloatin' in one of these lakes sometime. Maybe as long as the spring thaw.''

Bultman took off his cap, ran a wide hand through his stubbly crewcut. "You might be right,'' he sighed, "but we can't take that for granted. Let's eliminate everything above ground before we worry about what's below. And let's just hope those two who were taken out can tell us what happened down there.''

He pointed off along the ridge, in the direction of the big painted rock. "Smith, take two of the men and go that way. We'll take the other flank and should meet up with the others just past the far end. Spread out into the woods and be as thorough as you can.''

Cooper nodded and took his tracking des Flandres by the lead. Once they knew they would not be forced into the valley, the dogs were more than anxious to go along.

Bultman and his one remaining man started 'round the other way, but he stopped and looked back over his shoulder at Davejac. "Are you coming or not?'' he snapped.

"Might as well,'' Barton grumbled, motioning the elkhounds along before him. Though he knew deep down that they would never find Tucker or Covey. A cold tinge of clairvoyance, perhaps. But it was clear and concise and chilled him to the bone.

Sacking groceries at the Foodland . . . Right now it didn't sound too bad at all.

FIFTEEN

AT THE MUNICIPAL AIRPORT IN THUNDER BAY ON A BENCH near the front entrance to the main terminal building, Janet Wilhoit sat with her hastily packed suitcase at her feet. She watched the passersby impatiently, and her mood kept shifting by the minute from irritation to worry and back again. Dammit, she fumed, stubbing out her fourth Vantage in the pedestal ashtray she'd commandeered upon sitting down. They knew what time I'd be arriving. The least they could've done was have someone here to pick me up. I can't sit around wasting time like this, not when Steven needs me.

She checked her watch again. Five more minutes. Then I rent a car and find this Atikokan place myself.

She sat there a while longer and continued to watch the travelers who happened by, those either nervous or thrilled or bored with the notion of air travel. And they all blurred together. They seemed almost transparent, a parade of ghosts before her numb and unblinking eyes, and she began to question whether it was happening at all, whether she was actually there or just dreaming. Please let it be a dream, she wished. A simple nightmare so I can wake up and be back home in my bed, so there was no phone call last night and Steven's fishing trip is still going fine. But this wasn't a dream; the nagging fear in her stomach would not even allow her that momentary illusion. The numbness was just lack of sleep and nothing to eat since last night and a lifetime of worry, all rolled into less than twelve hours.

She caught herself shaking another Vantage from the pack and wasn't surprised, not after last night. She'd been doing so well before that, almost four days without one smoke. Steven would've been so proud. But then came that one phone call, and her resolve melted away in the blink of an eye.

It'll soothe my nerves, she justified. And by God they need some soothing. Besides, if anything's happened to Steven, it won't matter anyway—

No, don't talk like that. I don't want to hear it!

She'd known something bad was going to happen all along—she must have. It explained why she was so livid with Steven that first day, why she couldn't sketch a single illustration without seeing him in it, in danger. It explained why she knew the phone would ring even before it did, how a sudden chill caressed her shoulders and told her it will not be your mother calling or your publisher or a salesman pestering you to change from AT&T to MCI. It will be Steven—no, *about* Steven—and that realization hit her like a fist in the stomach. Her vision swam even before the ringing started and her legs went rubbery and she almost didn't make it across the room to pick it up . . .

The woman's voice over the phone still echoed in her ears. "I'm calling from Atikokan, Ontario . . . there's been some trouble up here . . ."

What kind of trouble, she kept asking herself. This Bailey woman had been so noncommittal, not only then but when Janet called the hospital back to confirm that she would be on the first flight to western Ontario and would arrive first thing in the morning in Thunder Bay. That wasn't too far from Atikokan, the woman told her, and she agreed to meet her there and bring her the rest of the way. But she wouldn't tell her anything else. Not until they were face-to-face.

Be rational, she told herself. What kind of trouble can you get in to on a fishing trip?

A million things. Drowning. Boating accident. A skilletful of bad fish, a hook in the eye—

All right, all right. That's quite enough, thank you. I've got plenty to worry about the way it is. C'mon, Bailey, get your ass in gear!

Someone came through the door then. Janet turned and stood, hoping to find a woman standing there. But it was a large man instead, imposing in jeans and a military field jacket, a ski cap pulled down over his ears. She sat back down, fuming with impatience. This is insane, she decided. I'm not waiting another minute. She fumbled in her purse for the credit cards, prepared to head straight for the rental car desk . . .

"Excuse me. Mrs. Wilhoit?"

It was the tall man she'd seen come in, now standing right beside her, looming over her in fact, and startling her with his closeness. The features were broad and rugged, matching the football-player shoulders, and she would have been a bit nervous in his presence had not her curiosity been so piqued. Because the voice that had called her name was strangely incongruous with the figure before her. And its tone had been one she somehow remembered . . .

The big person took off the ski cap just then and let a cascade of greying hair fall into view. The rugged man was suddenly a homely woman in her late forties, though a warm smile softened those features immeasurably. She seemed almost apologetic upon seeing the other's surprised reaction. "Sorry about that," she said, taking a step back. "Didn't mean to give you a jump. I'm looking for a Janet Wilhoit." The older woman held out a small photograph. "This is you, isn't it?"

Janet didn't have to look hard at the picture. A glance told her that it was one of the wallet-size from the Olan Mills packet. The eight-by-ten sat on the coffee table in her studio.

"You got that from Steven's wallet?"

"Yep. I wanted to be sure I could recognize you. My name is Bailey. We talked on the phone, remember?" She extended a wide hand, one in which Janet's seemed to disappear.

"Do you have any more news for me? Did this Davejac guy ever get back in?"

"Sorry. Barton's still out with the police, searching for the other two men—"

"Tucker and Covey."

"I suppose."

Janet sighed with frustration. "I was hoping I could talk to him. I mean, I don't have the faintest idea of what's going on here. I want to know what's wrong with my husband. I mean, did it happen while they were fishing, or on the way there, or—"

"I can tell you as much as I know, Jan," Bailey said, reaching for the other woman's suitcase. "But we can do that on the way, all right? I expect you're anxious to see your husband."

Janet nodded. "The sooner the better. Just lead the way." The big woman turned and they both headed through the terminal door, out into the late September chill. "Just how long will it take us to get to Atikokan?"

Bailey stopped and put an arm around the smaller woman's shoulders as they walked, like a big sister lending support. "Now I don't want you to get too upset. But Steven's not in Atikokan anymore. They had me fly him here to Thunder Bay last night. We tried to call, but you'd already gone. Right now he's over at Bay General—it's not that far from here."

Janet's eyes widened at her first assumption. "He's that bad?"

"I ain't no doctor, so it wouldn't do for me to be making guesses. But you gotta figure it's natural to move him—I mean, Atikokan's got a nice little hospital, but that's just what it is. Little. He'll get more care over here. Bay General's got some damn good doctors, you know. My daddy got his bypass done there a while back, an' they treated him like a king. So don't you go borrowing trouble, okay?''

They crossed to the short-term parking lot, where the big woman gently herded her toward a wood-paneled station wagon that was not in the best condition. "It's cheap," Bailey said shrugging. "The rental company didn't have many in my size." She ushered Janet to the passenger side, tossed the suitcase into the back, and then climbed in herself. Even the station wagon was a snug fit for her. "So," she said as she slipped the car into gear and headed into the thriving confines of Thunder Bay. "Did you have a nice flight?''

"Look, Ms. Bailey—''

"Now don't start that. It's just Bailey, least to most people.''

"Okay. Bailey. But what I'd really like to talk about is what's been going on up here. You said you knew something about what happened on this fishing trip—''

"Hunting trip, you mean.''

Janet blinked at her, wondering if they were on the same subject or even wavelength. "No, I mean a fishing trip. Steven and the others were coming up here to fish. My husband doesn't hunt. He doesn't even own a rifle.''

"Well, he had one up here," the woman was adamant. "All of them did. You see, that's what Barton does. He's a hunting guide." She saw Janet's doubting expression from the corner of her eye. "It doesn't surprise me, you know. I've seen a lot of hunters come up here over the years, and some of them are just what you'd expect; big beefy guys a tad shy on the intellect side, who go into the woods with a rifle in one hand and a cooler of Molson in the other. But the rest are quite a bit different. There are the serious hunters, the ones who are really good and come up here because they know that Ontario has a lot to offer in the way of game and a good challenge. And then there are the amateurs like your husband. These are guys you'd never expect to see in the woods, and chances are they'd never see themselves there

either. But going hunting, just once, is an irresistible fantasy
for most of them. They go, not necessarily to kill, but to find
out why everybody else is having so much fun.''

"That's not Steven," Janet said flatly.

Bailey shrugged. ''Well, you know him better than I do.''
But the tone in her voice said, *Do you really?*

Janet was beginning to wonder.

"Anyway," the other woman continued, "this is all I
know, wrong or not. Barton took the four of them back into
Chalako Lakes, a hunting parcel between here and Atikokan.
They were gone for three days or thereabouts. Then, yesterday morning, some cutters for Ati-Kut Timber got to their
bush camp along the Chalako boundary just as Barton came
staggering out of the woods. He said he had two men injured,
and two missing. Well, I fly a helicopter for Ati-Kut, and
it's one of the few in the area, so they radioed me and I flew
out and picked Barton up. Then he showed me where he'd
left your husband and that other man. We dipped down and
picked 'em up and I headed back to Atikokan.''

Janet was hanging on her every word. ''You saw them
then,'' she said, ''close up. How did Steven look?''

Bailey weighed her words carefully, not wanting to upset
the younger woman. ''It looked to me like exposure, and
that's the god's honest truth. Maybe they were in shock
too—they were both out, and your husband was a muttering
under his breath the whole time. They were really white and
thin. Maybe hypothermia, though I didn't think it got down
that cold the last several nights. Now, I don't want to scare
you or anything, but the other man, Church, he had blood
all over him.''

Janet went pale.

"Could've been a gunshot wound," Bailey continued.
"But aside from some scratches and bruises, Mr. Wilhoit
was in good shape. Just . . . out of it.'' She looked over,
saw Janet staring out the windshield in a daze. ''Now don't
take everything I say as gospel. I ain't a doctor, remember?
Maybe you should just wait till we get to the hospital.''

"That damn Tucker's to blame," Janet grumbled angrily. "If he hadn't forced them into going . . . God, I always hated that man. Just the way he'd always look at you . . . it really gave you the willies. That prick." She glanced back at Bailey then, an angry glint in her eye. "And this Davejac character. What's his story? What kind of guide is he, anyway? Takes four amateurs into the woods and ends up losing two, and having to airlift the others to the hospital? Does he even have a license to do this, or is he just some bum they picked up along the way?"

The smile slipped from the older woman's face and her soft eyes changed, became defensive. "Whoa down there, girl. That's the wrong tact to be taking. I've known Barton Davejac for a long time, ever since I came to Atikokan. He's damn good at what he does—you won't find anyone better in the woods, period. So just watch where you're throwing your accusations. It can be hard up here, away from the city, and sometimes a man's reputation is all he's got to bank on."

"But the fact is—"

"The fact is that you've got a half-assed account of what went on, something you got secondhand. And until you know the whole story you'd be wise to keep such things to yourself."

Janet didn't respond right away, just brooded angrily in the passenger seat and stared out the window. But she knew the other woman was right. You're not in your element anymore, Jan old girl. This is their world, something you don't know anything about. So until you know your facts, shut the hell up. "Look, maybe I was jumping the gun a little . . ."

Bailey cut her off, pointed through the windshield to the large structure looming just ahead. "This is it," she reported. "Thunder Bay General Hospital."

Janet studied the building as they parked and was relieved to see that this was not some backwater facility but large and thoroughly modern. It was sure to have the latest in medical services and technology. At least Steven would be getting the best care imaginable. Whatever was wrong, they would doubtless know how to handle it.

Doubtless . . .

They went inside and passed the admissions desk with Bailey barely breaking her stride. She must know where she's going, Janet thought. It was a relief that someone did. She walked silently beside the taller woman and tried to remain calm. But that was not easy to do. She'd always been uncomfortable in hospitals, the few times she'd been in them in her life. Only to visit relatives when their conditions were dire. Perhaps that was the reason she automatically associated them with death—it was the only time she saw them.

Just don't think like that. 'Cause this time it's Steven and he's never been sick a day in his life and he's strong, he'll pull through whatever this is.

Her eyes followed the arrows on the floor, the signs that pointed to OUTPATIENT SURGERY and RADIOLOGY and MATERNITY. And the one directly ahead of them that read simply INTENSIVE CARE. Be strong, she counseled, breathing evenly. Don't give up the fight. And she kept saying that as Bailey passed the sign entirely, ignoring the arrows on the floor. False alarm, Janet sighed, and she took some solace in that. At least he's not that bad then.

"Just where are they keeping him?" she asked.

"Upstairs" was all Bailey would advance.

She led them to the elevators, where they boarded alone. And when the doors slid open again on the top floor, the sign directly across the hall read ISOLATIONOBSERVATION. Bailey followed the arrow this time, while Janet's eyes lingered on the words. "Isolation? I don't understand . . ."

"I'm not sure either," the big woman told her in a hushed hospital-approved whisper. "Until I flew up here with him this morning, I'd never been on this floor. From what I overheard, this is where they bring the, uh . . ." she considered her words, "unusual cases."

The words were cold on Janet's ears. The small relief she'd felt downstairs no longer consoled her.

They went through swinging doors to a nurse's station that anchored three hallways, left, right, and straight ahead. There were no visitors or waiting areas in sight. Only orderlies and nurses and attendants, all dressed in antiseptic white and, to a man and woman, wearing rubber gloves and skull caps, with sanitary masks draped around their necks. The nurse behind the station desk, a sturdy-looking young man, looked up just then and fixed them with an annoyed glare. "I'm sorry," he said, motioning them back toward the swinging doors, "you're not supposed to be in this area. Only authorized personnel—"

"It's all right, sonny," Bailey waved him off. "Just tell Dr. Bouvier that Mrs. Wilhoit is here."

The nurse still glared at them, but the name Wilhoit seemed to get a response. He picked up the phone and whispered into the receiver, glancing back at Janet as he did so. Then he abruptly hung up. "The doctor will be right out."

A door opened down the hall and another white figure stepped into view. This man wore a lab coat instead of a uniform, and he walked with the educated swagger of someone in charge. He was short and wore his glasses way down on his nose, all the better to peer over the top questioningly. His well-manicured goatee was as salt-and-pepper as the hair that peeked beneath his scrub cap. He approached the two women directly. "Mrs. Wilhoit?" he said with a light French-Canadian accent. "I'm Dr. Bouvier. I'm handling your husband's case. You didn't think to bring Mr. Wilhoit's medical records by any chance, did you?"

Janet was caught off-guard by the man's direct, no-nonsense approach. "No, I'm sorry. It didn't occur to me—"

"No matter." He nodded curtly. "If you'll leave us your doctor's name and number, we can simply have the papers faxed. Until then, I'd like to ask just a few questions about his medical history . . ."

"Just hold on a minute," Janet finally managed to override the doctor's momentum. "I'm not going to answer one damn question until I get to see my husband and find out what's wrong with him. Is that clear?"

Bouvier looked at her blankly, surprised at such defiance until he remembered that this was not some subordinate to be ordered about. He smiled as ingratiatingly as he could manage. "Of course, you're right," he allowed. "I'm very sorry, and I hope you'll forgive my brusqueness. It's just that the inconsistencies of this case have me a bit preoccupied."

"Inconsistencies?" Janet shivered. "I don't think I like the sound of that."

Dr. Bouvier started back down the hall slowly, motioning them to follow. "I'll be perfectly candid with you. At first it looked to be simple exposure, symptoms of hypothermia just as they thought in Atikokan. Which is perfectly understandable, given they were to my knowledge lost in the wilderness for several days. In fact, the cases seemed so cut-and-dried we weren't quite sure why they were transferred to us. But now that we've had a chance to look your husband and his friend over, I'm afraid I'm just as baffled as everyone else."

Dr. Bouvier stopped at a nurse's cart along the hallway and plucked unopened packages of rubber gloves from a box, as well as sanitary masks and caps like the one he himself wore. He handed them to the women. "Just a precaution," he said and waited until they put the articles on. Then they continued down the hall to the closed door of I/O Room 314. The doctor cast Janet one last glance over his shoulder, then opened the door and ushered them inside.

The room was not large, just enough space for the single bed and the bank of blinking monitors that surrounded it. Janet crept closer to see the figure on the bed, holding her breath against what she would find there. Steven lay on his back with an oxygen tube in his nose and monitor lines running from his arms and body like siphoning hoses. His eyes were closed and his arms at his sides. He would have looked fast asleep if not for the movement of his lips, fluttering slightly in a soundless mutter. His face seemed drawn and exhausted, framed with stringy hair. And, perhaps due to the stark hospital lighting, his skin color appeared pasty and drained. But at least he was whole, in one piece. It was a relief to see him this way; his condition was nowhere near as alarming as her imagination expected.

"Steven?" she whispered through her mask, approaching the bed. She reached out and tenderly touched the side of his face. And even through the rubber gloves she could feel the clammy chill of his skin. "He's a little chilly, isn't he?" she asked the doctor. "Can't you warm him or something?"

"We're trying," Bouvier told her, motioning to the heating blankets covering him. "But that's just the problem. Nothing seems to do any good. You see, with normal cases of hypothermia, the skin temperature falls drastically, especially in the limbs farthest from the heart. But in your husband's case, his core temperature—the heart, the lungs, the chest cavity—appears to be colder than his skin. And that just isn't supposed to happen. We have tests planned for the rest of the day, but at this stage, we're all a bit baffled."

"How's the other guy?" Bailey asked.

"Mr. Church is semiconscious, at least. But in many ways, his condition seems even worse. Would you like to see him?"

"Yes, of course," Janet replied. She sat down on the edge of the bed next to her husband. "I'll be right back, sweetheart. Okay?" She leaned over and kissed his cheek through her mask, felt her lips tingle at the cold. "I love you," she whispered into his ear.

If he heard her, he showed no sign. He just continued to mumble incoherently.

The women followed Dr. Bouvier back into the hallway, and there Bailey took Janet's arm to offer support. "How're you doing, kiddo?"

"I really don't know," she said honestly. "Ask me again once this all sinks in."

"Ladies," the doctor motioned them toward another door

at the end of the hall. "This way, if you please." He held it open, let them slip past him into a room that was identical to Steven's. Right down to the monitoring equipment and bed, very nearly to the figure upon it. The man there was sitting almost upright, propped by the elevated angle of the bed, but his head hung forward onto his chest as if too heavy to hold erect. He was covered with a heating blanket that he'd mostly pushed away, so they could see heavy bandages around his shoulder and peeking out from beneath his hospital gown. They couldn't see his face, though, only the tangle of hair that seemed every bit as disheveled as Steven's had.

"Do you know him, Mrs. Wilhoit?" Bouvier asked.

Janet stepped closer, tried to get a better look. "I'm not sure. I might have seen him around the plant where my husband works . . . But the name doesn't ring a bell. Can I speak to him?"

"By all means. If you can get anywhere with him, that would be a start. So far, since he woke up, he's been so disoriented he's barely uttered two words."

Janet crept to the edge of the bed. "Mr. Church?" No response. "I'm Janet Wilhoit, Steven's wife? Could you tell me what happened to you out there? I've got to know . . ." She reached over, took his limp hand in both of hers, and immediately dropped it again. It was even colder than her husband's had been. "Please, Mr. Church. What happened?"

The man's head bobbed a bit, then slowly rose to look at her. And for a moment Janet thought she had indeed seen Andy Church before, the short chubby man who'd argued with his wife at Tucker's office party last year. But then the impression quickly faded. For this could not possibly have been that man. This face was not fleshy at all but drawn, harrowed enough to border on the skeletal. The cheekbones and brow were prominent because of it, and the sockets so sunken that the eyes seemed to bulge and stare. Judging by his length in the bed, this Church was much too tall and much too thin to be the man she remembered.

Andy looked at her with reddened, watery eyes. But there was no such hint of emotion in the slack, white countenance. He opened his mouth and whispered something, and she had to lean even closer to hear.

His breath was cold against her ear. "I'm . . . hungry . . ."

"I'll tell the doctor to get you something," she assured him. "But what happened to you and Steven? You have to tell me."

The dull, wet stare did not change. "Hungry . . ."

The man's monotone grated on her ears, the single-mindedness of it, and suddenly she was uncomfortable being so close to him. Hearing his whispers. Having touched him. She quickly backed away from him and rejoined Bailey and the doctor at the foot of the bed. Andy's rheumy eyes followed her without expression or content. He just stared and mouthed the same message silently.

"What did he say?" Bouvier wanted to know.

"Get him something to eat," a shaken Janet replied. Then without another word or a look back at the stuporous, unsettling patient, she jerked open the door and hurried back into the hall.

Bailey came out right after her, lines of concern etched in that broad face. "Are you okay, Jan? What's wrong?"

"Everything," the younger woman said, fighting back the sobs that were suddenly so close to the surface. For that dull monotone still followed her, still haunted her. Only now, in her own mind, it wasn't Andy Church's voice anymore. It was her husband's.

SIXTEEN

"WIND   WIND

Steven's barely audible mumbling had begun to wear on Janet's nerves, which were already frayed beyond her imaginings. If only he'd say something else, she wished. If only he'd give some sign, something to show that he knows I'm here.

She sat beside his bed and squeezed his hand again as if to signal him of her presence. He did not squeeze back, but she kept hold of him nonetheless, just as she had for the past three hours since they brought him back from the last battery of tests. She had let go of him only once since then, to rub the feeling back into her numbed hand and to fish the leather gloves from her coat pocket. She needed them. His hands were so cold . . .

Just try not to think about it.

If only Bailey hadn't flown back to Atikokan to help search for the other two men. She could've used her support right then. For at least while she was there, Janet didn't feel quite so alone. The big woman had not only been good company and a shoulder to cry on, but she gave Janet a welcome ear as well, let her vent her fears and frustrations. And it sure felt good to do that. But now with Bailey gone, even at Steven's side she felt adrift, isolated. And afraid.

Dr. Bouvier and his staff had been little help to her so far. If they knew something, they weren't telling. Of course, they hadn't had very much time to analyze the results of all the tests, and there were so many of them. But her suspicions were beginning to win out. At first the doctor had allowed her inside Steven's room for only short visits, "At least until we know what we're dealing with," he'd explained. But when they brought her husband back the final time, the nurse had instructions that Janet could stay with him as long as she wanted. What had changed Bouvier's mind? she wondered. Do they know it's safe now, that I'm not being exposed to anything? Or is it worse than they thought? Are they giving me time with him because there's not that much left?

Stop borrowing trouble, she chastised herself. Dr. Bouvier doesn't look like one who'd worry about sparing your feelings. He's too cool and tactless for that. He wouldn't withhold any information. Not unless he didn't know himself.

Her eyes wandered to the door across from the bed, then above it to the small closed-circuit video camera she had failed to notice on her earlier visits to the room. It was trained on the bed, on Steven and her as well. And she wagered that the doctor was watching them right now. "I hope you're being straight with me," she said into the lens.

The camera continued to stare and gave no reply. At least not directly.

Within a few minutes, whether from coincidence or not, the door opened and an attractive, bespectacled face peeked into the room, strands of feathery blond hair poking from beneath her scrub cap. Susan Railsback was one of the friendlier members of the nursing staff who Janet had met since arriving. She was efficient and knowledgeable and did her job well. But it was her cheeriness and warmth, as opposed to Bouvier's aloof professionalism, that left an indelible impression. She not only had a quick reassuring smile for everyone, just as she wore now, but she treated Steven well. She was gentle and talked to him in a soothing voice, even if he didn't respond. Just that little thing gave her high marks with Janet.

"I thought you might like a cup of coffee," she said, slipping into the room with a steamy Styrofoam cup from the nurse's lounge. "Do you need cream or sugar?"

"Black's fine," Janet said with a smile. "Thanks." She took the cup with one hand while keeping hold of Steven's with the other, then wondered how she would get the plastic lid off the cup. Finally Nurse Railsback consented to remove it for her. "Sorry about that." Janet blushed. She held up Steven's pale hand. "It's kinda silly, I guess. It's just that . . . sometimes I feel like if I let him go, I won't get him back."

"It's not silly at all." Susan's smile broadened. "In fact, I think it's kinda sweet. I'd give my eyeteeth to love someone like that. I keep my fingers crossed, you know. So far nothing's worked out, but I'll keep trying." She looked over at Steven. "No change, huh?"

Janet just shook her head wearily. "What about the tests? Has the doctor found out anything yet?"

"Sorry," the nurse was very sympathetic. "We haven't heard anything about either your husband or his friend. But I promise, as soon as we do, I'll come tell you myself. Even if I have to knock the doctor down to get here. Okay?"

Janet laughed with her. Then the mention of Steven's "friend" piqued her curiosity. "How is Mr. Church doing?"

Nurse Railsback's normally bright features darkened somewhat, as if a cloud had just passed before the sun. "Not much change, I'm afraid. Though he is acting a little odd at times. He keeps telling us he's hungry. But every time we've tried to feed him, he just spits it back out. We even put an intravenous tube in him, but he jerked it loose." She seemed uncomfortable just talking about it. "And the way he looks at you, his eyes . . . I hate to say it, but he really gives me the creeps." She glanced over at Steven then, just for an instant, all pale and stricken in his bed. And the look of apprehension did not leave her face. "Well, I'd better get back to my station," she said abruptly, turning toward the door. "We're setting a room up down the hall for you to stay in tonight. It's not being used right now, so . . . Just give me a yell when you want to see it.''

"I will. And thanks for the coffee.''

"My pleasure.'' Then the nurse was out the door and into the hall, leaving Janet alone with her husband and even more disturbed than before.

The expression on Susan's face . . . It was still etched into Janet's mind, that look of dread. Of expectation. She had looked at Steven, but she was really seeing Andy Church and his glassy eyes, hearing his raspy, toneless voice . . .

It was the same reason Janet had avoided the bathroom mirror all day long. For she knew her reflection would be wearing that same hurtful expression.

She leaned over and laid her head on Steven's barely rising chest, unmindful of the warmth of the heating blankets and the cold beneath. "You won't be like that, will you, darling?'' she asked tearfully. "You can't leave me, Steve. Promise me you won't leave. 'Cause I don't know what I'd do then.''

Steven would have comforted her had he been able. He would have held her close and stroked her hair and back, whispered that everything would be all right. But unfortunately her words never reached him. Nor did he feel the touch of her hand or even know of her presence. For Steven Wilhoit was imprisoned deep within himself, lost in a miasma of fog and fear that seemed to stretch on forever. He didn't know what had happened to him or where he was or how long he'd been there. The only important thing was, no matter how far he'd staggered blindly or how hard he screamed, no one came to help him.

Hinman's *Complete Survivor* came back to him then, words that his eyes had scanned once unconsciously and stored for future reference. *If you get lost, just don't panic. Stay calm. And if you can, backtrack to the place where you took your wrong turn . . .*

That's it, he decided. If you're ever to find your way out of this place, first remember how you found your way in.

He closed his eyes to the void around him and retraced his movements. He thought back to the instant that his world went wrong, when his ears stung with the wailing . . .

. . . of the wind as it whipped around him, swirling dirt and leaves into his eyes, gagging him with its debris. He was in the valley again, in the clearing, his head down to the fury of the phantom zephyr that had sprung from the forest around them. Andy Church was there beside him, sputtering and shielding his face from the assault.

And then . . . Just as suddenly as it came, the wind was gone. It sailed on past them, through the clearing, and disappeared into the trees on the other side. The swirling leaves quickly settled in its wake and the sway of the tree limbs eased. Even the echo of its rustling passage died away, leaving the forest still again.

"What the hell . . ." Church stammered, wide-eyed and blinking like a punch-drunk fighter. A trickle of blood ran down his left temple where a sharp stick had grazed him.

Steven mumbled some kind of response as he wandered through the shattered timber of the clearing in a halfhearted attempt to follow the mysterious gale. He was still numbed by its startling appearance and equally abrupt departure, and his flesh still tingled with its lingering chill. And though it had seemed to last but a moment, he now questioned just how long he had stood there, head bowed to the sudden storm. Because something seemed different around them. Something had changed . . .

. . . Tucker's pale face and lunatic smile, posing for a snapshot with Paul Covey's head . . .

Jesus! He jumped back a step as if avoiding an attack, half covering his eyes from seeing the crazy old man or his trophy again. But even as he did so, he knew that was what had changed. He looked for Elton Tucker then, who had been standing not six feet away. But the old man wasn't there. Paul Covey's twisted and butchered body had disappeared as well, as readily as his killer. There was not even a dark stain to the soil where he'd lain gutted and steaming in the crisp air.

If you really saw them, that is . . .

Steven's momentary doubt was alleviated when Andy Church finally cleared his head and stalked over, gaping at the ground with equal puzzlement. He even wiped at the soil and leaves with his boot. "Now, dammit, this ain't right," he muttered in frustration. "I know what I saw. You saw it, didn't you? Tucker was sitting right there . . ."

". . . and holding Paul's head," Steven finished. "Yeah, I saw it too."

"Then where'd he go? I didn't take my eyes off him for more than a minute, maybe two. How'd he get out of here so fast?" The younger man moved around the immediate area, bent over, inspecting the soil. "No drag marks. That means he had to pick Covey up, all six feet plus, and pack him out of here. Tucker's stout, but he's not that strong."

"He's crazy, you know," Steven offered in shrugged explanation. "Sometimes crazy people can have superhuman strength—"

Church flared angrily. "This isn't just about some lunatic, Steve. There's something else here. Look, he didn't make those crashing noises, did he? No, he was with us then. And he couldn't have twisted Paul's head off like that, couldn't have thrown Paul's rifle back at us. Not that high, not that hard. He didn't push these trees over, did he? And don't you dare say it was the wind or I'll stomp a mud hole in your ass here and now. That gust was strong but it didn't budge the two of us. So how could it knock down a whole stand of trees? If it could, hell, why didn't it level a whole swath through here instead of just this little area? C'mon, man. Can't you see that it's this whole place? The whole valley's wrong. No animals, no life. No way out. First it took Tucker and then Covey, and we're next. Unless we do something about it."

"What do you suggest?"

"I say we get to hell out of here, that's what."

Steven laughed at that, sounding nervous and brittle in the silence. "Brilliant. Just brilliant. Tell me, Andy, what the hell do you think we've been trying to do all day, huh?"

"You got a better plan?"

Steven glared at him, then shook his head wearily. "I don't have any plan. None. I don't even know what the fuck is going on here." He turned away and stalked across the clearing, kicking the nearest stump in impotent rage. What the hell *do* we do? he wondered. Is there a way out? Are we trapped here, destined to go mad like the old man or be field-dressed like an animal? What the hell is happening!

In his desperation for answers, he unconsciously slipped Hinman's guide from his coat pocket and was leafing through the pages, as if hoping the solution would just jump out at him. Then he realized what he was doing and almost smiled at the irony. Almost. "Good job, Wilhoit," he chastised himself. "We've got a madman on the loose and a dead body that's disappeared and you expect to find the answer in *a fucking book?!* " With a growl he hurled the *Complete Survivor* as far into the trees as he could. When his anger was spent, at least for the moment, he turned back to Church. "You're right," he said. "We've got to get out of here. Or at least keep trying."

Andy nodded, then motioned to the seeming hole in the forest overhead, where they could see the perpetual mist thinning slowly and actually glimpsed bare sky. It was already a deep shade of red, darkening in hue all the time. "It'll be night soon," he said in a somber tone. "Let's hurry."

Summoning what courage they could scrape together, the two men walked back into the forest, Steven leading the way. And they found that night had already settled among the trees. They could barely see through the gloom and needed their flashlights to show the way. The bright beams were a mixed blessing. They illuminated the way directly ahead but somehow the rest of the forest seemed darker for it.

Steven could feel his shoulder and neck muscles bunching up, knotting from the tension that slowly grew within him.

The claustrophobia was coming on strong. His breath grew quick and raspy like a man walking into deeper and deeper water. The night closed in around them; not only from the sides, but from above as well, where the dense limbs and late-year foliage cheated them of the stars. He did see slivers of moonlight here and there, filtering to the forest floor like long strands of web that danced with St. Elmo's Fire. But they were few and far between. And the water was getting deeper all the time.

They walked for hours, or at least it seemed like it. Steven felt bone-tired, and his breath danced in a ghostly cloud between his eyes and the flashlight's beam, reminding him just how cold the night had become. He wanted to stop and rest; no, he wanted to do more than that. Pitch the tent and climb into the sleeping bag and hide your head, wish all of this away for a few hours. Just a few miserable hours . . .

Tucker's leering countenance flashed across his mind, the demented smile framed in Covey's blood. "I'm hungry . . . I'm hungry . . ."

A shiver coursed through him, one not born of the cold, and it chased any thoughts of resting from his mind.

Another hour passed. Maybe two. He did not bother checking his watch, for he knew it would just discourage him. Besides, he wasn't so sure that time meant anything in this place. More and more he was coming to accept Andy's impression of the valley, a bad place where the rules of logic held little sway, where direction and distance were ever vacillating . . .

A rustling sound. Andy reached for Steven's shoulder, pulled him to a stop. "What was that?"

"I didn't hear anything," Wilhoit lied. "Keep moving." He started off again, forcing the hesitant man to follow, and didn't tell him what the sound had actually been. Steven's foot had kicked something in the leaves, knocked it sliding across the ground. And he didn't have to shine the flashlight on it to know what it was. He could tell by the touch and the sound, the way it slid, that it was Hinman's *Complete*

Survivor. He'd thrown it away hours ago, yet here it was. Irrefutable proof that they had been walking in circles.

The Steven Wilhoit of a few days past, even a few hours, might have given up there, sank to his knees at the realization and surrendered just as Tucker had. But this Steven fought back. He got angry. Because he finally realized that these were not his mistakes. There was another player besides him in this game of solitaire, stacking the cards against him at every turn. Fuck you, he said silently, knowing full well that his opponent out there in the darkness heard him. You won't beat me. You won't.

A gunshot tore open the silence, so close that his ears rang with echoes of their own. He turned to see Andy Church standing a few feet back, his rifle shouldered and smoking, the muzzle pointed off into the trees to his right. Steven shone his flashlight on the younger man and saw a hard grin of satisfaction on his face. "I got the bastard," he said with a nod. "I got him."

"What are you talking about?"

"It was Tucker." He pointed back through the underbrush with his own flashlight. "I saw him standing back there, watching us. His face was in a slip of moonlight right over by that tree. It almost glowed . . . He was smiling." The thought brought a chill, but it couldn't override his triumph. "I got him. I know I did. Dead fucking center." He worked the bolt to chamber another round, then waded into the thorny brake. Steven went right behind him.

The brier bushes were dense there, thick with shadows, but it only slowed them down a little. Church had a determined stride, and his eyes seemed to be fixed on something ahead that Steven was only beginning to make out—a fine thread of silvered moonlight, piercing the dark ceiling above and descending at an angle, pinpointing the roots of the diseased old cedar directly ahead. They went right to it, shined their flashlights in every direction. But Tucker was not there.

"I just don't get it," Andy complained. "I know I hit him. I even saw him jerk . . ."

Steven swept his flashlight along the ground, stopped when the light glared off something in the nearest brier bush. He reached out with the Weatherby's barrel and pulled the limbs away . . . and gasped.

Andy came over immediately. There in the bright beam of both their flashlights he found a human arm, hanging suspended by the thorny branches of the bush. It was complete, from the shoulder socket down, and still sheathed in the grey nylon of a coat sleeve. The shoulder end was a mass of ravels and ligaments and leaking Fiberfill, and the bony ball joint extended just far enough beyond to be recognized. The hand itself was fish pale, almost glowing in the glare of their lights, and the rigored fingers were curled into a claw. It was a left arm. It had a wristwatch. There was no blood.

"That isn't Tucker's," Church said flatly. "He had a blue parka, remember?"

Steven swallowed hard. "Covey's was grey."

The younger man just nodded as he fought back his revulsion and leaned over the bush for a closer look. Steven did the same. But almost immediately he wished he hadn't.

The fingers were not all curled and rigid. Some weren't even there. The ring finger and pinkie were missing down to the second knuckle, and most of the thumb. But the bone of the latter remained, a rigid white stick that jutted from the palm. And even in the D-cell glow they could see the small notches set deep into that bone. Tooth marks. There was more flesh missing from the blade of the hand, another chunk from the wrist, just beneath the sleeve. Steven reached in, pinched the nylon, and pulled that sleeve back. He found it had already been ripped back on both sides like the peel on a banana, and pulling it revealed the long empty pits in the forearm where the muscle had been stripped away.

"Fuck me blind" was all Andy would say.

They backed away from the bush, each wearing a look of utter horror. *Hungry, hungry* was all that played in Steven's mind, but he refused to validate those fears. "Scavengers," he tried to fight it. "Just animals. They've been at it, they've—"

"Animals my ass," Church whispered. "There ain't any animals here. That was Tucker, man. I saw him. I shot him. And he dropped that . . . that . . ." He just pointed back toward the bush. "Jesus, did you see what he's doing? He's . . . oh, God . . ." His throat began to undulate at the notion. He leaned against the cedar, racked with the heaves but dredging only bile.

Steven stayed in control of himself, but only because he had to. His revulsion was tempered with the knowledge that the monster that did this, that had been Tucker, was still somewhere out there. Watching them. Waiting for them.

Hungry, hungry . . .

"Let's go, Andy," he said, putting a hand on the gasping man's shoulder. When Church stayed there, still retching after there was nothing left to give, Steven barked at him. "Dammit, let's move already!" He caught Andy's collar and pulled him around, dragged him back through the brier thicket. The younger man fought at first, but as they put some distance between themselves and the last piece of Paul Covey, his gagging subsided and he moved along under his own power.

"Get me out of here, okay?" he muttered under his breath. His voice quivered, almost sobbing. "I want to go home."

"Just hold on, Andy," Steven whispered over his shoulder. "We'll get out. I've got a plan."

They wended their way through the woods at a dead run now, at least as much as their fatigued bodies could manage. Church especially was having a rough time of it as his weight and lack of conditioning came to bear. He wheezed and sucked at the air like a dying man, winced as the night chill cut his lungs like a knife. But he didn't stop. He stayed as close to his partner as possible. Steven led the way, his flashlight beam dancing low to the ground to spot any fallen limbs or tangles that might trip them and break a leg. And he kept the Weatherby always ready. For with each twist and turn, each new shred of forest they came upon, he expected his beam to flash across the death-white countenance of Elton Tucker. He could see it now in his mind's eye, just as Andy described, only now he was wearing a bib around his neck, a knife and fork in each hand.

Hungry. Hungry.

"Steve—" Church called from behind him, just before a thud reached his ears. He turned with the rifle leveled, so smoothly and reflexively that it seemed an extension of himself. But there was no target to find. The younger man had simply tripped and now lay facedown in the leaves, not even able to budge beneath the pack on his back. "I can't make it," he sobbed into the soil. "I can't, I just can't . . ."

Wilhoit went back to the man's side, shucked off his own pack and bedroll before helping Church off with his. He cast them both aside. "Forget it, friend," he pulled the man to his feet. "You're going if I have to carry you. Got that?"

Andy wiped the tears from his eyes. "What about the packs . . ."

"Who needs them? We aren't camping anymore. Either we get out of here tonight, or we die trying. Right?"

Church forced a smile. "Right." They started their trek again, their run little more than an agonized jog now. Andy fell into second place, content to let Steven lead again. "I hope this plan of yours is a good one," he called after him.

Wilhoit nodded, gave him a thumbs-up over his shoulder. But inside he was asking himself the same question. Just how much of a plan is this?

Maybe none at all, he admitted. But it was the only thing he could think of.

He stopped, surveyed the landscape ahead with his flashlight. On one side the ground was open between the trees, not too overgrown, and would be easy to traverse. The other way was clogged with brambles and tanglevine, stretching down into a shallow ravine and up the other side. None too inviting, he decided. Which is precisely how it was supposed to look. In an entire day's worth of walking, round and round in that godforsaken place, he had failed to notice,

until now at least, how the landscape had been tailored to
their needs. No matter where they went in the valley, there
was always at least one path laid out for them. One avenue
where the underbrush was manageable and the stickers less
dense, where the walking would be easier. And they wanted
easy, they needed it. They weren't woodsmen. They couldn't
be expected to blaze their own way. So they took the path
of least resistance every time. Took the bait like four starving
fish.

But even a fish could wise up.

He looked the two paths over again, and without another
thought he took the more difficult of the two. Church watched
him plunge into the thicket and down the slope of the ravine.
"What the hell are you doing?" he called.

"Just come on. Trust me, okay?"

Andy was too tired to argue. He just shrugged and followed
along, fighting the underbrush to do so.

Steven repeated his decision at every turn, taking the hard
road over the easy, no matter how many fallen trees and
heavy brakes the geography put in their way. The going was
noticeably slower, more arduous, but at least he finally felt
in control. They weren't being led around anymore like rats
in a laboratory maze.

Still, he couldn't elude his own doubts. They haunted his
every move. What if it (whatever *it* is) realizes what you're
doing? What if it changes things and the easy ways are the
right ways after all, and you're just plunging deeper and
deeper into the valley . . .

Just shut up and keep moving.

He batted aside yet another groping branch and stepped
through the overgrowth, thrusting his flashlight out to illuminate the way. But it wasn't necessary; the ground directly
ahead shone bright and silver in the unobstructed moonlight.
The trees parted here and open ground lay before them, oddly
familiar but not from that vantage point . . . Then his eyes
reached to the end of the open corridor and saw the slope,

the weedy path of loose shale that he had traversed just once before.

He stood there, blinking his eyes, hoping that the sight wouldn't betray him and disappear. "We're out," he whispered as Church came lumbering through the trees, where he too froze at the sight. "We're really out! I don't believe it." He turned and grabbed the still-stunned Andy by the arm. "Come on!" he yelled, pulling him down the narrow clearing toward the grade.

Andy staggered at first, almost pulled the both of them off their feet. Then Steven's own footing became fouled. It was hard to walk as the soil beneath them began to shift—

Oh, Lord, he suddenly realized as he looked around hurriedly. He saw that they were standing in the shallow depression he'd first noticed upon entering the valley. The same circular patch he'd suspected of being a sucking place even then. And now he was proven right; the dirt and leaves beneath them were moving inexorably toward the middle, pulling them along . . .

"Move!" he screamed, forcing Church out ahead of him and slinging him as far as he could. Then he began to wade through the moving soil, scrabbling for purchase where there was none, even as he started to sink.

"Steven! Grab hold!" It was Andy—he had made it to the edge of the depression and was reaching back with his rifle, the barrel pointed directly at Wilhoit's chest. It was almost within reach . . . a little closer . . . Steven made one desperate lunge, for one was all he would have, and his hand just missed it by a fraction of an inch. But somehow he caught the long dangling loop of the shoulder strap and he held tight, almost pulling Church off his feet. Andy was a stout man, though, and he lowered his weight and leaned backward like the anchor on a tug-of-war, and Steven's sinking halted. Slowly then Andy started to back away, step by step, and towed Wilhoit from the sump hole.

By the time Steven reached the edge, covered with dirt

and leaves and the both of them exhausted from the struggle, he was laughing out loud, uncontrollably. "Fuck you!" he yelled to the forest, to the valley around them. "That was your last chance. The last! And we won!"

"Amen," Andy sighed and dropped onto his back, his chest heaving with the strain of unconditioned lungs.

Steven staggered over to where the other man lay, tried to pull him to his feet. "C'mon, get up," he urged wearily. "We're this close, we can't stop now." But Church was too exhausted. He wouldn't budge.

"Just . . . give me a minute. Let me get my breath . . ."

Steven sympathized; his own legs were numb, his arms leaden. And the Weatherby felt like it weighed a hundred pounds. But he had carried it so long now that it seemed grafted to his hands and he didn't consider putting it down. "Okay," he sighed. "You rest. I'll take a look." He stepped past the wheezing man and wandered down the clearing, testing the soil with a boot before committing his weight to each step. Soon he drew to the foot of the slope, where he looked up into the cold clear sky and saw the stars out in mass to greet their return. "Davejac!" he yelled as loud as he could muster. "We could use a hand down here! Did you hear me? Davejac!"

He waited for an answer. Even a dog's mewl would have been comforting, anything to tell him the guide was still present. But nothing came. "Probably went to get help," he guessed, turning back to Church. "Looks like we'll have to make this climb on our own. Are you up to it?"

"I'll do my damnedest," Andy groaned, climbing to his feet with pained slowness. "Anything to be rid of this place." He started forward on wobbily legs. And that's when the figure came out of the trees to the right and fell into line behind him.

Steven's eyes widened and his scrotum shrank at the sight. He opened his mouth to call a warning but his tongue seemed suddenly twice its normal size and jammed his throat and allowed neither words nor breath to pass. The thing drawing up behind Andy Church was at least seven feet tall and as thin as a rail, like a stick figure suddenly come to life. The blue parka and L. L. Bean trousers were now too short but still baggy on its scarecrow frame. Those familiar clothes should have been a giveaway, would have if Steven hadn't been so paralyzed by the stark, harrowing features that loomed above them. The face was bleach white and skeletal, the brow heavy, the cheekbones jutting. And the eyes . . . they were glazed and every bit as pale as the surrounding flesh. It no longer looked like Elton Tucker or even a man at all.

Steven staggered a step or two on unwilling legs, trying to warn his unsuspecting partner. But "Watch out!" was all he could manage before the gangly creature overtook Andy Church.

A long white arm, extending well beyond the elastic cuff of its coat sleeve, reached out and grabbed Andy by the back of the collar. The man was jerked off the ground as if he weighed nothing, shaken until the rifle fell from his hand and his senses were scrambled. Then the creature turned him around and held him right before its face, a cold breath away, and Andy had his first look at his attacker. He reacted naturally; his frame went rigid with shock, and he let out a soft mewl of abject terror. But then his natural survival instincts must have taken over. He began to thrash about, cursing and striking out at his attacker. His punches had little effect on the long, angular face before him. It didn't even blink when he jammed his thumbs into its eyes; they remained open beneath his fingertips, all hard and wet like ice cubes. That was when Church began to cry out for help.

Steven was fumbling with his rifle, each finger suddenly two inches wide and incapable of feeling. He seemed barely able to force one into the trigger guard as he raised the Weatherby to his shoulder. "Drop him!" he yelled, but the command came out a frightened whine.

Tucker, or what had been Tucker, looked over at him, at the rifle bore pointed its way, and those facial features did not move. But behind that facade, like looking through a thin rubber mask, Steven was sure he saw another expression. A smile behind an unmoving mouth, spreading farther than any human smile ever could. All the way to each ear. Then the creature looked back at Church, and the mouth finally opened. And kept opening. It went so wide that the corners cracked and split, and the fissure ran back through each cheek all the way to the jaw hinge. The big toothy yawn went just beyond ninety degrees before its owner pulled the screaming Andy to it and bit into his shoulder, through layers of nylon and flannel and into the flesh beneath.

Steven's finger jerked on the trigger, and his shoulder jolted with the recoil. The big gun's report roared through the small clearing, ricocheting back and forth, but he didn't hear it. He only saw the impact on Tucker's chest as the round shoved it backward, jarring Andy from its grasp. The young man fell to the ground, bleeding, squirming in agony. But the Tucker creature had not gone down. It still stood there, looming over him, trailing bits of flesh and clothing from its torn jaws.

Steven chambered another round and fired. This one caught the wraithlike Tucker just as flush as before, staggered it another two steps back. It finally turned and looked at Steven then with those hard, wet eyes, and even in its slack expression he could read the vehemence there. It made him fire again, pushing it back farther. And again, farther still. But it wasn't going down.

He worked the bolt, shouldered the weapon. And clicked on an empty chamber.

His heart jumped up into his throat as he fumbled with the rifle, opened the action, and dug at his hunting vest for more shells, not even realizing that the ammunition there had been meant for his Remington and wouldn't function in this gun. But it wouldn't have mattered anyway. The Tucker thing was standing not that far away, and it could be across the clearing and on him before he loaded a single round. He kept his eyes on the creature and saw that same hidden smile as before, like a leering skull behind a few millimeters of placid flesh. It lifted a long leg, started toward him . . .

And almost fell. The thing wavered a moment, off-balance, then looked down to see its own feet vanishing into the shifting soil. It had backed into the sucking place.

What was left of Tucker's face showed utter shock, then a cold rage as it roared *"No!"* It thrashed about impotently, lost its balance and fell to its knees, and sank that much faster. *"No no no no . . ."* it wailed as it was pulled toward the middle, caught in the vortex of the hole. It seemed to slide down into the dirt in one quick gulp, until only that pale face and one gibbonous white arm remained. It was still reaching for Steven, groping for him, when the earth swallowed it whole. The dirt continued to pour down atop it for a minute or so. Then the soil settled and was still once again.

Steven was too stunned to move. But he finally willed himself to Church's side. The younger man's face was contorted by pain, his teeth chattering as he clutched at his torn shoulder. The blood that stained his face and chest looked black as oil in the moonlight. "Hold on, buddy," Steven tried to sound soothing. "We'll get you out of here. Just hold on." Andy didn't say a word, just groaned softly as Steven pulled him to his feet and drapped the man's one good arm over his shoulder. They hurried for the slope then, with Wilhoit intent on carrying him all the way if he had to.

From the woods behind them, from the depths of the valley, came a soft sound. Like a guttural whisper, devoid of all inflection or substance. "Ste-ven," it called.

Wilhoit froze. He knew there was no one left to be calling him, that Covey was dead and Tucker was entombed and Church was right there beside him. No one was left.

"Ste-ven . . ."

. . . *go to sleep, boys and girls, or you'll hear the windigo call your name* . . .

"Stop it," he whispered, unable to cover his ears while holding Andy erect. *"Stop it!"*

The voice or whatever it was trailed off. Silence resettled, at least for a moment. And then the crashing sounds started. It was the same as before, the snapping of heavy limbs, the groan of toppling timber. And it was coming this way.

Oh, God. Oh, God . . .

He started up the slope three times only to slide back after a few steps, undone by the loose shale and the imbalance of Church's weight. But the noises from the woods were growing. He couldn't stop. On his fourth attempt he gathered his momentum and hoisted the both of them up almost ten feet to a slight ledge where he could at least rest Andy against a rocky outcropping.

Another tree shattered against the ground, this time close enough that the reverberations broke into the long clearing and reached his ears fresh. It's coming, dammit. Hurry up.

He made it another five feet, pulled Andy after him, then pushed the heavy man up to the next small ledge he could find.

Church was no longer trying to climb. He had curled into a ball and now sobbed helplessly. "Dammit, Andy!" Steven cursed. "Something's coming! We've got to get out of here, so start climbing, damn you! Or I'll drop you right here!" He even slapped the younger man to bring him around. But it did nothing. And meanwhile the sounds of ruination continued to build, growing ever nearer like the coming of a storm.

The crest of the slope was not far above them, twenty feet, no more. Move, damn you . . .

Crash! The trees were torn aside behind them as Steven felt the air displaced by something there, something huge, monstrous . . . He froze then. For he knew without turning that whatever-it-was stood right at the edge of the clearing now.

Don't look, he cautioned himself. There was nothing to gain from looking. He already knew of its size and he could feel the evil emanating from it as well, even across the narrow stretch of open ground. The air had turned frigid in just a few moments; the chill pierced him and left small ghosts of steam to dance before his eyes, the product of his own nervous panting. And worst of all, it seemed to freeze him to the spot. Steven couldn't move.

All was still. The two men were motionless more than halfway up the slope. Steven eyed their objective so close at hand and tried to will his legs to move, his arms to scrabble for purchase and drag them the rest of the way. But his limbs would not respond. It was as if his fear had shut down the nerve endings, shorted them out and left him quivering and useless . . .

Hungry. Hungry . . .

The warped image of Tucker flashed through his mind then, over and over like a stuttering old kinescope. But then the picture abruptly caught and held, and he saw that the face was different now. It was just as long and white and skeletal, the eyes still flat and rheumy. But this time he was looking at himself.

One fear overrode another. He began to clamber up the slope once more, dragging the stuporous Church with him. And as soon as he moved, the earth seemed to shake with a massive footfall. Another. Another. They echoed down the clearing toward him. And then a blood-chilling howl . . .

He gritted his teeth, fighting the blind panic that bubbled up from the depths of his soul. "Move it, you fat ass!" he cursed Andy's dead weight, even as he pushed and prodded and carried him up the steep grade. They gained a single foot of ground. Then another. Then five, ten. Almost there. And even as the thunder grew deafening and the cold presence drew ever closer, he saw the crest was now within reach. A spark of hope burned deep inside him. We're going to make it, he knew then. We're going to make it—

He was almost to the top—the lip of the valley was right there, just within his reach—when the inhuman howl came again and giant fingers of ice closed around his leg, almost jerking him from the slope. He dug his fingers in and clung there desperately, filled with terror and much worse. For with the viselike grip came an utter cold that penetrated his heavy denim pant leg, stabbing through the flesh to freeze the blood in his veins. He fought in blind panic then, clawing at the dirt and weeds and trying to drag himself to the top even as the howl grew louder and changed and became his name, his *name*, for God's sake. And that's when he tried to scream. But little more than a strangled sound reached his lips . . . a single word . . .

". . . *Windigo!*" Steven howled, bolting straight up from his deep sleep like a swimmer breaking the surface. He sputtered and gasped, shaking the dullness from his mind. But his wide eyes found only an arctic whiteness surrounding him. It disoriented him even further, and when he tried to get to his feet he found a dark figure looming over him, pushing him back down and holding him there. "No!" he growled, shoving his attacker away. "Stay back!"

There were other figures there suddenly, many hands grabbing him and forcing his arms to his sides, holding him prisoner. He fought them hard, even as the hypodermic slid into his nerveless arm.

"Steven!" came a voice that somehow pierced his confusion and struck right to his heart. So familiar . . . He stopped struggling then, let the fight bleed away as he blinked his eyes into focus, as much as he could without his glasses. The faces of the orderlies holding him were strange, likewise the nurse swabbing his arm with a cotton ball. But beyond them . . . Janet came forward, forced her way between two of the men, and kneeled beside the bed. She was holding her shoulder from where he'd thrown her to the floor.

"Steven, honey, it's okay," she said soothingly, stroking the side of his face. "Calm down. They're just trying to help you. Everything's gonna be okay."

Steven's eyes were wet. He wanted to reach up and touch that sweet face, to hold her tight. But his arms were still pinned at his sides. "Jan," he stammered. "I was afraid . . . I'd never see you again . . ."

"Are you kidding?" She tried to laugh, even as the tears burned her cheeks. "You ain't getting away from me that easy. You're in the hospital, hon, in Thunder Bay. So you just lie back and rest. You're safe now. Everything's going to be all right—"

"No, it's not," he exclaimed, straining against his captors. "It's all wrong. I know now. I know what it was." But his voice was already beginning to slur. It was a powerful sedative, and it took effect quickly. "No time . . ." he managed, his lids already sliding down. "Promise me . . . find Davejac. Tell him. Promise . . ."

Then the darkness claimed him. And the scenes from the valley began to haunt him anew.

SEVENTEEN

JANET GOT UP EARLY THE NEXT MORNING RIGHT AS DAWN cracked the murky Ontario sky. She showered quickly and then she went to Steven's room, where he was still under sedation. She sat with him for a while and held his hand again, only now it was strapped to the bed frame along with his other arm and both legs. She didn't particularly like it but she understood the staff's reasoning. Her shoulder still hurt from being thrown aside last night, and he almost broke the wrist of one of the orderlies who restrained him. She'd never known her husband to be so strong before.

After twenty minutes she left him alone. There was a lot to get done, and she wanted to hurry as much as possible. The longer she spent away from Steven's side, the more it bothered her. But she had promised him . . .

She called the operator for the number of a Barton Davejac in Atikokan. Then she tried him directly. There was no answer there on the first two attempts. But on the third try someone picked it up. The voice on the other end was sullen and a bit slurred, almost stuporous. Probably got him up, she surmised.

"Yeah, this is Barton Davejac," he answered her. "Who wants to know?"

"My name is Janet Wilhoit. Steven Wilhoit's wife? He was in your fish . . . I mean, hunting party?"

There was silence on the other end. Finally she heard the man swallow. "I'm not real sure, Mrs. Wilhoit, since I just got back from the woods last night. But I think your husband was sent on to Thunder Bay yesterday morning."

"Yes, I know," Janet told him. "I'm in Thunder Bay right now. I'm just calling because Steven wants me to."

"He does, huh? How is he doing?"

"Not well, I'm afraid. He's only been awake once, and that was to tell me to find you."

"To find me," he repeated after her. Another pause. "What does he want with me?"

"I'm not exactly sure. Look, Mr. Davejac, I'd like to talk about this in person. Could you by any chance come to Thunder Bay?"

"Now?"

"I would appreciate it."

"I'm sorry, Mrs. Wilhoit. But I'm not really up to driving."

Janet felt her anger rise. The nerve of the man . . . "Well, if that's too much trouble," she said with stinging sarcasm, "how about if I come there?"

There was a sigh through the phone, and she could almost picture him running his hand through his hair in exasperation. "If that's what you want," he finally said. "I'll be here."

He gave her the address, repeated it so she could write it down.

"One last thing," Janet wanted to know. "The other two men . . . did you find them?"

"No." Then he hung up.

Janet gritted her teeth as she laid the receiver down. What an asshole, she thought. Rude, insensitive, won't even get off his butt to come check on Steven . . . The whole thing's probably his fault anyway. She made up her mind then and there. She wasn't going to like this Davejac character, no matter what Bailey thought of him.

She checked the phone book for the car rental office nearest Bay General, called to check pricing, then ordered a cab to take her there. But before she left, she took one last peek at her husband.

He was still asleep, still motionless . . . She thought about kissing him again, but she didn't have a mask on anymore and wasn't anxious to feel the clamminess of his skin anyway. It would only remind her of how sick he really was, and then she'd never be able to pull herself from his side. Maybe I should stay anyway, she tried to argue. I mean, what can this Davejac do for him now? What if something happens while I'm gone, what if he takes a turn for the worst and I'm not here when he . . . When . . .

Promise me, he'd begged her. Promise.

She nodded as if answering him again, wiped her eyes, and started for the door. But as she passed the foot of the bed, her attention lingered there for a moment. Steven's feet were tenting the electric blankets all the way to the edge, maybe even hanging over a bit. She hadn't noticed that before. Was the bed that short? He certainly didn't reach that far in their queen-size at home. She made a mental note of it, and when she stopped at the nurse's station on her way out, she told them to get her husband a bigger bed. She also left Davejac's number, in case they should want to reach her.

The taxi was already waiting when she reached the street. It took her just a few blocks to the Hertz Rent A Car office,

where she put a Ford Escort on her MasterCard. The rental
agent was congenial and provided her with a free road map
that included Atikokan. Then he instructed her on the quickest
way out of Thunder Bay. She made just one more stop after
that, this time at a convenience store for a donut and a cup
of coffee to quell her empty stomach. Then she headed out
Highway 11, on her trek westward.

Janet half expected the drive to do her good, to let her
unwind and release some tension by just jamming the pedal
and driving away, at least for a while. And it should have—
all the elements were there. The clouds had receded and left
a nice sunny day, with just a bit of nip in the air. The scenery
along the way was picturesque, especially that late in the fall.
But she barely noticed. Her hands were locked to the wheel
as if cemented there, and her arms were getting sore from
the pressure she unconsciously exerted. Her eyes may have
been on the road, but all they saw was Steven on his bed,
strapped down like a lunatic. The wildness in his red-rimmed
eyes when he looked at her last night. The pleading in the
few short words he'd spoken . . .

She turned on the Escort's tinny radio for company, settled
on station CFOB out of Fort Frances. The music was a welcome change from the whine of the tires. But after a while
even that was drowned out by the nagging voice of her own
concern.

She wasn't aware of time passing, of minutes clicking into
hours as she watched the road but never really saw it. So
when a sign suddenly flashed by, it took her by surprise.
ATIKOKAN, it had read. NEXT RIGHT.

Wake up, Jan. You're there already.

She followed MacKenzie Avenue into the small town and
then turned onto a side street at random, for Atikokan was
little more than a dot on her map, and once within its limits,
she was at the mercy of chance. But once she was on Main
Street she followed it into the center of town until the sign
for O'Brien caught her eye. Turn right onto O'Brien, Davejac
had told her, and drive out like you're going to the airport.

Partway there'll be a gravel road on the right, with a nest of mailboxes. That's where you want to turn, and go all the way to the back.

Just as he instructed, she followed O'Brien out of Atikokan proper. And, sure enough, it wasn't a mile before she spotted a gravel drive on the right, winding back into a shallow band of woods. The mailboxes were lined just to the side of it, six of them in all, and as she drew closer and eased onto the shoulder of the road, she could see that the farthest one read DAVEJAC in uneven, hand-painted letters.

Janet steered onto that pitted, bumpy lane and drove back into the woods, accompanied by the tortured squeaking of the Ford's shocks and suspension. She passed several rustic cabins along the way, mostly hidden by the trees, but she kept going. All the way back until she reached the dead end Barton had described. From there it was just a few dozen feet to his front door.

This cabin's upkeep had not been as strictly maintained as the others she'd seen, for it seemed less suited for the hard Canadian winters. Its native lumber had turned dull grey and splintery over time, and its character eroded by the elements. The roof needed reshingling and the rain troughs were breaking down in a place or two, beginning to hang. There were no gaping cracks between the wall logs and the windows weren't broken, but one still couldn't shake the initial impression that it would be cold inside, especially once winter set in with a vengeance. But not everything was ramshackle about this property. Just to one side of the cabin and to Janet's complete surprise stood a satellite-receiving dish. It wasn't a newer model by any stretch of the imagination, wasn't even motorized, and had to be positioned by hand. But its presence was nonetheless incongruous.

Different strokes, she dismissed with a shrug.

She approached the front door and rapped on the fuzzy wood. No one answered at first. She knocked again. And this time a shrill voice answered her.

"Hold on, dammit, I said I'm coming!"

The figure who opened the door and peered out at her did so from behind thick glasses. The wizened old man who stood there regarding her was thin and bent with age, and unmistakably Indian in ancestry. Beside him in the doorway were what looked like two big bear cubs, though Janet finally realized they were some breed of sled dog.

"Yeah?" the old man snapped impatiently.

"You're not Barton Davejac . . ." she said hesitantly. "Are you?"

"Nope. George Wilson's my name. Who are you?"

Janet flushed with embarrassment. "Oh, I'm terribly sorry. I must have the wrong house—"

"Didn't say that," Wilson prompted. "This is the boy's house, just like I'm the boy's grandfather. But we still haven't decided who you are."

"My name is Janet Wilhoit—I called earlier? Mr. Davejac is expecting me."

The old man was already nodding along with her. "Yeah, yeah, come in then, hurry up. I'm missing my shows, you know." He turned and hobbled back into the cabin interior, favoring one hip over the other. Janet hesitantly followed, and the elkhounds came up behind her, sniffing with canine curiosity.

The living room had a distinctly lived-in look. The furniture was secondhand, covered with flowered sheets to hide the worn upholstery. The coffee table had been handmade from a log and none too well from the look of it. It was strewn with empty beer bottles and magazines, from Petersen's *Hunting* to *ORBIT*, the *TV Guide* of the satellite set. But the head of the room, the altar as it were, had to be the twenty-six-inch console television against the far wall, the perfect complement to the dish outside. George Wilson was there right now, settling into a Barcalounger opposite the set that looked to be vacu-formed to his precise shape. He settled in with rapt attention, utterly silent. For Bob Barker was about to speak.

"Rod Roddy, why don't you show them what's up for bids on *The Price Is Right*."

"Okay, Bob. It's . . . an Amana Refrigerator!" Wild applause, certainly more than was called for.

Janet perched herself on the edge of the couch, feeling very out of place in this strange setting. One of the bear dogs came right over to her, its tail going a mile a minute. The other just lay on the ground and eyed her suspiciously. "Mr. Wilson," she finally said, "I hate to bother you, but your grandson is here, isn't he?"

He pointed down a shallow hallway to the two closed bedroom doors, all without taking his eyes off the TV. "Back there."

"Is he asleep?"

"Probably. C'mon, honey," he told the TV, "bid nine hundred 'n' twenty, dammit! Oh, you stupid . . ."

"I'm sorry to keep bothering you, but do you think he'll be up soon?"

The old man didn't reply right away. But a commercial was soon in coming, and he finally pulled himself away from the set. "You want to talk to Barton? Do like I do." He yelled toward the hallway. "Hey, boy! You got company!" Then he swiveled his chair around to look at her. "He'll be out in a minute. You know, missy, you're a pretty good looker. You some new girlfriend I don't know about?"

"I'm afraid not."

"I figured. He's still pretty sweet on that girl works down at MacLeod's Hardware. Just who are you then?"

"My husband Steven was one of the men your grandson took hunting this last week."

The old man's face grew pensive, even more lined than before. "I'm sorry to hear that. I'll bet I probably met your husband, though I doubt I'd remember which he was. Tell me, did they bring him out or is he still missing?"

"They flew him to Thunder Bay. He's in the hospital there."

"Well, you can be thankful for that much, I suppose." The old man leaned a little closer. "Just what is it that happened out there?"

"That's kinda why I'm here," Janet confided. "He hasn't told you either?"

"Hasn't had time. The boy just got back from the search party last night. And he ain't been of a mind to talk much about it since."

The door opened down the hall, and a strong smell of liquor wafted out into the living room. It preceded Barton Davejac, clad only in his jeans and a flannel shirt, carrying a sack full of empty Moosehead bottles. He took it into the kitchen and set it beside the trash basket, then opened the refrigerator and took out a full one. "A little hair of the dog," he said softly as he came back into the living room and popped the cap, took a big swig. Then he dropped into a chair across from Janet and was silent for a moment. "Mrs. Wilhoit," he told her plainly, "I'm really sorry about your husband. I like the guy a lot, and I'd have done anything for this not to have happened."

Janet studied the man for several moments. She hadn't known that he was an Indian, but aside from that, he pretty much fit her expectations: stocky and muscular, the typical Neanderthal type, a beer constantly grafted to his hand. But his expression did not match at all. There was sincerity there, in his words as well as his eyes, and a lot of pain as well. It was no wonder he'd been unable to drive to Thunder Bay to meet her; he'd been trying like hell to drown his guilt, all night probably. And he was just now realizing that there wasn't enough beer in all of Ontario for that.

Okay, she admitted, so he's not the insensitive jerk I pictured. But there could just as easily be a reason for that guilt. And I want to know what it is.

"He's not doing too good, you say?" Barton asked.

"He was comatose until last night. Then he woke up and told me to find you. Find you and tell you."

Davejac massaged his pounding temples, as if that would bring on some sort of enlightenment. "Tell me what?"

"I don't know. He only said one other thing, and that was just when he woke up. He screamed something about 'where we go' or 'when we go,' something like that."

"Windigo?" George Wilson asked.

"I suppose that could have been it. What is that?"

Barton shrugged it off. "Nothing. Just a ghost story I told them around the campfire."

"It's more than that, boy," the old man cautioned.

Davejac shot him an irritated glance. "Look, old man. *The Price Is Right*'s on. You don't want to miss that, do you?"

Wilson sulked, turning his attention back to the TV.

"Mr. Davejac," Janet said firmly, "just what happened out there in the woods?"

Barton sat back in the chair, fingered the sweating bottle in his hand. The remembrance clouded his face. "To tell you the truth, Mrs. Wilhoit, I'm not all that sure myself. We were out two days and the woods were pretty bare— no game, that is. Then we came to this valley that I'd never seen before. And there was just something wrong about it. I don't know what, just . . . wrong. The dogs, they felt it too." He gestured to Yogi and the dog left Janet's side, crawled up into the chair with him. He scratched her thick pelt as he continued.

"I just wouldn't go down there. Period. And I told the others not to go either. But by that time Mr. Tucker was acting pretty crazy. He kept insisting there was a deer down there, that they just had to go get it. He ordered the others into the valley, and your husband went along. I told them to signal me if there was trouble, fire some shots, but I never heard anything. Not a peep. So I stayed there on the ridge of the valley all day and most of the night. And close to morning I found Steven and Andy wandering along the ridge there, white as ghosts. And no sign of the other two."

Janet waited for more, finally realized there was none forth-coming. "That's it?"

"What else do you want to know?"

"A lot of things. Like what was in that valley, for starters."

"Nothing. It's not that big a place. But all the search party found were their packs and rifles. The guns had been fired, and one was broken all to hell. But I swear to you as I sit here, I didn't hear a sound from in there. No shots, no nothing."

"Had you been drinking."

"No."

"Well, this just doesn't make any sense," Janet snapped, standing, starting to pace with frustration. She abruptly lashed out at the closest person she could find. "You were in charge, weren't you? Why did you let Steven go down there if you knew it could be dangerous?"

"No, I was not in charge. Mr. Tucker was. And no, I didn't know it would be dangerous—I just said it felt wrong, which is precisely what I told your husband. He went any-way."

"You could have stopped him."

Now Barton was getting angry. "What would you have suggested, ma'am? Should I have shot him in the leg or something?"

The bickering stopped for a moment as the two sides re-grouped. But in the interim George Wilson had turned his attention away from Bob Barker and the studio audience. He'd been listening to the conversation with a furrowed brow, and now he spoke. "This valley . . ." he said to his grandson. "Was there anything unusual about it?"

"No, old man. It was just a valley, it . . ." Then something clicked in Barton's memory. "No, wait a minute. There was something. A big rock along the ridge. There were picto-graphs on it. They were really strange, like nothing I'd seen before."

Wilson took a Bic pen from his pocket, the same ballpoint he used to mark things to watch in his satellite listings. He picked up a *People* magazine from the coffee table, and in the empty cover space surrounding Kevin Costner's head, he began to draw. The stick figures came out warped and ill-proportioned, made worse by the feeble shaking of his hand. Janet was looking at them upside down, but even from straight on they would have had little meaning. Just simplistic doodles. But the look on the old man's face showed he was dead serious.

He showed his work to Barton. "Did your rock have one of these?"

Davejac looked it over carefully. "Maybe. It's hard to tell, there were so many . . ."

The old man went to work again, this time came up with more arms and a longer neck. "This one."

"Closer. But I can't be sure."

Another drawing. And this time Barton took the magazine from him, stared at it. The ink figure was spindly and hunch-shouldered, arms impossibly long. At its feet were a crowd of much smaller stickmen. "I know this one," the guide said. "It was on the rock." He looked at his grandfather. "What's it mean?"

Wilson shrugged. "I'm not sure. Yet." He turned to Janet. "Just what is your husband's condition? His symptoms?"

"Well, he's very pale—"

"And cold to the touch?" the old man finished.

She was surprised. "Yes, but how—"

"And his chest, it's even cold in there?"

"Yes, exactly. Do you know what it is?"

George Wilson's face was dour. "I'm afraid I do. It's exactly what he was trying to tell you, Barton. He's been cursed by the windigo."

Davejac sighed dramatically, rubbed his face with exasperation. "Don't mind him, Mrs. Wilhoit. He gets like this sometimes—"

"Shut up," Janet cut him off abruptly. She turned back to the old man, giving him her full attention. "What is this windigo exactly?"

"Most would say an Ojibwa legend. The windigo is a malicious spirit or manito who haunts the deep woods, stalking and preying on lost hunters."

"Preying?"

"He means eating," Barton volunteered.

Wilson nodded. "They are a cannibalistic race, this is true. But often as not they would rather toy with their victim, torment and bedevil him rather than consume him. Sometimes to the point of insanity. Sometimes much worse." He considered his words, and when he looked up at Janet, his face was gravely serious. "The windigo most often takes the form of a giant skeleton of sheer ice, with a heart that is doubly frozen. It is that which has cursed your husband. And that which your husband will become."

"Old man, that's about enough. You're scaring her . . ."

Wilson pressed his point, looked her straight in the eyes. "Is he growing thinner? Taller? Is he?"

Janet withdrew and paced across the room with uncertainty. She was thinking of how drawn Steven's features had become, and how his feet stuck over the end of the bed. And when she laid her head on his chest, how the cold could be felt right through the heating blankets. "And his heart . . ."

The old man nodded. "It's turning to ice."

"Yeah, right," Barton said skeptically. "And just how did you arrive at that conclusion?"

"Because I've seen it before," George said solemnly. He fished on the coffee table for the remote control and turned the TV off. That finally got Barton's attention, for he'd never seen the old man do so willingly. He knew he was serious then. "It's funny," Wilson laughed as he settled back into the Barcalounger. "This all took place so long ago I'd begun to think it a story my own grandfather had just told me. But hearing about your husband brings the whole thing back to me now. I was about ten at the time, while we still lived up by the Chipachig River, just above Ten-Mile Gorge. One of the boys from the village wandered off one day, into a part of the forest where people were told not to go. Tainted land, they said. And he found that out, sure enough.

"He came back a few days later, and they said he'd gone windigo. That he was cursed. They wanted to burn him then and there. But my grandfather Crooked Wing said no, and his words held power. He was a midé shaman, and he was known for 'evil ways'—that meant everyone knew and feared his sorcery. But there was doubt that even he could face a windigo."

"Midé?" Janet asked. "What's that?"

"It means mystery. Mystic doings. The midéwiwin was a curative society. Medicine men, you'd call them. But they were also powerful sorcerers."

"And your grandfather cured the boy?"

"It was a struggle. I ought to know, I was there. He had to call on many Supernaturals, including the Thunderbirds. But he finally succeeded in driving the taint from the child."

"How did he do it?" she asked hopefully.

"Magic, of course."

Her optimism dimmed a bit, but would not go out. "Nothing else? No potions, no herbs or home brews?"

The old man thought hard about that, then shook his head. "No, not that I recollect. Just the migis shells. I think I still have those somewhere. Ol' Crooked Wing left them to me." He was suddenly up and moving toward the bedrooms, his momentary excitement lessening his arthritic gait. Once he disappeared they could hear drawers being opened and banged shut. Then the closet door. Then the drawers again.

"Do you need some help, George?" Barton called.

"Bingo!" Wilson came hobbling back down the hallway. He was unfurling a fist-sized roll of otter hide that was stiff with age and refused to hang loose. He had to hold it taut with both hands to show that it formed a long pouch with two strips of decorative fringe around the middle. It also sported several pictographic drawings, including the ones George had scrawled on the *People* magazine. "This is the wayan, where the migis are kept.'' He slipped the pouch open and poured a few of the contents into his hand, showed them to Barton and Janet. The ''shells'' were small and dull in color but shiny, like tiny pebbles polished in a tumbler.

''That's it?'' she asked, a bit incredulous.

''A migis shell is supposed to be ancient,'' he explained. ''Grandfather once told me they were charged with power by the Earth Supernatural, who conceived of the midéwi-win.''

Janet picked up one of the smaller shells, held it between finger and thumb. ''And these cured him?'' She abruptly asked, ''Could I take these back to Thunder Bay with me?''

The old man's face went from enthusiastic to guarded. Brilliant move, Janet chided herself. Just walk into a stranger's house and ask if you can borrow a family treasure. She quickly rephrased the question. ''What I mean is, would you come with me to the hospital, and bring your migis shells? We could really use your help.''

Wilson's face brightened. This was something he would consider. ''I don't know what I can do for you there,'' he said, cinching up the pouch. ''After all, I'm not my grand-father. I only know some of the old stories. But if you think it might help . . .'' He turned to Barton. ''You coming too, boy?''

Davejac looked at them through a squint, the farthest his hangover would let his eyes open. He didn't look any more prepared to travel now than before. But he agreed just the same. ''Count me in,'' he said weakly. ''Get your coat, George. It's a little chilly out.''

The old man nodded and started for his room, joined by the elkhounds who smelled a trip coming and expected to go along as well. ''Not this time, you dogs . . .'' Wilson was saying as he disappeared down the small hallway.

When he was out of sight, Davejac moved over beside Janet and whispered, ''You don't believe him, do you?'' It was more a statement than a question.

''I believe he knows something,'' she replied. ''He knew

the symptoms. He's seen it somewhere before. As for the evil spirit stuff, well, I don't know about that. But this is a start. Maybe the doctors can get something out of your grandfather that they can use. Anything's worth a chance." She looked up at him squarely. "What about you? Do you believe him?"

There was a look of uneasiness in his eyes. "I don't want to" was all he would say.

EIGHTEEN

THOMAS BOUVIER STOOD IN THE CORNER OF ANDY CHURCHS hospital room, watching him sleep. He had been there for several minutes now, not saying a word. Just thinking. And trying to understand his fear.

He's just a patient, the doctor told himself over and over. Someone with an illness, someone who needs your help. But he just couldn't seem to convince himself. The vagaries surrounding this case had already filled him not just with self-doubt but now a creeping paranoia that bypassed a lifetime's career in medicine. In med school he'd learned to attack a mystery, to probe and find out. That was just why he took this case in the first place. But now he'd reverted to his more adolescent tendencies. If you don't understand something, fear it. Shun it. Run away.

Is that why you're turning the case over to a research team, he asked himself. Are you running away?

Probably. And he expected some sort of shame or guilt for having admitted it. But in this case there was only relief.

The folder in his hand was stuffed with a whole sheaf of medical test reports, toxicology and blood workups and CAT scans and every other exam he'd thought to subject both Church and Wilhoit to since they arrived. The results were a mixed bag. Some had turned up completely normal. Some inconclusive. And some downright impossible. Since Andy Church's condition seemed much more accelerated than Wilhoit's, the majority of his results gathered at the latter end of that scale. Instead of explaining the man's condition, they only heightened the mystery. His blood pressure failed to even register now, and his heart rate had actually fallen to a quarter of the norm. His core temperature continued to plunge, was already well beyond the accepted mortality level. Yet he was still alive.

Worse yet, he was changing.

It had been subtle at first. But since last night the changes had become more pronounced. More startling. And in light of that, the nurses were already having reservations about even entering the room. Bouvier stepped closer to the bed where Andy Church was strapped down, hand and foot, so he could get a better look. And he was just as dumbstruck now as ever. The figure sleeping there did not even resemble the man they had brought in the previous morning. This patient looked more like a photo of a Holocaust victim. Church was emaciated, withered nearly to skin and bones. It was obvious even through the blankets that covered him. Even more so in his face. It was more skeletal than before, the cheekbones and eye sockets more pronounced, his teeth bulging beneath paper-thin lips. If this atrophy had been the sum of his change, Bouvier would not have been so alarmed. He might even have attempted to explain it in terms of malnutrition and vitamin deficiency. But it was not. Andy Church's face was not only thin and bony but much longer than earlier, at least half again the length of Bouvier's own. Indeed, his entire frame was elongating, growing at an incredible rate. His feet stuck well past the end of the bed now, and his head butted right up against the wall. Only an hour ago, they had measured him at six feet eight inches. A full foot longer than when he was admitted.

Bouvier had seen pituitary giants before, likewise diseases that mutated and warped the human bone. But not overnight. Not like this.

"Just what are you?" he whispered softly as that quiver of primal fear curled around his spine yet again. Suddenly he just wanted to be out of there, away from that room and that case and that hospital even. Maybe set up a private practice somewhere south of there. Like Florida.

He turned, was almost to the door when Andy Church said something.

The patient was still lying flat, barely lifting his pale head a few inches off the pillow. He muttered another garbled word or two, then let it fall. Dr. Bouvier walked back to the bedside. "I'm sorry," he said, though his tone was ever clipped and professional, "I couldn't hear you. What did you want?"

Church's eyes weren't even open. It was as if he were mumbling in his sleep. "Hungry . . ." he finally managed.

"Yes, well, we tried giving you food only an hour ago and you spit it out, remember?" The fear was subjugated for now by his customary impatience. "We don't want to waste the nurse's time, do we?" He looked at the restraining straps. "Although we do have you under control now . . . yes, I think it's safe to order another feeding tube—"

"Hungry!" Church suddenly barked. His eyes flew open and glared up at the doctor. They were teary and clouded as if stricken by cataracts, and they did not blink. To his horror Bouvier realized they didn't look like eyes at all. More like wet balls of clay, slipped into empty sockets. *"Hungry!"* he called again.

"Calm down, son," he tried to soothe even as he backed away instinctively. "I told you I'd let the nurse—"

Before he could say another word, there was a physical jolt. Andy had caught hold of his hand.

Bouvier couldn't understand who had grabbed him since

this man was clearly bound. But then he saw Church's hand holding his and the thick strap hanging frayed and broken from that bony wrist. The sight sent a chill rippling through his body, or maybe it was just the intense cold emanating from the man's very grasp. "Just . . . settle down, son," the doctor tried to be calm as he pried at the long steely fingers encircling his palm. "Let me go . . . Mr. Church, let go and I'll go get you some food right now, just . . ." He tried to jerk away, but his arm wouldn't budge. "Let go, dammit!" His eyes searched the bedcovers, looking for the remote button that would alert the nurse's station.

Church stared at the man dully, no emotion registering in those pale, filmy eyes. Then they shifted without blinking to the hand that he held in his own, squirming to escape. And something did pass through his gaze then. Something primal. Harsh. A look that filled the doctor with paralyzing dread. He couldn't move, couldn't fight back as Church suddenly pulled that shaking hand into his open mouth.

The pain didn't come right away; Thomas Bouvier's mind was too flooded with fear and disbelief to allow any other sensations direct access. But his auditory senses were still functioning. So there was no avoiding that sickening crunch that reached his ears, the delicate, brittle sound that small bones make when they are crushed or ground in two. Andy jerked his head then, twice, until something gave with an audible snap and Bouvier's limb was suddenly free. He staggered sideways into a bank of monitoring equipment, lifted his hand with drunken slowness, and found his thumb and index finger still intact. The rest was gone. From the first knuckle back to the wrist, the flesh was stringy and pulped, the muscle and bone peeking through between the synchronized jets of crimson. The wound was spraying like a garden hose, showering the equipment, the wall, the covers on the bed. Even Andy Church. The doctor glimpsed him sitting up in bed now and pulling his other arm free, breaking that strap as well. There was something sticking out of his mouth . . . two fingers, like long noodles steeped in surgical rubber. Then he repositioned a jawful and sucked them in as well and the crunching started anew.

The doctor just stood there, mouth open but saying nothing, staring at his gored limb. He was trying to yell for the nurses, the orderlies, anyone. But nothing would come. All that escaped his lips was a strangled mewl, and it wasn't nearly loud enough to alert anyone. He was slipping further into shock, he knew, and despite his medical knowledge, he was powerless to fight it. All he could do was gape incredulously as his life fluid belched out across the white tiling, as the gaunt giant on the bed struggled with his leg straps, straining . . .

Freeing himself.

Like a laser beam, that one thought pierced the cloud that seemed to traumatize Thomas Bouvier's brain, burned deep into whatever controlled his motor functions. And the primal instincts he'd decried only moments earlier now turned him around, sent him staggering toward the door on legs that could not feel the ground. His goal was miles away, at the end of a stretch of red-spattered tile that seemed to reach to the far horizon. But he moved for it just the same. Panting, he put his balance out in front of him and built his momentum until it was either reach the door or fall flat.

He collided with the jamb just to the side of the door, and the impact reverberated through the open nerve endings of his hand. Any scream that resulted was extinguished by the vomit that rose into his throat and nose and made it hard to even get a breath. The handle, he yelled at himself, just get the handle and pull it open and you'll be in the hall and somebody will come and everything will be all right . . .

He reached out with the dull, tingling fingers of his one good hand, managed to clasp them around the steel handle. Now, just one good pull . . .

He was hit hard from behind, shoved into the door and pinned there. A hand was planted in his back, just below his right shoulder blade, and the force it exerted against him robbed his lungs of air and made the door creak in its frame.

But it didn't stop there. He could feel those long, thin fingers working against him. Digging. Burrowing.

"My God, my God . . ." the doctor prayed, but it came out little more than a high-pitched squeak of agony. Then his body went rigid as the hand slipped inside him, broke through the rib cage with one hard thrust.

Thomas Bouvier was dying even then; the splintered ribs had punctured his lungs and tore his stomach open, pulled a kidney completely loose of its moorings. He was hemorrhaging badly, and his muscles began to spasm as he had watched terminal patients do so many times in the past. And he was aware of it all, every detail. He even felt the hand close around his heart.

It was so cold . . .

Andy Church jerked his arm from the twitching body, let it slide down the door in a heap while he held up his steaming prize.

It would do for now. But it would never be enough to satisfy him.

Janet and Barton stepped off the elevator on the I/O floor, but George Wilson moved with a bit less enthusiasm. "You smell that?" he said, sniffing disdainfully. "That soapy smell?"

"That's antiseptic, Mr. Wilson," Janet explained.

"I know what it is. But I don't like it. Just doesn't smell . . . natural, you know? No, sir, I wouldn't want to die in a place like this. When my time comes, I want to be at home in my chair, watching TV, just like usual. Did you hear that, boy?"

"Yeah, old man," Davejac said. "Loud and clear. Now can you pick up the pace a little?"

"I'm coming, I'm coming . . ."

As they approached the swinging doors of the observation wing, a steady electronic whine reached out to greet them. The three exchanged befuddled glances. "What the hell is that?" Barton wondered aloud.

Janet shrugged. "I'm not sure."

"On *Trapper John, M.D.*," George Wilson said, "that would sound like cardiac monitors going off."

Janet gave the old man a caustic glance, started to tell him that he watched too much television. But the sound was familiar, and when she admitted that, the implications set in all too quickly. "Steven?" she said in sudden panic, pushing through the double doors.

They were across the shallow hall beyond and halfway to the nurse's station when the stillness slowed them and the emptiness brought them to a halt. The large counter was completely unmanned. The hallways were empty as well. Not a doctor or staff member or patient in sight. Only that pulseless whine, much louder here. And from this close, they could tell there was more than one.

And then there were the red stains on the floor. Long streaks. Blotchy footprints. In front of the station, up and down each hall.

Paint, Janet tried to convince herself. Just spilled paint . . . "Susan?" she called, though she couldn't draw the courage for an outright yell. "Dr. Bouvier? Anybody?"

"That's blood, isn't it?" George Wilson said. "That's what it is—I can smell it. Ooh, I've got a bad feeling."

"So do I," Barton whispered. "Let's get the hell out of here." He backed toward the still-swaying doors. "We have to tell someone downstairs, call the police or something . . ." But Janet wasn't listening. She was already starting down the hall on the right. "Mrs. Wilhoit, what are you—"

"I have to see Steven," she called back, not expecting him to understand. But she kept going anyway. Seeing the wing deserted like this, the spattering of red on the tile, hearing the cardiac monitors wail at her from each door she passed, filled her with an icy dread. She picked up speed and was running by the time she reached the closed door to Steven's room.

Please let him be all right, please, God . . .

The door opened to darkness. She fished along the wall

for the light switch. A flick made the fluorescent tubes overhead stutter a moment, then spring to life.

Steven was still on the bed, still bound hand and foot. But he was fully conscious now, his pale face twisted with concern and worry. "Janet?" he said, "Thank God. The screaming brought me to, made me realize where I was. I was so afraid you were . . ." He sank back into his pillows, exhausted.

"Lordy, there's blood everywhere," Barton said from right at Janet's shoulder, startling her. He peered past her through the doorway. "Is he in there?" Then he saw the figure on the bed. "That's him?" he said, gaping in disbelief. "Steven? Is that you?"

"Go check on Church." She pushed the guide back into the hall. "He's down that way, last door on the left."

"Look, shouldn't we—"

"Just do it, Mr. Davejac. Please?" She went into the room with her husband and left him grumbling in the corridor.

George Wilson sidled up beside him. "About this Church fella," he whispered. "How far gone do you think he is?"

"I think we're about to find out." He looked down at his bare hands, shaking imperceptibly. "Lordy, lordy, I wish I had my rifle about now. Or a knife. Or anything."

"Maybe there's something," the old man said, pointing off to his left. Just across the corridor, parked haphazardly against a wall as if its pilot had just abandoned it, stood a small, two-shelfed dressing cart.

They went there in desperation and inspected its cargo. There were boxes of gauze bandage and roles of tape, jarlike beakers marked ALCOHOL and ACETONE, as well as one stuffed with cotton balls and another with Q-Tip swabs. There were scissors there too—that's what caught Barton's eye immediately—but of the several pair present, only one had a point sharp enough to be considered threatening. He checked the second shelf then, but there was only a plastic basin filled with recently removed bandages, some stained crimson and others pus yellow. He wondered which of the patients in this wing had shed them, and if their cardiac

monitor was now adding to the communal wail. The thought
made him shiver, and he hefted his new weapon for reassurance. But the small scissors did not provide much. "It'll
have to do," he grumbled, stalking down the hall, leaving
George Wilson to pick through the articles on the cart.

Church did all of this, an inner voice told him adamantly.
Because he's a windigo just like George says and you believe
him, you don't want to but you do just the same. And now
you're walking straight toward his room and he's gonna come
flying out of there and be all over you like stink on shit. And
all you've got are scissors. Just a pair of pointy little—

Shut up. Let me concentrate.

He knew the voice was right. He was walking right into
something very bad, and he was all but defenseless. This
wasn't like the forest at all—there was no cover he could
take, nothing to hide behind or shield himself with. Nothing
but the sterile white hallway and an empty gurney pushed up
against one wall and . . .

"Wait a minute," he realized. He went to the mobile bed
and pulled it away from the wall, tested its wheels to see
how well he could guide it before him. With it as a barrier,
he was partially covered, at least on one side. Under these
circumstances, it was the best he could hope for.

He swallowed hard, but only forced down a bit of his
apprehension. "Are you with me, George?" he said without
turning.

"Be right there," the old man replied from back up the
hall a ways.

Don't wait for him—it'll take too long. Just take a quick
look and get it over with so we can get the hell out of here.

Barton crept closer, damning the faint squeak in the bed's
casters, hoping the electronic whine would cover it. He drew
up to the last door on the left, just where Janet had directed
him, and he noticed two things. One, the door was standing
open. And two, the bloody marks on the floor, footprints and
blotches and snakelike streaks, were much thicker there. I'm
not going in, he promised silently as he positioned the gurney

between himself and the yawning doorway. I'm just going to peek inside and that's it. Just to peek . . .

The lights were on in Andy Church's room. So he didn't have to look very hard. The long bright tubes overhead displayed the scene in grisly detail.

The small expanse of open floor just inside the doorway looked as if it had been swabbed with blood. Not an inch of pale tile was left uncovered, and it gleamed with a waxy luster, still running and fresh. Behind that was a large pile of discarded clothing at least waist-high, looking like a huge clot of blood and white cotton. Until he realized with horror that there was also flesh and bone mixed in. A face stared out at him from beneath the pile, a man he didn't recognize, with shattered glasses and a goatee that framed a still-screaming mouth. There were other faces there as well, one on a detached head lying near the wall baseboard. It wore a scrub cap and a grimace of pain, and from those twisted features he could not tell whether it was male or female, let alone that it had once belonged to a nurse named Susan. There were other body parts in that pile, an arm in a sleeve, a crepe-soled shoe with the foot still inside. In fact, there were too many pieces. Enough for an entire nursing staff.

At the edge of the pile was an arm whose sleeve had been stripped away, and likewise most of the meat, from wrist to elbow. The bones showed clean and white, like a drumstick well gnawed.

Oh, lordy lordy lordy . . .

The stale beer from last night's binge was heaving inside his gut and demanding to come up. But Barton couldn't even retch. His muscles had gone flaccid and numb, paralyzed by the charnel-house scene before him, and his head was spinning madly. But not from the hangover anymore. From fear. He could only lean on the wheeled cot for support, trying to will his legs to move and get him the hell out of there.

An electronic whine rose from the room behind him, growing steadily louder. What, another death, he wondered. Is Church in there right now, rending another meal, triggering another cardiac monitor? Or has the machine been crying all along, muffled until now by the closed door . . .

Oh, shit.

Davejac felt the presence behind him then like a gust of cold air against his skin; it sent an involuntary shudder through his stocky frame, called every hair on his body to attention. In reflex he threw himself across the gurney and came down on the far side, away from Andy Church, for he knew that's who it would be. He turned, half expecting the roly-poly man he'd carried through the woods to be leering now in dementia, brandishing a butcher knife in the classic Halloween tradition. But the gaunt fish-white figure he found in the doorway bore little resemblance to the Andy he'd known. In fact, it resembled nothing he'd seen before. Not even in his worst nightmares.

Church stalked into the hall like a ghostly preying mantis, his head almost scraping the ceiling panels. He was naked, having shed his hospital gown, and with it most all allusions to his past identity. That looming marmoreal frame was far too spindly now, the arms much too long. And the face . . . Andy Church's few remaining features were dull and lifeless, like a thin film of dead tissue. The facial muscles had already atrophied and now hung in an expressionless mask. But behind that guise . . .

It looked down at him through Andy's dull grey eyes and a leer spread behind his face, so wide the lank tissue covering it had to move as well. It was only then that Barton saw the cheeks had torn, all the way to the jaw hinge, so the whole lower part of Church's face seemed to smile down at him. Cold. Taunting. The capering evil in that smile even translated to the last remaining vestige of Andy Church's humanity. The withered genitalia that hung between those rail-thin legs was standing erect now, rigid with delight. It was enjoying all of this. The slaughter. The feast.

Barton shrank in its presence, holding up the scissors in feeble defense, knowing full well how useless they would be against such a creature. He started back up the hallway and pulled the gurney with him, keeping it between the two of them. At first Church just watched, swiveling his sticklike neck to follow the man's movements. But then he followed, his frozen member pointing the way.

"George," Barton called, not daring to take his eyes off the monstrosity before him. "George, find me something to fight with. Hurry!" No answer. Church was catching up, almost to his barrier now. "Did you hear me? Dammit, old man, I need help!"

A long, thin hand caught the edge of the gurney and pulled it to a halt, casually flipped it aside as if it were a toy. The cot bounced off the wall and onto its side, leaving only a few feet of open ground between the Indian and his assailant.

Barton thought about running. It was his natural instinct, and he had to fight hard to conquer it. But he did not want this thing catching him from behind. As clichéd as it sounded, he was determined to at least put up a fight. So he drew back the scissors and tried to pick a vital target on something whose very mortality was in serious doubt . . .

Someone caught his arm from behind and plucked the scissors from his grasp. "Try this instead," George Wilson said, sticking a fat glass jar into his hand. The one marked ACETONE from the dressing cart. He looked at the jar, then at his grandfather. The old man was already thumbing the wheel of his Zippo lighter, birthing a flame there, turning it up as high as it would climb. "Throw it," he urged. "Hurry."

Church came for them then, in one long loping stride. Barton didn't have time for careful aim; he just lobbed the jar as hard as he could and prayed he was on target.

It tumbled through the air for no more than a split second before it shattered on Church's bony face, splattering the clear liquid across the floor and all down his chest and shoulders. But its effects were neglible at best. The creature did not even flinch with the impact nor blink an eye. It hesitated just a moment, then came straight ahead, reaching for them . . .

Barton ducked beneath a groping limb as the old man tossed the Zippo at the oncoming nightmare.

There was a flash. An acrid stench. And Andy Church no longer advanced. He stood uncertainly in the middle of the hall, disoriented by the sheath of angry flames that now enveloped his head and torso. At first he brushed at the fire like a bothersome insect, tried to shake it off. But then it must have started to burn, for his actions quickly turned frantic. He flailed madly and careened off the walls, screeching like no human throat could ever produce. But his tortured dance only fanned the flames even more.

Barton grabbed for the gurney as a shield. And when he had the chance, he righted the cot and shoved it straight into the shambling monstrosity. Church was blindsided; he sprawled across the cot as Davejac drove him through the nearest open doorway, all the way to the far wall. Then the Indian jerked the door closed and held it there, bracing his leg against the jamb for support. "George!" he yelled. "Get moving! I'll hold it as long as I can!"

"But, Barton," the old man was stammering, "look at the door!"

He glanced up for the first time, and his eyes finally found the red danger sign posted just above the handle he was gripping. OXYGEN IN USE, it read. NO SMOKING.

"Holy shit!" He pushed off the wall and threw himself over George, taking him to the ground and shielding him just as the room and much of the wall around it exploded. A gout of flame blew the door off its hinges and licked out into the corridor, blackening the tile and singeing the air. Sections of plaster and fiery ceiling panel rained down around them. And in the wake of the blast, there were two wails to assault their ears. One was the automatic fire alarm, echoing through the halls. The other was the inhuman cry of Andy Church.

Barton pulled his grandfather up and they faced the inferno that moments before had been a hospital room, shielding their faces to the intense heat. The bed and curtains were on fire and the ceiling fell in smoldering pieces. Flames even danced along the walls. And in the middle of it all was a gaunt figure, barely discernible through the shimmering glare. It was still standing. Still moving. Coming toward the door. They gaped in horror as it took one step, then another.

"Lordy . . ."

The thing stopped and loosed another wail. Then it shuddered, and in doing so changed once more. Whole sections of the figure seemed to drop away, sloughed off like a man shedding an overcoat. What was left was even thinner than before.

"Skeleton of ice," George Wilson whispered fearfully. "Windigo."

The thing wavered there in the blistering heat and seemed to dwindle before their eyes. It was then that the hissing started, like steam from a kettle. Like ice in a fire. But the thing kept coming. It came toward the doorway even as it shrank with each step, even as its long arms dripped away to nubs, until its legs no longer held it. It fell just a few feet from the hall, and the screaming stopped. But the hissing didn't.

"Let's get out of here," Wilson said, pulling his grandson by the arm.

They turned to find Janet Wilhoit standing wide-eyed in the hall outside Steven's room. From her slack expression they could tell she had witnessed it all.

"Snap out of it, Jan," Davejac took her by the arm. "We've got to get out of here."

But Janet resisted him. She motioned to her husband's room, and the two men finally noticed the figure standing in the doorway there. Watching them. Steven Wilhoit was dressed in a T-shirt that barely reached his waist and baggy jeans that now seemed too short.

Barton backed up a step defensively. The American didn't look nearly as bad as Church had—he was pale and haggard, maybe even several inches taller, but not nearly as cadaverous. Still, that was enough for the Indian. "He's one of them. Just like his friend."

"Not yet," Steven said weakly as he stepped into the hall. "I promise you that." He looked at the old man, pleading in his eyes. "Janet says you can help me," he said hopefully. "Can you?"

"I . . . I don't know," George Wilson said. Then he looked at his grandson. "There's no time to argue. We'll take him with us." He turned and hobbled back up the hallway, with Janet and her changing husband in tow.

"Great," Davejac scowled. "Just fucking great. How are we supposed to get him out of here, huh? Have you thought about that?"

But apparently they had. George Wilson had already located a wheelchair at the nurse's station, and a lab coat and scrub cap as well. Janet slipped those on, trying to look as much like a member of the staff as possible. Then they got Steven seated and threw a blanket over his chest and lap. Their timing was fortuitous: it was bare seconds before a steady stream of rescue workers and firefighters and orderlies from other floors came pouring through the entrance.

"What the hell's happening up here?!" called the first man through the doors.

"There's a crazy man down there," Janet told them even as she pushed the wheelchair through the throng with the Indians following right behind. "He's crazy, he started the fire. Please, get out of the way, we have to get the patients evacuated!"

The men nodded in agreement and let them pass, barely casting them any notice in the face of this emergency. They made it to the elevator unmolested.

"So far, so good," Janet said as the doors closed and they started downward. She handed the keys of the Escort to Barton. "You go on ahead, bring the car around. We'll meet you outside. And keep your fingers crossed."

When the elevator reached the bottom Davejac sprinted down the hall and out of sight, leaving them behind. Confusion ruled the hospital in the aftermath of the blast, and that blaring fire alarm only added to the strain. Police officers and security personnel were already manning the corridors, directing the flow of traffic as patients were evacuated in droves, just in case the fire spread. Janet and the old man slipped Steven's chair into the moving current of bodies and soon found themselves wheeling out the emergency-room doors. But to their chagrin they found the circular roadway clogged with rescue trucks and fire equipment. No sign of the rental car.

"There he is." Wilson pointed across the lawn to the nearest open drive. The small Ford was parked there with the engine running. But Janet knew that rolling the wheelchair up over curbs and through the grass would be difficult at best. It might attract attention.

She leaned down, whispered to Steven, "Do you think you can walk to the car?"

"I can run if I have to." He abruptly stood from the chair, a bit unsteady but moving nonetheless. They walked away from the emergency area and strode across the lawn to the car. No one seemed to notice their departure.

Steven squeezed into the back of the small compact, his knees up under his chin, and then Janet started to crawl in beside him. But Barton pushed her back. "You drive," he told her as he slipped into the backseat himself. "I want to get something straight first." He took a roll of surgical tape he had pilfered from the nurse's station and began winding it around Steven's wrists, binding them together. "I don't like taking chances," he said. "Now, let's get the hell out of here."

Janet slipped the car into gear and headed down the road, careful not to be too impatient and squeal the tires. They turned the corner, eased into midday traffic, and were gone.

NINETEEN

ONCE THEY WERE ON HIGHWAY 11 OUTSIDE THUNDER BAY, heading west, the cramped interior of the Escort grew silent. No one spoke for a long time. The horrors of the afternoon were finally soaking in on each of them.

Barton shivered in the backseat, despite the bright sunlight that bore in on him through the magnifying glass of a window. Sitting next to Steven Wilhoit was proving the next best thing to cuddling with a refrigerator. He glanced over at the pale man and found him sitting still and quiet, not even complaining over his doubled-up, near-fetal position. He was staring out the windshield. His face was slack and his eyes glassy. Unblinking.

That nonexpression seemed disturbingly familiar . . .

Davejac began to fidget uncomfortably and was about to direct Janet to stop the car immediately. But that's when Steven looked over at him from the corner of his eye. His head swiveled around to regard the Indian, and a slight smile curled the corner of his mouth. "Relax, Barton," he said in a soft monotone. "I'm still here. Just thinking, okay?"

"How're you doing, hon?" Janet asked from the driver's seat.

He hesitated a moment, a queasy expression on his face. But then he saw her eyes in the rearview mirror, watching him, and he forced a smile. "I'm all right, Pud. Don't worry so much."

"I can't help it." She shifted her reflected gaze to Davejac.

"You know, I've been thinking. And I'm not so sure we should be going back to your house."

"Why is that?"

"Because they might look for us there. I don't know if you noticed it or not, but there were cameras in each of the rooms in that wing of the hospital. They're bound to have tape of Church on his rampage. And because Steven's condition is related, they'll want to find him too."

"Maybe the cameras and stuff burned up," George Wilson guessed. "Maybe the whole area went up, and all them records are gone for good."

"I don't think we can take that chance. We've got to assume that they know about Steven, and that I'm up here with him."

"But how would they connect you to us?" Barton asked.

"Well, for one thing, you're involved in the case—you found them, after all. They might call you just to touch base. But more to the point, I left your number when I came to see you this morning. If they find that . . ."

Barton sighed, rubbed his face. Ever since that nightmare in Thunder Bay, his mind had been running on autopilot. Now, when he actually tried to think rationally, he found his thoughts clouded with confusion. "First things first," he told them. "Let's analyze this thing. What are we going back to Atikokan for, anyway?"

"So George can help Steven," Janet said matter-of-factly. She saw Barton's expression in the mirror, questioning. "I know, I was the one who wanted to approach this thing scientifically. But I can't explain what went on back there any more than you can. Right now, I'm willing to believe anything. If George really thinks he can help . . ."

"I'm not so sure I can," Wilson said weakly from the passenger seat. "I just don't know."

"But you said—"

"I said the migis cured that boy, which is true. But this isn't a pill or a shot in the arm. We're talking about re-

creating a midé ceremony, with Indian spirits and sweat
lodges and the whole shebang.''

Janet's tone still retained a hint of skepticism. "Well . . .
if that's what it takes . . .''

"But I'm no shaman," the old man protested. "I know a
few old stories, but that's about it. I don't even speak the
Ojibwa tongue anymore. My grandfather was midé, yes, and
very powerful. His spirit guardian was a Thunderbird, one
of the most powerful manitos. But my father was another
matter. When he came of age and went into the woods to
fast and attract a spirit guardian of his own, none would come.
He was 'empty' then, without spiritual aid. This was a shame-
ful thing for the son of such a revered sorcerer. So he moved
away in disgrace, took us to the city of Port Arthur where
he did construction work. That is where we became white.
We spoke no more of the native tongue, and we no longer
discussed the old ways. So all I know of these matters is what
I remember from childhood.''

The revelations caught Barton off-guard. "But you taught
me about the woods. I thought you'd been raised there.''

"I learned to hunt and camp from a white man," Wilson
said, a bit embarrassed. "As an adult I moved to Atikokan
to work the iron mines. Me and another guy would go into
the woods on the weekends, whenever we got the chance.
He showed me everything that I showed you.'' He hung his
head. "Sorry, boy. Guess I never told you that, huh?''

Davejac was thin-lipped. "I guess not.''

"Getting back to this ritual," Janet persisted. "Are there
any other shamans around these days? Someone who would
know what to do?''

"Maybe.'' The old man shrugged, but his tone was not
hopeful. "Though today not many seem interested in the past.
I've seen a few on the reserves, still practicing some of
the rituals and ceremonies, keeping the old customs alive.
But whether they actually believe in what they're doing is
another matter. You parade Steven up in front of them and

nine chances outta ten they'd shit their skivvies same as everyone else.''

"We don't have time to look anyway," Steven told them. "Mr. Wilson, it looks like you're the only hope I've got. We know this ritual or whatever it is works, or at least it did. Can't you at least try?''

There was silence for a moment. Then the old man gave a weak nod. "Guess trying won't hurt. Not that it'll do any good . . .''

"Now that that's settled," Barton declared, "what do you need, old man? Anything from the house?''

Wilson held up the wayan bag he'd been carrying tucked in his belt. "This is all I can think of.''

The younger Indian nodded. "Good. Then I think I know where we can go. Somewhere they won't think to look, least not right away. Just keep driving, Janet. I'll tell you where to turn off.''

It was another twelve miles until the unnamed dirt road appeared to the left of the highway, snaking off into the underbrush there. Davejac pointed it out in advance, so Janet would be sure not to miss it. The Escort's suspension protested mightily as they pulled from even pavement to rutted earth, and the jarring seemed to rouse Steven from another bout of stolid silence. He looked around, recognition setting in. "This is the way to Chalako Lakes," he said. A tinge of apprehension was almost detectable in his low voice.

"It's the best place I can think of," Barton told the three of them. "The search parties shouldn't be out in this area too much longer. When they dropped me off yesterday, they'd already convinced themselves that Tucker and Covey were swallowed by a sump hole.''

"Tucker did go down that way," Steven informed them, staring out the window. "But not before he killed Paul and attacked Andy.''

"I'm not following most of this," Janet said in exasperation. "What's a sump hole? Just exactly what happened in this valley everyone's talking about?''

After a bit more prodding her husband recounted the night-marish events of that night, just as he'd relived it countless times in his hospital bed. The others listened in rapt silence; the memory of Andy Church's transformation was still fresh in their minds, so it was not hard to visualize the horrors he described. And he described them all. He didn't leave out one detail, painted it moment by moment, right to the time when his leg was grabbed and he woke up in bed, screaming.

They waited for the rest of the story, but there was none forthcoming. "And?" Barton tried to lead him. "How did you get away from it?"

"I'm not sure. I'm pretty hazy after that, up until I awoke. But I think it let me go."

"Let you go? Just like that?"

He nodded sullenly, disturbed by the thought. "I remember bits and pieces. And I can hear it . . . laughing. At least it sounds like that in my mind. Crazy, isn't it?"

"Not really," George Wilson observed. He was turned halfway 'round in his seat, regarding Steven with a curious eye. "A windigo is not like the shark in *Jaws*. It doesn't prowl the backwoods looking for food alone. If that were the case, we would never have known of the madness it inflicts. Lost hunters would simply have vanished, never to return. But they did return, just like the boy in my village. Because windigos are malevolent spirit creatures. Devils. Demons. And they take as much nourishment from torment as they do human flesh."

"Sweet Jesus," Janet sighed.

"Wait a minute . . ." A harrowed expression was suddenly creasing Davejac's face. He looked at Wilhoit with wide eyes. "You said Tucker grabbed Andy and cursed him. And that the original windigo touched you and gave it to you . . ." His mouth was too dry; he dredged up just enough saliva to finish his dark thought. "I carried you both to the helicopter. I touched you. Does that mean I'll . . . Am I gonna get this too?"

"Calm down, boy," George Wilson said, dismissing his

panic. "You haven't started changing yet, have you? It would seem to me that this affliction can't be passed until the change is complete. Until the windigo asserts itself. Mr. Tucker had already turned when he attacked Mr. Church, am I right?" Steven nodded in agreement. "See there? Don't worry so much."

"I'll worry if I want," Davejac snapped. "You said it yourself; you don't know the rules here. I mean, how do you know . . . that he hasn't already started to change? I'm sorry, Steve, but you do look pretty weird. And look how fast the others went—Tucker in one night, Church in about three. That's not good odds, eh?"

"Tucker was crazy before we ever got to that valley," Wilhoit reminded him. "That was his weakness, how it first started to work on him. As for Andy, he didn't have much willpower. He gave up before we even made it to the edge of the valley. They both gave up. But I'm not about to do that. I'm fighting it." He looked back out the window, averting the mask of mental exertion he wore. "It's hard," he whispered. "But I won't quit. I won't." He muttered it softly that last time, as if only to himself.

"Don't you worry, hon," Janet said. "We'll stay quiet and let you concentrate . . ."

"No, don't do that," he told her. "Keep talking. Sing a song, turn on the radio, anything. I don't care. Just as long as there's noise." He leaned his head against the window. "It was quiet in the woods. And I never want to hear that again."

"It's not much farther, Steve," Barton told him. "Just hold on, okay?" He started to reach over and pat his shoulder reassuringly, but thought better of it.

When the base camp finally came into view, they found it just as they'd left it. The two Land Rovers were still parked out in front of the cabin, since Barton had returned to Atikokan on one of the search team's float planes. There were only three canoes on the rack, the other two presumably still grounded at the portage half a day away. Janet, upon seeing the camp for the first time, was surprised. From all the horror stories she'd heard thus far, she half expected the haunted woods from Oz. But this . . . There was no two ways about it. This was beautiful.

As she drove toward the cabin, Barton told her, "Don't stop here."

She looked around. The cabin was the only thing in sight. "Where the hell do you want me to go? Into the lake?"

He leaned forward, pointed over her shoulder and through the windshield. She followed his finger to the dense tree line and strained her vision to see a rift of any size there. It was difficult; she could only make out the tire ruts in the grass that disappeared into a wall of vegetation. "Back in there?"

"That's where my cabin is. Just into the trees."

What they found back there among the cedars and pines was a cabin, all right. But even less of one than the structure they'd passed in the clearing. It was small and obviously one-roomed, with a single shuttered window. The structure was a simple shell of rough timber with handmade shingles and a stovepipe jutting from their midst. It would have been best described as a shed, but then they would not have had a name for the even smaller building that stood adjacent to it.

"Home sweet home," Barton declared as Janet shut the engine off. "This is where me and the dogs stay when we're out here hunting, or sometimes when I just want to get away and read. It's not as large as the other cabin, but it's a helluva lot warmer." He motioned for Janet to get out so he could push her seat forward, then he extricated himself from the backseat. The ride had put a crick in his spine that wouldn't allow him to straighten, at least not right away. "It's going to be dark soon," he estimated. "I'd better start the generator so we can have some light on the subject. Go on in, make yourselves at home." He took a crooked walk toward the little outbuilding alongside the cabin.

George Wilson noticed Mrs. Wilhoit looking around self-consciously. "Anything wrong, missy?"

"It's just so lovely here," she marveled. Unlike their drive in, she had no trouble seeing out of the forest. The other cabin was in sight and likewise the placid beauty of Beaver Lake. "I can't quite get used to this. I mean, am I supposed to be looking for monsters or something amid all this natural beauty?"

"Not around here. In the valley." He pointed off to the southwest. "Barton tells me it's off in that direction, about two days from here."

"Can't this windigo thing leave the valley and wander around? Or is it trapped there, imprisoned somehow?"

Wilson shrugged. "I guess it's possible that some other Supernaturals could have stuck this windigo there. But I tend to believe it doesn't wander for other reasons. Just suppose that valley is 'shared land,' a place where our world and their world—the midé, the spirit realm—overlaps. In that place the windigo is a spirit creature, very powerful. But once it comes into our world, it must take on mortality, become vulnerable. I have heard several stories of Cree and Ojibwa war parties catching one of them and burning them to death, or chopping them to pieces so they might take the frozen heart and melt it. If that was the case, would you risk leaving the valley?"

"I guess not."

"So," Steven was saying as he pulled himself from the back end of the Escort, unfolding like a jackknife, "are you saying that's what I've got to look forward to? Being chopped up like kindling?"

"Or burned down like your friend Church," Wilson told him point-blank. "I'm not gonna lie to you, son. If the midé ceremony doesn't take, it may come to that."

Steven's expression was sullen for a moment, and he bowed his head as if in defeat. But when he lifted it again, they could see a steely resolve there. "What are we standing around for?" he said, heading for the cabin. "Let's get on with it."

TWENTY

GEORGE WILSON WAS STILL AT IT STOOPED DOWN ON THE small area of tile before the wood stove where he could continue stoking the fire.

"Don't you think it's getting awfully hot in here?" Janet asked, mopping her brow.

The old man nodded. "That's the idea, missy. The hotter the better." He reached for yet another splinter of wood.

Great, she thought. After I puke, I'll let you clean it up. She leaned forward and put her head in her hands, tried to quell the nausea that was welling within her. She'd never realized she was claustrophobic before; that was usually Steven's domain. On the other hand, she'd never been cramped into a one-man cabin with three other people. There was only the single room with a cot and a rocking chair and a small table nearby, where an old kerosene lantern stood in dichotomy to the portable TV and VCR beside it. The real light for the room came from the electric bulb overhead, powered by the same generator that ran the TV. There was a shelf on the wall for videotapes and Louis L'Amour westerns, and a well-stocked gunrack, and on the counter across the room were supplies and a presslike contraption that Barton told her was used in loading rifle shells. And that was all there was to this cabin. That and the all-too-effective stove. The four of them were seated on the plank floor in front of it, just as Wilson had instructed, and had peeled off their outer clothing until all they wore now were jeans and damp T-shirts. And the heat kept building. Janet gasped for another breath, felt it burn her lungs. *I can't take any more of this, I can't . . .*

Settle down. Breathe easy. And think of Steven.

She looked over at him, sitting cross-legged on the floor beside her with his now bony knees jutting out and his thin arms folded across his lap. He was sweating profusely, staining the boards beneath him, and his gasping and pinched expression showed that he was even more uncomfortable than she. "Hey," she said, putting on her best optimistic face. "It's gonna be all right, Steven. Just wait."

He tried to smile back, reached over, and squeezed her hand appreciatively. "I'm trying, Pud. I'm—" Then he seemed startled, realized their hands were touching. He pulled quickly away. "It's not a good idea," he said sullenly.

"But, Steven . . ."

"No, Janet. Please." He folded his arms across his chest, hiding the threat that his hands might hold. And she could see the fear in his eyes.

George Wilson was explaining the background of the midé ceremony as he fed the stove, thinking out loud as if to get the memories straight in his head. "The Ojibwa view of life has long been that of a single man against unyielding nature, fighting to survive harsh conditions and faced with manitos such as North Wind who could be treacherous and unkind. To get by, each man had to fast and suffer, show himself worthy of the pity of one of these powerful Supernaturals. Once this was accomplished, the manito that answered his call could become his patron or spirit guardian and give him mighty visions, watch over him as long as respect was shown and gifts given."

"Did you have a patron, old man?" Barton asked.

George glared at his grandson for interrupting. "We moved before my time to fast came. And in the city, Father wouldn't allow it."

"Then which manito do we call to help Steve?"

"Old Crooked Wing's patron was Ginyu the Arctic Owl —I heard him call to the spirit when he worked his cure on the windigo boy. The owl is one of the Thunderbirds, the air spirits. The Thunders were often called for curative ceremonies. It's just that . . .'' He trailed off and sighed, obviously flustered.

"What is it?"

"There's so much I don't remember. And what I do recall can't be done. The midé curing ritual was supposed to take eight days, followed by a public ceremony. We don't have time for that. And besides, the shaman would have different officers perform certain functions.''

"Me and Janet could be your officers."

"But that's just it. I'm not even sure what it was they did. It's all so sketchy . . .''

Barton laid a hand on the old man's shoulder. "Calm down, George. Just do what you can. We don't expect any more than that. Okay?''

Wilson managed a weak smile. "I'll try." He went back to feeding the stove and dredging memories. "The sweat lodge was often used to address the manitos and gain visions. They used heated stones back then, kinda like a sauna. But this should accomplish the same thing. The heat clears the senses, and our discomfort will make us even more pitiable.''

"What happens if this owl character shows up?" Janet asked.

The old Indian held up the wayan bag, which had been sitting next to him on the floor. "We ask him to awaken the migis and guide their magic. I watched Crooked Wing hold up the bag and point it at the afflicted boy, and he shot him with the shell. It flew right into his chest, for it's inside the body that the shell magic occurs. As soon as it entered him the boy collapsed to the ground, unconscious, and the healing took place. Then when he came to, he was cured. Later on, he coughed up the migis.''

"Couldn't we just have Steven take a couple with a glass of water?''

Wilson turned on his grandson impatiently. "No, no, no!

The magic has to be awakened, the manito has to trigger it and help shoot it from the bag, he—''

"George, George," Barton restrained him. "I was kidding, okay? Lordy, you'd better loosen up or you're gonna have a heart attack or something."

The old man nodded. His shoulders sagged visibly, and he wiped a sheen of sweat from his weathered face. "It's time to start," he said, shutting the door on the stove. He leaned closer to Barton. "Did you bring the rope from the shed?"

"It's over by the door."

"Good. Help me up." Wilson stood with a great deal of difficulty and shuffled over to the cabin door, retrieved the coil of thick rope and then pulled the rocking chair over near the stove. "Mr. Wilhoit," he addressed Steven, "if you'll have a seat . . ."

The American obliged, moving to the chair even as Janet questioned their motive. "What's this about? You aren't going to tie him up, are you?"

"Just as tight as we can," George answered. "It's for his own good, Mrs. Wilhoit, and even more for ours. We're about to call on manitos. We may get some we don't want. And I guarantee you that the windigo inside your husband will come to the surface. For now it should be temporary, just until the ceremony is over. But we wouldn't want it getting loose while it's here."

"It's okay, Janet," Steven told her. "I'd rather not take any chances." As Barton dropped loop after loop around his torso and secured the rope with double knots, Steven looked straight into George's eyes. "Anything else you want me to do?"

"Just relax, sonny. Rest. From here it's out of your hands." Once the tying was finished, he moved back over near the wood stove where Barton helped him back to the floor. He motioned for Janet and his grandson to move closer to the heat so they were all seated right across from Steven.

Then he reached into his shirt pocket, got out his pipe and tobacco pouch.

"I'd like a cigarette myself," Janet said, "but shouldn't we get this thing started?"

"We are," Barton whispered to her as they watched Wilson pack his bowl and then sprinkle the rest of his tobacco in a line on the floor before him. "Gifts of tobacco are what's used to call the manitos." He saw the questioning in her eyes and shrugged. "I don't know why or how they arrived at that deal. Maybe these Supernaturals set the price a long time ago, back when tobacco was a valuable commodity, so the caller was sacrificing something to call on them."

"Or maybe they just like a good smoke?" she countered, trying to be flippant and unconcerned. But instead she just sounded worried and afraid and about to pass out from the heat. Barton put an arm around her shoulder to keep her sitting up.

"You two, shhh!" Wilson scolded in a soft voice. "It's time to begin." He drew on the lit pipe, let a languid smoke ring waft from his lips and into the air before them. "O manitos," he called, seemingly very loud in those close quarters. "See this sacred tobacco. It is for you, and in return we ask for an audience. Please, take it kindly and regard us gently."

Silence still.

"Is anything—"

"Janet, shhh!"

George blew more smoke into the hot, heavy air, till it was thick and grey and they had to hold a hand over their mouths to keep from coughing. "I call to you, great and powerful Thunderbirds, and to Ginyu the Arctic Owl who was the wise patron of my father's father Crooked Wing. Forgive our ignorance of the customs and the old ways. But we need your help. Please . . ."

The smoke in the air around them seemed to move, to swirl gently, lazily, as if the merest hint of night breeze were somehow slipping through a rift in the cabin walls. They had just a moment to notice it before the lights suddenly faded and went out.

"What the hell . . ."

"I don't like this."

"Both of you, listen!" At Barton's insistence they calmed down, held their breath. Silence.

"I don't hear anything," Janet said.

"Exactly. The generator motor isn't humming anymore. It's stopped. That's why the lights went out."

That brought a collective sigh. "Don't you have a flashlight or something?"

"My regular one's back in Atikokan. But here, I'd have to look. For now we can use the kerosene lantern. I think there's enough fuel in it." He fished around in his pocket for a book of matches, then got up in the dark and felt his way to the table.

Behind him Janet suddenly realized she was hugging herself, and that gooseflesh had crept all along her arms and back. "Has the stove gone out?" she asked. "Suddenly it's a little cool in here."

There was a hissing sound in the dark as Wilson cursed, sucked on his throbbing finger. "The stove's still hot, all right. But it does seem to be getting colder in here."

"It's gotta be your imagination," Barton said, striking a match. "The temperature just couldn't . . . drop . . ." He trailed off, watching his words pass before the match's flame in an opaque cloud. The steam hung in the air without dissipating. "Lordy . . ."

The match burned down to his fingers and he dropped it. The dark resettled immediately, and Davejac almost cried out. Panicked, he pulled another from the book and struck it, then grabbed for the lantern and fumbled with the glass chimney so he could get to the wick. It was well steeped and took the flame immediately, widening the match's circle of light a hundredfold. It illuminated nearly all of the room, and its brilliance was multiplied by its own reflection.

In the ice.

Barton looked all around him, his eyes growing wide with shock. The walls . . . They were cold and white, glistening with a thin layer of crystalline frost. Icicles hung from the rafters and the bookshelf and even from the edge of the table before him, like small stubby teeth but growing larger, longer, as he watched.

"Oh, my God," Janet gasped from behind him, echoing his sentiments. Only her attention was focused somewhere else entirely. "Oh, God," she sobbed, "Oh, Steven . . ."

Barton felt a cold chill race from tailbone to brain stem. Don't turn around. You won't like what you'll see. You'll be sorry. But despite his trepidations, he picked up the lantern and carried it back to the others. And saw what had them frozen with dread.

Steven Wilhoit was still seated in the rocker, most of his torso obscured by the binding coils of stout hemp. He hadn't moved at all since sitting down. But he was different just the same. His eyes were closed and his facial features lax and sleeping. But behind those features, something else was going on. There was another face behind his, as if his skull were growing, pushing forward, stretching the skin that enclosed it. But this skull had few human attributes. The jaw was long and underslung, and the teeth much too large for the dimensions of the head. Their sheer size, imprinted behind his closed lips, gave the impression of a leering smile that stretched from ear to ear. Literally.

Barton immediately thought of Andy Church, grinning, showing the splits in his cheeks that ran all the way back . . .

Steven's lids snapped open suddenly, but the eyes they revealed were not his own. These were wet and grey. Dead.

Janet started to get up, to go to him instinctively. But Barton held her down. "Steven?" she called to the thing in the chair. "Can you hear me?"

The mouth of the windigo moved first, and then Steven's opened in reaction. Davejac was sure the cheeks would tear, but it didn't go that far. "You. Called," it replied in a cold, distant voice. "We. Come. Hungry."

"Keep at it, old man," Barton whispered urgently. "Get hold of somebody, pronto. I've got a feeling those ropes won't hold him."

"Yes, of course," George Wilson said, looking around for his pipe before realizing it was still clenched between his gritted teeth. He puffed anxiously, gagged as the smoke burned his throat. "Oh, Ginyu, I raise my hands to the fabled Thunders. Please help us."

Steven looked right at the ersatz shaman, fixed him with a dull, lifeless stare. "You. Are. Dead. Old. Man. Dead." He laughed, his tone hollow, and it froze them even more than the chill in the surrounding air.

George tried to ignore the taunts but his mind was swimming. The smoke was making him ill, and despite the sudden cold, he could feel sweat running down his sides and beading on his brow. His ears were throbbing with his own heartbeat. "Thunders, hear us. Aid us now and we will hold a real midéwiwin in your honor, just as our ancestors did, just as Crooked Wing would have done." He held up the wayan bag and pointed the open end toward Steven's chest. "Guide the shells. Give him life."

They waited, watched for a migis to come shooting from the bag. But nothing happened. Steven laughed again, tried flexing his arms beneath the ropes. "We. Are. Hungry."

George was growing frantic. He thrust his hand into the bag, pulled out a fistful of the small pearls, and held them out bare inches from Wilhoit's chest. "Do not punish him for my mistakes," he pleaded. "I'm the one who forgot the old midé ways. I forgot the ceremony. Punish me for this. But this man is innocent. He did not know better. Please, help him . . ."

Nothing. His only reply was the windigo's mocking, toneless laugh. It smiled then with those big teeth, and Steven's cheeks began to tear like tissue paper.

You. Dead. Old. Man . . .

The pounding in George's ears skipped a beat, became erratic. His left arm went numb. Pain lanced through his chest like a drill bit.

Loosen up, old man, or you're gonna have a heart attack or something.

A smart boy, that Barton. Just like his mother . . .

Still clutching the migis shells, he staggered away from the grinning specter in the rocker and collapsed across Janet Wilhoit's lap. The pain was unbearable now, engulfing him and pulling him away from the world. He could see the woman and his grandson looming above, saw their lips move as they called to him. But he was sliding further and further away . . .

OU IGNORED YOUR PEOPLE.

It was a soft voice, a whisper in an ear that no longer heard. It came from nowhere and from all around him. And there was great power in its tone.

OU IGNORED YOUR PEOPLE.

OU IGNORED YOUR PAST.

UT YOU REMEMBER US.

OR THIS WE HEAR.

OR THIS WE GIVE PITY.

A burning erupted in his clenched right hand, chasing the numbness away. Waking his senses to a new kind of pain. It was even more sharp and jolting than that in his chest, like electricity stabbing through his muscles, making them spasm uncontrollably. He held up his fist. The migis—it had to be the shells! With concerted effort he forced his hand open, shook it to get rid of them and the pain they caused him. But . . .

They were not there.

"Look at his hand," he faintly heard Janet gasp. "Look!"

In the center of his palm were five small knots, like kernels beneath the skin, no larger than a pea. And they were moving. Across the heel of the hand and down the wrist. Following the bloodstream. From there they picked up speed, raced up his bare forearm, and disappeared halfway to the elbow.

And the pain moved as well.

It followed the same trajectory, up through the bicep and across, burrowing under the pectoral muscle until it overtook the other pain in his chest and consumed it. Only this was many times worse than before; it felt like someone had hooked jumper cables to his heart and was steadily turning up the juice. George Wilson's whole body went rigid and began to twitch uncontrollably. He didn't feel Barton holding him down, or Janet sticking the wadded tobacco pouch between his gritted teeth. This pain was so severe that it took his mind and his senses and left him adrift in a blinding whiteness.

But not alone.

He could feel someone there with him. Something. In fact, more than one. But this was not Barton or Janet, he knew that intuitively. He was in the presence of something ancient and elemental, like standing beneath a towering birch or watching the natural wonder of a waterfall. It filled him with the same awe. The same fear.

OU ARE CLEANSED.

OU LIVE.

HIS IS OUR GIFT TO YOU.

"Wait," he called to the Thunderbirds, if that was who these spirits were. "What about the white man? Can you help him?"

E DOES NOT KNOW THE OLD WAYS.

E DOES NOT REMEMBER US.

E WILL NOT HELP HIM.

Then he felt the whiteness dimming around him, felt himself being pulled back to the realm of pain and consciousness, and away from the elemental majesty of the Thunders. "Wait!" he called to them in desperation. "Is there nothing else for him? Is there no other way to help?"

There was no answer. The pain began to rise around him again, washing over him in numbing waves. But just before he was completely emersed, one of the voices whispered in his ear . . .

Barton and Janet were still leaning over George's stuporous

form when the hum of the generator sounded from the shed outside and the bulb overhead came back to life. Janet looked up for a moment, startled, and found the frost gone from the walls. The icicles had vanished, as if they had never been. The room was warm once again, almost steamy.

And Steven?

He sat in the rocker with his head hung on to his chest, no longer struggling with the ropes or moving at all. He was still pale and long-limbed. Still cursed. But at least the windigo had retreated for the moment, or so Janet hoped. She reached over hesitantly, tipped the head back . . . Steven's eyes were closed and his features slack. But the slits in his cheeks were now bleeding slowly, something they hadn't done at all before. Then his eyelids fluttered and he looked at her, not with hard muddy eyes but his own. "My mouth . . ." he whispered painfully. Then he looked down at himself, at his long gangly legs splayed out in plain view. And his spirits sank. "That's it, then," he said, dejected. "I'm finished."

"Not . . . necessarily," George Wilson croaked after he spit the pouch from between his teeth.

"Best lay back, Grandfather," Barton tried to keep him still. But the old man would have none of it.

"I'm fine, boy," he said, though obviously pained and very weak. "I'll be all right. But Steven must know this." He looked at the tall man still imprisoned in the rocking chair. "The Thunders will not help you. But there might be another way."

Suddenly the old man made a queer face, as if he tasted something bad. And he spat five migis shells into his open hand.

TWENTY-ONE

JANET HELD THE SMALL SHAVING MIRROR WITH TREMBLING hands as her husband kneeled down beside the table and studied his reflection. The angry fissures that ran from the corners of his mouth were the only hint of color in an otherwise pallid face. The bleeding had stopped so long as he refrained from opening his mouth too wide. He regarded the task at hand, then turned to Barton's emergency med kit and took out the antiseptic, a pair of scissors, a spool of heavy thread, and the curved suturing needle.

"Are you sure you don't want something for the pain?" she asked him again.

"No," Steven was firm. "The pain's not so bad. As long as I feel something, I know I'm still here." He looked up at her, tried to grin as much as his ruined mouth would allow. "Don't worry, Pud. It won't hurt any more than it already does." She watched him thread the needle with difficulty, his long fingers trembling. "I wish you'd just let me do this," she said.

"We've been through it, Janet. Remember? The less contact, the better." He knotted the thread, then sterilized the sliver of curved steel with a cotton ball. "Hold the mirror still," he told her as he pinched the two parts of his cheek together and started the first stitch. He flinched as the needle went in, then just set his jaw and continued the procedure.

"You're a better man than I, Gunga Din," Davejac said from the other side of the small cabin. "Takes real balls to sew up your own face. Lordy . . ." He tried to put the thought out of his mind by turning his attention to his grandfather. George Wilson lay on the nearby cot, looking withered and spent but even at that a hundred percent better than a few minutes ago. "Hey, old man," he said softly, perching himself on the edge of the bed, "how are you doing now?"

George regarded him through slitted eyes, then managed a smile. He reached out to pat the younger Indian's hand. "I'll get by. Don't you think twice about it."

"I've got to tell you, I was worried there for a minute. You looked like death warmed over. I was positive you were having a heart attack."

"I was," Wilson said matter-of-factly. "A bad one too. But the Thunders saved me. They brought the migis shells to life." He touched the wayan bag in his belt, where he'd returned the small pearls he gave up.

"They saved you, huh?" Steven stopped sewing long enough to observe. His voice was resigned, bitter. "How come they didn't help me?"

The old man shrugged. "Because you're white, I suppose."

Steven's laugh was cynical. "Too bad your windigo isn't so fucking picky."

"The manitos can be arbitrary and spiteful, that is for certain," Wilson agreed. "Why do you think the Ojibwa always considered themselves at odds with the forces of nature? Sometimes the game was plentiful, and sometimes they took it away. Who knows what they'll say or how they'll act. You just do what you can."

Janet interrupted. "You mentioned something about another way to help Steven? What was that about?"

The old man's face was a mixture of hope and dejection. "The Thunders told me you might still be able to remove this curse. But I doubt you'll be too anxious once you hear." He tried to think of some better way of explaining it to them, but he finally opted for the direct route. "They told me you must drink the blood from a heart of ice."

The three looked at one another quizzically. "What the hell does that mean?"

George fixed his gaze directly on Steven. "It means you must face the windigo that cursed you, melt down its icy heart, and drink the water. Then you'll be free."

"Is that all?" Barton sighed sarcastically. "Well hell, why didn't we think of that ourselves? I mean, it's so obvious." He cradled his head in his hands and moaned, wondering just what he was doing there and exactly when he would wake up.

Steven finished one line of stitches, knotted the thread, and clipped it with the scissors. Then he looked at his gaunt reflection in the small mirror, with one cheek badly sewn and the other gaping horribly. "I don't want to go back there," he whispered, his voice tinged with fear. "But if that's what it takes . . ."

"I'm going with you," Janet said.

"Oh, no you're not. It's too dangerous." He looked up and saw the hurt in her eyes, tried to make her understand. "You don't know what it's like in there, Jan."

"You aren't leaving me behind again," she snapped. "I'm going, no matter what you say."

"You'd better listen to her, Steven," the old man counseled. "You'll need all the help you can get. You're in control here, now. But what about two days from now? Besides, if this valley is a manito place, the windigo within you will be more powerful than ever there. It will take everything you've got just to keep your mind straight. And maybe your wife can help with that. Now, if you'll give me till morning, I'll be rested enough to come along—"

"Oh, please," Barton groaned angrily. "Spare me the bullshit, George. You know you're as weak as a kitten. You aren't going nowhere. And that leaves me, doesn't it?"

"No one's even asked you to go, Davejac," Steven said as he went back to work on his face.

"Oh, yeah? Well, how do you two get through the woods without getting lost? How do you find the valley again? You know damn well it boils down to me. And you know what else? I don't like it. Once is enough for me. I never even want to see that place again.'' He stalked around the limited interior of the cabin in frustration. ''Do you really know what you're talking about here? Just how big is this thing you're expecting to take down? The size of a tree? Bigger? And you're just gonna wander in and say, could I borrow that chunk of ice in your chest? I mean, wise up. We don't have any LAWS rockets or flamethrowers here, no heavy artillery. Just how do you intend to pull this off?''

''The Thunders gave us a weapon, boy,'' George informed him. ''They whispered to me Words of Power. They said if these are spoken in the presence of the windigo, the creature will be bound long enough for you to chop out the heart.''

Barton rubbed a hand through his hair wearily. ''Words of Power, huh . . . Let me ask you a question. How do you know they weren't lying? You said it yourself, manitos can be spiteful. How do you know for certain?''

The old man shrugged. ''I don't. But they saved me, didn't they? And besides, what other choice do we have?''

Barton simmered there, dredging up more and more rational reasons why they shouldn't even consider such a fool's quest. But he finally realized it was useless. This situation was beyond all rationality. ''All I can do is think about it,'' he finally allowed. ''No promises. Just think about it.'' He started toward the door, muttered something about taking a leak, and went outside into the night.

''Don't you worry,'' George Wilson assured the Wilhoits. ''He's a good boy. He won't let you down.'' Then a weary look washed over that deeply lined face, and he sank back into the pillow, exhausted. ''I just wish I could come with you. But the boy's right. I'd just slow you down.''

''It's just as well, old man,'' Steven warned as he stood away from the mirror, clipping the excess thread on his other finished cheek. His lips were now flanked with crisscrossed lines of black. ''You don't want to go there. Take my word for it. You don't ever want to see that place.'' He looked over at his wife. "I'd rather you stay here where it's safe. But I know how you are once you set your mind on something."

"Damn right." She managed a grin. "I've said it before, mister, you aren't getting rid of me. Not now, not ever." She reached out for his hand but stopped herself, knowing that he'd just flinch and move away. So she turned her attention to the man on the bed instead. "These Words of Power . . . Could anyone say them? Like me?"

Wilson shrugged. "They didn't say, the Thunderbirds, I mean. But I would expect Barton to have a better chance, especially after the way they turned their backs on Steven 'cause of his color. Besides that, Barton is Crooked Wing's direct descendant. Maybe there's a little midé magic in the blood."

"But if he doesn't come with us . . ."

George dismissed the notion out of hand. "Don't give up on him, missy. Barton's always done the right thing before. He took me in, didn't he? Not many kids these days would do that for an old man."

"He can go or stay," Steven said. "It doesn't make any difference to me. Whatever he decides, we're leaving at first light." He stepped back to the table and picked up the shaving mirror Janet had laid aside. In it he looked at himself, at the long, thin, laced-up face that was becoming harder to recognize. "I want this over," he whispered. "One way or another."

It was past midnight already, and Janet was still awake.

She'd drifted off several times since turning in, only to jerk back to consciousness within scant moments. Sleep was a stealthy prey this night, and it was eluding her at every turn.

It was the floor, she told herself, the plank floor. It was too hard for a bed, and it played hob with her back muscles. And it was cold, too, even though she was curled up only a few feet from the still-glowing wood stove. Combine the two and that had to be what was keeping her up. And George Wilson's snoring wasn't helping any. He was on the cabin's only cot, on his back, and his light breathing was raspy, like sandpaper on her nerves. And then there was Barton. He was still up, sitting on a stool at his counter with the kerosene lantern, tinkering with his tools and doing God knows what. All that clatter . . .

It was all of those things. And none of them. They were loud and irritating to be sure, but only because she made them that way, listened for them. Anything to blame, to get her mind off her worries. For that was the heart of the matter. She just couldn't shake the apprehension, the fear. Of what would happen. Of what wouldn't.

This insomnia was nothing new. She'd been experiencing lesser bouts for the past week, ever since Steven left. But her worries had been for such inconsequential things then— whether he'd twist an ankle or catch a bad cold, or whether he'd have too good a time and want to do this macho bonding crap more often, see more of the guys and less of her. Stupid things, in comparison to what she now felt.

What would you do without Steven?

She tried not to think about it, but there was no use. It was the foremost thing, the only thing, on her mind. And it demanded an answer.

I'd get by, she told herself. I'm strong. I'm self-sufficient. I'll always survive. But the one question I can't answer is, would I want to?

She thought of Steven then, not as he was now but as he had been. His quick smile and bad jokes. The way he'd peer over his glasses at her, just to get a smile. Even that infuriating stubborn streak. They were all things she loved so dearly. Losing him would be like giving up a piece of her heart, and how would she live with that?

The question came again. What would you do without Steven? And this time she had an answer.

I wouldn't. And I won't. I'm holding on to what's mine, and I'm never letting go.

She sat up and stretched, abandoning her hunt for slumber, and was about to ask Barton if he kept any coffee around there. But that's when she noticed that her husband was nowhere to be seen. He'd insisted on crouching in the far corner, away from the rest of them, but that area was vacant now. The blanket Barton had given him was lying on the floor. "Where's Steven?" she said, suddenly alarmed.

Davejac didn't even look up from his workbench. "He stepped out a few minutes ago, while you were snoozing. Said he needed to get some air."

"And you let him go?"

Barton chuckled at that. Sighed. "Hey, if I had my way, he'd be hog-tied in the corner. I wanted him bound, remember?" He shook his head and kept on working, left Janet to stand there and fume.

"He won't turn that fast, Barton. He said so and I believe him." She zipped up her coat, hurried to the door, and went outside.

The woods directly around the cabin were much darker than she'd anticipated, filtering out all but the most tenacious moonlight. She found herself hemmed in by shadows, tall and gnarled, perfect fodder for a vivid imagination. But her attention was focused to one goal only: finding her husband. Her eyes scanned the grounds, searching for the now-familiar flash of pale skin . . . There, out in the open beyond the tree line. A tall, gangly figure, visible for only an instant as it disappeared behind the other cabin. It had to have been Steven. It had almost glowed in the stark celestial light.

She came out of the trees to find a vista every bit as awe-inspiring as what Steven had witnessed on his first night at Chalako Lakes. Clouds edged the horizon but left the heavens overhead crystal clear, and she felt her breath catch as she took in the sheer immensity of that infinite field. But Janet Wilhoit was single-minded to a fault. She stood there in wonderment for only a moment or two, and then she was back on the hunt. She crossed the open ground and rounded the cabin, found herself on the shores of tranquil Beaver Lake.

Steven was standing at the edge of the water with his back to her, skipping stones with a casual sweep of his almost gibbonous arm. She wasn't sure whether to approach him or not. He appeared lost in thought, and she didn't want to disturb him . . .

"What's the matter," he said without turning, "can't get to sleep?"

"I saw that you were gone," she said, walking down to stand beside him. "I was worried."

"I just needed to get out. I couldn't breathe in there."

She laughed. "I know how you feel. I—"

"No, you don't," he interrupted flatly. That took her by surprise. He saw it in her eyes and tried to soften his demeanor. But little of it was under his control. "I mean, this isn't just claustrophobia. I need to be outside. I'm part of this now. This place, these woods. It's so hard to explain . . . Hell, I don't think I understand it." He pointed across the lake, into the shadows back there. "You see the crooked limb on that jack pine, the one with the knotty trunk?"

She peered across that distance, tried to discern anything in the blackness there. "I don't see anything."

"Exactly. But I do. And I'm not wearing my glasses. Get it? My eyes are sharper now, even in the dark. And that isn't all. Here, watch this." He bent and picked up a rock, flung it out across the water with only moderate effort. Still, she distinctly heard it impact on a tree trunk. Clear on the other side of the lake. "I'm changing, Janet. I'm stronger, I see better, I hear better. And it's scaring the shit out of me." He held up his long, thinning arms, stared at them in disgust. "This isn't me. This is some kind of fucking monster."

"Steven, don't talk like that." She moved toward him. He moved away. "It's going to be all right," she told him. "I promise."

"I wish I could believe that," he whispered. "I really do." He walked a few yards down the tranquil waterline with Janet following along, and perched himself on a stump there. "You do know I love you, don't you?"

She blushed a little in the moonlight. "I know. And right back at ya."

There was a slight smile playing on his face. In the silvery glare it looked almost bittersweet. "That's the worst part about this," he said somberly. "You know what I miss most? Touching you. I always loved that. I did it so much I really didn't realize I was doing it. But now I remember each and every time. Hugging you. Holding your hand while we watched TV. Kissing the back of your neck while we fixed dinner. I remember all of it. God, I miss that."

Janet blinked back her tears, determined not to cry. Be strong, she told herself. He needs that now. She held out her arms to him and took one tentative step. Steven stiffened warily.

"Don't, Jan. It's too big a chance."

"I'll risk it," she said as she went to him, put her arms around him, and felt how thin he had become. He held back at first, tense and afraid. But then he clung to her desperately and buried his face in her shoulder. And he started to cry.

Janet stayed there, holding him tight despite the cold he emanated. She rocked him gently and sang softly into his ear, even as her teeth chattered. And she did not let go.

TWENTY-TWO

DAWN WAS STILL WELL OVER AN HOUR AWAY BUT THE FOUR IN THE cabin were already up. They had to prepare for the journey.

After a quick breakfast of George's biscuits and gravy, Barton went out to search the shed while the others scrounged what supplies they could find and piled them on the small tabletop. Janet knew after a chilly night that she was not dressed for the outdoors, and promptly slipped into a chamois shirt and a pair of fatigue pants she found in Barton's cedar chest in the corner. Both were oversized but she managed to roll up the sleeves and legs and adjust the waist extenders to fit her lithe frame.

Barton came in just then, carrying a double-headed axe— "The better to chop out icy hearts, my dear"—and a ratty, nearly worn-out backpack as well. "It's the best I could do," he said. "My better pack's back home in Atikokan." He looked then at the pile of food and gear the others had gathered and shook his head. "Too much stuff. We'll be moving as fast as we can, so we'll have to pack light." He pulled the rocking chair over and sorted the necessary items there. A Rossi twelve-gauge shotgun, both barrels sawed off for ease in carrying. Extra deer slugs. A flashlight he'd found in the shed. Extra batteries. Dried food packages, more than enough for four days, two there and two back. A first-aid kit. The rolled-up blankets that would have to do in lieu of sleeping bags. Heavy winter gloves for handling the windigo's heart. A pot for melting it.

"What if that pot's not big enough?" Janet asked.

"It will be," he said, refusing to believe otherwise.

George looked over the meager supplies. "It ain't much," he observed.

"This isn't a camp-out, you know," Barton said solemnly. "We're either in and out, or . . ." He took out a fanny pack that held a flare pistol and extra flares, handed it directly to Janet. "In case we get separated," he said. "And take this too." He offered her a diminutive revolver, the Charter Arms Pathfinder.22 he sometimes used to put down wounded game.

Janet looked at the toylike weapon quizzically. "What will that do against a windigo?" she asked.

"Same as this," he said, hefting the shotgun. "Not a thing. The guns are just a last resort." He picked up the Rossi, put the barrels under his chin. "Know what I mean?"

"Oh." The thought was repugnant but she stowed the gun in her pocket just the same.

George Wilson began to load the backpack. But when he started to slip the medical kit into the bag's front pouch, Barton stopped him. "That pocket's for our special cargo," he said. He crossed to the work counter where he'd spent much of the night, picked up three Campbell's Soup cans and a bean with bacon. Each was now resealed with epoxy putty and sporting six inches of linen from a hole in the lid. "Home cooking," he said, motioning to the reloading equipment behind him. The big can of bullseye gunpowder was empty and lying on its side. "I even impregnated the fuses with powder so they'll burn good. If these Words of Power don't pan out, maybe we can blow 'em back to hell." He carried the bombs to the bag like fragile eggs and slipped them into the padded outer pocket. Then he handed the whole pack to Steven, who was standing silently nearby. "Guess who gets to be pack mule on this trip, eh?"

"Fine with me," Wilhoit grunted.

"While we're at it, come on outside with me. I've got something else to show you." Barton ushered Steven to the door, slung the shotgun over a shoulder, picked up the axe again, and followed him out.

Janet and the old man were left alone in the cabin. George sat down wearily on the edge of the cot. The preparation had almost been too much for him, and he was waiting for his breath to catch up. "Are you feeling okay, George?" she asked.

He waved off her concern, tried to grin in spite of his malaise. "I'll be okay, don't you worry. It's you that's important. How are you doin'?"

She started to say fine, a rote response that automatically came with the question any other time. But this wasn't any other time. She felt awful, she hadn't slept much, and she was scared out of her wits. So she just settled for a shrug.

"I wish I could do more, missy."

She reached out and took his hand. "You've done all that you could. We wouldn't be this far without you."

"Well, at least take this." He pulled the wayan bag from his belt, reached into it, and took out a handful of migis shells, five or six in all. He held them out to her.

"George, I couldn't . . ."

"Please. Maybe they'll bring you luck." He grinned. "Who knows? The manitos are fickle. They could change their minds."

She took the shells from him and slipped them into the cargo pocket on the thigh of her pant leg. Then she hugged the old man tightly and kissed his weathered cheek.

"Janet," Barton called from outside. "Time to get going."

She slipped her coat on and went out onto the porch, Wilson following behind. Steven was waiting on her. He carried the backpack over one bony shoulder and a double coil of log chain on the other. It was capped with a large padlock from the shed door. "What's that all about?" she asked, pointing to the heavy metal links.

"My idea," Barton said as he approached, carrying his axe over one shoulder. "I won't be able to sleep at night unless I know where he's at. Just in case."

Janet glared at him. "He's not an animal, mister. That's just cruel."

"No, Pud," Steven said softly. "He's right. Besides, it's not that heavy. Not the way I am now." He looked over at Barton. "You want the canoes in the water or what?"

"Can you get 'em by yourself?" Davejac asked. Then he realized he was staring up into a face that was by now almost a foot above his own. "Sorry. Stupid question. Janet, why don't you give him a hand." He watched them walk off toward the canoe rack. Then he turned to his grandfather. "Do you have the words, old man?"

George handed him a piece of paper from his pocket. Davejac unfolded it and stared at the unsteady scrawling there. He started to read it under his breath but the old man grabbed his arm. "No! Read silently. Do not speak them aloud or they will lose their power before you need them. Besides, the windigo might hear and know your plan. Then it would never show itself."

"This looks like gibberish, you know."

"It is the best I could do," George said. "They didn't spell 'em for me, you know. I had to write it down phonetically."

"Is it Ojibwa?" Barton asked.

The old man shrugged. "I recognize a few of the words, here and there. But the rest, they could be actual manito words. Ancient, like the rock paintings. That's where they get their power. Just remember—you can rehearse them, practice them. But only to yourself. Not out loud."

"I'll keep that in mind." He secured the paper in his shirt pocket, then zipped up his light parka. He looked away, unwilling to meet his grandfather's gaze directly. "Well . . . I guess this is it."

"I suppose."

"Take care of the dogs, okay?"

"I will do that thing." The old man held out a trembling hand. "You take care too, eh?"

Barton clasped the hand, held it tight for just a moment. Then he turned and headed across the clearing. He was almost to the lake before he heard Wilson call out behind him.

"I'm proud of you, boy."

He wiped his eyes to make sure there were no tears before he got to the boats. No need for the others to see, he thought. You're the leader here. You've got to appear confident. Even if you're not.

Because of Steven's increased height and gangly limbs, he was forced to occupy a canoe of his own. Janet was already seated in the other. Barton handed her the axe and shotgun, then made ready to push off.

"You're sure there's not a faster way there?" Janet asked in a whisper. "I'm worried about Steven—he may not be able to last two days. Hey, what about that log camp where you went for help? Can't we just drive in there, then hike the rest of the way?''

"I don't know the roads back there," he told her. "It could take us two days just to find our way. Besides, if they're looking for us like you thought they might, it's better not to be out on an open roadway where they could spot us from the air. Right?"

Janet nodded. His logic was sound, and she didn't say another word as he edged them out into the deeper water. Then they broke out the paddles and followed a course parallel to the shoreline, just as the hunters had done before. Within fifteen minutes both canoes were out of sight of the base camp.

"This is it, then," Janet whispered. "No turning back now." She nervously churned the water with her oar.

"We'll be okay," Davejac tried to assure her. "Just settle down. Keep a smooth, steady stroke . . . That's it. You're doing fine."

With the two of them paddling, Barton had expected that they would all but leave Steven behind and constantly be waiting for him to catch up. But he hadn't counted on the man's reach and newfound strength. With extremely long strokes that went all the way from bow to stern, he powered through the water like a whole collegiate rowing team and did not seem to tire from the breakneck pace. He stayed well ahead of Janet and Barton the entire length of Beaver Lake, and held up only after reaching the end of the open water. The mazelike rills and runnels of Chalako lay before them, and he would have to rely on Barton's experience from there.

As they navigated the narrow backwaters, Barton watched Janet for a reaction to her surroundings. He expected at least an awed gasp or some other acknowledgment of the natural wonders of the forest around her. But if she felt any of the incredulity that Steven had experienced before her, she did not give it voice. She kept her gaze pointed straight ahead, and the few times she did waver to search the banks alongside them, her expression was furtive, suspicious. Looking not at the natural beauty but what might be hiding behind it. And then he understood. After all, Steven had come to Chalako looking for wonderment, to be excited and experience a whole new world. But his wife came for a whole different reason. She was only there to track down her husband's attacker and destroy it.

No two ways about it. Between the two of them, husband and wife, she was the real hunter.

"Barton!" Wilhoit called from the other boat. He had pulled in his oar and was just drifting. A long finger was pressed to his lips, and he motioned for them to quit paddling as well. Once they had, his momentum brought his canoe right up alongside their own.

"What is—"

"Listen!" He cocked his head to the side, his eyes closed. Concentrating. Then he softly said, "It's coming this way."

Barton grabbed for his shotgun reflexively. For now he heard it too. A whistling sound, far off in the trees but growing louder. A powerful rushing of air. It was coming right at them, or at least it sounded that way. But then it turned and blew parallel to the stream, off through the woods in a new direction so that its soft howling reached their ears but denied them visual evidence of its passing.

The sound was enough. It alone had the hair on Barton's neck standing at attention. His arms prickled with gooseflesh. "The cold wind . . ." he muttered.

"So?" asked Janet. "A wind . . . what's the big deal?"

"It blows from any direction it wants," Steven told her in a hushed tone, as if not wanting the gust to hear him. "But it comes from just one place. The valley."

"George says it could be lesser manitos," Barton told them, "under the control of the windigo. Or . . ."

"Or?"

He swallowed hard. "The anguished souls of those it's killed."

They exchanged worried glances and waited for the sound

of the wind to die out completely. Then they paddled all the harder.

It wasn't quite noon when Barton pointed out the deer pictograph that had so fascinated Steven on their first trip. They steered into the shallow portage just beyond the rocky overhang and pulled their canoes ashore, parked them right next to the boats from the earlier expedition.

Janet helped Steven on with his backpack and his burden of chains. Then she checked her watch against the position of the sun. "I'm no Daniel Boone," she estimated, "but I'd say we're making pretty good time. Wouldn't you, Bart?" When he didn't answer she turned to find him staring into the trees before them. His face was lined with uncertainty. "What is it now?"

He snapped out of it, smiled a bit sheepishly. "I'm sorry, Janet. Just a little lost, I'm afraid." He saw her roll her eyes and hurried to correct himself. "I don't mean lost geographically. This is just the first time I've been out here without Yogi and Boo-Boo. It doesn't feel right without them. Oh, well . . ." He shrugged off his unease and shouldered the axe, headed into the trees. The others followed close behind.

Almost immediately they came to the clearing where the men had first camped. The fire pit marked the spot. There Barton sat down on the ground, reaching into an inner coat pocket for his pipe.

"We're not camping already," Janet was surprised. "Are we?"

"No," guessed Steven. "I think I get it. The baguck, right?"

Barton smiled. "Very good. You were paying attention after all." He gave Janet a quick summary of the legend, how offerings were always left to this small bird spirit to ensure a successful hunt. Only now it had a different meaning for him. "It was always a game before," he admitted as he packed the bowl of his pipe. "I was playing at my heritage, showing off to the people that came out here. But I never really put much stock in it. Until now, that is.'' He lit his pipe then and puffed with determination as he laid a patch of cotton material on the ground and poured out a small hillock of tobacco onto it. ''Hear me, O baguck, spirit of the hunt,'' he called between big puffs of smoke. ''Accept this gift from us, this token of sacred tobacco. And in return look favorably upon our hunt. Bring us success.'' He folded the material around the shredded leaf, tied it off with a piece of string. ''Sorry, no candy this trip. Maybe next time. If there is one.'' He stood, carried the small pouch to the nearest tree, and secured it in the crotch of a low branch. ''Well, that ought to do it.'' Then he retrieved his axe and pointed out the direction they should travel. ''We've got a lot of ground to cover before dark.''

Steven went first, jingling like an elf with a hyperthyroid condition. He would not be hard to keep track of with those chains, Barton acknowledged. An additional benefit to bringing them along. Janet followed close behind her husband, leaving the Indian to bring up the rear for now. Which was fine with him. He wanted to gauge her ease of travel, as well as how much Steven remembered from their previous trip. He'd take over in good time.

He was just leaving the clearing when he glanced casually to the rear and froze right where he stood. On the lowest limb where he'd stowed the offering sat a small bird, delicate and fragile, completely lacking feathers or flesh or anything else. There was nothing there but dainty hollow bones. A skeleton, not only complete and erect but *moving*. It turned, pecked at the pouch he'd placed there, then hopped up onto it. That tiny skull turned his way and with empty sockets it seemed to acknowledge his presence. The beak opened and closed as if trying to speak. Then it extended the frameworks of its wings and flapped into the air, the offering clutched in its talons. It crossed the clearing and rose up into the glare of the midday sun, disappearing from his view.

The baguck has answered you, Barton, he could almost hear his grandfather say. *Your hunt will be successful after all.*

But we're after a monster this time . . .

He couldn't decide if the manito had brought him good news or bad.

Janet had been right. They were making good time.

By the time they set up camp for the night they were, by Davejac's estimation, almost two thirds of the way to their destination. If they got an early start, they would make it to the valley by late tomorrow afternoon.

Of course, none of that mattered now. The only important thing was sleep. They were all exhausted from the forced march, especially Janet. She had been unprepared for the rigors of the trek, so it wore on her most of all. But she was a stubborn woman and would not admit defeat nor ask any quarter. She stayed right with them as they trudged along, and whenever they slowed to give her time to rest, she always scolded and shamed them into a faster stride. But those efforts had taken their toll on her. Before they could even get a campfire underway, she had curled into a ball and dozed off, her slumber so deep a thunderclap couldn't have cracked it.

Barton envied her that. For it was now well after dark, and despite his own fatigue, he simply could not get to sleep.

He missed the dogs. He never realized how much he depended on them until now. He was always so confident in their presence; if anything came around, their hypersenses would pick up on it in an instant, and then they would wake him in turn. But now, he had to rely on his own painfully inadequate faculties, and they were not at all adverse to the influence of paranoia. Every pop and crack in the forest, every drop of dew that slapped a leaf from on high, echoed in his ears like ground-level thunder. Some big hunting guide, he scolded himself. Take his dogs away and he's a scared little boy, hearing things—

He jerked up onto one elbow, raising the shotgun from beneath his blanket even as he asked himself what had alarmed him so. He couldn't remember a specific sound.

Couldn't tell which direction triggered his unease. But an underlying fear told him to check on Steven.

Wilhoit was still sitting against the nearest tree trunk, about ten feet away. His arms were locked at his sides, bound there by lengths of log chain encircling not only his torso but the bough he was leaning on. It, in turn, was secured in place with the big padlock. He was awake, or at least his eyes were open. They were staring off into the woods . . .

Wait a minute . . . He sees something.

"Steven," the Indian whispered. "What is it?"

Wilhoit remained still. Softly he said, "Over there," and nodded his head across the camp.

Barton's eyes searched the darkened woods around them, trying to sort one tree from another. That's when he saw movement in the needled arms of a pine, just where Steven had motioned. Something was standing just to the side of the tree, bending the limbs back with its presence. In the folds of shadow Barton couldn't make out its shape or appearance. But a stray beam of moonlight did show the big rack of antlers poised above it. A sixteen-pointer, maybe more.

"It's a little late for that," Barton sighed to the animal. "You should've showed up a few days ago. Maybe we wouldn't be in this mess now. Go on, get out of here! Get!" He shooed the deer with his arms, even grabbed up a rock and threw it.

There was a thud in the dark. The throw was dead-on. But the deer still stood there.

"Look closer," Steven told him in a calm, toneless voice.

Davejac's unease was building even as he reached for the flashlight—deers just don't stand there and watch you and they don't put up with a rock in the forehead so what the hell is this, eh? So he wasn't completely surprised by the entity that his bright beam found there. The deer regarded him quizzically, as if empty sockets could do so any other way. Its grey hide seemed to be sliding off the bone, but that did not keep the animal from standing erect or shaking its head, pawing the ground anxiously. He adjusted his light downward, caught a glimpse of the ropey lengths of intestine dragging the ground beneath it. And he remembered Steven's story, of how Tucker had tried to field-dress his deer.

The old man had left the job half-done.

Barton sat there, frozen, unable to lift the shotgun, unsure what good it would do him anyway. That's when Steven spoke up. His voice was still toneless and calm, but just a bit louder so as to be heard on the other side of the camp. "We will be along," he said evenly. "But in our own time."

The deer watched them blankly, eyelessly. Then, slowly, it turned and stalked off into the trees, dragging part of itself behind.

"A helper," Steven said even before Davejac could form his question. "It came to lure us, like it did Tucker. But we know now. We can see through the illusions . . ." He seemed to be lost in thought a moment, staring into space. Then his stark gaze returned to the Indian. "Go back to sleep. It won't come again."

"Yeah. Sure."

Barton laid down and pulled the blanket up around his neck. But he knew sleep wouldn't come now. And maybe not for the rest of his life.

TWENTY-THREE

"JANET GET UP THINK WERE LOSING STEVEN!"

The words burned the fog of sleep from her mind. She jerked awake, wide-eyed and full of dread, to find herself still in the forest. The early morning sun barely penetrated the shroud of trees around them, and that rendered Barton Davejac little more than a shadow kneeling over her. She couldn't see his expression. But the tone of his voice, and the worry in it, still rang in her ears like a dying echo. "What is it?" she stammered, hoping against hope that she'd dreamed those alarming words and he'd just tell her it was all right, to go back to sleep.

Instead he grabbed her by both arms, hauled her up off the ground, and nearly carried her over to where Steven was still chained. And she saw just what it was that had the Indian so concerned. Steven was slumped as much as his bonds would allow him, and he was staring vacantly into space. His features were even more slack and empty. And so were his eyes. They had glazed over with a dull film. They seldom blinked. "Oh, God," Janet muttered, moving closer. "Steven? Steven, don't you do this to me. Come back, please . . ."

"Not too close, Janet," Barton warned. "You don't want to touch him. Not when he's like this."

Barton was right. But she had to fight the urge just the same. She wanted to grab him and shake him from his stupor, hold him and help him through this. "Steven, you said you'd fight. You promised me."

His mouth opened then as if to answer, but no words came. Still, it gave Janet hope. "He's trying," she told Barton hopefully. "He heard me."

"You can't be sure, Jan—"

"Yes, dammit. I'm sure!" She leaned down, looked her husband right in the eye. "What is my name? What is it? Come on, honey. What's my name?"

". . . Ja . . . Janet . . ."

"Good." She kept after him. "And where did we meet?"

The lips quivered a minute, trying desperately to form words. "In . . . Indiana . . ."

". . . University, that's right. Do you still remember that day, sweetheart? I was sitting on the steps of Woodburn Hall studying and—"

"Ballantine," he said. "It was . . . Ballantine Hall." This time his voice seemed stronger, more distinct.

A smile of relief from his wife, even as a tear slid down her cheek. "I was studying," she continued, "on the steps of Ballantine and then here you come, Mister Business School Bigshot. And I dropped my books all over the place just to get your attention. Remember?"

Steven just stared. For a moment Janet feared she wasn't getting through, that her words were falling on deaf ears. But then he moved. His eyes finally blinked, not once but three times. He looked straight at her then, the grey film easing, and a slight grin curled the corner of his mouth. " *My* books," he said, his words slow and drawn out. "I dropped *my* books. And you fell for it."

"Hook, line, and sinker." She laughed tearfully. "Welcome back."

"Thanks," he replied, flexing his facial muscles as if to thwart their atrophy. "I guess I drifted off for a minute there. Scary stuff."

"You're telling me. Don't you do that to me again."

"I'll try not to."

She chanced touching him then, placed a light kiss on his forehead. "Sit there and rest a little bit. We'll be leaving soon." Then she turned away, averting her face, wiping her eyes as she went. "I've got to use the bathroom," she said quickly, starting off into the trees. Barton called for her not to go too far.

She kept fighting the tears even after she was out of their sight. She sat down on a log and fished out her cigarettes, lit one with a shaking hand. Keep calm, girl, she advised. Keep it together. But it was no use. She was tired and sore and her nerves were shot and the sobbing finally overcame her, racking her entire frame. I almost lost him, she finally admitted. It was that close. And what happens next time, huh? What happens when he can't remember our anniversary or his name and he won't even talk, just sits there staring. Becoming one of those . . .

She took another drag on the cigarette, tried to steady herself. But the unraveling had already started, and she couldn't even hold her head up. She curled over into a ball and cried, rocking gently back and forth, wishing there was some answer to this hopelessness . . .

Leaves rustled.

Janet snapped alert, one emotion shunting aside another as fear brought her up off the log. She poised there, searching the trees around her, ready to run . . . And that's when she saw movement about fifty feet away, up in the crook of a wizened old birch. An owl was perched there, watching her with big saucer eyes.

Janet sighed, feeling stupid. "Just a bird," she sighed. But it was a beautiful bird at that. It was about the size of a football, and its feathers were pure white. They ruffled haughtily across its chest, giving it a look of superiority, like a landowner glaring down at some lowly trespasser. "Pretty bird," she said, waving to it. "Pretty . . ."

We call upon Ginyu the Arctic Owl . . .

The Thunders are fickle. They could change their minds . . .

". . . bird . . ." No, it couldn't be, she rationalized. Then she looked at the cigarette in her hand, its spiral of smoke wafting into the air. And she remembered the smoke rings that old George blew, and how tobacco is a sacred gift. *Could I have called to it? Could it have heard me crying and decided to take pity?*

The owl just watched her. Stoic. Unmoving.

She stepped forward hesitantly, afraid it might spook and take flight and show itself to be just another bird. But it didn't move. Another step, carefully through the tangles of weed and brush. "Hello . . . Ginyu," she said hesitantly. "Please, we need your help. Here," she shook the last two cigarettes from her pack and held them up for the bird to see. "These are for you. Um, accept this sacred tobacco and in return I ask . . . Please help my husband. Heal him like you did the old man." She dropped the cigarettes and ran a hand into the cargo pocket of her pants, dug out the migis shells, and held them up. "You can use these. You made them work before."

The owl just glared.

Janet's emotions were so close to the surface that she couldn't control them. She shifted from grief to anger in an eye blink. "Look, we may not be of your people but he needs you just the same. Don't hold that against him. It was one of you manitos that cursed him. It's only right that you should bring him back." Then she began to sob again, sank to her knees before the crooked birch tree. "Please," she cried, "I'll do anything. I'll give you more tobacco, as much as you want. I'll hold a midéwiwin for you, whatever it is. I'll learn and I'll have one in your honor. But you've got to help. You've got to—"

"Janet?" someone called from the distance behind her. Barton's voice. "Are you okay? Where the hell are you?"

"Over here!" she called back over her shoulder. "Hurry, come and talk to them. Tell them . . ." But then she looked back at the birch, and found the crook was empty. There was no owl there, white or otherwise.

If there ever had been.

As Barton came through the underbrush he found her standing by the tree, reaching up to touch that split where the bird had appeared. "Janet?" he asked. "Are you all right?"

She nodded, wiping her face. There were no more tears; they had all been cried out. "I guess I was daydreaming," she muttered. Then she looked down at the migis shells in her open hand, thought seriously about throwing them as far as she could. But instead she just slipped them back into her thigh pocket. "Are we ready to go?"

"Yeah, we'd better get moving."

Janet nodded. She stepped past him and went to rejoin her husband.

They did not travel like the day before, in solemn silence. This day's trek was accompanied by the steady drone of voices. Mostly Janet's.

''What year did the Hoosiers last win the NCAA?

''What's your mother's maiden name?

''Who played Chekov on *Star Trek*?''

The questions were all aimed squarely at Steven. Jogging his memory had enabled him to fight off the windigo's effects earlier that morning, so Janet figured that constant stimulation of his conscious mind might help him to keep control. It seemed to work. His speech and reflexes grew smoother as they traveled, and it also made the monotony of hiking a bit more tolerable. Barton even joined in on a few occasions, especially since *Star Trek* was his personal raison d'être. But Janet shushed his answers, firmly reminding him who this wilderness version of Trivial Pursuit was for. This was not just a game, after all. For Steven it was a matter of life or death.

Steven was still trying to name the entire cast of *M*A*S*H* when they came out of the trees and onto a rocky escarpment that looked out over a sea of prickly green. The noonday sun reflected in the chain of small lakes in the distance. ''Remember this place, Steven?'' Barton asked. He pointed over toward the lakes. ''The timber camp's right over there. That's where I went to get help.'' He fell silent a moment, listened. ''I don't hear anything. No saws, nothing. That means they probably bugged out. But I'll lay ten-to-one odds that once this hubbub over Tucker and Covey dies down, they'll move right back in and take up like nothing happened. I've seen it before. In fact, I'll bet their machinery's still sitting down there, just waiting for 'em.'' He put a hand on Janet's shoulder. ''I've got an idea. When this is all over, we'll go down there and see if there's a truck that's operational. Then we can drive out instead of hiking, okay?''

Janet managed to smile, even though she knew he wasn't serious. False confidence had a bad ring to it.

The Indian checked the position of the sun, mentally measuring the distance he'd traveled on foot a few days before. ''If we keep on at this rate, we should be there before dark.''

He turned to the figure that loomed behind him. "Hey, big guy. Up to some more traveling, eh?"

Steven was still lost in thought. ". . . Loretta Switt . . . William Christopher played the priest . . . but who was the hairy guy with the nose . . ."

More walking. More forest. And the lull between Janet's questions began to widen. She had strip-mined her trivia vein and bled it dry; now it was Barton's turn to come up with some, and that left her free to survey their surroundings for the first time. Steven's game had kept her too occupied— she'd missed the subtle changes as they traveled, the transition from vibrant forest to dark, dead woods. The trees here grew tall and held their foliage against the threat of autumn, but it still seemed lifeless. There were no birdsongs, no sounds of any kind. Nothing. These, then, were the demon woods she had expected all along. True, there were no looming oaks with faces formed right in the bark, ready to grope after her. But they seemed haunted all the same. For it was easy to envision monsters here.

Far too easy.

"Clayton Moore," Steven was answering the latest question as they forded a small stream. "And Tonto was Jay Silver—"

"Wrong," Davejac razzed. "It's Silverheels, not just Silver. Man, you shoulda got that one . . ." He cast Steven a backward glance and found the man had stopped several feet to the rear. He was now frozen in place, his back rigid, his face turned skyward. And when he finally met the Indian's gaze, there was a strange look of agitation in his eyes.

"It's close," he said. "I can feel it. I don't want to go there, I don't want to . . ." He wore a look of real dread; his brow was knitted and his lip quivered fearfully. Barton would have sworn that he was about to turn tail and bolt like a frightened doe. But instead he abruptly stalked forward, continuing their advance. In fact, there was a strange urgency to his stride as he plowed through the underbrush. "No, I don't want to," he was still saying as he headed off through the trees.

Those sudden movements took Janet and Davejac completely by surprise. Before they even knew what was happening, Steven had gained a commanding head start, and was growing farther and farther away. "Steven, wait!" Janet called as they started after him at a dead run, as fast as the clinging undergrowth would allow. But even then they could not keep up. Her husband's extended stride took him deeper and deeper into the brush, until he was no longer in sight. Only the echoes of his plea remained.

"I don't want to go there! I don't!"

Oh, God, Janet thought as a cold realization settled. It's drawing him. That damn place is pulling him in. "Fight it, Steven!" she yelled, willing her already-numb legs to carry her faster still. "We're coming, sweetheart! We're coming!"

They beat their way through the weeds and bushes at a frenzied pace, even after the echoes of his voice had died away and there was nothing to follow, nothing but the silence. Still, they knew where he was going. Barton led the way, but Janet's mortal fear kept her neck and neck with him, would have propelled her past had she known which direction to take next. "Steven!" she called. "Say something!" But there was no answer. "How much farther, dammit!" she snapped to the guide as her panic neared the breaking point.

The next instant they plunged through the trees and found themselves on the edge of a startling precipice. The valley spread before them.

It did not look the way Barton Davejac had last seen it. It had been hiding its true face the day the search party came, concealing its mysteries with an air of normalcy. But no more. The rift was as he had originally found it, flooded with a shifting mist that hung thick in the upper limbs of the trees. The waning daylight made it almost opaque, a sea of clouds impaled on spires of jack pine and spruce.

"My God," Janet whispered next to him, stifling a shiver at its very appearance. "It's like . . ." But any initial reactions were immediately overridden by her concern for Steven. She went right to the edge of the land and found it almost a sheer drop into a void of tree limbs and pine needles and wispy whiteness. "He was moving so fast," she said, not wanting to believe it. "Could he have come through here . . . ran right off . . ."

"Ssh," Barton put a hand on her shoulder. "Listen."

At first the totality of the silence was like white noise; it hurt her ears. But then she picked up what Barton's sharper senses had already discerned. A murmur . . . A distant voice. It came from off to the right somewhere, beyond the trees that lined the valley shoulder. Janet seized that as her only shred of hope and ran after the sounds, with Barton close behind. And as they went, the voice became clearer to them. Low. Barely lucid. Rambling madly.

". . . Uh, uh, Buddy Ebsen was Jed, Granny's Irene Ryan, Max Baer was Jethro, and Ellie Mae . . . uh, Donna Douglas, yeah, that's her, but . . . who played Drysdale? Let's see, that was Milburn Stone, no, that's *Gunsmoke*, and Milburn was the character's name, Milburn Drysdale, not the guy who played him, I can't think, dammit, I just can't think . . ." Angrily, "No! No, I'm not going, I'm not!" Then, in a weaker voice, "Oh, God, what did I do to deserve this . . ."

They came out of the trees very near to where the hunters had first discovered the valley, bare meters from where Barton had pitched his tent that fateful night. And they found Steven standing on the ridge of the valley. He was pacing incessantly back and forth, his shoulders hunched, his head down, his fists balled and shaking at his sides. And he was still ranting about anything and everything that came to mind. ". . . Wait a minute . . . Bailey, Bailey, *Raymond* Bailey! That's it! That's it! But now what? Think of something, hurry . . ."

"Good Lord," Barton muttered. "He's gotta be seven feet tall!"

Steven jerked upright, swiveled to face them as if the whisper had been a cannon blast. His face was a frozen mask of terror, a thin veil of white stretched across warped and sinister bone. The cheekbones jutted, the jaw was more prominent. He'd even torn the stitches in his cheeks; they stuck out, taut and ragged, like cat whiskers. There was no blood this time. "Help me," he pleaded, hugging himself. His face twisted with mental effort. "It's so strong." He pointed at his chest, at his own heart. "It wants to go down there, and I can't stop it. Please . . ."

Janet started to go to him. But instead she went to the steep grade and peered down into the shadowy realm that awaited them. "We have to go now," she said flatly.

Barton's blood chilled. He'd always known this was coming. But now, faced with the prospect . . . "It'll be dark soon," he observed, hoping that Janet and Steven would be just as uncomfortable about descending in the dark and decide to wait till morning. But then he looked at Steven again, all seven feet of him, prancing about and talking to himself, trying desperately to retain the barest shreds of sanity and identity and losing on all fronts.

But if you go into the valley, you won't come back . . .

Aw, go fuck yourself, he told the voice. He shouldered the axe, took a deep breath, and committed himself with both feet. "Let's get this over with."

Janet nodded a curt thank you, then turned to her metamorphosing husband. "Sweetheart? Maybe you'd better stay up here until we can—"

"No, no," he said frantically. "I can handle it, I can. If we keep moving. I can, honest." He went to the slope and trembled a moment. But then he got his bearings and started down, beginning to mumble in an unstable voice, "Space, the final frontier . . . um, these are the voyages of the, uh, Starship Enterprise . . ." Janet went next, plunging down the slope nimbly and without a second thought. And that left only Davejac.

He patted his shirt pocket and the folded paper for reassurance. Then he begrudgingly followed after them.

They reached the bottom without mishap and found themselves staring down the narrow patch of open ground, same as their predecessors. "It feels . . . empty," Janet observed. "Which way now?"

"Three guesses," Barton said. He pointed to a major disruption in the even tree line, a swatch of broken boughs and shorn limbs at the end of the open alley. "It'll be like tracking a bulldozer."

The silence abruptly, and completely, resettled. For the first time since finding him, they realized Steven was not talking. Not even to himself. He was standing a few feet off to the side, his head cocked as if listening intently. "Honey?" Janet asked. "Are you all right?"

He looked tentative for a moment, dizzy and about to fall. But just as quickly the expression changed. He stood upright and took a deep breath, stretched as if testing new muscle, new vigor. "It's astounding," he said evenly. "I can see so far . . . It's like a big window, a whole other world . . . And I feel . . ." He turned and looked at them, his expression of wonderment growing into a sinister grin. ". . . Different. I can hear your hearts beating, you know? All the way over here. Thump. Thump. Thump." Then the schizophrenic shifting came again, changed to disgust to terror to bewilderment. He twitched and flinched and stepped away, seemed ready to race back up the grade. "I can't tell . . . how long," he stammered. "How long I've got, you know?" He handed the backpack to Janet and then dropped the coils of log chain, pointed to the latter. "Chain me up. Hurry."

Davejac did as he asked, wrapping the heavy links about him four times and closing the padlock. Steven sighed, reassured by his own imprisonment. Then he nodded that he was ready to continue.

They made their way down the narrow corridor of ground, with Steven guiding them around the sump hole indenture where Tucker had disappeared. Then they entered the path of ruination and followed it for some distance. But the easy travel it afforded them was short-lived; the signs of destruction gradually petered out, till the trees before them appeared completely untouched. It was as if whatever wrought this havoc had simply . . . vanished.

"I don't like this," Barton said, his grip on the axe growing more and more white-knuckled. "Not one bit."

"This way," Steven grunted and headed off into the underbrush, his forged bonds jingling merrily.

They were having a hard time following him. The valley gloom was deepening with the onslaught of night, and the shadows around them multiplied exponentially. Steven appeared unfazed by it and did not slow his pace at all. But his wife and the Indian had more trouble picking their way along a path they could not see. Barton fished out the flashlight and immediately cursed it for not having a wider or brighter beam. For wherever the limited light of the flashlight did not reach, his eyes told him there was movement. On either side of them. Back in the trees. Even in the limbs above. And the shadows that he imagined there were all too familiar to him; they seemed to have been peeled off the pictograph rock above the valley. A spidery figure on the tree he was just passing, clinging high up with multiple arms. Squat piglike forms that scampered soundlessly beyond the reach of his torch. Dark, eyeless faces that watched them pass with muted curiosity. Stop it, he cursed himself. Stop it right now. There's enough going on here to be scared of. You don't need to make it worse . . .

Janet moved up close to him, and in a choked whisper she asked, "Do you see them too?"

Barton felt his crotch shrink in near panic. He shifted the axe to one hand and unslung the shotgun from his back. "Pay no attention," he told her, though he knew it would be impossible to even try.

Then night settled completely. A palpable darkness closed around them, and the figures were mercifully hidden in its folds. They left just the flashlight, and the few moonbeams that managed to pierce both the trees and the cloaking mist.

Things moved in those slim arcs of silver. But they were easier to ignore.

"It didn't look this big from up on top," Janet said, weary and nervous. They'd walked for at least half an hour already, yet the lowland forest was as dense and oppressive as ever. "Steven, sweetheart? Where are we going?"

The jingling giant ahead of them did not reply. He just plunged onward, deeper and deeper into the primordial wood.

Slowly they began to see moonlight ahead, peeking at them through the trees, and more than just a few errant beams this time. An actual break in the valley cover, a place free of the cloying mist. They found the clearing littered with broken tree limbs and shreds of bark, a carpet of twigs and green needles. "What the hell happened here?" Barton wondered at the shallow patch of destruction. But then he remembered Wilhoit's harrowing account of his night in this place. "This is where you found Covey and Tucker, isn't it?"

Steven was not paying attention. He had sat down on a shaft of broken timber, his expression tensed, concentrating. "Get ready," he stammered.

"Here?" Janet asked. "Don't we have to find the windigo first?"

Her husband smiled through his cheeks at her, or maybe it was the creature within him. "Don't . . . worry. It will find you." Then he looked off into the wall of shadows that was the forest, piercing its depths with glazed and colorless eyes. "Unchain me," he suddenly ordered. "Something's not right . . ."

"In a minute," Barton said. "First things first."

He knelt down and swept an area clean of debris, then piled twigs and branches there, the drier the better. In just a few minutes he had a fire going. It was soon large enough to cast the whole clearing in flickering yellow. Janet brought over the backpack and took out the cook pot, and they built a sturdy spit that allowed it to hang out in the middle of the flames.

"What about these?" Janet said, taking out one of the Campbell's Soup bombs.

"Not so close to the fire!" Barton pulled her back several feet. Then he let her take out the explosives and keep two with her. The other he sat on the ground where he stood, right next to the axe. "Well," he finally sighed, pulling on the heavy gloves. "I guess that's it. All we can do now is wait."

"No!" Steven barked at them. He was struggling, straining against the coils of steel that bound him. "Let me loose! Let me loose!"

"I don't think so, Steve," Davejac said warily. "You've been acting pretty weird —"

"You don't understand!" he screamed, his features lit up. "It's coming!"

Beyond the wall of shadow, the crashing sounds began. Coming their way.

TWENTY-FOUR

JANET AND BARTON JUST STOOD THERE LOOKING AT EACH other, unsure of what to do next. And while they hesitated, the din grew worse. The thunderous report of the devastation was reaching them ever clearer; they were no longer hearing pale echoes but the real thing now, the initial impact of toppling trees, of branches being stripped aside. A bulldozer would not have made such sounds, not even by mowing down everything in its path. No, this cacophony was purposeful. Whatever was coming their way wanted them to know it. To fear it.

If that was indeed the intent, it was working only too well.

Steven's ranting could barely be heard over the clamor. "Let me . . . *go!*" he screamed, straining at his bonds. But the others were no longer listening to him. Their attention was riveted on the shadowy forest with stark terror and a morbid fascination.

"The words," Janet had to yell, even though she was standing directly beside the Indian. She saw her breath hang in a vaporous cloud, realized for the first time just how frigid the air around them had become. "Read the words!"

Barton took the paper from his pocket and unfolded it. He held the flashlight on it to illuminate the printed words there. But he would not read them. Not out loud. Not just yet.

And then . . . The crashing sounds stopped. Their echoes continued on into the forest like hounds out to bay some distant game, and a brittle silence took their place. Only the pop and crack of the flames could be heard.

Their eyes stayed on that one patch of forest, where the shadows gathered layer upon layer.

And a face appeared there.

It extended just beyond the darkline, just far enough for the fire to light its features. To reflect in them. It was a skull, or at least it looked like one. Only this was of monstrous proportion and seemed chipped from living ice. The shape was oblong, stretched from chin to crown. Longer than any human head. Craggy cheekbones flanked overlarge sockets, and two ragged holes were all that marked the nasal cavity. The teeth made up at least a third of the total face; their size alone gave it a sardonic mien. And the eyes . . . Spheres of solid crystal the size of softballs. They scoured the clearing, and their malevolence scorched all in their path.

Janet's lungs stopped working, refused to take another breath. It wasn't just the terror she felt at the specter's appearance. It was the familiarity she found there. It gnawed at the back of her mind. She'd seen that look before . . .

Perhaps peering out at her from behind her husband's face?

She grabbed Davejac's arm. "Read the damn words!" she whispered urgently.

But the Indian paid her no mind. "A little farther," he muttered softly. "A little farther . . ."

Two of the trees that edged the clearing were pushed aside with a terrific groan to allow passage of the spindly form that abruptly stalked into the clearing. The windigo's body was more than a match for its nightmarish face. Over fifteen feet of ambulatory ice, taking the approximate shape of a human skeleton. It stood there despite any noticeable ligaments or tendons, the things that hold such bones together and allow them to move. But there was no denying its reality. Janet's eyes immediately went to the angular torso, to what passed for a rib cage. Through the slots between the "bones," she could make out a particular chunk of crystal about the size of her head. In the slats of moonlight that reached it, the heart seemed to shine brighter than the surrounding ice. Almost glowing.

"Janet!" Steven screamed, louder, more frantic than ever. "Let me *loose!*"

The creature turned and looked at Steven, glared at him with lidless eyes. Its smile seemed to widen. Then it turned to the other figures before it, seemingly frozen in its shadow. And its gaze centered on Janet. Its mouth opened. It stepped toward them.

Barton began to read. And pray.

"*Ko-o ko ke o-oo. Te gala Ginyu ni ah-sa ichyoo. Ay la witiko ka-a chin . . .*"

The windigo stopped its advance even before it began. It looked dazed for a moment, confused. Almost dizzy. It dropped to one knee. Tried to raise an arm but could barely budge it. Then that death's head snapped up and looked not at the people before it but to the heavens above. For it knew then, and it wailed like a banshee as if to curse the Thunders for betraying such secrets.

Barton felt a surge of confidence. It's working! By God, it's working! He continued to read, careful to pronounce the words just as George Wilson had sounded them out on the paper. Not one slip. Or else. *"Aka-tan wicha paka-tan . . ."*

The wail of anger strangled off, became an inhuman whimper. It was all but a statue now, could barely move. Only its long hands churned the air, the sharp fingertips clicking together like castanets. That and the eyes. They fixed on Davejac with a primeval rage. He did not have to look to know this. He could feel the stare, burning into him.

Just one more line to read. One more and we're home free.

A frigid gust of wind came racing out of the woods then, its sudden appearance taking them completely by surprise. Leaves and debris swirled around Davejac like a maelstrom, filling his mouth and eyes, blinding him. He wrapped his arms over his head in a feeble defense. That's when the paper was ripped from his grasp. He wiped his eyes free just in time to see it flutter away on a current of air, disappearing into the depths of the forest.

Oh, lordy. Oh, my sweet Lord . . .

The windigo moved. It broke the invisible bonds that held it in check, stretched its spindly overlong limbs with a catlike languidness. It threw its head back and let out another call, only this was different. Gales of unearthly laughter spilled from its throat and rolled through the crisp night air, cutting right to the bone.

Janet moved away from Barton, knelt down beside the fire. When she stepped back, she was holding out a soup can. The fabric fuse was burning. "Laugh at this, asshole," she muttered and flung the bomb as hard as she could. The can missed the thing's protruding hipbone by scant inches and sailed past, landing at the far edge of the clearing.

The explosion seemed to jar the very air around them. It uprooted another tree and sent it toppling into its brethren. But it wasn't close enough to damage the windigo. All it did was attract the creature's attention. The thing whirled around and studied the plumes of smoke that remained, sniffing the sulfuric odor without benefit of a nose.

Barton picked up his own bomb and waved the impregnated fuse just close enough to the flames to catch a spark. Then, instead of throwing it like a projectile, he simply lobbed the can underhand like a horseshoe player, with a postlike shinbone as his target. It fell short of the mark, but an end-over-end bounce put it right beneath the instep of one splayed foot.

Whoom! Only this time the thunderclap was accompanied by the crystalline sound of ice pellets pinging off the trees around them. The windigo lurched off-balance to one side and tried to right itself, but only then did it seem to realize there was no leg there to support it. With a howl of rage it went crashing to the ground.

The fuse on Janet's last bomb was already burning, shorter and shorter. But this time, it was she who muttered, "Not yet, not yet . . ." She gauged the distance and the remaining fuse, and at the last possible moment she tossed it straight at that wicker basket of a torso. Then they both dove for cover as the *explosion* cracked the air once again and even more shards of ice rained down around them.

The echoes died. The air finally stopped vibrating. And in the aftermath, there was stillness.

Janet and Barton rose hesitantly, uncertain of what they would now face. As the smoke cleared they found the windigo sprawled on its side atop the already fallen timber. Its back was to them. It did not move.

"Is it dead?" Janet wondered aloud.

Barton hefted the big axe. "Just stay here," he said, stalking slowly across the clearing.

He had to step over its one good leg to get around the far side. But once there he could see the damage that Janet's last throw had wrought. The entire side of the creature's torso had been blow open; the rib bones jutted like tines of shattered glass. And that left the heart exposed. It just hung there like some arctic fruit, waiting to be plucked. This'll be easier than you thought, he told himself. One good chop and . . .

A trickling sound reached his ears. Cautiously he turned and found the skeleton's shattered thighbone *bleeding*. Except

no blood issued from the stump. Only water, clear and icy.
It poured from the limb in a torrent, splattered across the
debris-strewn soil and continued to run in a solitary rivulet.
And as it went, it began to solidify. To freeze.

Re-forming . . .

With a sudden all-encompassing panic he looked back to
the rib cage. It still gaped at him, taunting him with the
accessibility of the heart. But the hole was smaller now. And
as he watched, the rib bones extended, centimeter by centimeter, arching toward one another.

Go now, he yelled at himself, or you'll never get the
chance . . .

Davejac lunged. The axe whistled through the night air,
struck the ice with a riotous clatter. The blow reopened the
torso, bared the heart once again. But the regeneration continued, right before his eyes. The hole was closing even as
he raised the weapon for a second swing.

"Die, damn you," he grunted as he laid into it again,
putting all of his weight behind the axe, one chop after another. He was making headway, shattering more ice than
could be replaced. The heart was almost within reach . . .

"Barton! Look out!"

Janet's cry jolted him. He glanced from the corner of his
eye and saw that nightmare face looking down at him, smoldering with rage. At that same instant he threw himself backward. The ice hand that had reached for him missed by scant
inches. He felt the cold as it passed.

The Indian rolled to his feet with the axe ready and found
the windigo struggling to sit up. Its butchered rib cage was
already repairing itself, undoing the damage he had inflicted.
But his efforts had not gone unnoticed. It glared at him om-
inously, its intentions all too clear in those otherwise opaque
eyes. It tried to stand but the new leg was not completely
formed; water was still running down its surface, refreezing,
strengthening the icy bone there. But it rose enough to grope
for him again, this time more on target.

The grab was too fast for him to try to evade. So instead

he swung the axe and met it head-on, chipping the entire thumb off. It made another attempt and he met it the same way, this time cleaving off two other fingers. The windigo drew back, holding its hand and watching him. The digits regrew readily enough. But it seemed unsure just how to deal with such behavior.

"Come on!" Barton yelled, caught up in the surge of adrenaline that mortal fear and a hopeless situation can bring. "Come and get me!"

The skeleton picked up one of the sections of shattered trees that littered the clearing, a shaft at least a foot in diameter and over eight feet long. But the creature wielded it like a twig. It tried to swat the man, slamming it down at him once, twice. Barton dived aside both times, barely evading the knotty club. But the third try was a low and lateral arc. And it took him by surprise.

The impact made a sickening sound, laced with the crackle of breaking bone. Janet heard it all the way across the clearing. The blow pitched Barton Davejac into the air like a rag doll. He was at least ten feet off the ground when he disappeared into the trees. But the remainder of his flight was reported by dull thuds as he bounced through the tangle of limbs on his way to the ground.

"Barton!" Janet called in shock. But that only seemed to attract the monster's attention to her. Those eyes found her, bore right into her. And in them she saw something far different than what Davejac had seen. Not rage now. Only . . .

Hunger?

She backpedaled one step, two, putting the fire between her and the steadily regenerating nightmare. But then she bumped into something . . . Steven was standing right there, still heavily chained. He was looking down at her, and his expression seemed stark in the flickering firelight. "Let . . . me . . . *loose!*" he ordered in a gravel voice that barely sounded like his own.

"I can't! Barton has the key!" Then her eyes fell on Davejac's shotgun laying there on the ground. She brushed past her husband and picked it up, trained the twin bores on the massive beast and fired. One of the deer slugs actually punched a hole in the side of the thing's skull. But it barely even flinched. It just glared at her, and then the mocking laughter returned.

Janet stood there, feeling hollow, devoid of any spark of hope. There was nothing left. No magic. No weapons. Nothing but the flare pistol in her fanny pack, and the .22 revolver in her pocket. She took out the latter. Of the two, it alone offered an alternative. A last resort, as Barton had called it. At that moment she just wished it was a bigger caliber. Something a little more final. She looked over at Steven, who was no longer ranting at her but standing completely still, staring into space. She considered using the gun on him first, saving him from this curse. But it was no use. He was already too far gone.

The windigo was just testing its new leg, putting weight on it. Starting to stand. There wasn't much time left. "I'll always love you," she said to Steven as she closed her teary eyes. Put the barrel to her temple . . .

Snap! The sound was sharp, defined. But it wasn't the gun. She hadn't pulled the trigger. She opened her eyes just as it came again. *Snap!* Only this time she was looking straight at Steven and she saw the chain links break and pieces of them spin off in different directions. He suddenly shrugged his arms and the whole mess came apart, fell to the ground in a pile.

"My God," she muttered in horror as he turned toward her, gritting his teeth from ear to ear. A spindly arm snaked out and caught her shoulder, jerked her so hard the revolver was shaken from her grasp and her feet completely left the ground. She felt herself tucked under his arm like a small child and then suddenly they were moving, running into the trees. Escaping! And the windigo's angry howl filled the air behind them.

She caught one last glimpse of the creature before they left the clearing. It was on its feet now, shambling after them.

And then they were in the trees and moving through the underbrush with blinding speed.

Timber fell behind them. The demon was following, hammering aside all in its path. And if it caught them . . .

It won't, she promised herself. It can't.

Branches and vines tore at her face and hair; all she could do was cover her head with her arms and brave the ride. Steven was moving at an unimaginable speed, despite his rather awkward height. It was as if his feet barely touched the ground. She thought his efforts must have been a strain, for she could hear him grunting and gasping as they went. But then, somehow, she realized they were not sounds of exertion at all. He was singing softly, a tune recognizable only to himself. It was the one tenuous connection that allowed him to stay in control.

The crashing sounds were getting louder. "It's gaining on us!" she called.

"Out of the valley," Steven grunted, pointing ahead through the woods. "Maybe it . . . won't follow."

"But what if it does? What if it comes out of the valley?"

"Kill it."

With what, she wanted to ask. Our fingernails? But he was having a hard enough time just trying to elude that lumbering giant. She could see its white form through the darkness, illuminated by the moonlight that its devastation allowed in. It reached out once, missed them by only a foot or two. But the next time . . .

The trees disappeared abruptly—the silver blaze of moonlight was all around and she realized that they had broken out of the forest and were moving down the corridor of open ground they had traversed on the way in. Steven vaulted over the sump hole even as the timber behind them groaned and fell, and then they were heading up the slope. She clung to his bony frame as he let go of her and used both hands and feet, digging at the dirt for purchase and using their momentum to carry them up the sharp incline.

"No! Noooo!" the windigo roared, right behind them. But they went over the ridge anyway and on into the forest.

Janet risked a backward glance. The skeleton of ice was standing on the slope, just its sternum and shoulders evident above the ridge. The specter howled and shook its bony fists in impotent rage. But it did not advance. It wouldn't leave the haven of the valley. Or couldn't.

But Steven kept running just the same. He plunged on into the forests of Chalako, and they left the valley far behind.

"It's gone, Steven," Janet tried to tell him. "We can slow down." But if he heard her, he didn't acknowledge it. He kept right on running. Though the strange vitality that he'd seemed to draw from the valley was gone now. He was laboring despite his still-superior strength, almost stumbling at times. He no longer sang. He plowed through the underbrush in silence.

"Steven?" Janet called to him. A pervasive unease was spreading through her. "Steven, put me down."

No answer. He was too busy running, out of the trees and onto a rocky ridge and right over the precipice, down the steep slope beyond with long limbs windmilling madly. But somehow they didn't fall. They made it to the foot and were just as quickly back into more woods, a whole different patch of trees where the stickers and branches once again tore at her.

"Steven!" she yelled in panic. "You put me down! Put me down this minute!"

But her commands again fell on deaf ears. It wasn't until they next emerged into the moonlight, into a clear area, that Steven finally stopped. His foot caught on a tangle of exposed tree roots and he went sprawling, throwing Janet aside to keep from landing on her. She hit hard but managed to roll with the impact, so nothing was broken. But that was not to say she was in good shape. In the silvery light she could see that her coat and clothing were shredded, that she was covered with blood from a hundred scratches and tears. The stinging

in her face told her it had fared little better. But she ignored
the pain. As soon as she regained her footing she ran to
Steven's side.

He was still lying in the dirt, completely spent from such
an extended flight. His clothing had been tattered during the
run, and there were innumerable gashes in the skin beneath.
But like the tears in his cheeks, they no longer bled. In fact,
in the moonlight he did not look like a human being at all
but some giant dying spider, his great limbs curled in on
themselves, close to that fragile-looking torso. There was
virtually nothing of her husband left. The face was just a
shell of skin, barely concealing the demon that dwelt within.
But the eyes . . . She could see in them that Steven was still
there. Barely.

"Sweetheart," she said softly, unsure of what to do next.

He looked up at her pitifully. One long arm unfolded,
pointed away. "Run," he grunted. "Camp. Hurry."

She looked in the direction he referred and realized for the
first time that they were in the middle of a wide dirt road.
Camp, she wondered . . . He must mean the timber camp
that Barton pointed out from that ridge. Maybe we can get
some help there. "Come on then," she said, urging him up.
"We've come too far to quit now."

Steven tried to rise. But he only made it as far as his knees.
It wasn't just fatigue he was fighting now. His face was
twisted with mental anguish, the battle to keep control.
"Can't. Too hard. You run."

"Not on your life, mister." She grabbed his hand and
turned, pulling him after her. Despite his great size, his actual
weight had dropped so far that she could almost drag him
along. If that's what it takes, she decided stubbornly . . .

But then suddenly she stumbled forward. His weight had
given way.

But her grip had not.

She looked down at her gloved hand, saw that she still
held his. But it was all flesh and no substance, an elbow-
length glove of dead skin that was already crumbling in her

grasp. Stunned, she turned and held it out for Steven to see. But his eyes were elsewhere, glued to the spot where that fleshy shell used to be. A forearm and hand of naked bone now flexed in the moonlight, shining. The radius and the ulna were intact, the metacarpals and phalanges. But they were all things of pure ice.

Tears slid down Steven's face as he held the thing aloft, trying to cry out but unable to find a voice.

Janet fought her revulsion. It's still Steven, she reminded herself, over and over, as she quickly slipped off her coat and threw it over his denuded limb. "Come with me," she said in as even a voice as she could muster. "Come on, sweetheart . . ." She pulled gently, firmly. Brought him to his feet. "That's it. Come with me." She started down the road and he stumbled along after her, his expression numb. Lost.

Janet acted only by instinct. She didn't know if they were going in the right direction, or what she would do once they reached the camp. All she could think of was the decision she'd made back at Barton's cabin.

I'm holding on to him. And I'm never letting go.

TWENTY-FIVE

THEY STAGGERED INTO THE LOGGING CAMP IN THE CLEAR light of the moon, so Janet's view of the equipment there was unfettered. It looked like a still-viable installation; the big old trucks were still there, parked by the refueling tanker just as Barton had seen them, their flatbeds still almost half-full with stout timber for shipment. The trailer with the OFFICE sign over the door still sat next to the trucks. But beyond that was open land, stretching to the tree line. There were no campers or pickups this time. Nor were there any lights in the office windows.

Barton was right, Janet decided. The timber workers had bugged out. This place was deserted. But her eyes suddenly fixed on the office trailer, and on the radio antenna clamped to the window frame in plain view. "That must be where Barton called for help," she said. "God, I hope they left the radio." She turned, looked up into Steven's face. He was still distant, hollow-eyed. But his knitted brow told her the fight was still on. "You won't be able to fit in there," she said, motioning to the trailer. "I'm going to call for help. Will you be all right out here?"

He said nothing in reply. Just nodded weakly.

She let go of his arm but left the coat to cover it. "I'll be just inside, okay?" Then she ran to the trailer and up the steps to the door. Tried the knob. Locked, of course. But after all she'd been through this night, it simply wasn't enough to stop her. She backed off and got a run at the steps, lowered her head and collided with the door. It let out a groan that masked the pain in her shoulder, and it visibly sagged in the middle. Thank God trailers aren't built too sturdy, she thought. I'd never get through this. She put her shoulder to the task once more, and this time the lock bolt tore through the jamb and swung open. She spilled onto the floor inside.

It was dark in there. Only moonlight through the two windows gave her anything to see by. She felt along the wall for an electrical switch, found one, and toggled it back and forth. But nothing happened. The trailer must have been hooked to a generator, and now that wasn't running. How the hell do I find something in here, she thought in futility. But then she looked to the antenna again and spied the cord that ran through a hole in the sill. She staggered through the gloom and found the line, followed it by hand into the shadows.

Groping in the darkness, she came to a box that she couldn't see. But tactile senses told her that its front panel sported buttons and a tuning knob. And standing right beside it . . . a tall microphone, one of the old kind with a stem to hold on to and a TALK button at the base. Pray, girl, she cautioned herself. Pray that it's hooked to a battery instead of the generator. Because if it isn't, you're fucked.

She pressed a button. Nothing. Another. Nothing. Her unease was growing. One more . . .

A crackle of static. Then the radio came to life.

"Mayday! Mayday!" Janet called into the mike, hearing her voice as high-pitched and panicky. Calm down, or no one'll know what you're saying. She took a deep breath before continuing. "Mayday! Emergency! Can anyone hear me?" She paused, waited for a reply. But there was only static. "Please, we need help. I'm at a timber camp at Chalako Lakes, I'm not sure where but two men were lost near here a few days ago. Get hold of Bailey at Ati-Kut Timber, she'd know where. We need help and fast!"

Still crackling emptiness. "Can't anyone hear this?" she cried. Then she gave up on that channel in disgust, was just reaching for the tuning knob when a voice broke through. It was a man's, sounded thick with slumber. "I copy you, over. Please come again. Where did you say you're at?"

She was just about to squeeze the mike button again when a plaintive voice drifted through the open door from outside. "Janet" came her husband's voice, weak. Distant. "Hurry . . ."

"Come again, over," the radio repeated. "Where is the mayday?"

But Janet was barely listening to it. The tone of Steven's voice had struck a chord of mortal fear in her. And in that moment she realized she had been fooling herself. No help would come. At least not in time. She pushed the button and whispered "Chalako Lakes" into the microphone. Then she set it aside and ignored any further calls. She turned to the door, wondering if any part of her husband would be left waiting for her out there. Or would it be another of those beasts, a demon of ice and carnal hunger. Some twinge of self-preservation made her reach back and draw the flare pistol from her fanny pack. Not that she thought for a moment it would do her any good.

Cautiously she went back out into the moonlight.

Steven was not where she'd left him.

"Sweetheart?" she called hesitantly, stepping back into the trailer's doorway for cover. The pistol came up in both hands as she scanned the open ground around the trailer.

"Over here."

A white stick figure was hunched down by the first log hauler about thirty feet away. Steven had taken her coat off his arm, baring the icy bones. And as she watched, he stabbed that stilettolike arm into the metal tank just below the truck's passenger door. Gasoline belched out onto the dirt in a steady stream, forming an ever-widening pool and reflecting the moonlight into a rainbow of colors. Steven stood, stepped out into the middle of it. "No . . . more . . . time," he stammered, fighting to annunciate each individual word. Then he held up his fist, worked the thumb as if flicking the wheel on a lighter.

"No," Janet refused. "I can't . . ."

"Please. Pud. While . . . part of me's . . . left."

Her tears were flowing freely now. But there was no other choice. She raised the flare pistol, aimed it for the puddle of fuel at his feet. "I love ya, you know."

He nodded. "Good-bye." He took a deep breath, raised his eyes to heaven. And that's where he froze, staring up over the trailer. Gaping in surprise. "No," he stammered. "No . . ."

Janet saw his reaction and stiffened. She had to move away from the trailer steps to follow his line of sight. But there she saw it, looming above the roof of the office. That same hell-spawned skull, grinning down at them. It had followed them, crept up on them. All fifteen plus feet of it.

The windigo laughed hollowly and shoved the trailer aside, knocked it right off its concrete block supports so that the axles dug into dirt and it nearly turned over. And in an eye blink the creature lunged forward and grabbed Janet, its massive hand closing completely around her middle and lifting her off the ground.

She winced, and not just from the pressure the grip inflicted. A chill was seeping into her, the windigo's taint, and it infused her bones with a cold so intense her marrow seemed to burn. It wrung a scream from her as the monster held her aloft, its face lit with a mocking triumph.

She looked into that nightmarish countenance, into those glazed eyes. And aside from her pain she felt the same sense of gnawing familiarity as before. Only this time there was the terror of recognition as well.

. . . the way he'd always look at you . . . it really gave you the willies . . .

"Tucker!" she screamed at it. "You're Tucker!"

The windigo's smile grew even wider. *"Ja-net,"* it replied in an arctic tone as it brought her toward its face. Its mouth.

She'd forgotten till that moment that she still clutched the flare pistol in her hand. She brought it up in desperation, aimed for that yawning maw dead ahead. But before she could squeeze the trigger, something passed just below her, close enough that she felt the air from its passing. A large sheet of metal, spinning through the air like a Frisbee—she barely had time to recognize it as a truck door before it sliced through the windigo's arm at the elbow, shattering the limb and filling the air with a cascade of ice. Janet fell almost ten feet to the ground but the hand still around her bore the brunt of the impact. She wormed her way from its grasp and scrambled across the ground for cover.

The windigo held the water-dripping stump of its right arm and searched for its attacker. It found Steven Wilhoit standing near one of the log trucks, the one conspicuously missing a passenger door, and it howled at him in rage. Steven howled right back, and his tone was every bit as defiant. As inhuman. The larger demon did not wait for its shattered limb to reform. It leaped on Steven, caught his head in its massive

hand and slammed him back into the truck with such force
that it actually tipped up onto two wheels for a moment. The
windigo lifted its opponent up and dashed him to the ground
over and over, the air vibrating with each thundering impact.
Steven tried to fight back, but there was little he could do
against such an overpowering foe.

It drove him to the ground and clubbed him mercilessly,
laughing as it did so. Then it picked up his limp form and
hurled Steven like a missile, straight through the wall of the
mobile home as if it were cardboard. It was silent after that.
Nothing stirred in the ruined office, or on the open grounds
for that matter. Except for the towering skeleton, of course.
And the lone figure that now faced it.

Janet Wilhoit had stepped back into the open. She was
bloodied and bruised, and her body quaked with spasms from
the inner cold she felt. But she did not back down. She stood
her ground in the shadow of the windigo, and she held the
flare pistol in a taut two-handed grip, trained on that ever-
grinning face. "You sonuvabitch," she said to the thing that
once was Elton Tucker. "I never liked you when you were
alive."

The demon laughed from deep in its see-through chest,
mocking the woman's futile defiance. But then it saw her
smile. Confusion tempered its laughter, and the mocking died
away completely as it watched her alter the aim of her
weapon. The gaping bore of the pistol lowered from its face,
traced a line straight down its sternum and spine, all the way
to its feet. To the murky puddle they stood in.

Somewhere in that icy skull, deep within whatever passed
for a mind, a glimmer of realization must have burned. For
the windigo seemed to perceive the threat, actually tried to
step away. But not before she pulled the trigger. A red fireball
belched forth from the gaping tube of her pistol and shot
across the open ground, straight into the still-growing pool
of gasoline at its feet.

Whoosh!

Fire leaped up nearly as high as the monster's shocked face, and Janet felt the flash of heat as far back as she was standing. But a split second later the flames raced into the punctured gas tank of the log hauler and ignited it, as well as the sister tank on the driver's side. The truck went up in a plume of flame, lifting it off the ground for a split second and throwing it sideways, right into the windigo's legs. The skeleton fell forward and the truck came down atop it, pinning it down, spilling flaming logs across its back. *"Nooo!"* it wailed, thrashing wildly, digging at the ground and the burden that imprisoned it. *"Noooooooo!"*

Janet ran for cover as the second truck blew right after that, and bare moments later the tank on the refueling truck as well. Plumes of gasoline spilled across the flames, feeding them, until the fire became an inferno and there was no sight of the windigo at all. Only a weak voice as if from far off, like that of a lost child. "I'm sorry, I'm sorry . . ." it wailed. Until the roar of the flames drowned it out completely.

The pistol fell from Janet's numbed fingers. She sank to her knees, hugging herself against the overpowering chill. She was not even conscious that the clicking in her ears was the sound of her own teeth chattering together. Only then, experiencing it firsthand, did she begin to realize the torment her husband had gone through . . .

Steven! She had forgotten about him in the heat of the battle. She turned back to the battered mobile home with a gaping wound in the wall, staggered toward the door. "Steven?" she called. "Are you all right?"

There were sounds from inside. Debris falling. Furniture being shoved aside. And then a familiar figure came into the doorway, so tall it was bent almost double to clear the ceiling. Just glimpsing him, Janet sighed in relief. "Thank God," she said, "I was beginning to think—"

Then she saw his face. Or at least part of it.

Only the upper half of Steven Wilhoit's features remained. The hair and scalp, the eyes, part of the nose. But from there down the flesh had been torn away in the struggle, leaving only a skeleton's face. Extremely long jaw. Extremely large teeth. They seemed to grow for her into a capering icy smile.

"*JA-net,*" the mouth said as Steven's body stepped outside, having stripped away his remaining clothing to stand spindly and naked and white in the moonlight. He lunged at her but she jumped back and his icy claw caught just the front of her shirt, tearing it open.

"No!" she cried, backing away, feeling a wave of hysteria wash over her. "No! It can't end like this! We've come too far, we've been through too much! It can't end like this!" She tripped and fell to the ground and stayed there, crying, even as Steven's windigo loomed over her.

Somehow, in her ear, the roar of the flames grew quiet. All sound seemed to stop.

E HAVE HEARD

The words echoed through Janet's mind, as surely and as clear as if someone had spoken them directly to her ear. But no one was there. No one but her husband, and it had not been his voice. This was soft, commanding. Powerful.

She looked around for its source, saw that even Steven's windigo had stopped advancing. It had heard the voice as well, for it was now looking about, hesitant and confused.

And then Janet felt something. An odd sensation against her thigh, like heat building. It was coming from inside the pocket of her fatigue pants. The cargo pocket where she'd put George Wilson's migis shells . . .

Pain! It lanced into her thigh muscle like a red-hot needle, like a sizzling arc of electricity. She ran her hand into the pocket and found nothing there, nothing but holes burned in the backing, still hot around the edges. The pain was growing worse, so much that she tore the pocket completely lose and then hooked her fingers in those holes and tore that material as well. She found no wound on her bare thigh. Only several small knots just beneath the skin. Moving.

She knew then. And they had gotten it all wrong.

"No!" she cried out to the Thunders. "It's not me! It's Steven you've got to help! Steven!" But the pain kept growing. The knots had moved off toward the femoral artery, disappearing from sight. And the electrical jolts she felt were moving as well. Growing stronger.

In her pain-fogged mind, a thought suddenly formed, crystal clear. *Strong enough for two?*

It was all she could do to muster her strength, to fight the spasming of her own muscles enough to get to her feet and charge the confused giant that stood so close. Steven's windigo was still looking around for the Thunders when she leaped onto its back and wrapped her arms and legs around it tightly, pressed her bare chest to that unbearably cold flesh. Never let go, she told herself. Never.

The demon immediately began to thrash about and tried to throw her, reached back to rake her side with those long icy fingers. But she held on. Because she could feel none of that. The searing pain had already reached her heart, and that left her entire body in agony. She screamed but did not hear it, nor could she see anything. Senses overloaded and shut down. Darkness closed in around her.

She felt . . . nothing. No pain—she was beyond that. No cold. Not even numbness. She heard, saw nothing as well.

Am I dead, she thought.

OU HAVE COURAGE.

OU HAVE STIRRED US.

OU WILL NOT DIE.

But what about my husband, she called back. What about Steven? But it was too late. The limbo was receding from around her. She was already sinking back to her own world, back through the sea of pain. It washed over her like a red tide, and when it finally subsided the first thing she felt was . . .

Cold. Despite the hiss and roar of a fire close by.

She roused slowly. When she moved, her whole body screamed out; she knew then every cut and contusion she possessed, knew them intimately. And once she had their collective agonies under control, she could stretch her senses out and take stock.

Cold. But at least it was on the outside, not the inside. This was just gooseflesh brought on by the chilled night air. It made her snuggle even closer to the figure she was still locked around, appreciating warmth against her bare arms and chest . . .

Warmth? Oh, my God.

She unlocked her arms from around Steven's torso, having to almost lift him just to free her left wrist. They were lying on the ground, he on his stomach and she still astraddle his back. And he wasn't moving. But his stature was no longer extreme. He had reverted to his own size, his frame still lean but nowhere near its earlier skeletal incarnation. And his skin . . . it was not just pink but warm to the touch.

She took his arm and turned him over, unable to contain the tears of joy that were making her vision swim. The face she found there had no jutting cheekbones or translucent lips. It was instead the face she had fallen in love with years ago, made completely anew. Even the cheeks were unmarked, free of scar and stitchmark.

His eyes fluttered open, took a minute to focus. "Pud?" he whispered wearily.

She kissed him then, hugged him tight. "It's all right now, sweetheart. It's gonna be all right."

"I believe you," he said, chuckling. But a moment later he broke their embrace and pushed her back. He had a nauseated look on his face, and his throat was undulating.

"What is it? What's wrong?"

He made a gagging sound, spit up into his open palm. "What the hell?" he said as he wiped the saliva from his hand, leaving only the five pearllike shells. He looked at her, stymied.

"It's a long story," she said, putting her arms around him once again, thrilling to the warmth that their bodies generated together.

REMEMBER YOUR WORD.

She looked up, beyond his shoulder. There was something perched on the corner of the mobile home, silhouetted by the flames. She smiled with recognition and nodded. I'll remember.

The arctic owl stared at her, unblinking. Then it spread those great snowy wings and took to the air, soared off into the depths of the forest.

They retrieved Steven's tattered clothing and huddled together before the raging fire, holding each other tight and never feeling so alive. Janet knew they were going to be all right. Someone had heard the radio call. Help would be on its way. All they had to do was wait.

Still. . . something was gnawing at her. An ominous thought. *That Tucker-thing was not the one to curse Steven; he said it fell into the sucking place before it could touch him. But if that was true . . . what windigo did? And where was it now?*

She looked to the forest and shivered. That kind of chill, the remembering kind, would never go away.

TWENTY-SIX

BARTON OPENED HIS EYES.

There were figures standing over him. Shadows just the slightest bit darker than the blackness around them. They made no sound, just stood there. Watching. One craned a long snakelike neck to see him over the squat shapes in line before it. Another reached out a hand with far too many fingers, started to touch him . . .

"Leave me alone!" he cried out, even though the slightest movement stitched his side and chest with needles of fire. The outburst startled the shadows; they scurried away, melding back into the whole cloth of night from which they'd been cut. And that left Davejac alone with his pain.

He leaned back with a groan. Well, Barton, said a little voice in his head. You're pretty much fucked, you know it? Your left leg's broken, there's no two ways about that, and your ribs are pretty much busted too. And from the way you're gasping and coughing blood, you may have punctured a lung.

No, on second thought you're not just fucked. You're dead.

"Sez you," he grunted defiantly. "The fat lady hasn't sang. So don't count me out just yet."

He painfully lifted his head and looked around. It was dark back there in the trees, so much so he could barely see his hand before his face. But somehow he could still make out the figures. They had retreated a short distance but had not left entirely. Peeking through the weeds and around the trees, peering down at him from the limbs above. And there were more of them now. Staring. Watching him. How long would that last, he wondered. How long till there were enough of them to override their skittishness, to surround him again. He had a bad feeling that the next time they would not be scared off with a yell. Got to move now, he decided. Gotta get back to the clearing. To the light.

He reached out as far as he could, sunk his hands into the soil, and pulled. The exertion triggered a wave of agony all through his body, and a backwash of nausea right after. But he kept pulling. He moved through the fallen leaves like a slug, dragging his shattered leg behind him. And with every inch he gained, his momentum increased. He gritted his teeth and crawled all the harder toward the light.

And what will you find there? Janet's and Steven's broken bodies? Or maybe just pieces of them, a few drumsticks . . .

Shut up.

He was bathed in cold sweat by the time he pulled himself to the edge of the clearing and peered out from beneath the underbrush. And found nothing there. The fire had gone out, but the moonlight was enough to show that Janet and Steven were gone, and the windigo as well. How long have I been out? he wondered. What happened here? He thought of his last glimpse of the Wilhoits, and he desperately wanted to believe they were safe somewhere. But the chances were less than slim. More like none at all . . .

There was a sound just then, in the distance. Deep in the heart of the forest. A low tremulous call, like a bird seeking out its mate. But Barton was immediately alarmed. There were no birds in this valley. No normal ones at least. As he listened, it grew louder, slowly but steadily. Almost a voice, whispering, murmuring something indistinct. Three syllables . . .

He gasped, this time not from pain but fear. Frantically he clawed at the dirt and leaves around him, wadded whatever he could find and stuffed it into his ears, crammed them full. For he knew what the sound was then. The voice. And what it was saying.

Three syllables. Dav-e-jac.

Go to sleep, boys and girls . . .

My God. It's coming back!

He pulled himself out of the trees completely and into the moonlight, scrabbled like a crab over the fallen timbers and limbs that blocked his way. His pain no longer mattered, not in the face of the blind panic that gripped him now. For the voice was getting louder, its booming timbre even penetrating his plugged ears. And with it was an odd roaring sound, growing louder, filling the forest . . . He crawled for the campfire he had started earlier, trying in vain to find his axe or his rifle or anything so at least he could die fighting. But the cold awareness that gripped his spine told him he would never make it. The winds were back, whipping around the clearing and swirling the debris into a mad tempest. The roaring sound had become deafening, and when he dared to glance up from the corner of his eye he saw the moon and stars blotted out by a looming shape . . .

"Dav-e-jac. Are you down there?"

The glow of the moon suddenly brightened by a factor of ten, and Barton had to cover his eyes from the glare. He held up a hand, squinted against the brilliance from above to make out its source. And it was then that his pain-wracked mind finally began to assimilate the confusion around him.

The dull roar had a distinct rhythm to it. He quickly dug the dirt and leaves from his ears and could make out the *whup-whup-whup* of rotor blades beating the air.

"There he is," someone called. *"Barton, are you all right?"*

It was not some supernatural voice that had been calling his name after all. It was the big bullhorn on *Fannie Mae*, the helicopter that now hovered just above the clearing. If he looked hard beyond the spotlight, he could see the bubble of the cockpit and Bailey's big figure at the stick, balancing the machine delicately in the air. There were two others in there with her. He waved and shouted, but his voice was lost in the roar of the engine.

"There's no room to land. If I lower the ladder, can you hang on till we get you to open ground?"

He nodded his head dramatically to make sure she could see it. In answer he saw the side door on the Bell open and a figure lean out, the coiled rope ladder in hand. And he would have sworn it was Janet Wilhoit. She dropped her burden, and the ladder unfurled down into the clearing, slapping the ground only a few feet away. Bailey let the craft drift just a bit to starboard to bring the lower rungs right into Davejac's grasp. He moved as quickly as he could, pulling himself up far enough to get his good leg through the ladder and curling it around the outer rope. Then he tangled his arms in it as well, hissing with the pain that it caused him. There ain't no way I'm coming off of this thing, he promised himself. No way.

He waved to signal them all clear, then got a death grip on one of the rungs. And he started to pray as the helicopter slowly rose into the air and him along with it.

"Bar-ton . . ."

It was a toneless whisper from the forest, a bare vibration in the air. Yet somehow it cut through the din, the roar of the engines overhead, and found its way to Davejac's ears.

Cold fear sprouted in his stomach. "Hurry!" he screamed to Bailey. "Pull me up! Pull me up!"

A moment later the cold wind came rushing through the valley.

The helicopter lurched suddenly, started to spin, and with a less experienced pilot at the controls it most certainly would have gone down right then. But Bailey fought the stick, fought it hard. The Bell Ranger veered sideways over the forest, struggling just to stay aloft. And that dragged the rope ladder and its dangling passenger straight through the treetops.

Barton tried to bunch himself as he swung into the dense upper branches. But it did little good. The first impact was against his broken leg, and when he tried to cry out he got a faceful of pine needles for his troubles. The limbs tore at him and shredded his jacket and pants, gouged the flesh beneath. But he held on.

"Bar-ton . . ."

He looked up immediately. Something was coming through the branches . . . A hand, glowing icy white, measuring at least three feet across the palm. It was open, reaching for him. And he was swinging right into it.

Bailey jerked back on the stick then, put all of her weight and strength behind it. The Bell suddenly broke free of the wind and rose straight into the night sky, jerking Barton from the forest in a spray of leaves and broken branches. In an eye blink the woods and the hand and that damn whispering voice were gone from around him and he was high above the valley, steering away from there. Going someplace safe.

Barton hung on the ladder, numbed and bleeding, barely alive. He did not feel the pain anymore, nor the biting cold of the air that high up. But he did feel the terror.

"Bar-ton . . ." the whisper echoed below, carried on that damned wind.

He looked down at the forest that was falling away behind him. And just for a split second he saw something there. A face. It was cold and white and wore a capering smile, just like the windigo he had fought in the clearing. Only this was five times larger. And it was watching him through the trees.

The *very tops* of the trees.

Then it was gone, and the valley was far behind them.

EPILOGUE

In the days that followed there were many visitors to the forest. Doctors and researchers came all the way from Thunder Bay, looking for answers to questions they had not yet even formulated. They combed the valley and surrounding areas. But Chalako Lakes wore a different face that day, and they found nothing. Not one clue to explain Andy Church's madness. They finally went home unfulfilled, and after that, no one came for a long time.

Barton Davejac recovered from his injuries, but only after four months in the hospital. Once discharged, he went back to Atikokan and took a job at the sporting goods store. But it was too close there. The nightmares were too strong. So he finally packed up his grandfather and his dogs and moved them to Toronto, to the suburbs. He found work with a construction company and ran the dogs in the park on the weekends. And he never went into the woods again.

Steven and Janet Wilhoit returned to Indiana to pick up their lives where they'd left off, and they never spoke much of their experiences in the backcountry of Ontario. Janet finally managed to give up smoking. Almost. Once a month she would go out to the picnic table in the backyard and light up one cigarette. Just one. Then she would leave the rest of the pack behind. Sometimes they sat on the table for days. Sometimes they disappeared completely. But whatever the result, she never wavered in her dedication to that ritual. Because she always remembered her word.

Tucker Pharmaceutical had no use for a chunk of northern wilderness. But that's just what it ended up with, since Elton Tucker had seen fit to purchase the ground through the company and not with his own funds. They immediately put the parcel back on the market. But there were no buyers. Not even at a reduced price. Finally, as a charitable act in memory of their late founder (and for the resulting tax benefit), the board of directors offered Chalako Lakes to the province as a possible addition to bordering Quetico Park. The proposal met with broad support from environmentalists, and officials were even sent out to survey the property and evaluate the practicality of the idea.

They brought back glowing recommendations. Beautiful land, they said, filled with wildlife and geographic significance. The tourists and campers would love it.

The proposal edged ever closer to acceptance.

Tourists and campers . . .

The forest smiled at the notion and continued to wear its most tranquil face. For now . . . But it was eternal. It could wait.